GLASS BOYS

NICOLE LUNDRIGAN

GLASS
BOYS

a novel

Douglas & McIntyre
D&M PUBLISHERS INC.
Toronto/Vancouver/Berkeley

First U.S. edition 2012

11 12 13 14 15   5 4 3 2 1

Douglas & McIntyre
An imprint of D&M Publishers Inc.
2323 Quebec Street, Suite 201
Vancouver BC Canada V5T 4S7
www.douglas-mcintyre.com

Cataloguing data available from Library and Archives Canada
ISBN 978-1-55365-797-2 (pbk.)
ISBN 978-1-55365-798-9 (ebook)

Editing by Barbara Berson
Cover and text design by Jessica Sullivan
Cover photographs by Peter Beavis/Stone+/Getty Images (top)
and Chev Wilkinson/Stone/Getty Images (bottom)
Printed and bound in Canada by Friesens
Text printed on acid-free, 100% post-consumer paper
Distributed in the U.S. by Publishers Group West

We gratefully acknowledge the financial support of the Canada
Council for the Arts, the British Columbia Arts Council, the
Province of British Columbia through the Book Publishing Tax
Credit and the Government of Canada through the Canada
Book Fund for our publishing activities.

For my husband, Zoltán Deák

PART ONE

1

NO ONE IS chasing him, but the Glass boy's heart still pounds as he runs through the woods, soles of his canvas sneakers slapping the soft earth. When he reaches the other side of the forest he stops abruptly, removes his sneakers, steps onto a blanket of bright green grass. For a moment, he crouches to catch his breath, watches as a pair of pale cabbage moths flutter up from a dead stump. He hears a bird chirping, the branches moaning as they lift and fall in the breeze. The sun overhead is hot, and he closes his eyes, pulls a lungful of sweet air in through his nostrils. *Heaven,* he thinks. *This sliver of land just before the water is my private heaven.*

Using his hands to shade his eyes, he scans the woods, the visible length of the stream. He is alone, and he scampers to the edge, lays down on his stomach. Slides his arm over the grassy lip, and as his fingers wiggle through drowning roots, a handful of waiting tadpoles skitter and hide. He feels around. And for a moment, when he finds nothing, his heart strikes so loudly in his ears the sounds of the stream and bird and creaking trees sink. But then his hand knocks it. Hard and slippery. It's there. Grunting, he pulls the pickle jar from the water, heavy with the rock weighting it down. He notes it is intact, no rust on the lid, no evidence of water damage to the treasure inside. No sign that someone else has touched it.

After he dries the jar on his T-shirt, he looks around once again. Yes, yes. He is alone. Then he sits cross-legged on the grass, pinches the jar between his bare thighs, twists the lid with both hands. Even though he had washed the jar in hot suds, the faintest smell of vinegar still tweaks his nose. His breath is shallow as he reaches in, removes his tiny treasure. So valuable, but bought for only a handful of change.

He hauls a handkerchief from his pocket, blankets the rotting stump beside him, and examines each item before laying it down. Too much, now, to see everything at once. To have it all exposed, recklessly, where a gust could arrive without warning, pilfer a piece of his perfect puzzle, carry it off to someone who might destroy it. Hands shaking, he scoops them up, clutches them to his chest. Imagines, for a moment, they hear his blood moving through his veins.

Time folds, an hour dissolves, and the boy wonders if he might be missed. If the man might question his absence. He places the items in the jar, seals it. One last glimpse, his eyes, wide open, pressed to the heavy glass.

He is dizzy when he stands, and he nearly drops the jar on a flat rock. Even though he is still holding it close to his breastbone, he cannot help but see it smashed, a spray of glass, his collection scattered. The very thought makes his legs weak, and he does not trust them. Scrawny legs, even though he eats like a gannet. He shuffles, carefully, places the jar back into the stream, underneath the overhang of unkempt grass. The tadpoles are there again, grazing his knuckles with their quivering tails. Wanting him to stay and play. But he stands, whispers, "Not now, not now."

He searches the woods for blinking eyes, listens for footsteps or hollering. He stares at the sky, expecting to see the man's shocked face pressing down through the clouds. He knows the man is everywhere. An almost God. With the swoop of an axe, he has witnessed the man choosing between life and death. Witnessed it more than once. Head of a piglet flying in one direction, pink body in the other. Tiny hooves on stick legs twitching, still trying to run away.

But there is nothing. Nothing, yet. And he coils his excitement and guilt, like a greasy spring, presses it down, locks the trapdoor inside his mind. He stuffs his feet into his sneakers, stiff fabric heel flattened, and for a good distance he walks backwards through the woods. Gazing at the spot where his secret is guarded. And he tells himself, as he watches the rippling water, that no one will ever know. No one will ever find it. No one will ever get hurt. Then he turns, runs towards home. Towards the farm. Towards his life with the man.

AS SOON AS the cloud of mud settles to the bottom, the tadpoles push through the water, and tap the glass. They are children still, barely limbs to stand on. Eyes like black beads, they see what's inside the pickle jar, and don't know to look away.

2

SOMETHING WAS STUCK down there, something decaying, and the sour smell sat in the sink, billowed up whenever Lewis turned the tap. Shining his flashlight into the hole, he saw a slick black lump just before the pipe curved, like an eyeball, blinking every time water dripped over it. He had poured a half quart of bleach into the drain, rinsed with hot water, but once the stench from that dispelled, the rot crept back. This was his brother's fault, he knew. Rather than scraping a plate, Roy would press the bits of fish and brewis, corner of bread down through the opening. Lewis had seen him do it. More than once. And now, he was going to have to take the pipes apart.

Wrench in hand, he slid underneath the sink, started to tap and twist. Something kicked at his leg, and he craned his neck, saw a pair of loose jeans, fabric cross-hatched with guts and grime. A pair of worn boots, tongues hanging out. He eased his head around the sink, edged out onto the floor. And there was Roy, standing there, his youthful face grinning, cigarette clamped in his shiny teeth, cheeks and nose burnt a deep red from the morning spent out jigging fish. Nellie, his dog, stood behind him, her wet snout jammed into the crease of fabric just behind Roy's knee, sniffing.

"You got to be a plumber now, too?" Roy said, smoke flickering as his lips moved.

"Stick your nose down the sink. You tell me what I got to be."

Roy laughed, took a step backwards. "That I won't, then. You can have it."

4

"Well, it reeks to high heavens."

"I'm sure you'll put it to rights. Now, get your arse off the floor and come and have a drop with me."

Lewis came to his feet, let the wrench drop onto the countertop, gestured towards Roy's hands, the two paper bags, twisted at the opening. "Where'd you get that?"

"Morley."

Arms folded.

"Now don't you go getting all uppity. Morley made me swear you'd leave well enough alone."

"He did, did he?"

Roy laid both bags on the table, stuck his smoke in an overflowing dessert dish, then crunched down the paper to reveal two label-less bottles, crystal liquid. Plucking one up, he ran a slow hand down over the glass. "Christ, what magic he don't do with a bucket of potato peel."

"What else did he say?"

Bottle opened, Roy reached into an already open cupboard, retrieved two tumblers. "He says you should be keeping an eye on those vagrants wandering 'round. There's got to be some of those you can dog."

"We don't got no vagrants 'round here."

"Well, you know, you can make sure those lassies don't be wearing their skirts too long. Can we make that a law, Lew? Skirts no longer than," he held his hands a foot apart, top to bottom, "no longer than that?"

"I don't think so, Roy."

"Worth a shot, Constable Trench." He winked, filled the glasses with swift practiced pours. "But seriously now, Lew-Lew, I was talking to the fellers just the other day when we was fixing the cribbing up under Morley's stage. And they're not all that keyed up about some young fart bringing change."

"I can't help that." A squirt of anxiety darted through Lewis's stomach. He knew, even before Roy opened his mouth, that once he returned home, everything would be different. That the faults beneath his feet would shift, and he would be standing on new ground. His role in Knife's Point was clearly laid out, but the tactics he should employ were cloudy. Hard-nosed and they would hate him, laid-back and they would spin circles, until he was out there alongside them, salting the very fish they stole from the sea.

"You knows how the crowd was when the Ranger'd pass through."

"Yeah."

"And now, you. Having gotten the nod from some paper sorter up along. Not really much sense."

"What do that mean?"

"That's their words, not mine." Roy sat, legs straddling the back of the chair, and Nellie followed, lumbered underneath the table, turned and turned, flumped, lay her jowls on Roy's boot. In one fell swoop, he grabbed his glass from the table, emptied it into his mouth. Visual shudder, slishing sound through lips pulled back over pink gums. Nellie stirred, opened a single eye, tucked her muzzle underneath her paw. "Christ. That'd rip the hair off the rabbit," he hissed. Fingers dove in around his scalp, pulling black curls.

Lewis smirked, took the chair across from him, laid his palms on the table. "Or, the rabbit off the hare."

"Even better." Roy knocked a glass towards Lewis. "Now, go on with you." When Lewis hesitated, Roy looked upwards, growled playfully, "Christ Almighty, Lewdy-Lew. Don't be telling me you can't do nothing illegal in your own home. I means, if a growed man can't be breaking the law under his own roof, then where can he?"

"Shut your trap."

"But you got to see what they're saying. Most of them knowed us now since we was youngsters. Pissing in the grass."

"You're still pissing in the grass, Roy."

"Yeah, yeah. They just don't want you counting snares or following moose around or telling them what sort of stuff they can

6

or can't cook up in their cellars. Rushing in with your guns blaz-ing." Roy laughed, emptied his glass again. "That sort of thing."

"Ah." Lewis sighed. *One more go*, he thought as he looked at the temptation near his fingertips. *One more go before I settles in.* Then he lifted the glass, dumped the works down his wide throat. Audible gulp. In only moments, once the shock glided out through his flesh, he sensed that familiar tickling, a door creaking open, cavernous thirst hiding below. Deep and diffi-cult to get in under it. He tapped his glass for a refill. "I don't know, Roy, my son. I don't know."

"'Nuff yammering. You'll make your way. We always got on fine."

A second swig, smoother entrance this time. "I'm apt to be bored out of my tree."

"That's what we wants, Lew-Lew. That's what we wants." Leg cocked, Roy struck Lewis in the thigh with his stained boot. "You got her scald, my son. Hauling in a wad of quid for doing shit all. Good on you, if you asks me. Should've done it myself, but I idn't that smart."

"I wants to do a good job." Lewis clanged his tumbler on the table, and Roy filled it again until it rose at the brim. Leaning forward, lips touching glass, he slurped Morley's offering, let it coat his mouth, preserve his tongue. Several more swallows, and the questions that prodded his hackles were leaving. Flaked away, old paint in summer sunshine.

Roy pushed his nose with the heel of his hand, emitted a sound like a knife cutting through cabbage. He went the sink, snorted again. "Besides," he said and spat. "They takes what they can. That's human nature. Grab after the bit of elastic in my fucking underwear if that's all I had to give."

Effortless, old-time laughter erupting. "If some poor fuck was after your underwear, if they could manage to snap it off your dirty arse, they should be locked up, keys tossed in Gray-ley River."

"Only be so lucky," he replied, turning the taps.

"Christ, Roy. The pucking fipe is off." He wiped his mouth. "Fucking pipe."

"And?" Roy clomped back to the table, topped up his glass again, spilling colorless liquid over the wood. He took another cigarette from the pack hidden in the roll of his T-shirt sleeve, stuck it behind his ear. "Look at you," he said, slurring slightly. "Coming back with a paper, some boots, and enough airs to burst a pig's bladder."

Lewis grinned, and smacked the table.

"Here's to that." Roy raised his glass, clinked Lewis's harder than necessary, liquid spilling over his hand, wetting his wrist. Starting with his palm, his tongue trailed up and over the back of his hand. Then he bent down, slurped the spill from the table.

Lewis blinked once, twice, then grinned again. His brother was older by less than a year. Thinking back, he couldn't recall ever really being apart from Roy. Since they were children, they had trudged through the world together, occupying the same space. Complementary shadows, Lewis's leaning slightly towards the orderly, Roy's towards the thrill of upheaval. They were loved, too. Loved more than most, he knew. He remembered Sunday dinners, and he and Roy were always fed first, offered up the most tender morsel of meat or an extra scoop of cream on their pudding. Once, after receiving a thin scrap of bone-riddled fish, their father stared into his plate, shook his head, said, "Do you want to know when 'twas clear I was in for trouble? When 'twas clear you two gaffers had made off with her heart? Let me see." Picking bones from his teeth. "Two of youse, Tit and Tat, now, in your cribs, sticking your hands down your drawers, wiping shit on the walls. Do you know what she did? Your mother?" Shaking heads, wide eyes, mouths stuffed with food. "Washed your fingers off, and told you fellers what lovely pictures you gone and made. Pained her, it did now, to clear it off the wall. Pained her, I tell you." "Saints preserve us," she had cried, swatted the back of his bald head with a damp cup towel. "What garbage you don't get on with! And language! On a Sunday."

8

Their father lived a hard life, with an abundance of drinking and harmless carousing and gambling. Even with the trouble, he never allowed a cross word to curdle the air, and Lewis could not recall a single time their father's open palm kissed their oversized heads. Their mother tolerated it all, would only throw down her hands, shake her head, giggle over the foolishness of boots pushed onto the wrong feet, brandied fruitcake jammed into a pocket, thick eyebrows burnt clean off.

As soon as Roy could stand, he was down on the stage, kicking guts into the heading hole, rinsing fish in the dipping pan. Midget amongst the fishermen, he would grapple a fish, cart it over and spread it out on the boughs, douse it in salt. Mimicking hand motions. Learning how to flick. Back and forth, every season, every year, until his body was sinewy, teenaged shoulders broad and brown. Sips here and there, but the first time they offered him a mug, Roy swallowed like an awakened baby, comical desperation. Once he dozed off, they poked him underneath a flake, in the triangular patches of shade, curled on his side so he wouldn't choke on his own vomit. Common phrase bestowed upon him, "You're your father's son." Roy worked hard to verify that appraisal.

Not that Lewis didn't like a drop. Only his binges were far less gritty than Roy's, and Lewis rarely left the stool where he drank, mostly kept his consumption within the hours of darkness. Roy placed no such limits on himself, and in recent years he had developed a reputation for falling whim to his stomach, giving free rein to his wandering feet. "Gut on two legs," he was often called. Any given time of day, folks knew Roy might be banging on a patio door looking for a slice of molasses bread, or stealing the few scraggly tomatoes tied up in the garden, or dozing on the steps of The Good Fryer waiting for someone to drop a chip. Occasionally, people let him in. Sometimes they left him, and sometimes they carted him home. The afternoon Lewis was leaving for training, he passed his neighbor wavering along the road with a loaded wheelbarrow, Roy's splayed body being the contents. "Bringing him back, is all, now." Resting on Roy's stomach were two blue platters, one turned upside down over the other. The neighbor had noticed Lewis staring, said, "That's nothing. Roy never got to his bit of stew. Missus took pity on the poor bugger, sent it along."

Lewis looked across the table at Roy, shook his head as Roy licked the outside of his glass. With a teasing scowl, he said, "Someone got to try to fix you, my son."

"Only thing that's going to fix me, now, is a good woman."

"And where's you going to find a woman willing to take on that type of labor?"

"What type of labor?"

"You, that's what."

"They be lining up once I puts my sign out."

"Yeah, clamoring for cruel and unusual punishment. She'd have to have some awful strong stomach on her."

"Some broads go in for that."

"The only broad that's going to fall for your charms, now, is Nellie."

"Oh, yes," Roy reached down, rubbed Nellie's head with vigorous strokes. Leaned and poured an ounce into Nellie's water, and she hoisted her fat trunk off the floor, clicked a few steps, lapped. "That's all you'll be having, too, Miss Nellie. Don't you be looking for more. We're the ones wants to be slobbering around on all fours. You're already there."

"How come is it," Lewis said as he glanced at the tools in front of the sink, "that you'll borrow something broken just so you can fix it, but you can't do a tap 'round the house?" Head leaning towards the drain.

Roy crossed his eyes, cracked the second bottle. "Who needs a woman, Lew-Lew, when I got you?"

THE RUNT. Where was the goddamned runt when there was work to be done?

Eli Fagan looked up, scanned his fields, the grassy backyard. No sign of the child. Then, as he continued to work, the hammer came down onto his thumb. He cursed, threw the hammer, squeezed his pulsing digit inside his fist. *Bloody Christ.* All morning he'd spent hauling old felt strips from the roof of his barn, and now he was trying to get proper shingles in place before the rain arrived. But the work was hampered by the afternoon heat—the shingles were sticking together, and he could see his boot prints in the softened asphalt. His shirt clung to his sweaty back, salt blinded him. Made his hands unreliable. And now, because of the godforsaken runt, his thumb wanted to explode.

He didn't ask for the runt. The child came with his wife. Eli had married her quickly, and there had never been any mention of a boy. She said he must've known, but he didn't. Unless he'd been so inebriated over the course of their courting, he failed to remember. No matter how much warm whiskey was skipping through his veins, wouldn't a man remember something as significant as that? A child? He decided his wife had tricked him, and that should not surprise him. After all, his wife came from Split Rock, a crotch hole of a town an hour north of Knife's Point. There were sayings about the quality of girls from Split Rock, crude sayings, and Eli wouldn't repeat them. Cursed himself for not heeding them. Cursed himself for rushing headlong, letting his infantile desire for a warm meal and soft flesh overpower him.

Spending every day on a farm, Eli knew what was normal, what was right, and that boy was about as unnatural as a beast with two assholes. He watched his wife taking care of him, bathing his scrawny body and scraping a comb through his feather hair, and the very sight of it made Eli twitch. When she fed the child honest meals, smaller servings of what actually appeared on Eli's own plate, well, that made him angry. Eli sensed there was something bent inside the boy's head, and he had to insist by way of a few smacks that the boy never look him straight in the eye. When his wife once stood behind the boy, hands on his shoulders, and said, "He is your son, now," Eli reached for a junk of wood, threatened to strike her. Frightened her enough to shut her up. There was no way in hell he'd take on that boy. Make him a Fagan.

Eli sat back onto the roof, wiped his handkerchief across his forehead. He felt the urge to put his throbbing thumb into his mouth, but wouldn't dream of actually doing it. During the summer months, it was tough to get much good out of the boy, but if Eli hollered loud enough, knocked him between his shoulder blades a few times, the boy occasionally carried a few pounds of his own weight. Lately, though, the boy had been disappearing. Every afternoon that was halfway fit for working, he was nowhere to be found. At first, he'd wander off for fifteen or twenty minutes, and Eli would assume he was lingering in the toilet. He was prone to that. Or hidden around the side of the house, chewing on a large wad of paper stuffed into his cheek. He was prone to that, too. But nearly three hours had passed since he saw the boy jamming two halves of a sandwich into his face at once. And Eli very nearly went after him then, put the boots to him, for such a brazen display of gluttony.

Eli stood again on the roof of his barn, one leg up, one leg straight, put his uninjured hand to his eyes to block the sun. "Boy!" he hollered. "Boy! You get your skinny arse up here." But the runt did not appear. He did discover his wife, though. Through the open door of the house, he could see her yanking open cupboard drawers in the kitchen, sliding stuff off the counters, slamming the drawers shut with her hip. He hated that, the mounds of hidden clutter. Could feel it when he walked into his own home, orderly on the surface, dirt beneath. He called to her. "Hey, Missus! Hey!" She glanced up, quickly slipped out of his line of vision, and Eli watched the door creak closed as though a ghostly hand was pushing it.

Eli crouched, opened his fist, saw a purple mess beneath. Took a knife from his pocket, flicked open the blade, steadied his thumb and stabbed the nail. Pressed and twisted. Blood seeped up through the slit, and the pressure released. He would lose the nail, no doubt about it. He sighed, licked away the blood, and then something caught his eye. In the slanting afternoon sunlight, Eli spotted a trampled line of grass. A paler green of bent blades. Leading across the backyard and into a clump of overgrown dogwood bushes. A sure path, and Eli knew he'd find the runt at the end of it. Probably wasting time, playing in the stream. Fury made him light-headed. He dog-crawled backwards off the roof, lumbered down the ladder, and made his way across the yard. Followed the narrow trail into the coolness of the woods. Towards the tinkling water.

MINDS STUNNED BY the contents of the second bottle, decency dissolved and replaced by something visceral, something that wanted to hunt. The boys were out, Lewis no longer reluctant, slogging behind Roy and his straying stomach. His gut on two legs. With wobbly strides, they waded through Wilf Stone's field of vegetables, leaving a trail of torn cabbage leaves, uprooted heads. Once his legs were freed, Roy toppled headlong into the spindly potato stalks, and as he righted himself he tugged on a plant, beige globes popping out from the soil. Plucking one up, Roy jammed it into his mouth, crunched down on raw potato, dirt, and pebbles.

"That's theeevery," Lewis slurred as he fell hard on his knees.

"'Tis, Cunts-stu-bul."

Swaying, Lewis jabbed an authoritative index finger in the air. "Let you off with warr-ing," he managed before he sat back, slapped his thigh, mouth hanging wide open, soundless laughter banging about against his teeth.

Sprayed beige chunks, hands gripping his knees, crumpled over. "C'mon, Lew-see, 'ress me. Ah-ress me."

"That I 'llows, you l'il fucker. T'row you slammer. Swallowa key."

Lewis lunged forward, coiled his arms around Roy's legs, and the two of them tripped, rolled, crushing the fluffy tops of a row of carrots.

13

"Fuh you-self." Roy yanked a carrot from the earth, held it like a dirty dagger, pretended to stab Lewis in the neck. Then, bit the tip, sputtered, "Whassup, Doc? You're a 'appy wabbit?"

Lewis curled onto his side. Joy pulled all of his muscles inwards, and for a moment he imagined he was a caterpillar, enormous godly finger stroking his belly. Oh, so good it felt to be free. Free. Just for these instants, floating high above newborn responsibility, toes skimming the surface of sober expectation. Just he and his brother and all this foggy air and blurry horizons and spin-top antics. Angling his cheek, he stuck his tongue out the side of his mouth, edging, edging, touching. Soil coating his lips, and he exhaled. The earth was still there. Still beneath his cheek. Strong and ready for when the whirling stopped, when his body would once again be at rest.

"Up and out," Roy bellowed as he booted Lewis in the back. "Needs find you lass. Kiss that. Lips's softer an dirt."

Lewis swiped the specks from his mouth and cheeks, crawled onto all fours, then up again, lumbering forward. Side to side, gravity drunk. Up on the gravel road, they rolled along in the heat of the late afternoon sun. Roy's chest was bare, his shirt lost somewhere along the way. Limping, one boot now missing, black sock sliding down over the pasty skin of his heel.

"You smell sum-um?" Nose rooting the air above him, huffing, nostrils flaring.

Lewis swaggered alongside him. "Sssmoke."

"Meat. Burning. Meat."

"Chri. Some nose on. Jus' smoke."

"Gone, buddy. Starved. Eat my fuckeen boots."

"Only got a one."

"Tongue the tongue." Eureka moment, and Roy struck Lewis with his fist. Lewis faltered, righted himself. "Lez go."

"Nuts, my son. I idn't go Eli Fagan's. Apt to shoot you come through the woods. Say you fuckin' moose."

"Ah, c'mon. Nab a bite him."

Something in Lewis alerted him to the fact that staying away from town was a wiser choice, and he did not protest. Trailing close behind his brother, he tumbled down over the embankment, across the mucky ditch and through the woods. His limbs burned with boozy ammunition, face unaware of the damp whipping boughs. Roy like a banshee in the near distance, loping along, swinging from low lying branches, body flying through the cool air. One bare foot flashing in the shadows, stomping onto slippery exposed roots, soft moss.

They were about to pull off the greatest heist ever. Lewis could picture it all, and he could barely contain the electricity that had crept into his marrow. First, enter yard, then wrestle man, steal meat, bound off into the woods, canines clamped down on juicy reward. But before Lewis reached the edge of the woods, Roy had already burst out of the brush, and into Eli Fagan's backyard. Panting, Lewis stopped, wrapped his arms around the bubbly trunk of a fat spruce, laughter firing out from his cannon chest, legs weakening, as he watched Roy charge towards the smoking barrel where Eli stood. His bloodshot eyes watering, his diaphragm hiccuped inside his chest, and he leaned, tried to catch his breath.

Sensibilities smashed, the brothers were unable to clearly see what was happening in this backyard. They did not notice young Garrett Glass's face, the pink welt that caused his left eyelids to kiss, purplish bruise that spidered out from his cheekbone. Or that Eli Fagan's wife was holding her diminutive son firmly by the straps of his wet overalls, and that he fought her, writhing, gnashing his teeth. They did not see her catch his wrist, twisting, his knees buckling until he squatted down, subdued, on a worn hump of grass. They did not heed her face, lips pale, eyes numbed and drowning inside their sockets, how her rake hand leapt to cover her mouth when Roy and Lewis appeared at the edge of their yard. They failed to see the fragments of broken black plastic, the shards of glass from a shattered pickle jar, lying in the grass near Eli Fagan's feet. Or that he was stabbing his arm into smoke and flame, poking, poking, deep into the rusting barrel with a sharp kitchen utensil. They did not know he was deafened by the crackling, the snaps and pops, and they never sensed the depth of his anger, how it cranked his shoulders up, how it enabled him to drive his hand into ripping fire without feeling a single pinch of pain.

Arms flailing, an exchange of some sort when Roy reached Eli. Lewis could not make out what was being said. The words, after bumbling across the yard, were distorted and watery. As Lewis watched, the two men seemed to embrace, hold each other for a moment, like old friends. But when Lewis caught sight of Eli's face, it was hot poker red. And then Eli shifted, and Lewis saw Roy's face, his features pulled back in a strange sort of smile. Then, an altogether different sound showering down from up above. A sound a young deer might make, if shot, but only wounded. Lewis scanned the woods, then looked towards his brother, whose head was arced backwards now, searing cry erupting from his mouth. Hands to his bare stomach, and brightness tumbling from somewhere beneath his fingers.

Mind shocked sober, body slower to respond, Lewis stumbled across the yard, falling forward, knuckles grazing spots of grass, then gravel. He caught his brother as he collapsed, back bowed, pinning Lewis to the ground. "Jesus Christ. Help him," Lewis tried, but the phrases were trapped beneath his tongue, sounding nothing like they should. Thin liquid poured down over Roy's abdomen, belly button filled, fish-stained jeans soaked, soil drinking. Lewis cranked his neck, looked this way and that. Eli and his wife were gone, and Garrett, the boy, was beside the barrel, eyes slit by smoke, trying to hook something out with a serving fork. Hugging Roy as best he could, Lewis tried to whisper into his ear, "Shush, shush. Someone's coming for you. Someone's coming. Going to be alright." Wrapping his arms around Roy's waist, Lewis moved his hands over his brother's muscle and skin and thick pelt of fat. As he gripped, two fingers slipped into a hot opening in Roy's flesh. He'd located the source of the rapid blood loss. Lewis pressed hard, tried to plug the hole. But it was a useless consummation.

3

THE AIR INSIDE the courthouse was cold, and smelled of paper and wood. Lewis sat in a hard-backed chair, fingers knotted together in his lap, rib cage shivering and sweating inside his dress coat. "I don't care what he says. I know what he did." Fourteen months Lewis had waited for this day, and he was struggling to stay seated.

"But did you actually see him commit this act?"

Lewis mumbled. "I saw."

"Okay." The lawyer paused. "I will rephrase my question. Do you remember? Do you remember seeing your brother die?"

"I was there." He let his nails bite the backs of his hands. "I was right there."

"Yes, sir. That is not in dispute." The lawyer stood directly behind Eli Fagan, then leaned forward, gripped Eli's shoulders, continued. "But is there anything you can tell us that contradicts the sequence of events put forth by this gentleman? That what happened so long ago was an accident. An accident. An honest and tragic mistake."

"A man is dead."

"Yes, sir."

"He knows what he did."

"Your opinion, Constable Trench." The lawyer released his hold on Eli, clapped his hands lightly. "Forgive me for saying so, but in this particular case, that doesn't count."

ON THE STONE steps of the courthouse, Lewis heard statements like a loudspeaker bellowing inside his head.

"Might've had a fighting chance," Dr. Doke had testified. "If he hadn't of been so inebriated. Potato whiskey. With a substance like that, there's no telling the alcohol content of what you're consuming."

"Not a good start, Constable Trench," Eli Fagan's lawyer said calmly. "Not a good start to your career."

Then, the judge. "This is not just a man's life here, but that of a family. Mr. Fagan has demonstrated he is a hardworking individual, and a dedicated husband and father to his wife, his stepson, and his newborn daughter. I accept Mr. Fagan's testimony. That Mr. Trench and his brother, Constable Trench, trespassed onto his property. In an inebriated state, Mr. Trench accosted Mr. Fagan, and following a brief tussle, Mr. Trench fell upon the tool Mr. Fagan was utilizing at that time. Furthermore, I accept Mr. Fagan's plea that in no way did he intend to cause bodily harm to Mr. Trench." The judge licked the tips of his fingers, turned a page. "While the loss of life is no doubt tragic, further destruction of this family would only serve to compound the misfortune. Moving forward, you both need to return to your homes in Knife's Point, live side by side as neighbors, find some way to forge a peace between you. And begin again."

Lewis waited as Eli Fagan emerged through the doors, taking each step with a heavy foot. His gray suit was snug and covered in pills, and the legs of his trousers rested an inch above his ankles, revealing mismatched socks. Underneath the oversized collar of his shirt screamed a gaudy tie, bright and, Lewis thought, disrespectful. Lewis had never known much about Eli, other than his reputation for being a son of a bitch. But Lewis had stared at him so long and hard in the courthouse that he could describe everything about the man now. How his hand twitched whenever a lawyer spoke Roy's name, how a dozen coarse hairs curled out of his ear holes, how he turned the ridged base of his empty water glass around and around, clinking it against the wooden table. Lewis saw him as a dog, fighting against being caged.

"I hope you rots in hell," Lewis said quietly through clenched teeth. "The entire load of you."

Eli stopped. Turned towards the swinging doors of the courthouse. His wife paused there, wispy and stern, a fat bundle splayed in her arms. But Eli didn't appear to notice her or the new baby. Instead he seemed to focus on the boy, his stepson Garrett Glass, already standing on the steps, gnawing at his cuticles, spitting. The boy squinted, but did not stare back. He had grown so quickly, torn away from his boyishness, almost overnight. Lewis watched as Garrett touched a shadow of hair creeping along his jawline, twisted a few of the longer strands between his fingers.

"Needn't worry," Eli said, and he coughed, wiped his shiny forehead with a handkerchief. "We will, Constable Trench. We will."

4

DRIVING IN A rattling pickup with his mother and stepfather, Garrett Glass was on his way home. They were heading north, away from the city, away from the courthouse, back to their farm in Knife's Point. He was perched on the hump in the cab between his parents, his damp body jiggling even when the pavement was smooth. Garrett kept a hand cupped over his mouth, could smell dirty metal on his skin. If he threw up now, Eli would certainly pull over, kick open a door, toss him out onto the dirt shoulder, and tear on over the highway. No flicker of brake lights. Garrett swallowed constantly, kept his head turned away from Eli, and scanned the rocks and barrens and clumps of straggly trees. Imagined how he would survive if the acid and the mangled French fries spewed onto the worn floor below.

He would be alone in the woods, with the bears and foxes and the moose. But, Garrett told himself, he might be okay. He had some smarts. His father, his real father, had taught him plenty of things when Garrett was a small boy. How to make a snare from a stretch of spruce root or some wire, how to strip bark from a birch to kindle a fire. How to sleep comfortably on dry boughs, away from the wet ground. Garrett ran his hand over his pockets, felt nothing. No perfect coil of wire appearing out of thin air, no fishing hooks, not a candy to tease an empty stomach. He didn't even have his pocketknife. "You can't take that into a courtroom, for God's sakes," his mother had said when she saw it in his hand, and she'd grabbed it from him, tossed it into an overflowing drawer.

20

Garrett tried to distract himself. Thought about the farm. Thought about school. He didn't have a single friend. He had tried to blame it on the white scar that snaked from his upper lip and right nostril, or the red flaking patches on his elbows and knees. Perhaps his clothes were too small, sweaters darned, white worn line where the hem on his trousers had been let down. Or that his shoes were oversized, paper stuffed in the toes, and he clomped when he walked. Maybe it was because his mother insisted on shaving his scalp so he wouldn't catch ticks. But he couldn't deny there were other kids who wore worse clothes, had worse haircuts, and they still managed to find their pack.

In the woods up behind the school, older boys often surrounded him, pulled crushed stone from their pockets and chucked it at his head. If Garrett couldn't escape the enclosure, they might pin him down and let long strings of slime hang from their mouths, dangle just an inch from his face. Or, roll him over, jam a hand down the back of his trousers, grab his underwear, tug until his private parts chafed and burned. They ignored his cries for mercy, chanted "hinbreed, hinbreed, you're a hinbreed," made him crawl home on hands and knees, torn cotton up around his ribs, sharp sticks and pine needles stabbing his palms.

Once, in a moment of bravery, he asked what it meant to be a hinbreed, and this fellow named Willie called him a dickhead, told him he was the spawn of boy cousins poking girl cousins and brothers poking sisters. "You knows," Willie had said with a filthy wink, and he rammed his index finger into his loose fist, gave a few throaty snorts, hips bucking in time with his fingers. Blood going sour, he said. Babies with their feet on backwards. Fingers for toes. "That's why you got donkey ears, stupid-ass. And your snout is like a bloody faucet. Shit, you're lucky your eyes idn't crossed. You're lucky you got eyes t'all. Some hinbreeds only gets holes and they sticks marbles in their heads."

Growing up on a farm, Garrett knew all about poking, and, in the case of two beagle dogs his stepfather Eli kept in a chicken wire pen, the occasional getting stuck. When he asked his mother for the truth, if his real father had been her relative, and if she knew she was going to grow a hinbreed, her mouth hung open for a moment, then she cried, "You, my son, is fortunate to have your feet on this earth."

"That's not what I asked you."

"Of all things. You are a perfectly fine little boy. Perfectly fine. Can't you think for yourself?"

"I am thinking. Thinking I'm a hinbreed."

She sighed, and Garrett knew that sigh was her final word on the subject.

They were smart too, those boys. They were the ones who were quick to stick their hands in the air, math problems solved, while he was still counting his fingers, and finger-like toes, underneath the desk. So he knew they weren't just spouting lies.

One wheel of the truck struck a pothole on the highway, and Garrett listened to a stream of curses, saw a bubble of Eli's spit on the steering wheel, a second bubble land on the dashboard. Garrett closed his eyes, thought about the item tucked into his back pocket. Miraculously, that tiny scrap had somehow survived in the barrel, even after the fire had eaten everything else. Garrett had raked his hands through the black ash, and there it was. Buried underneath a warm rock. Such a gift. And whenever Garrett felt especially lonely, he would hide in his bedroom, stare at it, put it to his mouth, pull the acrid odor into his lungs. Then, carefully, he'd hide it away, and make a silent vow that he would never get caught again.

Just thinking about it now, Garrett felt nervous, longed to slip his hand behind him, to feel around. But he wouldn't dare, wouldn't risk that Eli'd notice his body shifting. So, he closed his eyes and remembered when the pickle jar was whole, safely hidden under rushing water.

Garrett bowed his head. Yes, he was different, and that was why Eli Fagan hated him so much. Garrett guessed Eli never knew that truth when he married Garrett's mother, but he certainly knew now. And Garrett was helpless to change who he was. A hinbreed, after all. Born that way, like a goat with three horns. No making him into someone else. Even though his peculiarities had caused a lot of trouble. Had caused a man to really die. Really, really die. Not just pretend.

Shapes whizzing by just outside the window, and Garrett was feeling worse. He shifted his focus, stared at his mother instead. He willed her to reach over and touch his forehead, ask if he might want to stop, breathe in something other than the bluish smoke trapped in the cab. Maybe a chocolate bar to pull the taste of someone else's cigarettes off his young tongue. But, no. Since they'd left the courthouse, his mother was like hardened wax, barely registering when they rode the gravel or swerved around a turn. She held her bundled baby girl in the crook of her right elbow, hand rigid, and he saw her nails were ragged, like his own, bitten down to the quick. Near the top button of her dress, he could see her ribs beneath her skin. Her eyes were closed, and if he hadn't noticed the single blue vein pulsing on the side of her neck, he might have wondered if she were frozen. If she were dead.

As he stared at her, he heard the faintest growl coming from her throat. She moved her left hand to cover a scorch mark on the fabric of her dress.

"Please don't look at me, Garrett."

"I idn't," he whispered.

After another moment, "I still feels you looking at me, my son."

"I said I idn't, then. I'm watching the outside."

"That you are. Now give it up. I'm beat out beyond."

"I swears, Mom. I was watching for moose. Idn't you supposed to watch for moose when 'tis dusky?"

He felt a sudden sting on his scalp, then his ear caught and twisted, head changing direction without his permission.

"Did your mother open her mouth?" Eli.

"Yes, sir."

"And what do that mean, boy?"

"I- I keeps mine shut."

"You wake that baby with your yammering, and your tongue'll be in a pot."

Eli released his grip on Garrett's ear, and as Garrett stared at the dash he heard that familiar sigh. He didn't dare turn to look at her, or reach up to rub the burning spot. Instead, one hand held the other, and he silently counted the number of melted circles in the plastic where someone had missed the ashtray. His eyes watered, but at least the pain had pressed down the nausea. He no longer wanted to throw up. Instead, he only wanted to cry. And for the rest of the drive home, he looked straight out the window, mused about how he might feel to see the end pummeling towards him. Dull eyes of a nodding moose, branching antlers too heavy for the head, smashing through the glass to say hello.

5

AFTER HE LEFT the courthouse, Lewis did not go home. With his charred heart, he roamed the streets of the city. Like a stray, darting this way and that, up dark alleyways, down cobblestone streets, over cracked sidewalks, pot-holed pavement. He could not bring himself to make the long drive to Knife's Point. To an empty house. No parents. No brother. Even Roy's dog Nellie had run off months ago and not returned. All he had now was a job as the keeper of order, and the upward battle of regaining lost respect. But what could he expect from his neighbors? How could they abide by him when the first thing he had done was create the foulest kind of chaos? Events that led to the death of his brother.

Eli had meant to do what he did. Even though everything was a blur to Lewis, he believed that one fact without a shred of doubt. Any other conclusion would leave some room for forgiveness, and Lewis would not allow that. It was much easier to curse Eli than to curse bad fortune.

Now, what was Lewis going to do with the hate that coated his insides? Hate for Eli, hate for himself. Like a mug of rancid cod liver forced down his throat, and when he burped, he swore he could taste the hate on his taste buds. No matter how he tried to expel it, drifting until his legs ached, ankles raw and weeping from rubbing against his shoes, he could not find a way to leave his emotion on the street. He could not let it out. And when the sun began to move down behind the buildings, he decided to tamp it, tamp it until he could make it no smaller. Tried to bury the hate, that ebony kernel, in some recess of his mind.

Threat of drizzle realized, and the sky began to spit down on Lewis. Icy pecks that pricked his skin. He ducked into an alcove, stared out at a world of gray and brown, cement and brick. Everything was dull, and he understood there were months of dullness ahead of him. He sighed, leaned his head against the window of a store, closed his eyes, and prayed. "Dear Lord," he whispered inside his head. "Please show me one thing that is beautiful. One thing that is perfect. If you do," he bargained, "I will never make another mistake. I will do everything right. By the book, Lord. By the book."

Lewis shuddered, and he opened his eyes, read the sign on the storefront, an arc of painted letters on a slab of swinging wood. "The Curious Urchin. Please come in." He pushed open the door, cowbell clanging, entered a quiet world of dolls' heads, used books, glassware, candle holders, wood planers, doilies, and fishing nets. A horse's saddle hung next to moose antlers. Bobbins and yarn, Chinese checkers and empty bottles. Two-tone pottery jugs. Everything imaginable, displayed in painted bookshelves, all coated in a fine layer of dust. Something about the clutter, the desire to preserve, to find value where none might exist, made Lewis's broken inner filament reconnect, glow ever so slightly.

An old man sat in a corner, white hair, beard, filing the teeth of a saw. He glanced up, nodded. Lewis shuffled in, clicked the door closed, and when the old man laid the saw aside, Lewis noticed the store was almost completely silent, except for ticking clocks and the thump of his own heart. Then he heard movement coming from the back, behind nailed wood shelving. He moved sideways, spied something that surely didn't belong. Tucked amongst shovels, pitchforks, and one-eyed teddy bears was a young woman. Tweed skirt and neat white blouse. Brown leather shoes and thin calves. Shiny black hair in a low pony-tail, and a pale round face. She was leaning over a mess of junk, watering a row of orange flowers in chipped pots.

As Lewis watched her, the black soot began to peel off his heart, drift into forgotten corners. Revealed, a deep pink organ, new, and pumping vigorously. She was precise, delicate, and he held his breath as he followed her long white fingers, prodding amongst the leaves, pinching a dried one, crumbling it in her fist. He could not move his watery eyes away from her, and believed, in that moment, that God had brought him there. In through the doors of The Curious Urchin. A way of showing him that in an empty world, there was always a flicker of hope.

Lewis patted his hankie on his damp forehead, then plucked up a glass bowl, apricot-colored, fluted edges, and carried it over to her. He felt like a fool before he even opened his mouth. He couldn't help but think of his mother and her books, tucked into her knitting basket, covers depicting brawny men, supine women, sheer fabric draping their bodies, faces locked in a perpetual state of ecstasy. "Sometimes it do happen," she'd say. "Love at first glance. Though most time you got to think about it for a spell." And here he was, tongue dry as though he'd just peeled it off a flake, thoughts scrambled, young heart suddenly swollen with the rushing of blood. But he had to say something. Could not leave the store without speaking, without seeing her lips move.

"What do you think," he said when she turned towards him, "of this dish?"

"Lovely," she replied, her smile like a salve.

"Would you like it?"

"Of course;" she replied. "Any woman would be happy to have it."

"Then it's yours."

She laughed, narrowed her green eyes, angled her head. "And the catch?"

"Storage," he said. "The bowl'll stay in my kitchen. But it'll be yours when you gets there."

She laid the watering can next to the flowers, dropped the dead leaf fragments in a small bucket. "Has anyone ever told you you're a brazen one?"

Left hand in his hair, he shook his head. The shyness that normally silenced him had vanished. Even though he could not meet her eye, words spewed forth as though his voice box were possessed. He held the bowl, edge of it jammed into his stomach. "Has anyone ever told you you're beautiful?"

She tittered, covered her mouth with a hand. Her expression was one of mild embarrassment, but Lewis was looking down at his shoes, the spaces between the floorboards. Never noticed that she did not blush.

WILDA BURRY HAD agreed to a drive. He rushed to the motel, showered and changed, bought a small box of saltwater taffy from the display at the front desk. Returned to the store in forty minutes flat. He could see her through the bay window as he parked, leapt out, rapped his nails lightly on the door. Just beneath a kitschy handmade sign that read "Closed for Business, Curiosity Seekers Come Again."

She turned the knob, let him in, then said to the old man, "I'll be going now, Francis."

"Your father?" Lewis asked.

"Oh, no, no," she replied. "Um... my uncle." Then to the man, "You're my uncle. Right, Francis?"

The old man hobbled forward, applied extra weight to his cane, murmured, "Well, yes, Wilda." His voice was like an instrument in the hands of a child. "Though not in the traditional sense."

"Who wants tradition?" she said, and tugged her ponytail out from the neck of her coat, twirled the black rope through her fingers.

Eyes lost among happy wrinkles, he turned to Lewis. "She's my mermaid, you see. Wilda is my mermaid."

"I idn't surprised," Lewis replied. He pictured her then, sprawled on the steps of the shop in summer sunshine, endless iridescent tail, caudal fin curled just so, long wet tresses barely disguising her naked top. "Idn't surprised," he repeated, and dove his hands deep into his pockets, willed the flush to stay beneath his collar, cuffs on his shirt.

"Found her, I did." Nodding in Wilda's direction as though she were another curiosity.

"Francis. Stop."

"Offered a pretty penny to part with her. But she's my most precious discovery."

"Francis!"

"Ah, I was only tugging your leg. You got good strong ones, can use a little tugging."

Strong legs. Again, he could picture them. Not just ankles and calves, but all the way up. Creamy thighs, gentle curves and joints where limb met flawless bottom. Lewis felt the flush creeping past the desired boundaries. "We should go," he managed. "Before I loses my– my way."

"Yes, yes. You young folks. Go on and have a time for yourself." An easy smile, and Lewis thought the old man's light brown teeth appeared to be made of wood. A hundred years old. A homemade surprise he might have dug up in a long forgotten drawer. Focus on the teeth, he told himself. Focus on the teeth.

She wrapped her arm around his shoulder, kissed his cheek. "Don't stay up past your bedtime."

"You never knows who might come knocking in the wee hours," he replied with a wink.

She coughed lightly, tugged on her coat. "You don't need to answer any more doors."

"I suppose you're right. I got my mermaid, and I got my Barley. That's more than enough for this old gaffer." A fat wheat-colored cat climbed out of a half-open drawer, dragged its body around Francis's legs, leaving a trail of fur on his dark trousers. Ignored, the cat went up on its hind legs, batted at a limp hand. Francis hunched, grasped the end of the cat's tail, shook it. "Idn't that right, Mr. Barley."

Lewis watched their banter with bright amused eyes. Their relationship was one of ease and comfort, that much was obvious. But Lewis was certain he would remove her from this picture, extract her, even if it was to the detriment of the

29

gentleman. He needed to bring her home; he'd decided that the moment he laid eyes on her. The moment she laid her eyes on him, her stare lasting just a moment longer than what he might consider ladylike.

He would offer it all to her. And she would accept, wander through every inch of his home, over every square foot of his land. Over the past year, that place had permitted entrance to too much sadness, too much darkness, and he was certain this woman, with her magic, would smoke out the evil eye, fill his home with light.

6

DARKNESS HAD SETTLED by the time Eli Fagan and his family pulled up to the farmhouse. He changed, ate a quick meal of cold ham and bread, then tromped out to his fields. After working for two hours by the light of an orange moon, he stood straight and cleaned moist grit from his blade, folded it and placed it in his shirt pocket. Hands on his hips, he surveyed his progress. Along the neat rows, immense cabbage heads lay on their sides, their severed stumps glistening. He plucked up one head, two, balanced them under his arms, and started walking home. As he neared the edge of the field, he glanced up at the farmhouse, and saw the curtains shift in the window of the boy's room. Eli stopped, stared hard at the narrow pane of glass, waited for the spying face to re-emerge.

SHORTLY AFTER HIS wife had moved into the farmhouse, Eli noticed a dozen or so planks of wood piled onto the floor of the upper hallway. Silver nails sticking upwards, just asking for a fleshy foot.

"What's this?" he had hollered.

"I took them down," she'd replied matter of factly. "To see."

He said nothing, but shook inside at the surprise of it, the cheek of the woman he had married. That door had been battened up for over twenty-two years, since the day Eli buried his mother and he had rightfully inherited the home. He had fixed sturdy boards across the door frame, nailed them to the molding on either side. But she, his wife, had somehow pried them off. She had entered the room, cracked the window, and washed the walls. Hung old blankets on the line, beat dust from the rug, scrubbed gray stains from the mattress. Plumped a feather pillow, brought in a brown teddy bear, a quilt of navy boats on a white sea, a wooden box filled with painted wooden blocks. She stole into Eli's old bedroom, she did, without a single thought, and made a space for her boy.

Those were the worst moments for Eli, to pass by that room, see the door open wide, that boy crouched on a braided rag rug, running wooden trains along the coils. Or reading a small book, acting like he was a fine child. A son to make a father proud. Sometimes Eli caught a whiff of the boy's smell. In the paste on the wallpaper, now, the sheets, the floorboards. Sour, as though the boy's very skull was a putrefied potato. Eli imagined squeezing the boy's head, his thumbs bursting through the tight skin, sinking into the yellow filth. The odor reminded Eli of his uncle, a man who lived with Eli and his family when Eli was a young boy. A grubby fucker, and Eli wouldn't think twice about slitting his throat if the bastard were still breathing.

Whenever the air in the room crawled out and drove itself up his nostrils, he'd skid down the stairs, back of his boots barely grazing each step, belt already undone. He'd find his wife, and no matter what she was doing, he'd clutch her hips. Haul down or yank up, tear aside, and with a suffocating urgency, he'd locate that warm space. Struggle with his own body until those two knots, one between his ears, one between his legs, were untied. Smoothed. As he let go, he'd arch his back, strain his face towards heaven, wanting to cry out, "I am this. I am not that. Do you see me, you bastard?" A few moments were all it took to remind himself. All the proof he needed.

Night after night, Eli dreamt of trapping the boy in that room. Bricking up the narrow window that looked over the field. Bricking up the doorway. The boy inside, and still alive. A slow madness, a slow death. And Eli would awaken, coated in sweat, overwhelmed by the need to soothe himself, once again, with his wife's body.

32

He could despise the boy but, he reasoned to himself, he could not move him from that room. A perfectly acceptable place for a child, and his wife might question. Not force an answer of course, she was incapable of that, but she would spy his flustering. The heat in his skin. Eyes averted and suspicious. So instead, he held his breath when he passed the open door, and after weeks, he collected the boards of good wood. Brought them out to the barn and hauled the nails out with the claw of a hammer. Laid bent ones on a stone, tapped them straight. He piled the boards in a corner, and so as not to waste, he collected all of the nails in an old jar.

NO OTHER SIGNS of movement in the room, and Eli kicked the earth with his left boot, then started walking again. He hated the thought that the boy, from the dimness of his bedroom, had been watching Eli work. But what could he do about it now? Too late, too late, for so many things. With practiced elbows, Eli squeezed the cabbages until their outer leaves squeaked. They were solid and heavy, a good harvest, and he tried to be grateful for the late frost, the predictability of his soil.

7

LEWIS AND WILDA drove out towards Crowley's Lurch, an expanse of flat rock that eased upwards and upwards, then dropped off into the ocean. A man from the motel had told him this was a popular spot, even though it was haunted by the ghosts of two young lovers. "Our own Romeo and Juliet," he said. "Story goes, one young chap was a bit of a scoundrel, up there on the lurch with his missus. Right crazy in love. He goes over the edge, let's out some sort of scream, and then she's calling to him, frantic-like, and not a sound. Just the water. And then she, thinking he's dead, tosses herself in after him. Strikes the rocks below, washed right out to sea, never seen again. He, now, gets up from the perch where he was hiding, couple feet down on a rock that sticks out. They calls that Romeo's plank, nowadays. Well, he sees what he done with his horsing around, and dives in after her. Smacks the rocks, and he's done for. Good-bye. But, tangled up with the wind, you can still hear the screeching coming up over the edge of the lurch. Wants other young lovers to join them. Two gets a bit lonesome after a time, I reckons. A bit dry." He glanced over at his wife. "No matter what sort of love you starts out with."

"Is that true?" Lewis asked.

"Sure as there's hair on my chest, sir."

Wife sidled up alongside him, patted his bald head. "Wouldn't go betting the farm on it, though," she said with a snicker. Leaned closer to Lewis, elbows on the counter, chest rising up to touch her chin. "You likes this lassie?"

"Uh-huh."

"You could try a fairy ring. Wander about over the rocks, and you'll find these odd circles of broken stone. People 'round here says good fortune'll befall lovers if they stands in one."

"Look who's talking nonsense, now," the man scoffed. "No more to that than the freeze and thaw of rocks."

Undeterred. "But the circle can't be broken, though, Mister. So, watch where you steps."

"Yes, now," he said, nudging his wife out of the way. "If you don't get blown over the cliffs first."

"Best hold tight to her good." She scratched out a map on a piece of paper, folded it and slid it across the counter to Lewis.

Lewis pulled into a row of cars dotted over the rock, noticed a pair of visitors out trying to stroll, but clinging to each other. The stretch of land was barren, swept clean, except for a few crippled trees that were gnarled and spread, branches pushed down into the stone. The engine was turned off, but the car still shivered as winds whipped up and over the cliff. Lewis listened for the screaming, though the wind sounded closer to moaning. Breathy ohhs, ahhs. As though Romeo and Juliet were down there, in the inky blackness, right out in the open, engaged in frothy saltwater penetration.

Lewis shifted in his seat, parts of his body suddenly bound inside fabric. Yanked at the knees of his trousers, blurted, "Have you ever seen a UFO?"

Her hands were folded on her lap. "My word. Not that I know of. You?"

"I don't know. I likes to think that I did."

"Here?"

"No, up north. My brother and myself. In a camp a few years back. Moose hunting."

"You have a brother?"

He reached up, gripped the steering wheel. "Yeah. I do." That discussion could wait.

"Just what did you see?"

"Bluish lights. Just hovering." He left out the part about the empty bottle between them, or how Roy had fired several shots straight up into the night sky.

"Oh."

"'Twas pretty. Sort of." Mind straining for something poetic. "Pretty like a, like a . . ."

"A blue light?"

"Yeah."

"With all this talk of flying objects and Francis with his mermaid, I feel like I just tripped down after Alice."

"Alice?"

"You know. Wonderland?"

"Oh."

He laughed hesitantly. This was his attempt at being playful, and it was clear he was failing. "The old rabbit hole, hey?" Stupid. Stupid. Invisible heel of a hand hitting a forehead.

"We ought not to worry about things so far away. There's enough right here."

"Yes, yes," he said. "Of course." Quickly changing streams. "Your Uncle Francis. Now there's a man who could make a decent living as a department store Santa Claus."

"Oh no, not really."

"No?"

"He's far too frail."

"Must be a lot of work. Looking after him."

"No, no. Not at all. He doesn't need me."

"I thought you said he needed help."

She touched her cheek, looked away. "Around the store. That's all. More than likely for a bit of company. He doesn't need much." Quiet for a moment, then she said, "So. Constable Trench. That's a serious job to have."

"Yes, yes. Can be. Did my training up in Ontario."

"Why did you leave?"

"What? Leave Ontario?"

"Yes, there."

Lewis frowned, leaned his head to one side. "I wanted to come home, of course."

"Really?"

"Don't we always want to come home?"

"I– I don't know."

"To settle down. Have a family. Be close to everything familiar."

Her head was turned away from him, and he couldn't see her face.

"Don't you want children?"

"Do I want children?" She laughed lightly. "Oh, gosh. Do children want me?"

Lewis groaned inside, stomach flip-flopped. This talk of children, and he could not control the flashing images of the act that led to their creation. He coughed into his fist. "Have you always lived here?" Words like squawks, someone plucking his feathers.

"Long as I care to remember."

"How many years have you been there? With your uncle?"

"Six. Maybe five, about. He needed help."

"Do you like it here?"

"Yes. I do. It's quiet. Calm."

"And before that? You lived—"

"Nowhere important."

"Maybe I know it. I'm good with geography."

"It's a good distance away. Barely even on the map."

"Let's see if I know it." Louis rubbed his palms together.

"It's nowhere, really."

"You sure are secretive."

She placed a hand on the button near the top of her coat. "You sure do ask a lot of questions."

Lewis stopped then. He was probing, wanting to know everything, but he risked silencing her. "I'm sorry."

"Don't be. My life. Life there, and then here. The store, Francis. Yard sales and markets and people's front porches. It would just bore you to tears."

"I'm certain it wouldn't, then."

She laughed again. "I'm certain it would."

"Well." He shifted in his seat. "We'll have to agree to dis-agree." The air had grown cold inside the small car, and he noticed that her arms were folded across her chest. Perhaps bringing her here had been a mistake. Maybe he should just have taken her for tea. A single slice of cake, two forks.

But first. He stepped out, came around to her side, and opened the door. Held it, as the wind tried to tear it from his grip, buckle it backwards. "Are you sure?" she said.

"Just for a minute," he replied. "Something I wants to see."

He took her by the hand, and they walked over the rock. As smooth as a sloping dance floor, though the tilt made worse by the coaxing winds. Drawing them closer to the edge. He found a stone circle, quick check of the circumference, and he lifted one foot, then the other, and stepped inside it. Guided her behind him.

Using the gust as an excuse, he put an arm around her belted waist, held her. He stuck his nose in her neck, her hair. Two dis-tinct smells trapped there. Something fresh, like tea roses, and something old, like an attic.

"I have to leave tomorrow." He spoke directly into her ear.

"Yes."

"But I can come back. A week or two. Not much more."

She never answered, and after another moment, he spoke the sentence he'd been thinking all day long. "To think I found you in a curiosity shop. That beats all, Wilda Burry. That really beats all."

Stepping back, she laughed, shook her head. "Found me? You and Francis. Who says I don't want to stay lost?"

Hand in hand they stepped out of the circle, Lewis first, and Wilda following. He cleared the stones with no trouble, but Wilda tripped slightly, and the tip of her shoe struck the lip, scattering chips of rock.

PART TWO

8

A KNIFE. THESE past years, Garrett Glass rarely went anywhere
without one. He always kept a shiny blade folded and slipped
into his pocket, or an open blade pressed against his lower
back by the band of his trousers. He felt stronger, more capable, when there was a knife at the ready. Ready for what, Garrett
didn't really know.

Garrett discovered his adoration for knives on a summery
afternoon when he was six and a half years old. Standing on a
stepstool near his mother, he watched her move metal down
through a hunk of bloody meat. The meat itself was interest-
ing, the shape, long and red, barely able to resist the sharpness
when his mother flexed her forearm. But it was not nearly as
fascinating as the tool of destruction, the knife that sliced and
chopped, turned that loin of muscle and fat and gristle into
pieces he would soon fork into his mouth. Power in that blade,
and Garrett could barely blink as it flashed before his eyes, edge
just missing his mother's knobby thumb.

When she turned to wash her hands, Garrett slid the knife
off the countertop, placed it inside his striped T-shirt, against
the flesh of his belly, and strolled cautiously out into the woods.
Privacy found inside a clump of dogberry bushes, and he tugged
up his shirt, removed the warm blade. Instantly, the skin on his
stomach sensed the absence of the metal, and he wanted to put
it back. First, though, to study it. He crouched, knife on the forest floor in front of him. He flicked away the bits of meat, then
stared at it. Turned it over and over. Caressed the worn wooden

handle, eyed the perfect hook of the edge, the forked tip that could pierce through a hide. Crack through a bone.

Fingers wrapped around the handle, he punctured the earth, felt the blade cut through dead leaves, grainy soil, pebbles. After several slashes, he looked around for something else to cut. A damp desire moved through his body, and he felt possessed by a need to alter something. Permanently. Nothing but trees surrounded him, growing up out of the earth like split hairs on a filthy scalp. Weeks ago, when he was reading the encyclopedia at the back of his classroom, he had come across a section on trees. They required water and sunlight to flourish. They pulled nutrients up through the soil using a complicated root system. If the roots were harmed, the tree would die. The tree would die. The tree would die. He had read that line three times. Then the fourth. The tree would die.

He chose a smaller tree, trunk straight and proud, wrapped in young tan skin. With sawing motion, he stripped a ring of soft bark near the base to label it. Then, on his knees, he worked his way around its base, scuttling backwards, inch by inch, cutting through root after root, as deep as the blade would go. When he finished, he buried the knife under a pile of stones, and promised the child tree he would return. Faithfully, every afternoon. So that it would not be alone as it withered away.

Frustrated that his tree still flourished, Garrett invented other games a lone youngster could play with a stolen knife in summertime. At first he removed his shirt, coated his stomach with lines of mud, then darted from tree to tree, knife poised, stabbing the wooden enemies that got in his way. He shaved long peelings of bark from a birch, wore them like primitive necklaces and bracelets. Pretended he was a feral animal, popped a wriggling earwig into his mouth, then spat it out for fear it might scramble through the holes in there, travel up to eat his earwax.

One summer evening, as the sun was setting, Garrett watched his stepfather spit on a whetstone, glide his hunting knife over it, one side, then the other, and test the sharpness of the blade against the back of his arm. As soon as Garrett saw this, he knew he would try it the very next morning. The knife he kept in the woods was dull, so he tossed it into the creek, and quietly returned to the kitchen, extracted his stepfather's knife with its bone handle from the drawer. Looking both ways, he scooted across the backyard and into his wooded play space.

He unsnapped the leather case, removed the knife, and stuffed the case up underneath a rotting log. Then, as his stepfather had done, he scraped the thin blade across the soft hair on the back of his hand. As he shaved the baby fur, he blew it, watched it scatter into a shaft of sunlight. Holding the knife, Garrett shivered, and his skin prickled with goose bumps. There was a thrill there, metal against flesh, and he panted, tongue jutting out, while he squatted, let the blade glide over his calves, over bony grooves and joints, effortlessly removing patches of hair.

As he moved the knife up his shins, he felt fierce, in control, and he imagined that this self-possession was what pulled a boy towards manhood. He belonged here, in these woods, away from his mother and stepfather. He was powerful and free, even though he was only a few steps away from the slaps and the ringing ears and the wooden spoon with the godforsaken hole in the middle. Finally on his own, and he could control any inhabitant that resided near him. Every worm and forest flower and maple sapling that might burst through the dead layer would live in his realm. He could punish them if he wanted. Slice them in half, slice them down. Or live among them as their leader. His choice. He laid the knife aside, licked his finger, rubbed the saliva into the whitish marks where the knife had been. Then threw his head back, hooted with unfettered joy.

Pressure down below, and Garrett stood, dropped his shorts, dull gray underwear, kicked them away from his ankles. Relief now as he arched his back, allowed a stream of his animal piss to coat the purplish testicle flower of a lady's slipper. *Aahhh.*

He watched the flower shudder, then bounce back to position, dripping. He scooped up the knife again in a dagger hold, swung around, weapon poised towards an invisible enemy that was creeping up from behind. Spitting and snarling, he slashed the air, screamed, "Die, you stupid thing." Hacked open its imaginary belly, ducked as the maggoty guts came spraying out. Knees bent slightly, he turned a full circle, seeking out any other creatures that might come up against him. "Dare you," he cried. "Double dare." Nothing appeared. No beast was brave enough to emerge from the ether and challenge him.

Garrett leaned back against a tree. In those dusky woods, he could be a hero. But out in the light was another matter. Though he tried, he was unable to quarantine his stepfather's words, would say them inside his mind whenever his bladder threatened to relax on the stained fabric of his pungent mattress. Those words were there now, even though he did his best to leave them at the forest's edge. Must have been hiding, he realized, inside the pouch of the lady's slipper. He heard them blaring, and he was suddenly aware he was still standing there, with his bottoms missing. What would his stepfather do if he came upon him like this? What would his stepfather say?

Trembling hand, Garrett let the blade hover over his parts, bent his head to see it, said in his gruffest stepfatherly voice, "If you wets the bed once more, my sonny boy, I'll hack your flicker off." Garrett raised both hands above his head, stomped his feet. He scanned the canopy for signs of arrival. His stepfather was supreme. That man could be anywhere. Was everywhere. "I'll hack your flicker off." Hysterical drunken laughter, replaying in Garrett's mind. "Come 'ere, boy." Point of a knife between his stepfather's two front teeth. Picking away a strand of meat. "Come 'ere, I says. Turn you into a lassie." *No, sir.* Garrett poked the sky with the knife. *No, sir. That you won't.* But there was little conviction in his high-pitched voice.

A shriek from a crow. "Garrett Glass! What in God's name are you doing?"

He jumped, nicked the flesh near the crease of his upper thigh. His mother standing there, between two scarred trees. "Idn't doing nothing, Mama," he squeaked. Knife dropped from his frightened hand, hidden underneath the broad wet leaves of the lady's slipper.

"You could cut yourself something fierce, horsing around like that."

"Clothes got wet."

"Well, they better get unwet. If Eli gets back, finds you haven't done what he ask, you'll feel the switch, my son. And you knows nothing I says'll make a difference."

9

SURE, LEWIS HAD dangled a fistful of carrots along with his proposal. But he wasn't the first man to do so. Alan Firsk, who called himself a pop artist, had offered up a silver band only a short time before she met Lewis. Wilda was his muse, Alan told her, and he couldn't abide a life without her. He was handsome, kind, and quirky, but it made her nervous when he sketched distorted line drawings of her face, images strained and haunted, smeared charcoal shadows in places that should have been shadow free. She disliked the enormous representation of her head made with a collage of clippings from old comic strips. Hated when he took snapshots of her, showcasing her attempted smiles, and strung them with cat gut inside a rusty bird cage. "These are your essence," he called it, but she did not want to see her essence. Did not want Alan attempting to capture it on paper or otherwise.

She had been carrying around his ring in the front pocket of her work apron for nine days, his proposal unanswered, when he gave her a handmade card. Bright white paper full of pretty silver fibers. He likely made it himself. On the cover was a single phrase, "My heart bleeds for you," and beneath, a miniature painting of a bright red heart, tilted on its side, anatomically correct with veins and arteries arching upwards. And beneath that, several droplets, frozen mid-drip, traveling down to a tiny pool, complete with spatter. She slid the card into the pocket of her apron, along with the ring, but all afternoon she kept removing it, staring at it. She thought she felt it beating against her lower stomach, heard the card, too, those fat drops letting go, whizzing through the air, splashing in an ever growing pool of liquid.

Such a horribly familiar feeling as she imagined the blood staining the hem of her skirt. Her tiny feet. Then, a swelling of words pressing behind her eyes. Her mother's voice, high and tight and filled with fury.

Wilda snatched the card out of her pocket, tore it into a thousand pieces. Dropped the ring into the penny slot of the cash register. When he next came to see her, she fled to the small bathroom at the back of the store. He rapped, several times, but she would not emerge, and he was forced to speak through the door. "Come on, Wil. A joke, is all," he said. "Meant to be dramatic. I thought you'd find it funny. A good laugh."

"I don't care."

"Did you even open it up? See what I wrote inside?"

"No. Now leave."

"But, Wil."

"Leave." The card was a sign. Wilda knew a vaporous bridge had formed between her present and her past.

And then, two weeks later, Lewis arrived, with his gray eyes and determination. Over the course of several months, sporadic visits, he lured her with many promises. He had some acreage, he said, a fair bit of it, and enough money to go along with it. There were spruce woods where she could roam, a warm stream to wade in during summer, and a tidy house that she could make into her own. Wallpaper and an electric stove and a robin's egg blue soup tureen that had belonged to his dead mother. She could have it all if he could take her home. Said that if she didn't agree, he'd club her over the head and drag her there anyways.

Francis told her not to worry. "Go on," he'd said. "Love when you're young. When 'tis easy."

Leave it to Francis to turn a snarl of emotional yarn into a neat skein. But it wasn't that simple. Even though she had grown used to Lewis over the months that he traveled back and forth to see her, his eagerness made her nervous. As he spoke of home life and family and any number of fat smiley babies, she noticed the soles of her feet starting to twitch. Her legs became restless, wanting to carry her away from those possibilities. To leave Lewis, and pretend she'd never met him. That would be easier. Before he realized what kind of things she had done.

She decided to marry him anyways, decided the moment when she noticed someone had strolled across that bridge. She had been walking to the bank on a March afternoon, and passed a man she recognized. Six years since she had been home to Teeter Beach, but she still knew his face. Not that this particular neighbor had meant anything to her, but it was another sign. Anyone could be next. She was not willing to wait, a sitting duck, to see who or what might emerge, materializing at the crest of the bridge, riding through the fog.

10

"HERE'S GOOD."

"Here?"

"Let me out."

"Your father might need you."

"He idn't my father."

"Still. You got work to do, and you best do it. You don't question him, Garrett."

Garrett nodded. On a cloudy morning in May, he'd gone with his mother to the drugstore, picked up yellow pills and toothpaste and tins of canned milk. He had planned to go straight home, but now, seeing that the harbor was full of pack ice, he needed to get out. "Early this year," he said.

"I don't like it."

"I think it's beautiful."

His mother never responded, but he saw her chest rise and fall in a silent sigh.

"Tell him I won't be long."

She gripped the wheel with wooly mittens, cuffs of her dark green coat worn. "No good comes from dwelling, my son."

"I idn't dwelling, Mom. Seeing idn't dwelling."

"Still. Steer clear of it. Steer clear of the water."

Garrett stepped out onto gravel, slammed the car door, heard her pull off the shoulder, drive slowly away. He went to the edge of the cliff, sat on the frozen lichens, let his legs dangle over. Out in the bay, huge shards of ice had crowded in, sharp layers lifting and buckling on the ocean waves. His heart skipped a beat when he saw three young boys dressed in navy parkas skipping from pan to pan. Arms out, balancing, and Garrett could hear them squealing. Maybe some cusswords, but he couldn't be sure. Watching them through slit eyes, he pretended they were fleas, popping about on a clean bluish sheet. He projected himself out there next, spread eagle on the cold sheet, and the young fleas sprung over, grateful, weaseled their way underneath his layers. He would allow this, allow them to take what they wanted, wouldn't think of nipping their hard shells between his two thumbnails.

As he daydreamed, Garrett felt a familiar fever clamber across his body. He put his hands beneath his thighs, pressed them into the rock. His thoughts bounced back and forth, volleying, one side explaining how he might go down to the water, step onto the ice. Play. A second side telling him to stay put. Leave them alone. Move now. Don't budge. Move now. Don't budge. The opposing positions, like hot tea sloshing about inside his mind, and Garrett's head swayed from side to side. Stay put. They were not fleas. They were young boys, and building friendships was not that easy.

But what if one of them slips? What if one of them drowns? There is no one else around. No one but you, Garrett.

He stood up.

Garrett remembered how his mother told him that Morris Murphy had hauled him out of the water when he was four. When Garrett explained he remembered it all, his mother said that was impossible. "Morris assured us you was completely unconscious." And Morris was the son of a doctor, so Mrs. Fagan gave no weight to any other scenario.

Still, Garrett insisted he was fully aware. That those moments changed his entire life. He could easily recollect the face that peered down through the surface. The light surrounding the head. Every detail was right there, on a shelf, tucked away behind other thoughts. The truth that he, Garrett Wesley Glass, had touched the mouth of God.

In the harbor surrounding Split Rock, Morris Murphy had been playing with his brother. They'd pushed shards of thick ice with sticks, laughing and stomping, until Mrs. Murphy tromped to the end of the wharf, holding her cardigan against the wind, told the boys that lunch was on the table. She said, "Tomato soup and crackers." Garrett remembered that because he was hungry, as he often was. He imagined the thick red liquid spilling over his guts, warming him from the inside out.

When no one was looking, Garrett had edged onto the wharf, walked to the end, and lowered himself down onto a slippery chunk of ice. Then he stepped gingerly onto the next broken hunk. The pans wobbled, but not nearly as much as Garrett had feared, and within a few minutes he was leaping like the boys had been. He glanced over at the Murphys' saltbox, and wished, wished, wished for the Missus to appear as she had, call him in for some soup. Some crackers. Garrett hollered and leapt, head twisted towards the house, waiting for the curtains to shudder. Arms straight out, dancing over the ice, he moved confidently, but the clouds divided, and for a second Garrett was blinded. An irritable wave, the shards bucked, and Garrett jumped as high as he could, came down onto a patch of slob ice, alarm triggering when nothing solid touched his feet. A hidden mouth, opening wide and swallowing him. Dreams of hot soup and crackers shot to the moon.

A shock of icy water had stabbed through his clothes, and Garrett was instantly numb. Twisting in the water, he saw the blackness below, shadows skittering, and above, a broken blue blanket. He floated upwards, mittens gliding over slick undersides of the pans, head knocking against a solid ceiling. Lungs bursting, only seconds until his muscles released, chest accepting the salt water, breathing it in and out like liquid air. Cold and scorching at the same time. Minutes passed, and he dozed in a limp sitting position, suspended in a dark place he could not describe. Where he felt nothing, no fear. Then, he noticed a bright window in the ice, and the face of a boy, plump cheeks, full lips, golden glowing halo around his head. Fingers of light reaching, reaching. Garrett turned away only for a moment, saw his father in the water behind him. Coming for him. But as much as he craved the comfort of his father's arms, it was nothing compared to the warmth the boy was promising. Garrett could not turn away from the light. Like a fish now, fins renewed, Garrett managed a kick. He felt his foot hooking into his father's neck, pinched for just a moment by his father's collapsing chin and shoulder. A second kick, striking his father's face with his boot, a burst of bloody ink snaking through the water.

Hands on his coat, tugging, yanking, some other force moving him up and out. The ocean agreeing to release him. The boy wanted to be part of Garrett, wanted Garrett to be part of him. Garrett felt it through and through and through. And after that, even though his mother repeated "'Twas only Morris Murphy," Garrett clearly recalled this other boy, a child, asking him to wait a little longer. And instead of taking him upwards, he kissed life into him. Kissed him back home.

"Hey fellers," Garrett hollered, hands to the sides of his mouth.

The boys stopped, looked up, yelled back. "What do you want?"

"Come here," he called, scooping the air. "Come up here."

"Says who?"

"Says ... says ... says me."

Silence for a moment, and they gawked at Garrett, gawked at each other. And next, childish laughter galloping up on the wind. Tongues stuck out, and then one of the boys turned, bent, hauled down his trousers, flash of pink skin. "And who's you?" one screamed. "Who's you? Telling us what to do."

Garrett felt his fever break. He was present again, fully inside his body. Shivering. He realized they were older than he had anticipated. Not children at all. Would not listen to him. Wouldn't understand. Only viewed him as a newly sprouted teenager, suddenly tall and sinewy and awkward. If they came closer, they would see his cheeks and forehead, covered with scabs and whiteheads, his face an oily joke he tried to hide with a mess of orange hair.

He turned, tucked his hands into his coat, strolled down over the rocky slope and up onto the laneway. He leaned against a picket fence, dipped his chapped hands into the pockets of his jacket. Inside the left one, his fingers found his small knife, a crumpled glove, a plastic bobber, three lumps wrapped in waxy paper. He pulled out a lump, removed the molasses taffy and popped it into his mouth. Then, in his right pocket, he retrieved the one item with which he would never part. Blackened edges, but no longer any trace of smoke. He pinched it between thumb and forefinger, looked only for a moment. Just enough to drive the cold out from his bones.

MRS. FAGAN DROVE up over the crest of the hill, pulled her car out onto the rocky cliff. Edging forward slowly, she stopped just as her front wheels touched the fat log. When she looked out over the dashboard, it appeared as though she were airborne, heading into the heaving sea. She wouldn't hesitate to admit (but only to herself, of course) that the thought was not altogether displeasing. But she wouldn't, wouldn't ever. Who would look after Garrett?

Taking a deep breath, she could smell the wet wool of her coat. Yes, her winter coat. Still. She hated spring, the false promise of it. How a bud or two swelled on the trees, teasing her, then, before she knew it, ice bullied its way down from the north, clogged up the harbor. Days or weeks of frosty gales, crystals in the wind, not a blue wave in sight. Icebergs stranded, wedged in by their girth beneath the surface.

Cold, cloudless days like this reminded her of troubled times. Reminded her of the day her first husband, Wesley, drowned. He had been trying to save Garrett, who had wandered out onto the broken shards that filled the harbor. Minute after minute passed, before Garrett was hauled out of the sea by their eight-year-old neighbor. She watched him lying there, crumbled on a drifting pan, clothes freezing to the ice. Life pushed back into his body through his willing lungs.

"A miracle," she called it, but others weren't so sure. Ruthless rumbling that God had met the boy, rejected him. People wondered why. "Well, He liked Wesley well enough," Mrs. Glass, as she'd been known then, offered in weak retort. Handsome and clever, she thought that man was, and he remained at large for several months. She maintained a foolish hope until the spring thaw, when his body, bloated and damaged, skin slipping like a loose wet glove, was finally spit up onto the rocks.

If she twisted in her seat now, she could just make out the form of her son. He wasn't down on the beach like she'd feared he would be. Not like those foolish children out jumping pans and squealing. No, he had listened to her, and was seated up high, on the cliff. She placed her damp mitten over her mouth, felt the sharpness of a burn mark in the wool. She couldn't fathom it, how her son might be feeling. To witness the arrival of something that nearly killed him. To be mesmerized by it. She could only dream of the sort of torment trapped inside.

11

CHEEKS HOT, HAIR standing on end, dozy Lewis Trench lay his head on the shoulder of his wife.

"Tell me the truth, Mrs. Wilda Trench," he said playfully. "Tell me who you really are."

"You're being silly," she said, patting his hand.

"We've been married a year, now. Don't you trust me?"

"Of course." It was easier to lie.

"Are you really a mermaid, Mrs. Trench?"

"Do I have a tail, Mr. Trench?"

"I believes you do. One perfect lovely sexy tail."

"You'd better watch I don't swat you with it."

He lay down, nestled his head onto her lap, and his breathing grew steady, reliable. She leaned back against the pea green chesterfield, and watched the reflection of the flames in the sheen on his forehead. May had been a cold month, and Lewis had lit a fire almost every evening. Used up the last of the birch. As she stroked his soft hair, she whispered a phrase from the children's story she'd just been reading from a thick book Lewis had owned as a boy: "Is your eyes awake? Is your eyes asleep?"

He smiled, but kept his eyes closed, and she tugged a blanket off the chair, smoothed it over him. Crackling fire, wind scraping a branch against a windowpane, but beyond that it was quiet. No one was asking for her help. No one was showing her what she'd done. Telling her she was responsible for a black stain in the mud. Perhaps here in this little house, surrounded by woods and gently rolling water, she might be able to lock away the past. Perhaps she should try. So, while he lay there on her shoulder, mind lost in deep sleep, she finally told her husband the truth. Part of it, anyway.

EARLY ONE MORNING, seventeen-year-old Wilda Burry stood smack in the middle of the only road leading out of Teeter Beach, her plaid skirt hiked to upper thigh. She was waiting for one of the few men who owned a car to pass. But no one was out for a drive, only Old Mackie, who edged up beside her with his creaky wagon, two dusty horses. "Put yer leg away, for the love of God," he said. "I kin cart ye over to Spoonie Bay without none of that." She hoisted herself and her father's kit bag, stuffed with a sealskin coat, up and over the wooden boards, and plunked herself down on a pile of freshly cut logs, bark skin still slick with a nervous sweat.

"Nothing wrong with cutting out, Wilda maid," he said as he stopped near the stage and waited for her to jump off. He grimaced when the wind lifted her hair, and he saw the bruises on her cheeks, split bottom lip. He waved to his son, and Baby Mackie bounded up from the broad flake. "Ouch, maid. Who took der boots to ye?" Then, glancing up at Old Mackie, he nodded, said, "Lucky day, darlin'. 'Bout to aul 'er up for the winter." Baby let her sit on the damp floor of his skiff, flattened kit bag beneath her backside, and she gripped the sides as they skipped and bumped over waves, skiff taking flight, striking water, salt spray coating her cheeks, stiffening her hair. Old and Baby understood she was leaving everything behind, and never coming back. And they didn't blame her, wished her the best. No child would be untouched after having a mother like she had, and witnessing her father stumble so brutally into the afterlife. Most agreed Wilda was as good as she could be.

She'd planned to keep traveling until she hit Florida or California or someplace warm. But she had little say in the direction of her journey. On the main roads, drivers slowed, eager smiles, and without any money she would oblige them with her small hands before accepting another fifty clicks of transportation or a night at Aunt Whoever's, or a motel just off the highway. Sometimes food from a cardboard dish or brown paper. Once a silver dollar hamburger from the lunch counter at a gas station.

Several days of travel, she headed south with a truck driver, and south some more with another, and then a bit east with a man and briefcase and a vacuum, and then south, and further east with someone named Dicky who had a wineskin that was always plump. "Wrong way," she said or thought as she dozed, a hardened towel balled between her head and the vibrating window. Teeth clinking. But she never got out of the warm car that smelled of leather and cigarette butts and spilled whiskey.

When she reached the city, she tripped onto a sidewalk and soon realized the folly of her plan. November was not a time to take flight. In those couple of days, temperatures had dropped, skeleton trees now lined the neat streets, and powdery snow was drifting into damp corners. She blinked with the glare of sunlight on the harbor, kicked Dicky's car door closed with the thick heel of her shoe, and wandered. She had never been to the city, and she liked the bigness of the place. Each store window offering her something that might make her happy, from knee-high boots with zippers to oily fish and chips. But she didn't have any money, only a handful of change in a drawstring purse, now coated with eye shadow that had opened when jostled about.

She unzipped the bag, and the smell from the old coat, contained for days, assaulted her nose. Still, she slid it on, buttoned up against the cold, and walked quickly along the roads, thankful that the gusty winds tugged the odor away from her. Though she dared not admit it, she felt hopeful in this new place where nothing was known. Hopeful for the first time in her life.

Bells tinkled when she entered the jewelry store, but the man with the gray flannel suit and his daughter in the sweater set never acknowledged her. She tried fine clothing, musical instruments, timepieces, lady's shoes, yarn and fabric. But her inquiries were answered with clicking tongues, giggles, and once just a glare, shot out over the rims of lowered tortoiseshell glasses. Even in the shop where they sold milk, bottles of home-made jam with cutesy labels, and lobsters carved from pine, the owner behind the counter shook his head, averted his eyes, covered his nose with the back of his hand. Said, "Maybe you should wash yourself first."

She roamed, taking a street here, a flight of stairs there, another street, moving further away from the water, her direction unknown. Pausing in the shadow of an alleyway between two buildings, she crouched and touched the tips of her shoes with cold fingers, stuck her nose into the prickly lapel of the coat. Closed her eyes, and inhaled that musty odor, the scent of dead animal, hint of rot. Well, maybe more than a hint. The air was a mugging, as though someone had clapped a dead hand over her mouth. But still, she accepted it into her lungs. The coat had belonged to her father. Along with the rest of his belong-ings, she found it stuffed in a box, abandoned in the barn. Water had seeped in around the clothes, handkerchiefs, his khaki housewife, and nourished an orange mold that streaked all the fabric. She noticed evidence that mice had resided in amongst the folds, and when her fingers slipped through a tear in the lining, the back of the seal pelt felt soapy. Wilda still wanted it though. Wanted to keep something that belonged to him and treasure it.

When she was little, she would hide inside the coat. Open-ing the wooden closet with ill-fitting doors, she would step on old shoes and boots, worm her arms up and in, dangle, com-pletely obscured by fur. Her mother might open the closet, jam her own coat or hat inside, never notice that Wilda had trans-formed. That there was a seal in the closet that was fatter and sillier. But her father would notice. Haul open the door, and she would hold her breath when he'd exclaim, in his melted way of talking, "Lor, Jays. Nev woulda fathomed." Uncontrollable snicker when he squeezed the coat with his two big hands. "We got us-selves real live wilda-beast. Jessie, come see." With that, her mother would strut over, yank open the front panels of the coat, surprise, child revealed. Smacks about the head. "Wilda Burry. Get your bloody arse out of there right this instant fore I tans your hide. Always at where you got no business."

When she stole it from the box in the barn, she didn't allow an ounce of guilt to settle. It should belong to her now; it was an important feature for so many of her memories. Her father was always wearing it when she thought about him. Sliding down the back of Old Mackie's land, the two of them on a long wooden sled. Making perfect holes with the auger, lying flat on their bellies, foreheads touching, watching fish nibble pale worms. When she arrived at the woodpile on any given blustery after-noon, he would always wink at her, then abandon his crosscut saw for the two-man. Memories like this made her glad, and she ignored the fact that she could not recall ever seeing the coat on his back. Or that he never did any of those things, and was long dead when she thought them up. But they would have been real, she was certain, if he had of stayed around. If, as her mother always told her, Wilda had gone to find help, instead of running off to play on the beach.

Wilda dug into the pockets, found the bent cigarette she had pinched from whatever-his-name-was. Lit it, took sev-eral deep drags, let the smoke curl out from her nostrils, waft upwards. Her eyes watered, dripped. They were allowed to do that, as long as they weren't crying. Picturing the store own-ers, she snarled into her knees, "I wouldn't fuckin' work for you if you paid me." But what did she expect, with her sour breath and disheveled hair. Bare legs, mess of blue veins. Stench like a puffy carcass rejected by the water. She could hear her mother's voice, and knew it was true. "You looks like something a mutt tossed up. And don't even get me started on the smell."

Her mother was a seamstress, making skirts and aprons for the women in Teeter Beach. Wilda made no attempt to learn how to sew, not that there was much opportunity. She didn't linger at home. Most days, after her few chores were completed, she was out strolling, along the beach, up and down the laneways, wasting her hours. She liked to play a game with her eyes, pretending to look at any disturbing scene in Teeter Beach, and see it a thousand times at once. Men hacking heads from fish, golden balls mistakenly severed with a scythe, a young boy screeching, his free spirit tethered to a stationary clothesline via an inhumane length of rope. She tried to turn a single image into a mass of them, all butting up against one another, each identical and now meaningless. Over the years, Wilda had learned that if she could only see through fly eyes, she would feel nothing.

Visits to Eddie Quick's shack helped with this illusion. Eddie told Wilda he was in the distillery business, but she noticed the majority of his product went to serve his own needs. Smiling, teeth like burnt twigs, he'd offer her Whiskey Daisies without the daisy, or in wintertime he'd give her a mug jammed with snow, liquor poured over the top. "Dat's me famous Whiskey Shiver." And he'd shake for effect. When she wanted more, Eddie waved his half a hand, three fingers lost to frostbite, cautioned, "Too much, and trouble'll find ye." Pincer grasp towards her chest. "They's still there, mind you. Me fingers. Ye just can't see 'em." "Yeah, yeah," she'd always reply. "Just like everything else." He never expected much in return, just a few minutes' work. "Let's make it quick, Mr. Quick," she'd slur as she pushed her hand past the band of his trousers, tugged and tugged.

The day before Wilda left, her mother received a package of luxury fabric she had ordered to sew a fine dress for the reverend's wife. Wilda untied the string, tore the brown paper off the box. Inside was a silky heap of material, aqua paisley print on a cinnamon background. She ran her hands over it, in among the cool ripples, and was certain it was a sin to clothe the overstuffed carcass of Mrs. Hatcher in something so divine. After smoothing the fabric on the kitchen floor, she lay on top of it, blue chunk of chalk in her hand, and traced an outline of her body. While her mother was at the neighbor's house letting out an old gown for a "boom-boom" wedding, Wilda used those sharp thin scissors, worked the machine with her feet, and made herself a dress.

She was trying to squeeze her arm into a too-tight sleeve when her mother arrived in the kitchen, dropped her basket at her feet. Crying out, she knelt on the floor, scooped the slivers of material in her hands, looked at Wilda, who had the fabric pinned to her clothes, draped over her shoulder. "Jeeesus, good Jeeesus. 'Tis ruined. Do you know what that costed? Why oh why oh why?" Wilda replied coolly, "I wanted to make something. Have something new." "Something new?" Shrill crow in the room, flapping up now from the floor, beating the air with her arms. "Something new? You don't deserve nothing. Let alone something bloody new." Her mother reached across the table, clutched a pair of pinking shears in a clenched fist, and raised them in the air. Wilda curled her arms around her head, loose seam on the sleeve splitting. "Go easy, they says. Go easy." Her mother struck Wilda's head and back with the handles of those shears. "After what you seen happen to your father. They says. No one goes easy on me. No one helps me make bloody ends meet." Over and over again. Pain coming to Wilda in the most magnificent colors behind her closed eyes. "You stupid, stupid girl. You was born stupid. Born stupid. Do you think no one knows what you does? Going 'round like a drunken whore? Bringing shame down on me?" Through a clenched white beak. Wilda cried through her forearms, but her mother only saw fit to strike her harder. "You coulda helped him. Coulda found me. Stead of jus runnin' away." Her mother collapsed then, shears lost in a fold of her skirt.

Down the alleyway, Wilda heard silly laughter, and she turned to see two women slipping out of a house, the doorway invisible from her current angle. She stood, crushed her cigarette against a slab of stone, and moved towards it. Found a black door, no bell, no neat sign to the left or right. Somebody lives here, she thought, but pushed open the door, descended a steep staircase, and arrived in a dark open space, low ceilings, walls coated in red paint, a stretch of wooden bar, a few cheap tables, linoleum floor, chairs and stools. The smell of smoke and something else made Wilda's heart beat a little faster.

She walked over, stood beside a woman at a nearby table, hunched over a paper tray of limp fries. "What's this?"

The woman leaned her head backwards, rolling chins. "What's what?"

"This place."

"Nothing for you to be concerned about." Three fries poked into that black hole all at once.

Wilda's mouth watered. "Who do I talk to?"

"Honey, any man that slogs through that door, if you asks me."

So as not to reach out, and once again snatch what was not hers, Wilda made fists, shuffled her feet, waited.

"Ahh. Right over there. Vincent. From Montreal, he is." Chewing, licking her fingertips. "Thinks his shit don't stink."

Wilda twisted, saw the owner leaning back against the bar, body stumpy with slicked black hair, pink cheeks, skewed nose, tight trousers cutting into his crotch. One of his ears was ragged and discolored, like an oyster shell. She went and stood before him, never wavered as his gaze moved over her every swelling and crevice, his tongue wetting his bottom lip. But instead of speaking, he turned his back.

She tapped the flesh over his ribs. "I wants to be here," Wilda announced, feet spaced. "Do something."

"Bah, do what? What can you do?" he scoffed over his shoulder, cigarette waving in the air. "Liddle girl. Go find your maman."

"I needs money."

"Don we all?"

"But, Mister."

"But, non." He turned, poked a dull button on her coat, frowned. "Mes monsieurs don want for le phoque from the village. Go, bébé. Your mommy wait."

62

She looked at his hands, saw the dimples, nails like neat squares of waxed paper, and fingers so fat they were forced apart. "I idn't no fuck, sir." Steadied her voice, tried to keep the desperation out of her tone. Though she knew that outside, darkness was beginning to take down the light. "And besides," she lied, "my mother's dead."

"Ah," he nodded slowly, rubbed his shiny chin. Smiling, now, too. Few moments of staring, mulling, then, "Okay. Okay. I think thing for you to do."

"Oh, thank-you," she squealed. "Thank-you, thank-you." Well, then. Gainfully employed. "I can do it. Bring drinks. Sell cigarettes. Whatever you wants, Mister. What ever you wants."

He snickered. "You have nice face, but what I want first is put coat in garbage. Where belong. C'est dégueulasse."

She went through another door, rolled the coat and stuffed it back in the kit bag. Then, she found a toilet and sink, washed her face, scraped the corner of a towel across her teeth, pinched her cheeks. Rubbed her bloodshot eyes. Finally, someone was giving her a chance. Someone who had no idea about her life. She could be anyone she wanted now. She could be someone completely new.

Wilda returned to the bar, and Vincent smiled at her, flicked his head to another man, and three fingers of whiskey soon arrived in a glass in front of her. Buzz from the ride with Dicky having dissolved, she clutched the gift, and gulped it. Liquid coating her shaky insides, pressing out the ice crystals that inhabited the skin over her scant flesh. "Thank-you, Mister," she whispered. Wilda Burry was now a woman with good manners. Elbows off the table. When she clanked the glass down, it was full again. She stared at it, scraped her tongue against her teeth to make sure she had really drank something.

"Vas-y," Vincent said, wide welcoming smile. "Is good for you. Meat on bone. Hair on chess."

She picked it up, thought of Eddie Quick and his half a hand, and raised her glass to his distant memory. To you, Mr. Quick.

Who was always quick. Never one to waste good time. Gulped it down again.

Vincent leaned in towards her, sleeve of his shirt touching her bare arm. Voice soft. "Why you come here?"

Insecurity caged, she stared at his wet black eyes, considered her response. Lost soul or adventurer? She choose neither, responded with a question. "What happened to your ear, Mister?" Reached up, stroked the rippled skin over damaged cartilage. She had the urge to lick her finger, touch it again.

"Come," he said, taking a bottle and the two glasses. "Sit. Speak."

At a table, they sat side by side in a corner, and he poured her a full glass, eyes never moving from her giddy face. "I fight. When I were young boy. Strong. Boof-boof." Pretended to assault his ear with his own fist, once, twice. "Like that. Big fight." Then he laughed, patted his stomach, hollow sound. "Not now. Not today. Too fat. Old, now."

Wilda laughed along with him, touched his arm with one hand, locked her other hand around her never-empty glass. Drank. A cheers to Vincent, this time. Cheers to herself the next. Cheers to adventure, arriving this new place. Cheers to possibility. Cheers to leaving her ghosts behind. Wee, wee, mon-stur. Giggles. Wee, wee. "Non, non," he replied, "C'est 'mih-sieur.'"

People emerged from the shadows, shook hands with Vincent, and she nestled in, wide awake and sleepy at the same time, felt the heat radiating out from his armpit. In a blink, the place was crowded, loud, women and men standing beside her, pressing against her, coats and jackets abandoned. Fine wool skirts and loosened ties. Ladies perched on laps, head thrown back in fits of uncontrolled laughter. She tried it herself, leaning her head back. Wide mouthed smile. Haze of smoke in the air, sweet music, and as she gazed about, eyes struggling to focus on any one thing, she began to see the movement as fluid. Slow motion. Buttons on a tight blouse, a lipstick-coated mouth, soft fawn curls, greased ducktails, a silver watch. "If ever a devil was born without horn," Vincent sang along with the blaring record. "Ever angel fell. Was you." His breath spiraling through her ear into her brain, made her breathe a little faster, her backside throb against the seat. She laid her head on his shoulder, closed her eyes, pressed her mouth into the warmth of his jelly neck.

"Come," he said, and he gripped her wrist, and she floated up from the seat, struck her hip on the table, followed as he led her through the gaggle of happy socializers. Tripping over feet, smiling at backs of heads, trying to skip up a staircase like she was capable of being graceful. Like she was still a mystery, when she was drunker than she'd ever been in her entire life. He opened a door out into a pitch-dark alleyway, and she couldn't sense the cold as it wrapped around her thighs, pushed up her skirt. One knee hoisted, hooked over his elbow, and Vincent whispered, "Ah. Ma liddle Jezebel," and she hung onto his neck, slumped, as he fumbled with his pants, found his way, pressed against her, ground her bony wings, curve of her backbone, into the stone wall. Slipping sideways, and he wrapped a strong arm around her ribs, righted her, pressed her harder in place, grunting, grunting. Bump, bump, bump. A dirty rag doll with its legs pulled apart, stitches broken. "You love me?" she slurred, bump, bump, and inside her head she tried to crawl away from the wave of blackness that weighted her edges, shaking her down. "I keep you for this night," he moaned, full weight shuddering against her starfish frame, and she disappeared, spiraling eddy of darkness.

She awoke on a wooden floor, saw the wide back of Vincent bent over the open door of a woodstove, one knee on the floor. Prodding something with a metal poker. Hard to see. She stretched. A mound of gray and cream inside the stove, something dead, flames dancing around it, not wanting to consume it. What was he doing? She sat up, hands slapped on the floor to steady herself. A peculiar ache resided in her joints, her limbs. Then, she fell backwards, squeezed her eyes closed. There was dampness between down below, and she was sure she had soiled herself. Eyes open again, she watched the creature inside the stove as it gradually succumbed, began its conversion into soft ash.

Smell like burnt remains. Reminded her of a fire on the beach, when Baby Mackie's son, Clipper, had peeled a rotting mound off the rocks, tossed it in for a joke. Thought forming, forming, alarm triggering in her chest. A minute or two to comprehend, remember where she was. Who she was. Glanced about, and sure enough, near her bare feet, her father's kit bag was unzipped, fabric flaccid. His seal fur coat gone.

Like an insect, two legs amputated, she scuttled across the floor towards the stove, tried to reach into the flames. Vincent knocked her away, and back she came, crying, "Nooo, nooo. Mister." He slammed the iron door closed, rammed the handle of the door downwards, locking it, and growled, "Stop, beetch. Bring garbage to ma home. Make ma floor stink."

"Nooo, nooo." Down on front paws, begging, a submissive wolf.

"Is gone, now. Is gone." He clamped a firm hand around her skinny upper arm, bone bending as she was lifted to her feet, front door opened, and flick of a feather, she was on the street with no coat, no shoes. Sensation of a snowball between her legs.

Plunked down on a sidewalk, heavy slope, row of pretty painted houses, and no idea how she had gone from wherever she had been to where she was now. Empty kit bag in her arms, she stood, raised one foot, then the other, soldier legs taking the easiest path. Down, down the hill. Past men and women, arms locked, singing and laughing, dapper hats and fine coats. Clicked their tongues, said "Hey, Miss. You'll catch your death." But she rolled onwards. Weaving, stepping onto the road, smacking into rough brick, hands out to steady herself as the sidewalk lifted and buckled, knees marching high on this strip of rippling cement.

From up above, she could see herself staggering, then lurching. Mumbling. Nowhere for her to go, every way she turned led to nothingness. She was on a street of stores, doors locked, lights out, and beyond that were the rough rims of the earth. Over the edges, watery blackness moving up and down. She would go there, throw herself in. No one would notice a slip of a girl floating amongst the rusting boats. Just one step. Not much at all. You can do that, Wilda-beast.

Yeah. I'm coming.

She turned herself around, and was taking a second step closer to the harbor when an icy gale shot up the tunnel made by the buildings, lifted her hair. Frost invaded every pore, and she began to shake, a little at first, then violently. Teeth clanking, hands waving, she was blown sideways first, several steps backwards, then up and into a dark alcove. The entrance of a small store. Her head struck against the colored window of the door.

One sharp knock. Bone against glass. A sound even the deaf would hear.

Hands on her now, warm, gentle hands, guiding her through a door towards comfort. She knelt on the floor, and opened her eyes, looked up into the face of God. Silver tufts of hair by his ears, baggy skin around his veiled eyes, half-moon glasses dangling on a tarnished chain looped around his neck. "Hello, Lord," she slurred when she first looked into the face of Francis. "Hello."

"THOSE ARE THINGS I did, Lewis. Things I did. I don't blame anyone but myself." She stared at the flames, thought about that open oven door, her father's coat burning. "And then, after all that, I struck my head against his door. Struck my head against the door of the Curious Urchin." She sighed. Francis had told her that in all his years, he'd never seen a woman in such a state. Like she'd been swallowed by a whale and spit back out. She closed her eyes, could see her younger self staring back at her, summertime clothes in November, thin skin blue, scrapes on her feet and legs, patches of broken blood vessels near her neck, shoulders. Filthy fox bites, her mother would have called them, and the mere thought of those words made her want to vomit. "I was nothing more than a streal. Francis said the smell of liquor was so strong, he moved his candle to a higher table."

"He was not my uncle at all," Wilda whispered in Lewis's perfect ear. "That was my first lie to you. He was a stranger." She paused. "A bedraggled saint. Hauled me in off the street for no reason at all. Not a single question.

"He offered me a room and a job. Asked for nothing in return except that I don't leave him alone in the evenings. An easy request, keeping away from darkness." She put the back of her hand to her mouth. "I didn't own a thing. Not a thing. It is a debt that almost strangles me."

Wilda shifted backwards, pulled the blanket off of Lewis, pushed it underneath his head. "Do you hear me?" she whispered. He opened and closed his mouth several times, desert tongue smacking the roof. "Do you hear me?"

Watching his face closely, Wilda looked for some sign that her words had been absorbed. But his eyelids did not flutter, and there was only a playful dreamy smile at the corner of his lips. She kissed the tip of her finger, touched it to the end of his nose.

Both palms on the coffee table, Wilda stood, waddled to their bedroom. Closed the door behind her. The air was icy, as though a wall was open to the outside. She waited there, in the darkness, for a long time. Listening to sounds that had grown no more familiar even though she'd been living there for more than a year. And now, she could identify something else, something new, mixed in among the creaking frame, few flapping shingles on the roof. She heard a whirring, her own voice reverberating her humiliation. Murky echoes that didn't lose any momentum no matter how often they pinged off the walls, bore through her head. A mistake letting her secrets out into this open space. She recognized that now. Unloading her wretchedness inside a perfectly good home.

She stayed in the blackness minutes longer. When her child kicked, she looked down, rubbed her stomach, whispered, "I don't know what you were thinking. Choosing me." Then she reached up her arm, swung it, caught the crocheted string hanging from the light fixture, and yanked.

12

CONSTABLE LEWIS TRENCH could not turn a blind eye. Could not look away when he saw the young Stick boy taking a sharp turn, cut off the road and down onto a path that led towards Grayley River. Duane Stick's behavior looked suspicious, glancing about, then darting away like a deer that suddenly realized it was out in the open. But it was the fishing rod draped over his shoulder, silver tip glinting in the sunlight, that made Lewis turn on his heel and follow.

Lewis moved slowly through the woods, path soft and slippery, walking toe to heel, toe to heel. The trail that led to the river was narrow, and he shifted his body to avoid sappy spruce branches dirtying his jacket. Taking a deep breath of crisp autumn air, he could smell the forest floor, leaves and pine-cones and needles breaking down into soil. There was the faintest scent of wood burning, acrid, but it made him think of homes and fireplaces and cords of cut wood, and he paused for a moment to take another deep breath, and recognize his good fortune. One day, he would bring his son here, into these woods, to this river, show him how to land a big one. But only when the time was right, when the salmon were in season.

Wood burning replaced by the smell of cigarettes, human exhaust, and Lewis got moving again. Faster now as the rumble of the river was growing in intensity, and his steps would not be heard. As he came around the final turn, he saw the black water, fifty, sixty feet across, coursing happily over rounded stones, pockets of absolute calm tucked behind larger rocks, eddies twisting into eddies behind smaller ones. Lewis stayed just beyond the tree line, in the shadow of a row of fir trees, and he watched Duane.

Skinny, jeans stuck into black lace-up boots, oversized sweater with a too-big neck falling off his shoulders. Lewis knew the Stick boy, knew the family. Father was a drunkard, a gambler, would sell the seat off the toilet if he thought he'd make a dollar off it. The lot of them lived about a mile into the woods, at the end of a pot-holed road, parts of the clapboard on the ramshackle house rotted away, tattered tarpaper exposed. When Lewis had last carted Mr. Stick home, he recalled thinking that the family was in for a cold winter. Nothing much to keep the heat in.

Duane was there that early evening, head stuck underneath the hood of a rusted heap of junk, wheels gone, chassis sunk into muck. He never so much as hauled his head out when Mr. Stick tumbled from Lewis's car, fell sideways into the house, nearly squishing one of the half dozen children. Duane was the oldest son, and unlike his father never caused a scrap of trouble. Until now. Lewis watched the boy settle in beside the river, tie a leader onto his rod, then bring it to his mouth, sever the line with his front teeth. And as he tracked the boy's every movement, he wondered if Duane Stick, living the harsh life he was, had ever experienced joy.

That question was soon answered. Yes.

Lewis crouched down, sat on his heels, eyed Duane for several more minutes as the boy fished. Rod in his hand, Duane arched his arm behind his head, let his line whip back, snap the air, then sail forward, kiss the water. With each cast, Duane quickly peered over his shoulder, then tugged his line between thumb and forefinger, lifted the tip of his rod again, line released. Perfect casts, line floating through the air in wide curves, stroking the surface. Over and over, patiently, edging closer to bank, then up a short distance, then back down. Finally, snag, and Duane jumped a little, let the dangling cigarette tumble from his grinning mouth. Brrzzzz from the reel, fish fighting, Duane bent his knees, leaned backwards, tip up, reeling, relaxing, reeling, relaxing. In shallow water up over his boots, Duane guided the fish towards him, grabbed the line, lifted the salmon up and out of the water, caught it underneath its silky belly. Back on shore, Lewis could see the boy's open-mouthed smile, could hear him saying, "Well, I'll be. I'll be." Laid the fish on the rocks next to his rod. Lit another cigarette, proud manly drags. "Good supper tonight."

"Just what do you think you're up to, young man?" Lewis stepped out from behind the fir trees, put his hand to his brow to block the brightness. The sun's attempt to support Duane.

Stammering, Duane stared down at the fish, up into Lewis's eyes.

"Throwing in my line, is all. Practicing."

"With what?"

"Nothing, sir."

"Nothing idn't what I sees."

"A bomber."

"A bomber?"

"Well, close." Shade of dignity. "Made it myself with a length of Mother's yarn."

"Aiming to catch something, I reckons."

"No, sir. No. Nothing."

"Snag something, then?"

"I means, yes, sir. I was."

"I was what?"

One boot lifting, mud and gravel sucking at the sole. "Aiming to catch something."

Duane had the fish in his hands now, and Lewis couldn't recall the moment when the boy had bent to retrieve it. Grip on the tail secure, the other open hand supporting the throat, and the fish opened and closed its ancient jaw, stared out from its ancient eye. Witnessing this jig between man and almost man.

"Can I say something, sir?" Duane turned his head sharply, wiped his reddened nose on the upper sleeve of his sweater. "Can I say something?"

"Don't dig yourself no deeper than you already is."

"My mother," he stuttered. Words like the river, churning over rocks. "The youngsters. There hasn't been much these past six or seven days. Father's gone off, took the jar that mother had. She's too proud to come out and ask for something. And 'tis just the one, sir. Just the one. I swears."

"What's your name?" he asked, even though he knew it.

"Duane. Duane Stick, sir."

"And, Mr. Stick, do you know that poaching is illegal? Against the laws we got here?"

"No, sir. I means, yes, sir."

Lewis continued his standard spiel. "Do you know that the fines is hefty? And if you can't pay your fines, they can toss you in jail for a good long time? A good long time."

"No, sir. 'Tis one fish, sir. Just to have a dinner. Coupla meals. With Father gone, and all."

"Don't matter if 'tis one or one hundred. All the same in the eyes of the law."

"I don't got no money for a fine, sir, honest, sir, and I don't know what Mother'd do if I was gone off. I won't do it no more. I promises I won't."

"That's right, you won't."

Silence for a moment, and they stared at each other, Duane still lifting and dropping his feet, likely icy in soaked boots. He began to retreat, fish's tail still snug in his fist.

Lewis rubbed his face, pressed his temples with thumb and middle finger. He'd caught so many men poaching, mostly young, good stories tumbling from their lips, and never once did he waver. This was the first time he wished himself back behind those fir trees. Wished he could just close his eyes, let the boy walk away with his dinner. But he pushed out the words. "I can't let you keep it."

"What?"

"I can't, Duane."

"But. But."

72

"You have to put it back."

"Mouth is tore, sir. Tore on my fly."

Lewis clenched his jaw, scratched his forehead with hard nails. Rules were rules were rules, and Lewis had made an oath to follow them. He had no choice, and his insides ached, something akin to hunger pain, but not. Lewis stood still as Duane did as he was told, squatted near the edge of the river, moved the fish back and forth in the flowing water. But the fish never shook free from Duane's grasp, never spread its gills or flicked its tail, splashing freezing water up over his wrist. Duane twisted his neck, looked up at Lewis. Lewis whispered, "Christ," closed his eyes, nodded once. And Duane opened his hand, waited as the fat salmon rolled onto its side and began its lazy descent downstream. Then Duane crept backwards, not watching his step. Boot came down on the thinner part of his rod, cracked it. And he left the remains on the banks of Grayley River, bolted through the woods, disappearing into shadows.

Lewis never followed the path of the boy, just stood there with his frowning face towards the glittering water, squinted eyes following the dead fish. Tumbling over rocks, its brilliant belly flashing, flashing, until the river deepened, and the fish was swallowed by the thirsty current.

13

IN A GROCERY store aisle containing biscuits and canned veg-etables, a pair of rickety carts clanged together. Two women, both with evenly rounded bellies, feet swollen inside unzipped winter boots, collided with some force. But only one woman glanced up with flushed cheeks, hand to mouth in apologetic gesture.

Mrs. Fagan, the older of the two, did not lift her face. Of course she didn't. Had no desire to display her forehead cov-ered with fine wrinkles, cheeks and mouth white, emotionless. She adjusted her cart, continued to scan the shelves, searching for gingersnaps. Pretended the harsh sound of metal scraping against metal had never happened.

She was not born like that, dour and flat and mostly sound-less. Void of civility. Once, in a time of her life she could barely stand to remember, she and her sister had liked to dance, could do the foxtrot together, swing. Even tap a little. Holding hands, swaying on the old wooden floors of the Legion, edges of their full skirts brushing, both aware how many eyes, both men's and women's, were fixed to their trim whirling calves. That was when she'd been a Glass. Married to Wesley, tall and skinny with a mop of bright hair. Smiled incessantly. Even in his sleep. Sometimes she imagined him smiling at the sculpins while he was drowned.

Shortly after he died, her sister met a man of some affluence, and she moved to Cape Breton, into a brick mansion with a peaked roof and a sunroom. Perennial garden full of phlox and dianthus. And Mrs. Glass was alone then, with young Garrett, and not two pennies to rub together. She soon discovered that her perfect smiling husband owed every cent they had saved. Not even enough left for a few cups of flour. Requests for loans from her sister were eventually met with silence. Unanswered letters. Unreturned calls. Miss Piddle, the landlady, threatened to kick mother and son out as soon as the first leaf turned green. "I don't rent for free," she snipped. Mrs. Glass would have to send the boy away, go to the city, find work. A plan was beginning to form, until she received a half nod from Eli Fagan. The man from Knife's Point, who sat in the smoky corner of the Legion, never danced, but decided to take a wife to cook and clean, alleviate the frequent throb that tormented his dreams. She knew about Eli Fagan, but her options were limited—who was going to take on a woman with a young son? A young son who had gone a mite queer in the head since the day he was plucked from the sea. And as her mother always said, "The devil ye knows is always finer than the devil ye don't." Few words from the reverend, and she transformed from a Glass to a Fagan. Wanted the boy to switch too, but Eli wouldn't hear of it, and the child remained a Glass.

But that business was neither here nor there. No point to wallow when it made no difference to her current state. A husband who was like a kettle perched over an uncertain flame. A son who spent most of his days lost inside his head. A five-year-old daughter who already knew how to use her doe eyes and snarl of brown hair to get just what she wanted. And now, a third child on the way. Another girl, Mrs. Fagan suspected. Girls made her sick for the entire nine months, wide band around her neck, driest of heaves, and all she could keep in her gullet was package after package of Purity gingersnaps soaked to a golden mush in bowls of warm milk.

No, she didn't intend to look up, see the pretty face of the woman who had blocked her way. Felt no need to feign embarrassment or utter an excuse to someone who would only view her shabby clothes and saucy daughter with pity or anger or disgust. Not a common square inch of ground between them, she and Mrs. Trench. Yes, she knew who the woman was, could identify her in her side vision. Married to the last member of the Trench family, and Mrs. Fagan understood full well that her own husband had helped finish the second last one off.

WILDA TRENCH, cheeks shiny and plump from another pregnancy, needed two packages of gingersnaps. She had a recipe for squares that used a base made of butter and crushed cookies, quarter teaspoon of a spice she couldn't remember, but was certain she'd find in the varnished wooden rack that hung beside the stove. Lewis would like this dessert, she was certain, and he would sneak bites of it continuously until the glass dish was empty. Although she had never learned how to break an egg, she could feel the results of her efforts when she hugged her husband, his skin stretched and taut, nourished stores of fat expanding beneath.

That part of her life, slicing moose and sifting flour, scrubbing floors and darning socks, was not difficult. In many ways, she enjoyed the continuity. A bed made, slept in, messed, remade. Easy, simple, and it gave her a sense of purpose. But her newfound well-being teetered after she had her son. Even now, seated inside the grocery cart, three-year-old Melvin was watching her. With his patient eyes. Legs folded, seed-stitch hat and mittens laid neatly on his lap, he followed her every move. Each time Wilda would touch the edge of the cart, his small hand would reach up, rest lightly on her fingers. Always trying to connect with her, always trying to catch her eye. Not with the intent of gaining a sweet, as most children might do, but with an earnestness that made her squirm inside her boots.

Don't look at me like that, she wanted to say.

Like what?

Like I got hold of your heart.

He had been that way since he was born. She had arrived at the hospital's glass doors with a hardened stomach, stabbing pain in her back, awoke hours later, groggy, cramps a hazy delusion, stomach now an undercooked cake, stomping near the oven door. A nurse handed her a swaddled parcel, only five pounds, face wrinkled like a dried scrap of apple. And she held it reluctantly, stared in quiet panic as the old man hand wriggled free from the swaddling and five tiny digits, impossibly long, curled firmly around her own finger.

In those early days with her son, she frequently thought about nutty Rosie Crowder, roving up and down the laneway in Teeter Beach. Limp hair parted and tied in bows, chubby cheeks marked with dollops of bright pink rouge. In her arms, Rosie always cradled a blanketed rock. Desperate for a real child. Screaming out to any man who was within earshot, "I loves backseat bingo. Plays for free, I does. C'mon, now. C'mon." Legs spread, skirt held up to her waist, slip askew, hips swaying. "C'mon, fellers. Put a dollie in me. I wants a dollie." Some days, she'd be gripping a fence, rollicking back and forth, crying, "Me eggs. Me eggs. They's lettin loose." And the neighborhood youngsters would pelt her with slippery caplin they had plucked from the waves, chant, "Rotty Crowlegs got a henhouse in her drawers. A henhouse jammed up her arse."

One Sunday morning, just before communion, Rosie rushed to the front of the church, spread herself out on the floor in front of the pulpit. Announced to the wooden ceiling beams and the astonished congregation that she was after Mary's secret, would take one from Jesus, she wasn't fussy. Tugged at the neck of her dress, buttons jumping like grasshoppers, cleavage revealed. Audible gasps and clean hands rising up to cover loose wattles, and father and cousin dashed towards Rosie, helped her to her feet, and guided (hauled, rather) her out the side door. Then, shortly after that, Rosie vanished. Carted off to somewhere padded, an institution where she wouldn't trouble anyone. Wouldn't plant any more seeds in the minds of the impressionable youth of Teeter Beach.

During those couple of years, Wilda had paid her no mind. The woman was simply background buzz, barely registered, as

Wilda roamed about in a pleasant state of moderate inebriation. Perhaps because of Rosie, no one bothered Wilda. Wilda's actions were merely breezes while Rosie's were full gale storms. But now, it upset Wilda that Crowlegs took up residence inside her mind, with absolute clarity, during those early days as a mother. Troubled her for ages. Why would this woman's need, soaked with such agony, fill her head? Every time Melvin whimpered, and Wilda's hands patted him with mechanical motion, she would see that woman's hands, vigorously stroking the bottom of her cradled mound. Complete devotion to cold rock.

When Wilda and Lewis took Melvin home, the nurses were sorry to see him go. "He's a real honey ham," they said. "Never so much as squeaked." But Wilda heard them saying, "What Rosie wouldn't do to get her hands on that one." When alone, Wilda would place him in the crib, watch his arms flail, his hands trying to find her. And then she would chastise herself—what was wrong with her? Why did such helplessness water the knot of fear in her stomach, making it swell and flourish? She thought of Rosie, offering continual loving pecks on her stone's flat face, leaning in to inhale the saltwater smell trapped in the miniscule holes of its body. Her eyes wild and weepy. Bottom lip quivering with exaltation. These images made Wilda close the bedroom door, and pray that Melvin would be transformed into someone spiteful and aggressive upon waking. That he would develop an unending wail, like a siren that would pierce an eardrum. A baby that even Rosie would want to abandon on the beach with his millions of rounded brothers and sisters chattering in the waves.

"OOPS," WILDA SAID, when the carts struck each other. She glanced upwards, saw Mrs. Fagan standing before her, belly ripe, young girl in hitched tights, hugging a naked plastic doll with shorn hair, eyelids and lips painted with childish streaks of crayon. "Oh, I'm sorry. Not watching where I'm going."

Wilda knew only a little about Mrs. Fagan. She knew that Mrs. Fagan's husband had some undefined hand in the death of her brother-in-law, Roy Trench. If she ever crossed paths with a Fagan, Lewis had instructed more than once, she was to say nothing. Turn and walk the other way. "Devil got his hand on every one of them," he'd said. But when Wilda saw Mrs. Fagan now, up close, carts touching, she felt curiously drawn to the older woman. As though, in some antique time, there was an unspoken kinship between the two of them. That perhaps, if they were able to speak freely during an afternoon of tea and cards, they would find a common strand in their life stories.

Wilda put two fingers to her mouth, then lowered them. Eyebrows raised, she said, "Mrs. Fagan?"

The woman jumped slightly, as though startled by hearing her own name, then glanced up, met Wilda's eyes for only a split instant. She made no response, other than seizing three packages of biscuits, clutching them to her bump, grasping her daughter by the wrist and trotting towards the registers. Boots battering the floor. Left her cart, still blocking the aisle.

Wilda blinked several times at the empty space where Mrs. Fagan had been standing. She could still see the woman's eyes, hovering there, in a phantom head, row of canned peas as a backdrop. Wilda looked down at her fingernails, ends nibbled clean away, though not enough so anyone would notice.

It was foolish of Wilda to have spoken, to have momentarily wished for a response. In that flash before she opened her mouth, she imagined that she and Mrs. Fagan shared common ground. Both outsiders in Knife's Point. Both throwing something off into the air, some strangeness that let the other women know they were not raised here. That they did not belong. They had somehow stolen in, mixed in with the compost, potato plants sprouting among the cabbages.

Placing a hand to her abdomen, Wilda took several deep breaths, then removed the required gingersnaps from the shelf, dropped them in beside Melvin. He did not miss the opportunity to graze her hand as it moved past him, but Wilda did not acknowledge his touch.

She slid Mrs. Fagan's cart to the side, waited another moment until the woman had left the store, and made her way to the checkout. Paid with a handful of warm coins from her skirt pocket, and wobbled out into the slippery lot, almost empty with only a few cars. Melvin toddled along behind her, arms out in an open hug.

Wilda shuddered as snow found its way underneath the knot of her hair, floated down the folds of fabric near her neck. It had grown darker, sky like lead, and she had the sense that more snow was coming. Hurrying, she helped Melvin into the front seat, layered the few brown paper bags in around him.

She had seen something in Mrs. Fagan's dull dry eyes. A kind of passive detachment. A nothingness. And even though Mrs. Fagan barely met her stare, they were familiar, those eyes, as though they were offering a sneaky reflection of her own inner thoughts. Wilda realized that Mrs. Fagan's face was the exact opposite of Rosie Crowder's. Both women lost, one from complete lack of desire, while the other was overwhelmed by it. Why then, Wilda wondered, did she find some wisp of comfort in the flatness of Mrs. Fagan's expression? Why couldn't those mental images of Rosie's adoration nudge Wilda in that mothering direction? Wilda didn't want to know, and she pinched her mind as it began to wander. "You good?" she asked Melvin, and when he nodded, his chin scratching the opening of a bag, she closed the door, shuffled across the gravel lot to her side, and drove home with the radio on.

14

"WHAT IS RAPTURE, Mama?" young Garrett once asked his mother as they trudged over the dark snow-covered roads. He had been thinking of the young boys in their church clothes, each holding a candle, their voices melting together as they sang Christmas carols. Standing side by side, swaying slightly, they looked so heavenly, Garrett had to hold his jaw closed with wet mittens. When their mouths formed perfect O's, Garrett couldn't bear the joy that peaked within him, and he had to stare down at the glossy tips of his winter boots.

"My Lordie," she said. "Now there's a word."

"Do you know rapture?"

"What a foolish question." She increased her speed, soaked boots slamming into mounds of slush, making them spray. "None of us knows that, Garrett Glass. And none of us ever will."

But Garrett knew his mother was wrong. Garrett did know rapture. He had felt it deep in his flesh. And though he had wondered if his devotion was wicked, one morning at Sunday school, the reverend had explained it all to him. Explained to ten-year-old Garrett that love was something special, something pure.

During much of the jumble of Garrett's childhood, he had attended Sunday school. After the first ten minutes of service, the children would quietly leave the church, head outside to the newly constructed church hall. The boys were separated from the girls, and Mrs. Nearly, their particular teacher, would read stories to them or talk about being good Christians. The complexities of being good young men. Sometimes she would bring scraps of brown paper and broken crayons, let them color pictures of the animals marching up the wooden ramp to Noah's ark. Or read them Bible stories from a book with yellowed pages. One week, she surprised the group and pulled out a dozen small black balls. "If you youngsters is well-behaved," Mrs. Nearly said, "we'll play a game." "What game! What game!" "'Tis called Fightin' Sin." Well, they were as good as could be, and she let the balls loose on the concrete floor. Explained to them that each ball represented an offense, and, "You got to give that sin a good kick." The children ran about screaming and weaving and striking the hard balls with their shiny Sunday shoes. "Stay away from Cussing. Don't Steal," she'd shriek. "Good one, Sammy. Knock Disobedience right into next week!" Garrett was slow and awkward, tripped over his tight shoes, and he was struck in the thighs and backside, his left cheekbone, his shoulder, by sin more times than he could count. When the game ended, nine of the twelve were lying at his feet.

"Well, Garrett dear," Mrs. Nearly said as she gathered the balls, dropped them one by one into her sack. "Seems you're a magnet for sin. A real magnet. You best mind you're not led astray."

That day, Garrett wandered home, trailing a good distance behind his mother, and when she rounded the last bend before home, he stopped, fell onto his knees in the middle of the dirt road. He closed his eyes, pictured the smugness sitting so high on Mrs. Nearly's face, and he prayed to God. Fingers clasped tightly together, pressed to his chest, "Dear God," he whispered. "Dear, dear, dear, dear God. Is I full of sin, God? Do I think bad things? Do I? Is you listening to me?"

Wind moving through his hair, and something stung his head. The back of his mother's hand. He hadn't heard her turn, clip along the road towards him, didn't notice her shadow creep underneath his eyelids. "Of course He idn't, you silly child. No one's listening to no one."

"Why do we go to church, then?"

"Do you really got to know?"

"Yes."

"To breathe different air, Garrett. To breathe different air. Nothing more sacred than that."

Garrett's face turned red, but he did not cry. Then she put her hand on his head, sighed, said, "Look, I didn't mean to crack your ear. Pray all you wants, my son. Just not in the middle of the road."

Garrett was not swayed by his mother's crabbiness, and he waited for some sort of indication. He knew it would come, he knew God was there. Listening. Following his steps. Bringing him to the watery surface each time his head slipped below.

His answer arrived the following Sunday, by way of Mrs. Nearly's son. Eddie Nearly, already twelve years old, had been gifted with the ability to draw with near perfect accuracy. "We're going to have him illustrate some spiritual stories for the smaller children," she had told the boys. "'Tis a fine and honorable thing to do." The other boys didn't agree, called him pussy baby, pussy baby, said his pointy nose was jammed so far up the reverend's arse he could smell what was stuck in the old man's teeth. To redeem himself with his classmates, Eddie Nearly created a homemade deck of oversized cards, and when his mother's back was turned, he handed them around for all the boys to see.

Each card depicted a woman, in varying states of undress. There were pictures of bare torsos, breasts randomly attached, bulbous mounds with starfish perched on the tips. Women lying on their stomachs, backsides like smooth beach rocks, clinging to arching backs. The queen of spades was nothing more than a pair of enormous branches heading in opposite directions, curious seaweed arrangements where they met. And the queen of hearts had a dried jellyfish tucked between her bent legs. Tiny tentacles that might ensnare an unsuspecting male. As the cards passed through Garrett's hands, he felt a hitch inside his stomach. But that didn't stop him from studying them carefully.

83

He couldn't fathom that these were actual lady parts, how the underwater world had imprinted itself so blatantly upon a woman's body.

"Pass 'em along, pass 'em along, Dumb-ass Glass."

But, once again, Garrett was slow, and he thought about those black balls, and how sin stuck to him, so why should he rush anyway?

When one of the boys groaned, Mrs. Nearly's ears perked up, and she whipped around. One lunge, and the cards went from scattered to collected inside Mrs. Nearly's vice grip.

"Oh," she breathed as she held one up. "Oh, oh, oh." Her face grew ashen, and huge pink hives broke out on her neck. She placed a hand over the slight dip in her dress, covering her collarbones. "Oh, Eddie," she cried, and fled the room.

Mrs. Nearly did not return, though after about fifteen minutes, the reverend entered the hall. He wore a woolen jacket over his black gown, and with each deep step Garrett could see a flash of seal fur slippers on his feet. The reverend took a seat amongst them, and folded his hands in his lap.

"Boys. Boys. Boys."

"Hello, Reverend," they murmured.

"I believes 'tis time enough to talk to you boys."

"Yes, Reverend."

"Boys. Did you know we are made in God's image?"

Grumbling, nodding. "Yes, sir. We does, sir."

"Do you know what that means, boys?"

"Yes, we does, sir."

"Well, just in case there's some misunderstanding, let me clarify that for you. The human body is a sacred thing, boys. Sacred. Not a source of amusement. Not the brunt of a joke. Our bodies are beautiful things. Works of utter art."

"Yes, sir. They is, sir. Beautiful things."

"Scary, too," the youngest boy, Darcy Brown, exclaimed.

"Sssshhhushhh!"

The reverend rubbed his face, and Garrett caught a faint whiff of sweat.

"I don't want to come in here and snap down hard on you fellers. Like part of me thinks I should. I told Mrs. Nearly to keep the transgression to herself. And considering 'twas you, Eddie," he shifted to face the boy, "who created the filth, I'm sure she'll abide by my wishes."

Eddie coughed, tugged at buttons near his shirt collar. "Uh-huh."

"But, all you fellers had some hand in this. All of you took part. And I want to say a few things before I turns you out. Are you listening to me?"

"Yes, sir."

Garrett sat up, had a feeling something important was on the way.

"You are on the verge of being young men. Good young men. Decent young men. You should all know by now that physical expression of love is a gift from God. Do you know what I means by physical expression? 'Tis a gift, boys. A gift. A private gift between two people." He paused, dark hooded eyes looking around the room. "I won't try to kid you fellers, and feed you some line that 'tis all about making babies. Cause it idn't. That discussion is best left between you and your dads. But I will say this." Slowly and carefully. "Having that form of relationship with someone else, well, now, it takes a great deal of courage and trust. Courage. And. Trust. We need to share ourselves, boys, when the time is right, and accept another if we ask, and they are willing to share themselves with us. That's one of the most sacred things on earth. To look upon another's body, well, that's to look upon God."

Garrett nodded slowly, pinched his leg. Tears were welling up behind his eyes. "God's will," he repeated.

"Do you fellers understand?"

Plenty of snickers, and elbows bumping, and no one looked up. Except for Garrett. Who looked the reverend straight in the eye, replied firmly, "Yes, sir, I does."

"Alright, then. Get on out of here. Be good, and listen to your mothers."

Garrett left church, never flinched when he saw his mother waiting at the edge of the church grounds, face scowling, tongue clicking in her mouth. He skipped alongside her all the way to the farmhouse. Finally, he was happy inside. After lunch, a withered drumstick, potatoes like glue, he stole his stepfather's magnifying glass. Went deep into the woods, found a sunny clearing, and burned a cross into the flesh of an old birch tree. As a small thank-you. Thank-you, Lord, for blessing me.

PART THREE

15

MY DEAR FRANCIS,

I know it's been ages since I wrote to you, unforgivable ages, but life has gotten busier than I even thought it could. Lewis is working hard to keep the peace here in Knife's Point. Even though you'd think otherwise, there is always something going on. Tombstones smashed, a car stolen, fistfights on Friday nights. He tells me all about it, and you'd think we was living in some big city. Just last week, we had our own missing person case. An elderly woman, gone for four days. Having a few dollars to her name, I guessed she'd run off, but when Lewis suggested that, her two sons insisted that was out of character. She would never leave her things. Never skip a church service.

They found her, well inside her home. Well, not well, really. She was crushed under a pile of packed suitcases. She wasn't leaving, though, she just had full suitcases. Apparently, she never threw a single thing out, and had what her sons called a "sincere affection" for catalogue shopping. Parcel or two every day. They searched through the house, stuff piled up against the walls, sweaters and scarves, serving dishes and porcelain dolls, magazines—old garbage, too, mounds of it to the ceiling. Fifty-odd years of collecting. A lot of junk—good for nothing. Seems she was trying to find something in a back room, and the whole works tottered and came down upon her. Died with no water after a short while. Killed by the very items that made her happy.

Sad as it is, I thought of you when Lewis told me—thought you might like to get in at it, sift through it all. I imagine you'd learn a tremendous amount about that woman, and find a load of treasure for the store at the same time. But, her sons wasted no time in selling it all off. Never saw such a spread of goods on someone's lawn, and the crowds arrived from as far away as Idle Boot Bay. A hoard of hungry ants on an abandoned cake.

On a more pleasant note, the boys are growing and growing. They get along so well together, sometimes it surprises me. They never fight, other than some typical joking around boy business. Melvin is making great strides at school, and his teacher loves him. He is ahead in his math and spelling, and they're not sure what to do with him next year. Toby turned into a little man overnight, I really can't believe my eyes. He is very independent and often dresses himself in a mixture of plaids and stripes. He'd make you proud with his unique fashion sense.

Thank-you for the lovely card and gift you sent for Toby. He loves his books, as does Melvin, and though they carry some nice titles in the shops around here, it's a real treat to get something from the city.

I must close as I have to make some lemonade for the boys. I often wonder where your kindness comes from, Francis, and I'm certain it's not an earthly place.

As always, with affection,
Wilda

Seated at a small oak desk, Wilda laid her pen aside, folded the pages into thirds, creasing each edge with the back of her nail. Stuffed it into a white envelope, patterned interior. Then she dug through a drawer, located a stamp, pretty sailboat picture, licked it, and fixed it to the upper right-hand corner. In practiced script, she wrote out his address. Blew on the ink so it would not smear. "There," she said cheerily to Toby, who was cross-legged in front of the big box set, squealing each time someone hollered "yabbadabbadoooooo."

She stood, paced back and forth for several minutes, fanned herself with the letter pinched in her fingers. Of course, she realized what she should have written once the envelope was sealed. She should have spent more time describing her family life, Lewis, the boys, the vegetable garden, and a lot less time on that hapless old woman and her houseful of junk. She squeezed her hand, heard the crinkle of paper inside. Perhaps, if the saliva was still wet, she could peel back the closure and reread it. Just to make sure.

Fingers prying at the seal, but the glued paper began to tear. Evidence of tampering. So, she took a deep breath, tore it open, and the neatly folded letter popped out of its enclosure as though it was relieved to be free. She scanned it quickly, eyes jumping over her script, "My dear," "I thought of you," "your kindness," "with affection." Phrases lifting off the page, and her cheeks grew hot as waves of embarrassment moved through her. She crumpled the letter in her fist, suddenly aware that Toby was only several feet away from her and his program was ending. What if he looked at her, somehow discovered the childish game she was playing, sensed her humiliation?

Wilda could not explain these emotions, her slight shame whenever Lewis arrived home with the mail, presented her with yet another letter or parcel from Francis. Early on in their marriage, they repeated the same conversation: "Why don't you ever invite your uncle to visit?" "He's too old to travel." "Well, we could go, it's not that great a distance, you know." "Too busy, Lewis. Maybe next year." And now Lewis simply handed her each letter with a smile, some sort of trivial comment. "Business must be good. He got his own letterhead." And with her thumb, she would quickly cover the whimsical urchin now seated to the left of his return address.

Francis had only ever been kind to her. Beyond kind. A godsend. There was no confusion about that. He never asked for a single thing, only an ounce of companionship as he went about his daily rounds, buying other people's treasures, shining them up, and reselling them. But Wilda could not deny the fact that when she left him, when she kissed him goodbye on his dusty cheek that last time, she felt an odd sense of relief to be out from underneath it all. The damp sensation that accompanied being loved.

Since she moved to Knife's Point, she did not welcome his letters, the monthly reminder of his misplaced fondness. Wilda had tried hard to move forward through her life, and she kept a stiff broom at her back, made wide sweeps to obliterate each footstep. Always existing in the present moment. How else could she be expected to survive? But her broom was unable to disrupt his reasonable claim on her. And there, in the distorted tracks behind her, she could see his ignorance. He was unaware that she was a fraud.

From the top of the refrigerator, she retrieved Lewis's brass lighter, and then went to the fireplace, moved the screen away, tossed the letter onto the empty grate. She knelt down, flicked open the lid, thumb bringing forth the flame, and she lit the corner closest to her. Within moments, the letter curled inwards, and her highfalutin thoughts were transformed to ash and dust.

Before she prepared a picnic for her and the boys, she scratched a hasty second letter. A few quick thoughts—comfortably empty. Propped it up against the half-empty cookie jar, and it would wait there until Lewis mailed it.

Dear Francis,
It was so nice to hear from you, and thank-you for the birthday gift for Toby. He really adores books, and is just beginning to recognize a couple of letters. I hope you are well.
Yours,
Wilda Trench

Seated side by side on a matchstick quilt, they each held a sandwich in their hands, soft bread roughly halved. Bright orange Tang in Mason jars secured between their thighs. While Wilda and Melvin nibbled gingerly in a shaft of sunlight, Toby bounded down the muddy slope towards the water. Stripped down in a flash, shorts and T-shirt cradled in a low spruce branch, he hauled a black swimming mask on over his eyes. Stomping newly grown reeds, he waded out to the center of the stream, plunged beneath the surface. Even from her distance, Wilda could see his red shoulders, knew the skin was peeling and that she should insist he keep his T-shirt on. But she didn't call him back, watched him dance in the glistening water, pale blue underwear hanging off his backside.

"Dis is goo," Melvin said, lifting his sandwich, smiling at Wilda. "Jus de righ mound of everydin. Don sti do de roo o yo moud."

"Mmm," she replied, smiling back at him. She could tell by his garbled speech that the peanut butter was indeed firmly stuck to the roof of his mouth. Lunchtime had passed by the time she'd dealt with the letter, and she had slobbered it on the bread thickly, hastily, spared the near empty bottle of rasp-berry jelly along. "Mmm," she repeated. Full of little lies, that one. Lies spoken in an attempt to make her feel better about all her mini-failures—bathwater that was too cool ("Sure, that's some refreshing!") or a sloppy cake ("That's the best one ever!") or clothes stiff from too much soap ("Helps me stay upright.").

Inside, Wilda felt mildly raw from writing to Francis, and she had little patience for Melvin's softness. Many times she wished Melvin would just speak the truth, rather than trying to mold it into something warm and wonderful. Making her shortcomings all the worse, all the more obvious.

Wilda glanced down the slope, saw near-naked Toby twirl-ing in the stream, a cat's tail clutched in either hand. Each time he would wave his blossom stalks, conducting the watery music, Wilda could see fluffy bits released, drifting up into the sunlight. Toby was like those bits, floating without care, rising and falling at the whim of the wind. If only Melvin were simi-lar to that. Ignorant to subtleties. Bounding through life like a regular boy, climbing trees and skinning his knees, entranced by bright cartoons and the wonders of a handful of mud. Melvin was so attuned to her body, even if she altered her breath, permitted the slightest sigh to escape her lips, he was beside her, touching her, offering up a lemon cream or a glass of milk.

Wilda swallowed her last bite, sighed without meaning to.

Melvin edged ever closer, held up his sandwich, said, "Do yo wan my?"

Inner sigh. "No, thank-you, Melvin. You finish it."

She brushed crumbs from her dress, a picnic sort of dress, full flowered skirt that just covered her knees. She tried to stare at nothing, but her eyes settled on her bare calves, and she noticed they appeared slightly swollen. She could see every pore in her pale skin. Kicking off her rubber sandals, she studied her feet as well. Wiggled her toes. A yellowish callous had formed on the side of her left foot and both heels were covered in cracked skin.

Melvin laid his head against her upper arm, "You have beautiful feet, Mommy."

Yes, when he read her mind, that troubled her as well. "Thank you, Melvin."

"They've taken you a long distance."

"How do you mean?"

"You've lived on those feet for big number of years. Done a lot of things."

She swallowed, could still taste peanut butter on her tongue. "Yes. Yes, I have."

"So, you should be proud of your feet. Happy with your feet."

"I am."

"They's good feet," he said, between slurps.

"Indeed." She looked down at his small face, pie-plate eyes, joker smile from the orange crescent left by his drink.

"Mommy?"

"Yes, Melvin?" He was lying back on the blanket now, staring up at the leafy canopy.

94

"I knows where Nanny and Poppy is."

"That's nice."

"Don't you want to ask me where they is?"

"Okay. Where is they?"

"Up there." Skinny arm pointing heavenward. "Singing with the angels."

"That's nice, Melvin."

"But I was wondering where's the Nanny and Poppy that comes from you?"

Heart beginning to beat, she kept her voice level. "Well, they idn't here."

"Is they gone?"

"Yes, Melvin. They's gone."

"Gone off far?"

"Mmm." She stared up at the leaves, counted to three. "Pretty far."

"Is they with the angels?"

Bending her knees, she tucked her feet underneath the cotton fabric of her dress.

"Well?"

"So many questions," she said. "Just like your father used to be."

"I'm seven now. I wants to know about my tree."

"What tree?"

"Family tree."

"Oh." Wilda felt tightness building in her calves, a desire to walk towards the water and clean her feet. Feet that she'd lived on for a big number of years. She cleared her throat, kept a hand on her folded legs. "Your tree don't got that many branches. But you can grow it better when you're older."

"Is they with the angels?"

Legs straightened now, achy. "Poppy Burry is with the angels."

"Did he get there while he was sleeping like Nanny Trench?"

"I– I don't know, Melvin."

"How can you not know?"

Why didn't the fresh air make him nap? Every other child napped. Instead, he was exercising his little fingers, reaching into places they did not belong, poking, prodding the walls of a dark papery hive. Her heart thumped in her throat. After two even breaths, she replied, "I just don't."

"You was young?"

"Very." But not that young.

"Did you ask?"

Firm. "That's enough about Poppy Burry."

"Okay."

"Good, then."

Half a breath. "And what about Nanny? Do she play the harp up there?"

Wilda closed her eyes, twisted to grip her legs with both hands. "I don't believe."

"You don't know?"

"Haven't a clue, darling."

"Why?"

"I don't know."

"Why don't you know?"

She leaned in, hoping to offer enough to satiate his curiosity. "Can I tell you something Melvin? Swear you'll never tell another soul."

He sat up quickly, crossed his legs. "I swears, Mommy. On my ticker." Clenched fist thwacking little ribs.

"Do you remember when I read Hansel and Gretel to you?"

"Mmm hmm."

"Well, my mother, your nanny, was worse than the wicked stepmother."

Jaw dropped. "Oh, wow. She wanted you to cart you off to the woods?"

"In a manner of speaking."

"Was she your real mother?"

"Yes, sir. That she was."

He shook his head. "That's the worst kind, Mommy. A real mother that's a stepmother. That's the very worst kind."

"Mmm."

"Did you take any white pebbles? Any bread crumbs?"

"I weren't near as smart as you, Melvin."

"So you was lost?"

"I guess I was lost. In a way."

"Your dad didn't want to do it, Mommy. Didn't want to leave you there."

"Perhaps."

"Oh, sure. That has to be the truth. That's how the story goes."

"You're right."

"But, that won't never happen to you again, Mommy. Getting lost like that. I'll make sure of it. I'm a full growed boy and I got brains enough for the both of us."

"Okay." She pinched his chin, and then straightened her legs. Done for now. "Finish your sandwich, and that's it for today. You got me that grilled, parts of me is burnt."

Melvin wrenched his neck, glanced behind him. There it was, again. Heavy boots crunching through their woods, snapping twigs, crushing pinecones, coming closer towards their picnic spot. Snappy whistling that arrived in his ears in distorted strains.

"Mom?" Melvin whispered.

"I'm sure 'tis just your daddy," Wilda replied. "Lewis?" she called. "Lewis, is that you?"

Melvin jumped up, fists clenched and lifted, ready to defend. From the long shadows, Lewis emerged, waving his hand. Wilda waved back. He was still wearing his work clothes, but had a ball cap perched atop his head.

"Whoa, whoa, young feller. Stand down." Lewis said to Melvin with a pleasant chirp. Nudged him, and he scrambled back to his mother. Then, to Wilda, "I was wondering where you folks got off to."

"Not far," she said, smiling. "Too hot in the backyard, so we came here for lunch. You want a—" she began, then said remembered her sandwiches and said, "there's nothing really left."

"No, no. I'm best kind."

He sat down on the quilt, crossed his feet at the ankles, and Wilda noticed he kept the soles of his shoes just beyond the edge so that any dirt and needles would not land on her clean blanket. Something he didn't even have to think about, Lewis was just that way.

"How's the flies?"

"Not too bad. I guess they don't like the way we smells."

"I likes the way you smells," he murmured, leaned his face into her neck.

Melvin pressed in closer to Wilda, knotted his fingers in through her hand, fake sneezed. Twice.

"Speaking of smells," Lewis said. "What a day I had. Got a call from Gordie Tripp, three sheets to the wind, telling me someone made off with his best sow."

"How can you make off with a pig?"

"I was thinking the same thing. Just wrap a rope 'round her neck? Someone'll see you meandering down the road, right?" Lewis tapped a cigarette from the case, cupped his hands to light it, replaced the case in his shirt pocket. "Well, you wouldn't believe it, but I was driving down Belty Street, and lo and behold, a young feller cruises past me with a most unusual companion riding shotgun."

"Not the sow!"

"Yes, ma'am. Sitting up all prim and proper like the nastiest looking prom date."

Wilda put her hand to her mouth. "Well, I never."

"I goes after them. Hauls them over. Three of them. Three, plus the missy." Leaned back on his elbows, several deep drags, smoke curling from his nose, mouth as he spoke. "Turns out, they says, Tripp gave them the pig for a few bottles, bought and delivered. But then she went right wild when they jammed her into the backseat. Wouldn't have none of it. Only way to get her home was to let her ride up front, blast Janis Joplin or some such garbage."

"Well, what do you say to that?"

"Yes, what do you say? I told them to bring her back. Make it right with Tripp. No discussion."

"Now that don't seem fair to the boys."

"Give him his pinch of snuff," Melvin announced proudly. "Barber, barber."

"Yes, Melvin." She patted his knee, and he peered up at her, all smiles.

"Or fair to the missy. Her run cut short like that. And she was getting all kinds of annoyed without her music. Grunting and huffing, pawing the dash with her hoof. I told them to swing her around for a burger, plate of chips, and have her back in jig time. Make sure they don't break her curfew."

"Quite the story, Lewis. Poor pig. They should've just let it be."

"Stench so bad, now, my eyes is still watering." He tossed his cigarette towards the base of a tree, watched it smolder beneath a dead leaf, then stood, went over and crushed it. "'Tis good to be away from it all. Find a bit of peace here." Reaching down, he scooped up Wilda's jar of Tang, gulped it after she nodded. Scanning the branches, he said, "Where's Toby anyways? Up in a tree?"

Wilda turned her head sharply, stared down at the water. "Not today. He's . . ." looking up and down the length of the empty stream before her, "he's in the water."

Lewis dropped the jar, took two deep steps. "What do you mean he's in the water? Where in the water?"

Wilda was on her feet then, Melvin too, an extra appendage growing from her side. "Down there. Wading in the stream. It idn't even above his knees, Lew. He's just 'round the bend, I'm sure. You can hear him."

All three of them silent for a moment, holding their breath, Wilda willing the sound of splashing to rise up from the water below. But there was only silence, other than the rustling leaves, squirting sounds from Melvin's stomach, and an incessant chick-a-dee-dee-dee from an invisible bird.

"I don't hear nothing." Lewis stomped down the slope, heels of his boots sinking into the muck. Hollering over his shoulder.

"Is that what you does? Is that how you takes care of my son? Lets him alone in the water?"

"We was talking." Her voice faint, legs rubbery. She placed her hand over her mouth, spoke into the cup of her palm. "Me and Melvin was talking." For how long, she couldn't say.

Lewis waded out to the middle of the stream, water frothing around his pants. "Tobe," he called, voice gentle, panic controlled. "Tobe, where's you at, my son?" Turning, turning, and it occurred to him that this was the very area he used to play duck, duck, goose with Roy, and the loss of his brother somehow oozed out of its container, made Lewis's heart constrict. "Tobe!" he cried. Then he saw the tiny body, face down, stubby legs extended, a million iridescent bubbles tangled around his floating hair. Toby's bare backside bobbed slightly with the current. Sunlight penetrated the watery ripples, making Toby's skin appear bleached and dead. Panic in his limbs, Lewis leapt forward. But the water refused to solidify, to withstand his weight. And each time he kicked, his boots slipped through the surface, struck the greasy bottom. Distance between him and Toby expanding into miles. "Tobe! Oh Tobe!" But Toby never lifted his head, and a silent roar ripped through Lewis's mind all because he failed to notice the orange band at the tip of his son's snorkel.

Grabbing a cold skinny arm, Lewis hauled the entire body out of the stream. Never expected it to stay up on its own. He already pictured it crumpling down, back to its watery grave. But instead, a surprised child, gasping and sputtering, stood before him, blinking wildly when Lewis knocked the snorkel and mask off his head.

"Why don't you answer me?" Lewis blurted, his contorted face only inches from Toby's.

"Watching tadpoles. Didn't wanna scare 'em." Toby spoke in rapid fire. "They was trying to play with me." Toby wanted to tell his father that he stayed so still, they were tapping the glass of his mask. Peering in at him with their black bead eyes.

"Playing with tadpoles. Jesus Christ. I thought you was drowned."

"I'm a good swimmer, Dad. Better than half those tadpoles. Banging about."

"Yes, but you're too young to be on your own."

"Do I got to come out?"

"That you do. Right this second. Your lips is purple." Eyeballing the rest of his little boy body. "Not to mention other parts of you."

"Awww."

"Not a squeak, Toby!"

Toby glanced down at his once crystal-clear stream, saw the muddy water, mossy gunk scratched off the bottom. No sign of his mottled green friends. He pouted. All that stomping and stirring of the water had scared them away. His teeth began to chatter, his head ached, and he rubbed the reddened rectangle around his eyes and nose.

Lewis picked up Toby, carried him on his hip, forearm underneath the boy's bare backside. "And where's your underwear?"

"Around."

"Around, hey?"

"They kept slipping. And they fell off in the water."

"A good man keeps track of his underwear."

"I knows." He put his face down on the warm fabric, tucked his hands in, and made the tiniest mental note, filed it under "Ways to be a good man."

Up on the bank, Lewis gathered Toby's clothes from the spruce branch, then strode up the incline and said through locked jaw, "Melvin!"

"Yes, sir."

"Is that how you looks after your little brother?"

Wilda stepped forward. "'Twas my fault, Lew. Don't blame the boy. I wasn't paying enough attention." Even though Toby was safe, now, panic still lingered inside Wilda's stomach.

Fluttering upwards, making the skin on her neck flush bright pink. The memory of that afternoon with her father was in there, too, still churning inside her stomach. How could she make such selfish mistakes? Standing still when she needed to move. Walking away when she needed to stay.

Lewis ignored her, lunged forward and gripped Melvin's shoulders, applied enough weight to test the child's knees. "Is that how you look after your little brother, I asked?"

"No, sir."

"You got to be responsible."

"Yes, sir," Melvin replied. Then, his standard catchphrase whenever Lewis chastised him, "I won't do that again."

Testing. "What'd you do?"

"I weren't rees-ble, sir."

Voices springing into Wilda's head.

Re-re-re-pons-ble, maid.

I don't know what that means, Daddy.

Help me, Willie.

While Melvin stood tall under the pressure, Wilda's legs weakened, and she reached her hand out to touch the warm trunk of a birch tree. She wanted to say something to Lewis, say it wasn't right to put that sort of strain on a child. It could change who they were. Who they were becoming. But she said nothing. Watched Toby, naked, cut-off jeans and line-dried T-shirt wadded up underneath his arm, toddling off through the woods towards home.

ONCE THE BOYS were changed, completed half-hearted attempts to scrape the yellow film from their teeth, Wilda went into their shared bedroom, new book tucked up under her arm. As soon as she entered, Melvin pounced on her, locked his hands around her neck, dangled. "You are a perfect mother," he said. "Stupendous. Splendiferous."

Back straining, she dropped the book, tickled the taut skin over his ribs, slightly harder than necessary. "You're just showing off, now. You and your big words."

102

"But you is, Mommy," he said, letting go, squeezing her waist to the point of pain. "You're the bestest mommy in the world."

"Well, maybe in Knife's Point," she said, and wedged herself free, took a small bow.

"No, Mommy," he continued, hands on his flat hips. "In the world. Say it."

"That's enough."

"C'mon. Say it."

"Stop that."

"Say it, I said."

"Stop that, Melvin."

"Say it, Mom!"

"If you don't quit addling me, I won't read nothing. You hear me? And you'll spend your night in here in the dark with God only knows what type of scary monster crawling 'round under your bed." As soon as the words were out, she winced. Silence in the room, her older son stared at her, his smile punctured. Some moments, there was no disguising it. She was simply rotten.

"Well, now," she said, smoothing her hair, weak smile. "Shall we start in on the book? A new one from Francis. I flicked through and it does look like a lovely set of stories."

Melvin slunk over towards the bed, and when within two feet of the edge, he leapt, pulled his legs up, and landed near the middle of the mattress. Wilda sat between the two boys, and after a few moments they crept up next to her, each nestling into a side. She read several short stories about two best friends, a frog and a toad. Each had a distinct personality, Toad being a little slower and carefree, Frog a bit more intellectual and considerate. She read about a new season, a lost button, a letter written for a friend. All three of them giggled when Wilda recited the story of when Toad went swimming, and his shyness over his ugly swimsuit.

"Toby didn't mind his swimsuit," Melvin squealed.

"What swin-soot?"

"That's right!" Melvin rolled onto his back, feet and arms straight up, dead bug pose.

Toby looked up at Wilda. "What swin-soot?"

"Well," she said. "Toad didn't need a swimsuit. Just like you. Come to think of it, you are a little like Toad, and Melvin is a little like Frog. You'll be friends forever."

Melvin jumped up, bed converted into trampoline, achieving impressive heights in his alligator-print pajamas. When airborne, he cried, "You're just like Toad." Bump. "Naked Toad." Bump. "Sun cooking your arse red."

Wilda stood, allowed Toby up into arms. "Now, Melvin."

"Frog is the smart one." Bump. "Mother said so herself." Bump. "She admitted it." Bump. "You're a toad." Bump. "Toad-head." Bump. "Warty toad-brain."

"Melvin! Don't be mean to your little brother."

"You loves Toad-in-the-Hole." Bump.

"Frog would never, ever jump on a bed, Melvin."

Frog froze, mid-leap, returned to earth in a wrinkled mound of abused sheets. With immediate seriousness, he smoothed the bedding, climbed beneath it, squeezed his eyes shut, lips puckered to obliterate the smirk.

"Is I a toad, mom?" Toby spoke directly into Wilda's ear.

"Not, really. I was just joking."

"I don't wanna be no toad."

She hauled back the covers on his side, slipped him in, kissed his smooth forehead. Leaned in closer. "Frog may be wise," she breathed. "But my little Toad will find his own path. You wait and see."

At the door, she turned, made sure the two lumps were still in the bed. Yes, they were, and she flicked out the lights.

In the darkness, Melvin said, "Good night, Toadstool."

Toby never responded, pulled his feet up closer to his body. Though he felt overheated on the inside, his sunburnt skin was covered with goose bumps. As he lay there, he could feel his mother's words, swirling down into the drain hole of his ear. His own path. His own path. Even though he didn't quite understand what it meant, those whispers made him panicky. How could he ever exist on a path where Mellie did not?

104

WHEN SILENCE FINALLY arrived inside the boys' room, Wilda tiptoed back in, stood at the base of the bed. Open curtains, a waxing moon threw light into the room, and she could see her sons, a picture composed of a myriad of gray tones. They were sleeping, face to face, covers kicked off, backsides jutting out, knees and toes touching. Joined, like two halves of a lopsided heart. She watched their chests, rising and falling in opposing rhythm. Melvin gradually exhaling, Toby gradually pulling that very air into his pink lungs. Toby exhaling, Melvin's mouth drawing it back in. Over and over. A single breath shared between them.

And Wilda considered then they weren't as fragile as she often imagined. They weren't made of thin clear glass. If she opened her hands, let them go, they wouldn't shatter on the floor. Surely, they wouldn't. In the golden moonlight, she saw that each one was just enough for the other.

16

EVER SINCE LEWIS Trench was a little boy running amongst the stalls, he had always loved the fall fair. He believed that during those two days, a magic was trapped in the damp shadowy barn, transformed with lights dangling from high rafters, the proud smell of hard work. Nothing much had changed over the years—quilts and homemade sweaters were still displayed on the walls, loaves of banana bread and supper rolls and jams and sweet cucumber pickles still graced the makeshift tables. Enormous heads of cabbage and bulbous turnips waited patiently to be measured. As Lewis wandered, everyone was smiling and laughing, farmers and fishermen and store owners coming together. Children tearing about, begging for a pinch of Miss Nettie's fudge or Aunt Bertha's peanut brittle. Lewis's mother had been a frequent winner of the baking contest, and each year they reminded Lewis of the loss they felt when she died. How much they still mourned her, and her perfect pastry recipe, long gone to the grave.

Lewis searched for Wilda, found her standing silently among a gaggle of aproned ladies. A variety of pies on the table before them. He waved, but she shifted her body, folded her arms. It was Lewis who signed her up for the contest every year, and this time he'd pressed and pressed and pressed until she gave in, agreed to participate. And why not? He thought it was an easy opportunity for her to connect with the neighbors, show them that she was capable. "Better late than never," he'd said to her frowning face. "You'll see." Lewis found it odd that Wilda showed no interest in meeting the other women of Knife's Point. When his mother had been alive, the door of their house was always swinging, visitors coming and going. Cups and saucers empty on the table, crumbs scattered on the floor beneath.

Over the course of two weeks, Wilda made nine or ten blueberry pies. Not a one to her liking. Crust too thin, too thick, too hard, too goopy, filling either liquid or firm. Lewis had counseled her not to take it so seriously, "'Tis only a bit of fun," and she complained, "How do you think I feels being around those ladies?" "You feels happy?" "No! I feels like this," and she picked up her latest effort, top burnt from bubbling sugar, and dropped it into the sink. Lewis would never admit to her that seeing the pie destroyed was a relief. Somehow, he and the boys had managed to consume each of her labors, and they confided to each other that they all had the troubles because of it. Runs the color of midnight.

"Woot, woot for Wilda's pie!" Lewis called out, and the ladies turned, stared at the redness as it filled Wilda's cheeks.

"Oh, no," she said, one hand to her mouth. And Lewis laughed. Sometimes the shy ones just need a more forceful shove.

He wandered over to the stalls where the church ladies—The Tiny Trio, they called themselves—were fundraising. Signed his name down and paid for four church suppers, slices of ham, potato salad, coleslaw, beet. Maybe a leaf of lettuce and a slice of under-ripe tomato. For a quarter, he got to guess the number of Purity taffies stuffed into a jar. Prize was a lovely set of handkerchiefs, white tatting on the edges. "Tobe, Tobe," Lewis called out, as his son tore past. "How many do you think?" Toby stopped for a moment, ring of chocolate around his mouth, cried out, "two three gazillion," and then he continued his rampage, sticky fingers reaching for a young girl's pigtail. Lewis couldn't help but smirk, said to The Tiny Trio, "how many zeroes do you think that got?"

A few feet over, perched on a low wooden stool, old Dolf Neary hollered, "You got a live one there, Lewis. Startin' young, wha?" Dolf had spent his life on the water, and his face was like wrinkled leather, eyes smiling.

"That's right. He's my boy."

Net draped across his lap, Dolf's fingers held needle and twine, worked to repair broken mesh. "Just like Roy, he is. Roy coulda shat him out."

Squirt of vinegar to Lewis's gut. "You think?"

Dolf coughed, lifted his ball cap, scratched his bald head. "I minds when Roy was that age. And he do, he looks right like him."

Lewis sighed, nodded. "I knows, Skipper," he said. "They both do. Some days I finds it tough to even look at them."

"Like you would," Dolf replied gently. "Like you would, my son."

The two men watched Melvin, nuzzled in amongst the judges who were sampling the pies. "Delightful," one judge announced as he took a bite of Dolf's wife's pie. And Melvin stabbed his hips with his fists, hollered, "You just wait! My mom's pie is the more delightful. And I should know—I ate a dozen of them!" Dolf and Lewis roared, shook their heads. "Now I believes that's undue pressure," Dolf hollered. "Cause for disqualification."

Wilda appeared mortified at the attention, and Lewis couldn't watch her. Couldn't watch her lose the contest. If they gave her an honorable mention, the pity ribbon, that would be worse than no mention at all. So he clapped Dolf on the back, meandered down through the barn, past a table that held salt fish, another table covered with doilies and Barbie doll tissue box covers and crocheted snowflakes for future Christmas trees. On the wall was a grand display of string art from Miss Squire's elementary class, and Lewis searched for Melvin's. Wasn't hard to find. While all the other children created simple circles or single-colored tear drop shapes, Melvin's was intricate, layered, shape inside shape. Blue and red and yellow and black. Lewis leaned in closer, saw neat penciled words on the painted wood. "For MOM. Gods eye to watch you." Shaking his head, Lewis didn't know whether to smile or scowl. He wished

Melvin would let go of Wilda's apron strings, spend more time kicking the ball around. Like a real boy.

After days of drizzle, the late September sun was shining all afternoon, and Lewis leaned against the wooden frame of the barn door, one foot up, lit a cigarette. Lifted his face to the heat. So rare, he thought. So much had changed since he was a boy. Knife's Point was no longer innocent and isolated. The outside world had stepped right up, found all the front doors unlocked, and entered without so much as ringing the bell. But, this one event, these two days every fall, seemed to have stayed exactly the same.

Just a few feet away, he watched as Garrett Glass rubbed a rag over the large wheels of a tractor, then scattered handfuls of hay on the ground around it. Lewis could see that Garrett had rapidly grown into a young man, now tall and strong, strangely delicate in the way he bustled about. Feminine, almost. Greeting each boy, lifting him up onto a tire as though the boy were fragile. His red mop of hair was down over his eyes, and as the children approached, he kept his head down, like a shy but steady workhorse. Nothing like the boar of a man who had raised him. Lewis took a deep drag, closed his eyes again, and saw the orange glow permeating his lids. He could, if he wanted to, focus his hatred only on Eli, let the boy slip through. After all, here he was, volunteering his time. Making it a better day.

Then Lewis saw Toby crawl up the side of the tractor, settle onto the seat, feet dangling, hands gripping the enormous steering wheel. "Vroom, vroom, chuggachuggachugga!" Lewis tossed his cigarette into the dirt, stomped it with his boot. Stood for a moment, then hollered, "Hey, Tobe." The boy looked up, along with several others. And Garrett too. All of them staring at Lewis, waiting for something further. Lewis hauled his bottom lip in over his teeth, bit down. Then said, "You having fun, mister?" And Toby grinned, nodded, bounced on the seat. "Vroom, chugga!" Lewis waved his hand, waited until the boy waved back, and then went back inside the barn in search of an egg salad sandwich.

GARRETT GLASS didn't slouch at all as he drove the tractor down the shoulder of the road towards the community barn, a grinning scarecrow balanced on his lap. The place was bustling, and people stepped aside as he chugged nearer to them, parking the tractor just outside the door. He deserved this afternoon, he told himself. Deserved to have the children playing at his feet.

For days, he had begged Eli to allow him to borrow the tractor. It was newish, Eli's pride, blood red body and shiny silver grill. Thick tires that weren't yet dimpled or cut by sharp rocks. Garrett promised to return it in better shape than when he took it. Worked past dark to finish extra chores, gain free time. But it wasn't until Garrett explained the business sense of participating that Eli conceded. "These people purchase what we grows, what we butchers. Nothing's more important in this place than being sociable. There's always another farmer. Other vegetables. Other meats." Eli nodded, plucked the cap from his head. Said, "Get on with you, but don't expect me to have no part in it. And if I sees even a single footprint, a single nick, 'tis your goddamned skin'll be hanging on the line to dry."

"Yes, sir."

Garrett took a soft rag from his pocket, polished away the fine layer of dirt, spatters of muck from the fields. He cut the twine on a bale of hay, spread it around. When his set looked complete, he took the scarecrow he'd constructed out of an old shirt and pants, painted-up flour sack for a head, stuck the sharpened post in the earth.

His stepsisters lingered nearby, the older girl whining and writhing as though a worm were moving out through her bulky flesh. But DeeDee did not aggravate Garrett, not like the younger one did. Touching the tractor, running her girly fingers over the wheel, over the shiny body. He hated Angie. Eli's little treasure.

"Get away," he hollered, leaning forward, shaking his fist. "Get on with the both of you. Bloody pests."

"I'm hungry," DeeDee moaned. "I neeeeds food."

"I wants to work the tractor." Angie, this time.

"That you won't, then." Garrett dug into his pocket, placed a coin in each of their sweaty palms. "Take this. And don't let me see you again 'til you hears me calling for you. Not one second sooner. Or I'll- I'll- I'll skin you both."

DeeDee tore off, in through the doors of the bustling barn, dragging Angie so she nearly tripped on her own feet. Good, Garrett thought. Free at last.

He glanced about, saw two curious boys watching and waiting. Girls, generally, had no interest in big tires and tractors and scarecrows with crooked faces, and for that, Garrett was relieved. He didn't want to have to deal with the twittering and the squealing that accompanied braids and pierced ears. The awkwardness of lifting somebody who was wearing a tiny skirt, flashes of loose pink underwear. He waved his hand at the few boys, said, "C'mon with you, then. Have a look, sure." And they scrambled forward, nudged Garrett out of the way. As one kicked the large tires with rubber boots, the other jumped into the sturdy seat, pulled the steering wheel, and made screeching sounds. "Easy does it," Garrett said. "Whoa, now. This is a powerful machine, fellers." But there was no irritation in his voice, and as more boys stepped up to investigate the tractor, Garrett's intestines began to quiver. Like he'd drank too much of the cold coffee still sitting in the percolator, and he had the sudden nervous urge to find a toilet.

When he returned, he saw a boy standing off to the side, maybe eight, maybe nine. Hair that needed a trim, jean shorts, snug and blue, and a white and navy striped T-shirt. In his arms, the boy held an enormous turnip, and he stroked the clean purplish skin. Garrett felt faint, lost his breath for just a moment. He reached for the wood horse that pinned the barn door in place, and when his hands found it, he sat down. A dozen children were hanging off the tractor, trying to unhitch the snaps that held the body closed, testing the bolt and nut on the steering wheel, but Garrett didn't notice. Everything was haze, except for that one child. Who was stamped, now, upside down on Garrett's retina, and glowed with brilliant clarity.

SOME INNATE ABILITY, maybe, Garrett wasn't sure. But he was able to scan an entire group of children, and identify the odd one out. The youngster who was desperate for a connection, longing for a few kind words. Maybe it was the way those children kept their gaze locked on the touching tips of their shoes, or how they shrunk ever so slightly when any grown man spoke. Or maybe how they stretched their spines whenever a positive phrase drifted down upon them. Like an animal tucked inside a burrow: shine a bright light into the black hole, and that creature would look up.

Once he caught his breath, he pushed his hair from his eyes, went and stood beside the boy. Not too close, but just close enough so that the boy would sense he was there. Without looking directly at him, Garrett said in a light, gentle tone, "Wow, that's some kind of big turnip you got there."

The child squinted, held the ball with its thick root a little tighter.

"Did you grow it all by yourself? I'm guessing you did."

Foot kicking the dirt.

"I bet you took good care of it. Watered it and weeded all 'round it. Turnips don't grow big unless you treats them nice."

"Yeah. I done that."

Ah, his first words. A feather tickling Garrett's abdomen, and he slid a hand in through the front placket of his overalls, up underneath his shirt, rubbed his muscles.

"I knows that stuff. I farms too. That's my tractor over there."

"That's yours?"

"Yup."

"Oh."

"'Tis hard work. Farming. Man's work."

"That's not what my daddy says, Mister. We just moved here and he works in the bank, and he says men with real brains don't need to get their hands filthy digging up potatoes or

112

feeding slops to pigs or smelling the stink of filthy chickens. That's only if you got no choice you does that."

Well. Not so quiet after all. Not as nice as he'd imagined either. "Is your daddy here?"

"Here?"

"Yeah."

"No."

Garrett shifted from one foot to the other, jammed his hands in his pockets, adjusted himself though the thin fabric. "Where'd you get that turnip, then? Steal it, did you?"

Eyes wide. "I never stealed nothing, Mister, honest."

"Then where'd you get it."

"My mom. She got a little garden. I helps her every day, I does. I really does."

"How come?"

"I wants to be a farmer when I grows up."

Garrett knelt down, put a hand lightly on the boy's shoulder. "I likes the way you thinks, my son. What's your name?"

"Alvin."

"Alvin, hey? Like the chipmunk?"

The boy blushed. "Yeah."

"Well, Alvin. My bet is on you. You'll take the prize, my son."

"Yeah? You think?"

"What're you going to do with that fifty cents, saying you wins and all?"

"I'm going to save it."

"Not buy nothing?"

"No, sir."

Garrett liked being called "sir." "Well, I never seed such a young gaffer with such good sense. I woulda spent it in jig time, if 'twas me. Candy and junk like that."

"My dad don't let me eat candy. Your teeth got to last 'til you're dead."

"Mine neither," Garrett lied, and his tongue darted out for a split second, touched the scar on his upper lip. "But you don't got to listen to your father all the time. Some day you got to be growed up, and make your own mind. Decide stuff. You know, decisions."

Whispering. "I don't want to get into no trouble."

"You won't."

"My daddy says I was born in hot water. And never got out of it since."

"Yowch. That must hurt."

"He's always mad."

"Well, of course he is. I understands."

"You do?"

"Sure. He wanted a son, and he got a soup instead."

The boy giggled.

"C'mon now."

"C'mon where?"

"Some candy. I got some. Right here in my pocket." Garrett patted the front pouch of his overalls.

"What kind?"

"'Tis a surprise. You got to come with me."

"But they're coming 'round. My turnip."

"We won't be long. Besides, what I got is better than some dumb prize."

"Really?"

"But you got to be a gambling man. Is you a gambling man?"

"I s'pose. But I idn't supposed to go off with grown-ups I don't know."

Garrett laughed, then closed his mouth to hide the black molars. "I idn't a grown-up. Sure I'm still mostly a boy. Like yourself. And you knows me already. I can tell you're a good judge of people. Just like I is. And you know what? I likes you, Alvin. I just knows you're good at keeping secrets."

Garrett slid the turnip from the boy's hands, walked over and tucked it behind the wheel of the tractor, covered it in hay.

Like a magnet now, the boy was right beside Garrett.

"Can I sit up on the tractor first?"

"Sure," Garrett said. "You betcha."

114

"Can you lift me?"

"I can try."

Garrett tucked his hands around the boy's birdlike ribs, lifted. Felt the thump of the child's heart just beneath his rough fingers. The child leaned back, his shoulder blades pressing against Garrett's chest, his small feet climbing up the deep grooves in the tire, smell of his hair, like wet rocks by the river, curve of a thin white neck, T-shirt sliding and lifting, smooth skin of a belly, bumps of a perfect, perfect curved spine. Oh God, a small ripple of fat just beneath the belly button. Could this be, could this be, could this be the beginning of love? Garrett's breathing grew shallow, and his mind took rapid snapshots of the boy, edging up the tractor, slender hand gripping Garrett's hairy forearm, innocence of dirty fingernails and knotted hair, and the boy slipped, fell a few inches backwards. For a single moment his full weight rested on Garrett's chest. His full weight. And Garrett arched his back, held the boy up, the two of them touching, body to body. Back to front, front to back. Warmth commingling. Garrett panted. Oh. Oh. A quick recovery, too quick, and the boy's hand reached for the shiny steering wheel. "Almost," the boy sang, and he grabbed the wheel, pulled, broke away. And Garrett felt a sudden involuntary pulse in his pants. Looked at the boy, looked at the woods behind the barn, looked down at the lump of candies in the front pocket of his overalls. Spell snapped, and that sick wet feeling of loneliness began to spread, a mouth without edges yawning just underneath his skin.

"Can you get me down?"

"Find your own way."

"Hey, Mister. Can you get me down? I wants to go now. My turnip. I wants my turnip."

Garrett turned and walked towards the woods, left the boy perched on the tractor, short legs swinging. He came to a tree, leaned against the trunk, body frozen. Gradually the earth slid upwards, and Garrett found himself seated. He felt around him, in the dimming afternoon light, located a sharp stick, and jabbed it into the fleshy part of his thigh. Over and over until the skin broke, and he could see a stain seeping through the fabric of his overalls. He wouldn't think about it now, wouldn't allow himself to reflect. He would wait for a day or two to fold away, wait until the emptiness was pale, and then he'd dip inside his mind, and see the boy again.

"LET'S GO HOME," Wilda said.

"But, sure the fun is just getting started up. They're going to clear a space so the folks can have a bit of a dance."

"I don't want to dance."

He nudged her arm. "Of course you do."

"I'm tired, Lewis."

"You're too young to be tired, maid. And the boys'll love it."

"On my feet all day, barely a morsel to eat."

"What? Sure there was loads of food, left and right of you."

"I didn't want nothing. Didn't want to have a lunch with that crowd."

"What crowd?"

"All the people."

"There's lots of good people, there. I knowed most of them all my life."

"And I don't know most of them at all."

"That's 'cause you never gave no one a chance."

"I haven't, have I?"

"Not really. You're the one coming into their world, Willie. You just needs to find some inroads."

"I don't want inroads." Her voice was flat, quiet.

"You don't got to be like that, Wilda."

She shook her head, and Lewis knew he wouldn't win. Understood now that Wilda was just looking for excuses. They often had such discussions when he was trying to prod her into action, into joining. He thought she was lonesome, even though she repeatedly explained that lonely and alone were two separate things.

116

"C'mon, Wilda. Give it a go. For the boys."

"No, Lewis." She crossed her arms over her chest, hid her fingers. "I'm tired."

Lewis looked out across the fields, towards the thin strip of water on the horizon. Saw fog sneaking in, trails of it gliding over the bright harvest moon that hung low. He looked down at his two sons, blueberry-stained lips pinched, breath held, hopeful hands clasped. No chance of a turnaround, and he scooped up Toby, took Melvin's wrist, and started walking. Spoke over his shoulder, "You been tired since we met, Willie. I'm ready, I really am, any time you wants to wake up."

A LIGHTBULB DANGLED from a wire, burned in the center of the barn, but Eli relied on his lantern to inspect the tractor. He leaned in close, held the lantern to the shiny metal and the large wheels, searching for a nick or a scratch or a cut in the rubber. But he could find nothing, and some tiny part inside of him was disappointed over the absolute lack of damage.

Rustling behind him. He turned, lantern lowered to his thigh, and saw Angie, his younger daughter, standing in the door frame, her feet stuffed into a pair of his old boots. Even in the dimness of the barn, he could see the sides of her skinny body through the sheer fabric of her nightdress, and he laid down the lantern, took a sweater hanging on a nail, and tugged it on over her head. Groaned slightly as he bent on a sore knee to roll up the sleeves.

"Too cold to be out like that," he mumbled. Her hair was wet, and he could smell soap. "What's that woman thinking?" Reaching behind him, he grabbed a length of old rope. "Arms out," he said, and knotted it around her waist in a makeshift belt.

"I just come to watch you."

When she leaned against him, he felt her shiver, and he tugged off his own plaid coat, placed it over her shoulder, lifted the collar. "There now."

She laughed, "That's heavy. I can't lift my arms."

"Don't want you catching cold, maid," he said, and gave her freckled cheek a tiny pinch. This child never grated on him like the other girl, who was pushy and pouty. He had often let the soft one ride to the dump with him, had let her hang around as he hammered together a bench or fixed the hinges on a door. He'd even accepted a hug from her slender arms after he'd tied a tire swing to the branch of a tree. Eli knew who he was, and knew it was ridiculous to even conjure the notion, but in all his years, this was the closest he'd ever come to adoring something. So small and sweet and perfect.

"Daddy, I wants to see the tractor," she said.

"You seen it today."

"I never hardly, then. I wants to see it now."

"What do you want that for?"

"I wants to be a farmer when I gets growed. Didn't you know?"

"What?"

"A farmer. Like you is."

He stood up, stepped away from her, stared down at the tiny elf girl drowning in layers of wool and plaid. She stared back, and her face was bright and open. No wetness in her eyes, no fear of him. Something else there instead, and Eli's heart fluttered, felt as though it were filling and draining at the same time.

"A farmer, you says."

Big smile and nods.

He looked behind him, at his tools, and his barrels of vegetables, dirt still clinging to the skin. He glanced at the dark corners where he had severed throats, wrung necks, culled litters. He inhaled, smelled the sour stench of hens, uneaten scratch clawed into the mud, rotting. "That you won't then."

Pinprick, face falling. "But, I, me—"

"Don't let me catch you in here. Or out in those fields."

"But, DeeDee, she do."

Slight snarl. "That don't matter."

The child never asked why, never whined. Slipped out of the coat, handed it back. "Here," she said. "Don't want you catching the colds neither." Then she toddled away, dragging her feet in the boots.

"Angie!"

She stopped. "Yes, Daddy?"

"I. Well, I wants to tell you something, now," he said, and pinched his nose, swiped thumb and forefinger on the leg of his trousers. "I wants to say something, and I wants you to tuck it away for later."

"Promise, Daddy."

He went to her, bent again on his aching knee, plucked splinters of wood from the nubby sweater. Cupping her chubby cheeks his bear paws, he said, "Some people don't need dirt to grow something good." He coughed to loosen the words, caught in the thick tangle of netting around his heart. "Some people is bound for better things."

17

WILDA WAS SEATED at the kitchen table, flipping pages in the newspaper, when several words lifted off the page, made her stomach drop, mouth go dry. Leaning in closer, she scanned the page more carefully, found what her heart had already seen. The obituary section. Shallow breaths through parted lips, she blinked rapidly as her gaze sped over the entry. Mrs. Jessie Burry. Suffered from heart disease. Predeceased by her parents, Mary and James Smith, her husband, Edward, and infant son, John. Survived by her sister-in-law, Anita Andrews (Wayne), and her daughter Wilda. And that was it. A scant summary, laid out in neat black font. Wilda closed the newspaper, folded it, pushed it to the other side of the table. Those were the bare bones of her mother's life. The bare bones of her dead mother's life.

She felt light-headed, poured a glass of juice and sipped, waited for some sugar to seep into her veins. Teeter Beach was such a small village, why had her mother's obituary been published province-wide? Staring at the newspaper, she was certain her aunt, a decent woman, had wanted word of the death to reach Wilda. To know the blood tie had been severed, the mind tie might follow. But, sitting there, Wilda could not grasp the possibility that the woman was really gone, even though she sensed the knowledge was hovering around her, pricking her, wanting to find its way in.

Laying her face down on the cold tabletop, she closed her eyes, hoping her dizziness might fade. She shook slightly when she thought about her mother. This was something she had never told Lewis, and never would. There was no way to mouth these words. So snarled throughout Wilda's flesh, handfuls of rusty hooks, pulling them out would completely ruin her.

Wilda was only seven years old when her mother dragged her into an empty barn. Made her look at the sticky puddle in the middle of the pig pen. "That's your doing," she had cried. "Your doing. He loved you. And this is how you look after him?"

Her mother had said, no, no, no, for God's sakes, not in his state, but little Wilda still nagged her father to kill the pig. She sang out the words, roast and gravy, chops and hocks, roast and gravy, chops and hocks, until her father hoisted himself up off the worn stump beside the wood pile, stumbled into the barn. Her mother yelling out to Wilda, "Watch he don't hurt himself." And her father laughed, said, "Oh, she's re- re- re- pons-ble, maid. She got 'old of me heart."

She remembered when he struck the pig between the pink ears with a mallet, tying the tiny ankles with rope. Once airborne, the pig was swinging slowly to and fro, and it gently bumped Wilda's father as he approached, almost knocked him over. He found a knife, stuck into a support post, and he wriggled it free, slurred, "Close down yer, close down yer h'eyes, Cookie." Gripping a wee hock with one hand, he pressed the blade into the neck with the other. Slicing back and forth, blade moving with rapid, sloppy strikes, and after a moment's hesitation, blood squirting, splattering on the muddy floor. He leaned in, several more slashes, head nearly severed. Her father swayed, rich color pouring over his hands, onto his shirt sleeves. And then he stopped, dropped the blade, held out his arm, and turned his face towards Wilda. Expression of drunken confusion. He stared down at his hand, his wrist. But all Wilda could see was that the sharp blade had cut clear through the plaid fabric of his sleeve.

Wilda watched that day. Watched as her father reached for the pig, clutched its jaw, fingers slipping, then lunged for the ankles, up high, grasping the end of rope that trailed down between the pig's pinched legs. Blood spurting, spurting from the flank, and Wilda could not understand how her pig had been cut all the way up there, in the very place where her father was holding. "Help me, Willie," he said. "God, help me." His voice sounded like it was coming from behind her, above her. His face had turned gray, and at that moment, he let go of the rope, and collapsed.

She did nothing. Nothing. Besides skip outside into the warm sunshine, find her twin dolls in the overgrown grass. She was giggling, playing house, and at the same time her father slowly died in the barn.

Wilda jumped up, glanced at the boys, their backs to her, like two small strangers plastered together on the chesterfield, watching cartoons, giggling. "I don't feel... I've got to—," she mumbled. "I've got to go out for a spell. Some air." To calm myself. They hadn't heard her whispers. But no matter. She wouldn't be gone long. Just enough to sooth the agitation in her legs, her racing pulse. She lifted the keys from the hook, and slipped out the door.

WINTER MONTHS WERE slow on the farm, and Garrett Glass spent most of his days working at Clarey's Paints and Carpets. Mr. Clarey gave him two dollars and seventy-five cents an hour, and after Garrett had worked there for nearly five months, he also gave him a key. Made of brass, red braided string knotted through the hole, Garrett kept it inside the buttoned pocket of his only dress shirt. He took his new responsibilities very seriously, opening the store not a minute before nine, and locking it at five on the nose every evening. He was meticulous with the money, keeping note of every can of paint sold, every brush, and felt a rush of pride each time the cash register shot out, bumped gently into that area beneath his hips. Garrett had big dreams, hoped someday to stop working the farm altogether, and to keep his fingernails clean while managing Mr. Clarey's shop.

Though Mr. Clarey might not approve, several nights Garrett had slept there. But only if the snow was particularly heavy, and he couldn't tolerate the long trudge home to the farm. He would flick off the fluorescent lights, and once the gray light had faded he would hide down between the enormous rolls of carpet and linoleum, cover up with his winter coat, drift off while imagining he owned everything that surrounded him. That he was a young man of real substance. An attractive man that the young ones might admire. Sometimes, in the middle of the night, his bones would begin to ache, and he would unroll a few feet of carpet, fold them over, sleep on the soft charcoal sponge that covered the underside. He would lay his face directly against it, rub his fingers over the smooth rubbery surface. There was pleasure in the fact that no person had ever touched his feet to this product. It was pure and completely clean.

The night before, the clouds had been heavy and the wind was making the building gripe, so Garrett locked the door and switched out the lights. He ate the rest of his bologna sandwich in silence, drank handfuls of water from the sink in the bathroom near the back. Removed his good shirt, hung it on Mr. Clarey's vinyl chair in the office. He lay down in his secret place, and soon drifted. Only to be awoken by drunks stumbling home from the lodge, a man even stopping in the entryway of the shop to piss. Then a woman squatting, her girlfriends hooting with laughter. Garrett felt his heart bang in his chest, angry at the shamelessness, even in the light of the street lamp, faces clear through the window, liquid spattering door and step. He recognized them, but would never say their names. An hour or more later, after he had calmed down, he was startled again by the knob rattling, and he peered out from beneath the roll, saw a man and woman tucked into the small space, her dark coat and open palms pressed against the glass in the door. They were kissing for minutes and minutes, her head knocking against the door, and then, when they stopped, continued to linger, Garrett could hear her giggling, the sound creeping in around the wooden frame, reverberating in the empty store. The man grabbed her bare hand, tugged her up the street to God knows where to do God knows what. And Garrett lay there, wide awake, hands pinched between his bony thighs, lower half throbbing uncomfortably, and he wondered, *What kind of love is that?* Nothing like Garrett had ever experienced. Or would ever want to. Animals. No better than pigs barred up in a dirty pen.

In the morning, Garrett was stiff and sore and his eyes were swollen from lack of sleep. After he had dressed, washed his face, and put his shirt back on, he cracked open the front door. Several inches of snow had fallen, and Garrett took the shovel and the bucket of salt, cleared the steps, stained snow, layer of ice beneath it. His stomach turned, and he wanted to sluice hot water over it, but that would only freeze, make it treacherous. So, he turned his nighttime visitors into unusual dreams, bad dreams, nothing more, and closed the front door.

The store was empty until nearly noon, when Mrs. Pyke came in with her blond-haired son. Charming cowlick on his forehead, freckles spattered across his turned-up nose. With a terse nod from Mrs. Pyke, Garrett offered the youngster a lollipop. The boy accepted, and Garrett watched him peel off the waxy wrapper, lick and lick. "His room needs something," Mrs. Pyke said. "Got to be easy to clean." Though Garrett continued to be shy, his tongue shone the slightest shade of silver whenever he had to recommend flooring for a child's room. Especially when it was a young boy. Garrett could talk a tightfisted mother into upgrading from indoor/outdoor to luxurious shag. Didn't she want the best for her son? Could she imagine his poor knees, playing for hours with cars and blocks on such a rough and inexpensive surface? "If you only splurge in one room, Mrs. Pyke," he said with a genuine smile, "have it be your boy's."

"I got to be able to wash it, now. He makes an ungodly mess."

"You'll be careful, now won't you?" Garrett said, placing a hand on the boy's shoulder, and the boy looked up, mouth open, lips and gums green from the lolly, and nodded.

124

"What about this one here?" she replied.

"That gets very cold in the winter. Touch it."

And she hauled off her mitten, hand to the back of the linoleum.

"Hm. What about this?" She dug her fingers into a sample of pale blue shag.

"Yes, this one is nice. Has a long tuft, excellent quality yarn."

"Bit much for an eight-year-old, I suppose."

"Not at all," Garrett replied, giving it a good rub. "He only has one childhood, Mrs. Pyke."

"Don't we all?" she said, rolling her eyes. "Is it on sale?"

"No, ma'am."

"Where's the owner?"

"Mr. Clarey won't be in today." Garrett stood a little taller. "Do you know the measurements for the room?"

"No. Mr. Pyke will be taking those." She ran her hand over the shag once again.

"Well, when you know that, I'll see what I can do about the price. I'm sure I can shave something off it." Garrett knew he could always take five, even ten percent off the purchase price without angering Mr. Clarey.

"Alright," she said. "Alright. Okay. I doubts I'll be back today. With this weather. Likely Monday. And you lays it?"

"Yes, we do. We does it all ourselves, Mrs. Pyke. Whenever it works for you."

She purchased a mop and left. Garrett watched them through the front window, mother moving at a good clip, boy marching on the sidewalk behind her, mop hoisted onto his shoulder. He saw Garrett, and saluted him, and Garrett smiled, saluted back. What a delight! What an imagination! The child was worthy of such a fine floor covering, no doubt, and Garrett made a silent wish that she would return to complete the purchase. He could just picture the boy lying on the carpet, freshly bathed, and reading comics.

Garrett perched his bony backside on the edge of the window frame, stared up at the pinkish sky. The first few sprinklings of snow were drifting down, and then in a blink, lid on the jar loosened, the air was full of fat flakes. With this weather he was certain he'd have no more customers that afternoon, and Garrett went to the counter, found a dust rag, paused for a moment to listen to the lights buzzing, mice scratching and gnawing in the walls.

Though most might be bored, Garrett enjoyed these quiet times the best. What could be better than getting paid just to stretch his legs, wander about, and play games inside his head? One game he often played was Find the Child. Garrett would walk around the store, glancing this way and that, calling "Come out, come out, wherever you are." He only played it when he was certain he would be alone, as he had the penchant to lose himself completely in his fantasy. He glanced again at the snow batting the front of the shop, then he ran the dust rag over the counter, started down the main aisle, cleaning metal stands, rolls of linoleum.

Before long, Garrett invented whimpers coming from the very back of the store. The floor creaked as he circled around, and there, in a dim corner, he conjured a small child, maybe the Pyke boy, lost and crouching. "I knew it," Garrett said aloud. "I thought I seen you come back." But without his mother, the boy would be timid, would not meet Garrett's eye. "It's alright, you can come out."

If the boy moved forward, what would happen? Garrett thought of a dark puddle spreading on the floor, and his heart squeezed. In his nervousness, the boy could have peed, and it was now up to Garrett to respond. He could reach into his pocket, remove the carpet cutter that was always there, and expose the blade. Scrape his thumb across it, then waggle it under the boy's nose. "You're worse than a bloody dog. One flick, my son, and you'll never piss again." Then, of course, the child would cry with abandon, maybe even leak some more, and Garrett would haul back his words, kneel down and comfort him. "Shush, shush. I was only joking around for God's sakes. Being silly." Or, instead, he could suggest the boy slip out

126

of his wet clothes, offer a small towel to wash himself, dangle the promise of an icy mug of cream soda when he was dry.

For today, Garrett would imagine the second approach. From the bathroom, he tore the hardened towel from the rack, went back to the scene, and held it out. "We'll call your mommy later. Let her worry a bit, hey?" he said to the empty corner. "Serve them right." And Garrett's tongue grew sandpaper as the dream-boy edged forward, stood, stains on his corduroys reaching his knees. With perfect small fingers, he didn't hesitate as he unsnapped his trousers, bent and pulled.

EVERY MONTH, like clockwork, a letter would arrive from Francis. When six weeks has passed with no word, Wilda began walking to the mail every afternoon to check. In sunshine or slanting rain, she often left the boys playing tin soldiers on the carpet, and walked down the lane, up onto the main road, and into the corner store. Past all the canned foods, bags of bread, freezers filled with Popsicles and Drumsticks, she would slip into the shadowy back hall. Box sixty-one. Twisting the key, she'd bend, peer though the tunnel and into the office hidden behind, a counter with brown-papered boxes, an abandoned sandwich on a plate. Most days, the box was empty, or holding only a bill or a curled catalogue, but on this particular afternoon she spied a cream-colored envelope. She reached in, let her hand and wrist cover it, slowly slid it out with her fingertips. A letter. For Mrs. Wilda Trench.

Nothing like the regular notes she would receive from Francis. This was a formal envelope, typed address, printed business-style stamp rather than a licked square. At first she believed it was related to her mother. Perhaps, in the weeks since the woman had died, someone had decided to track Wilda down. But when she looked closely, Wilda saw the return address: The offices of Johnston and Eddy. A letter from the city. Francis, then. Oh, oh. Francis. She held it up to the low-wattage lightbulb, squeezed the quality paper. There was something hard inside. Something that was surely a key.

Envelope tucked into her pocket, she hurried home in a downpour, stopped on the mat in the kitchen, water dripping off her coat, splatting near her feet. She looked at the papered walls and painted cupboards, the red plastic tub in the sink still filled with iridescent bubbles. The dusty glass light fixture hanging over the table, the linoleum, hexagonal pattern, the two small heads blocking the television set. As she stood there in her sodden clothes, everything suddenly felt foreign. She could not identify a single trace of herself. As though, all those years ago, she had stepped into a world fully formed. Had existed in it ever since.

She placed her hand against her abdomen, heard the envelope crinkle. Her head began to pound as a stampede of emotions charged her. Recent news of her mother's death clanging against her awareness that Francis was gone. Missing from this world. The two thoughts, opposing spectrums, smashing, disintegrating, leaving Wilda curiously numb.

Toby squealed, cried "slug bug, slug bug," and she saw him punch Melvin in the arm. Wrestling now, they dove into the displaced cushions, laughing hysterically and pinching each other. In moments, she knew one of the two would be crying. Likely Melvin, and Wilda slipped quickly into her bedroom, closed the door, drew the curtains. She could not be a comfort, now. Could not do the motions, bending, kissing, cuddling, when her chest was bruised. Seated on the edge of the mattress in her cold coat, envelope now beside her on the peach-colored bedspread, her hands shook, she did not trust herself to open it, reveal the certain opportunity inside. She bit her nails, waited, listened for the crying, and when none came, she plucked up the letter. Began to search for a place to hide it.

Over the next few weeks, Wilda moved it frequently, on top of the dusty refrigerator, over to her drawer with underwear and stockings, tucked into the fabric band that held back the living room curtains. If she couldn't see it, she reasoned, the constant ache inside her legs would fade.

128

18

"CALM DOWN, MRS. VERGE." Lewis pinched the phone receiver between his shoulder and ear, slipped his hand underneath the tangled cord, scribbled notes. "A letter, you says? What'd he write?" Pause. "Yes, yes." Another pause, high-pitched mangle of words gushing through the phone line. "Sounds like your garden variety teenaged garbage, Mrs. Verge. Garden variety." Pause. "No, ma'am. Don't mind in the least. He's apt to be up there playing cards with his buddies. Joking about giving you a jolt." Final pause. Then light laugh. "No, Mrs. Verge. You don't need to bring me a casserole. I'm just doing my job."

Lewis cleaned snow from the windshield with the sleeve of his coat, slid into the driver's seat, and let the car idle for a minute. Windshield soon coated again, and he flicked on his wipers, revved the engine. Of all the days Terry Verge had to choose to make threats. Couldn't he have waited until spring? According to Mrs. Verge, Terry's girlfriend had broken up with him—for good, this time—and Terry was beyond distraught. What with her husband having passed last year, she was at a loss on how to deal with Terry. All her advice just hung in the air around the boy, she said, none of it sinking in. He took the truck, a good length of old rope, and headed out to the fishing cabin just off Jebineer's Line. Lewis had been there before. A solid thirty-minute trek in fine weather. It would take him an hour or more in this storm.

Easing up onto the highway, car sliding over invisible lines, he wondered what he was going to say to the boy. Would he chastise him when he found him, or would he be gentle, encouraging? This predicament wasn't entirely the fault of Terry Verge, but of the community as a whole. Everyone letting things slide by, no one speaking up. And all the youngsters, having oodles of time on their hands and nothing to do. No one was interested in clearing a pond anymore, skating over wind-rippled ice with a couple of sticks, a beat-up puck. Or hammering together a birdhouse or building a fort in amongst a few trees. Or, heaven forbid, helping out a neighbor in need. Sawing up a few logs, clearing a driveway, slapping a coat of paint on a fence. Not without a wad of dollar bills waved in front of their snouts. No, sir. Lewis shook his head, gripped the steering wheel. How times is changed.

Lewis turned off the highway, slowed to a crawl along Jebineer's Line. The road had been partially cleared, but in the newly fallen snow he could still see the tracks of the Verges' pickup. When he rounded the bend, Lewis arrived at the end of the tracks, discovered the mustard-yellow box lodged in the ditch. As though someone had gunned through a heap of snow on purpose. He pulled up next to it, parked, and got out. Looked around. A few feet more, and he would be stuck like the devil, no chance of getting out of this place until the thaw. He hauled on a hat and gloves, tucked his pants into his boots, and crawled up over the mound, wiped snow away from the cab. The truck was empty.

Only a short trek to the cabin, though parts of him were beginning to sweat as he lifted his feet up and into what he believed were Terry Verge's prints. The air was cold, and snow drifted into Lewis's face, stinging his cheeks. His leaking nostrils fused momentarily whenever he took a deep breath, making him curse the boy. A swirling gust, and Lewis could smell the acrid smoke pressed downwards by winter's cold palms. As he rounded the bend towards the cabin, clapboard the color of wet stone, he could make out a dying wisp rising from the chimney. The bugger's cooking himself up a meal, Lewis thought. A bottle of moose, molasses bread.

He knocked first, "Constable Trench, here. Open the door," pressed his ear to the rough wood, but there was silence. He was going to knock again, louder this time, but some sense of urgency arrived in his muscles, and his hand reached for the latch, clicked, clicked, no avail, and his shoulder banged against the heavy door until the lock broke, door open. There was Terry Verge, hanging from a rope he had wormed up and around a thick wooden ceiling beam, rickety chair tipped. Fingers curled over the rope, face and scalp like a swath of stately velvet. With an improperly tied noose, the rope had slipped, and he was left dangling there, tip of his right winter boot pushing down on the worn wool rug, slipping, pushing, slipping. His hazy mind clearly changed. The boy was alive, alive, but only by the thinnest of margins.

Lewis moved quickly, up righted the chair, fixed it underneath Terry, "Stand up, my son." But the boy's knees buckled, and Lewis had to abandon him for an instant to find a knife. Through cupboards, drawers, tossing spatulas and stirring spoons aside, where was a knife when you needed one, a can opener, bottle opener, forks, a knife, please, butter spreader. Finally. A bread knife, shiny serrated edge. He sawed through the taut rope, and Terry Verge, very nearly a ghost, fell forward into Lewis's outstretched arms.

"What the hell was you thinking, my son? What. The. Bloody. Hell. Was. You. Thinking?"

But Terry was unable to respond, even though his mouth was wide open, swollen tongue, only hoarse bawling emerged, then retching sounds, finally full-body sobs that made Lewis tighten his grip, keep the armload of teenaged bone and flesh from bursting apart.

"It'll be alright, my son. Shush, now. Shush, shush." Lewis knelt, loosened the rope, up over the tiny skull, flung it. Bruising and scratch marks all along his jaw. Ear rubbed to pearly rawness. Lewis stood, still holding Terry, and took an afghan from the back of a chair, wrapped it around the boy's body. Out through the door, pushing his legs straight through the snow this time. "Someone got their hand planted on you today, my son." He opened the back door of his car, laid the boy inside. "Reckons you'll see a print on your shoulder."

OVER THE WEEKS, an urgency spread across Wilda's skin, in through her ears, strapping her brain. A family of aggressive creepers, and eventually she could focus on nothing else besides the letter. So easy, so easy. And everything would be alright. Of course it would. She could picture the boys playing. Doing their schoolwork. Helping Lewis with the birch and clearing dead trees. Young brothers. Good brothers. Strong. Everyone would be just fine.

When the first storm arrived, blanketing the entire house, Wilda could resist no longer. She slit open the top of the envelope. Standing on the back stoop in slippers and beige cabled cardigan, snow falling soundlessly all around her, she dug out the letter. Unfolded it and read each word slowly, carefully. Read it once again. Refolded it, and then placed it neatly into the side pocket of her sweater. It was exactly what she had imagined. Still, shock seized her, made her clumsy, and the old brass key she had held so many times before slipped out from between her stiff fingers. She dropped to knees, plunged her bare hands into the fluffy snow to retrieve it.

A few yards away, Melvin and Toby were constructing opposing walls of snow. Melvin's was a smooth and sculpted semicircle, Toby's a fat mound that offered no protection from Melvin's pelting snowballs. She put her hand to her mouth, was going to call out, but she saw Toby was enjoying himself. Plunked down behind his crude barrier, he snorted, rolled like a hyper puppy, gnawed away the clumps of snow that stuck to his wooly mittens.

She stepped back inside, kicked off her slippers, hung her cardigan on a wire hanger. Gathered up her boots, her long coat, her gloves. Rolled up the good red shawl Melvin had given her last Christmas, tucked it into her purse. Lewis's Polaroid camera was sitting just next to the canister set, and once she was dressed, ready, she plucked it up, tromped out to the boys, calling for a momentary truce between the warrior and the target.

"Why do we got to stop? I idn't hurting him." Melvin packed snow between his mitts, and when Toby turned, bent over, Melvin let it fly, battering Toby's rump. "See, he loves it!"

"I know, I know," she said, almost whispering. "I just want one photo is all. Let's make one perfect picture."

"What do you need that for? You can look at us every day."

"I just want one, Melvin. One." She crouched down, fumbled with the snap on the hard brown case.

"No pictures, today, thank-you, ladies." He put up his mitten, in stop sign fashion. "Put your cameras away."

"Please, Melvin. Won't take a minute. One. That's it. I promise." Snow landed on her shoulders, patted her face, making her blink over and over and over.

Melvin cocked his head, stared at her. "Well, okay. Just the one, though." And he scrambled, four-legged, towards Toby, grabbed him by the scarf, yanked him in with an overzealous spurt of brotherly love. Icy red cheeks plastered together, they both hollered, "You're feet smells like stinkeee cheeeeese." Several teeth missing, they held their patchy grins, even though it hurt. Frost penetrating empty gums, baby enamel.

"Thank-you," she said after she'd clicked. She held her hand to the camera as the picture slid out, watched the dark square until the boys' image emerged.

Then she went back inside, tracked snow across the linoleum, and dropped the camera onto the table. Photo nestled inside a clean handkerchief, she placed it in her purse, then stooped to brush the crystals from her slacks. The clock chimed, a dozen tinny signals. She had to hurry if she was going to make it. Couldn't count on delays just because of the inclement weather. She did not look over her shoulder as she rushed out through the back door.

Just as she reached the bottom step, Melvin blocked her way.

"Where you going?" he asked. "With your purse."

"I needs to, um... I don't have a... I just... A little air, is all, Melvin. I needs that."

"We's going, too," Melvin replied. "Yes, siree, we's going wherever you're going."

"Okay, okay. But only for a bit."

"A bit of what?" he asked, but she didn't answer.

In the shed now, Wilda nudged Toby into the stroller. Fiddling with straps, pushing in damp fabric, she struggled to close the clasp. She shoved the stroller out through the door, wheels turning sideways, resisting the growing layer of snow.

Melvin watched her, shaking his head and smiling. "You're being silly. Strollers idn't built for snow, Mom. Why don't you use that?" He nodded towards a corner of the shed. Long plastic sled propped against the wall, straw-colored rope tied to the front.

"Oh yes," she replied, unbuckling Toby, straps flying backwards. "Yes. What was I thinking?"

"Not that he got to get a ride. He idn't so fat he can't walk."

"But he's so slow." She lifted Toby's feet over the edge, dropped them. "He wanders. You two don't even need to go, you know. I just wants air. A nice winter walk."

"Sure, I likes air. You and air is my two favorite things."

She bit her bottom lip. "And Toby?"

"He don't count, Mom. Toad's the same as me, and everyone's got to be one of their own favorite things, right?"

Snowflakes landed on her eyelashes, melted. "Let's get going," she said.

They trudged down the driveway, Wilda and Melvin pushing through a drift of snow, Toby holding the sides of the sled and squealing as it sprang forward with a jerk, then stopped. When they made it to the road, it was easier to move, the ground was level, free of drifts.

"Where is we going to anyways?" Melvin said. He was behind the sled, stomping hard into every one of Wilda's boot prints. "To get the air."

"Not far, darling."

"What do we got to be out for? Couldn't you just wait for Dad?"

"No, Melvin."

"This don't make no sense. I wants a hot chocolate. My feet is froze."

"Sometimes things don't make sense." Switched the rope to her other elbow, hauled with fresh drive.

"Do you want some breadcrumbs in your pockets?" he joked.

She did not smile in return.

At the end of the laneway, Melvin and Toby were allowed to go no further. Toby climbed out of the sled, stood side by side with his brother, and together they watched their mother leaving them. "We'll wait," Melvin had said to her.

"No, Melvin."

"We's waiting." He crossed his arms, spaced his boots. "Until you comes back."

"Please, Mom. On the side. Case the plow comes by."

"No, boys."

He stared straight into her face then, but she would not return his gaze. One last attempt. Gently. Softly. So perfectly. "Please, Mom. Please. Let us wait for you. My feet is wonderful warm. For hours. We'll be good as gold. Better than gold. Right, Toad?" Arm slung over his brother's shoulder, an irresistible team.

"We'll be good as, as, as good as hamburgers. Fat juicy ones." Biting the air. "Harrumph."

"Okay. Okay, yes," she finally said. A beguiling smile lit up her lower face, though it did not touch her eyes. "You fellers can wait."

Melvin's heart leapt, then plunged when he heard her say, "Until you gets cold."

And when she turned, so close to him, Melvin could feel a sharp wind coming off her, and even though he was still young he knew it was a door slamming shut.

They could not see her feet moving, and she appeared to be floating over the snow in her ice blue coat. Floating, until there was no way of knowing where the storm ended and she began.

Melvin's arms went out, navy mittens waving, as though he thought he might find her among the crowded air, bring her back. But she was long gone, and his arms soon returned to his sides. Toby reached up, and Melvin's hand opened wide, one damp mitten closing around the tiny other. Finger pinching fingers.

"I don't see her no more," Toby murmured. "Do we got to wait?"

Melvin stood there, staring.

"She'll be back, Mel. After she finds some bread. Or eggs. Or butter. That's what moms does. Looks 'round for milk and stuff."

He never wavered.

Toby sensed something different, now. He wiggled. "I got to pee." Pressed his knees together. "Bad. Real bad."

"Go home, Toad." His voice crackled. "Go home."

When Toby could wait no longer, he brushed his brother, nudged him towards the sled, and Melvin did not resist. He sat in the sled, then lay down, and Toby lifted Melvin's legs in, folded his arms across his chest. Toby stepped into the rope, hauled it up to his hips, and began to walk. One step after the other, don't stop, don't stop. Made his way through the snow. "We're going home, now, Mel. She'll come back. I knows she will. She got to." And the words, this new need to take care of his brother, propelled him forward, even though his bladder had let go, and the cold jean was rubbing his thighs.

ON THE DRIVE to the hospital, Lewis had to keep his window cracked, icy breeze numbing his watery eyes, his exposed neck. He felt sick to his stomach. If he'd been any more dismissive of Mrs. Verge's claims, this young life would have been extinguished. He glanced into his rearview mirror, saw the curled form of Terry Verge on the seat. Though well into his teens, he appeared small, deflated. No one's life should be so bad that they'd give it all up for a girl. Let alone one of the Chafe sisters. Witchy women, the lot of them. Lived in a rundown trailer,

136

hiked onto cement blocks, sour drunk of a mother and four daughters. He'd heard the oldest one provided a kneel-down service for gentlemen in the storeroom of Stubby's Pub, but he'd yet to catch her. He would though, and for a moment he thought to say something to Terry about his choices, but stopped himself.

He rolled up the window, considered that Terry might be cold. The nausea was passing, and what lay beneath it was tender awareness that he was blessed. By his wife, his two good boys, their cozy clean home tucked away from the drone of the small town. This sort of turmoil would never happen to him, not these days. Together with Wilda, he would raise his boys up properly. Not with slaps from a belt, but with unambiguous expectation. Clear guidance. A good example. They would grow up to be good men. Contributors to society. Nothing like the trash he scraped off the sidewalks or hauled up out of ditches every second day. Or worse, the lost souls, wiping their arses in the grim reaper's cloak, taunting him. Catch me if you can you dirty bastard. For no good reason whatsoever.

"You alright back there?" Craned his neck to see Terry's swollen face. "You doing alright, my son?" Eyes off the road for only a second, and Lewis glided over the hidden yellow lines, almost striking a bus that had formed out of a thick swirl of snow, barreling along in the opposite direction. Quickly, he corrected himself, swerved, backside of his car shivered, then straightened. "Jesus," he said, the word a single breath out. Two eyes, two hands on the wheel. From here on in.

Pulling into the hospital, he unloaded Terry, told the tale, said he'd make the drive over to see Mrs. Verge, bring her along as soon as he was able. Back in the car, he leaned his head against the steering wheel, closed his eyes, and there on the inside of his eyelids was a likeness of the bus. When he nearly collided, his police mind had taken a snapshot, the many rows of empty seats, a single person, familiar silhouette, seated two-thirds of the way back. A flick of bright red, a scarf perhaps, covering a head. He opened his eyes, looked out at the road.

Turned the key. Desperate to get where they're going, Lewis thought, as he turned out onto the road. Or else, desperate to get away from where they already was.

MELVIN SENSED HIMSELF lurching forward, gliding, lurching again. He thought about his new rubbery cowboy boots with the furry lining, boots he'd been so excited about only two hours earlier. And now he wanted to fling them into the woods, go barefoot. He wondered if he lay there long enough, would the snow cover him? Cover him completely? Make him disappear?

Though he no longer felt part of it, he could still hear the world, snow compacting beneath him, the crunch of his brother's boots, grunts from exertion. He closed his eyes now, sides of the sled cupping him, and he imagined his withered form moving over the snow-covered laneway in a bright yellow open casket. Breathing slowly, icy air entered and exited his functional lungs, but he was unable to shift a single muscle. Melvin had watched her leave, but he wondered if it had all been a dream. If that was really her moving away from him, if she'd even been there at all.

When Melvin pulled open his eyes, ice on his lashes, he was aware of the snowflakes whizzing through the air above him. How could they travel at such speed, for such a distance, and never collide? Each unique crystal maintaining a perfect orb of personal space. An hour earlier, he might have expected them to touch, some of them to stick, journey through the uncertain sky in unison. One flake guiding the other. With love. But right now, he wasn't at all surprised by the nature of their rejection. Selfish as they were. As he moved over the earth, dragged by his brother, Melvin was aware of something new expanding within him. Something outside of the realm of his childhood. A loathing, deep and cold. Not for the snowflakes themselves, but the spaces in between.

PART FOUR

19

"**HOW 'BOUT A BLUE** charm?" Lewis settled into the creaking chair in front of his desk, took a deep breath, and smiled. "What do you say? Blue charm's a good place to start, and I reckon you're big enough now to give it a try."

"Alright," Toby said. "A blue charm."

"Thatta boy." Sliding open the bottom drawer, Lewis selected some feathers and floss and laid them on the desk. He twisted the screw on the bottom of the vice, secured it to the edge of the desk.

"Haul your chair over a bit closer," Lewis said as he opened the miniature metal jaws, slid a single hook in place, clamped it.

"Can you jig a squid with that?"

"What?"

"A squid. Haul it in. Squirt his black juice right in your eye."

"Nope. I don't do squid. Salmon, my boy. Big tasty salmon. They can't resist it. Blue charm's a real charmer." Lewis laughed, rubbed Toby on the head, neck wobbly. Toby drew the corners of his mouth straight back in a flattened smile. "This here's where my dad used to show me how to tie flies. Right on this very spot with this very vice."

Lewis had thought of his father often, these past couple of years. Dig, my son, or be buried. That was what he'd always said. And Lewis did his best to put that old adage into practice.

At first he was angry when Wilda left. Savage, actually. How could she do this to her husband and children? Were they not good enough? Did they not deserve better? What words he'd plan to spew when she returned from her extended outing. But as the days passed, and her homecoming seemed less and less likely, a quiet relief had gradually elbowed its way into his heart. The distance that existed between them for so many years was no longer coiled into the space of a few feet. It was stretched out into almost nothing. A strand of weakened netting. And whenever his mind lobbed memories at him, her earlobe between his teeth, ends of her thick hair tickling his nose, the taste of her carrot cake for breakfast, he took a wrench to the valve, twisted until the screw was stripped. He reasoned Toby and Melvin should be strong enough to do the same.

"Really?" At eight years old, Toby now understood when to nod, when to agree. "With this vice?"

"What do you say, big guy?" Over to Melvin, now. "What do you think of that?"

Melvin was in the corner, spread feet pushing his chair back on two legs, arms folded across his chest. "You told us already. A hundred million times."

"I have?"

"Uhh, yuh-aah."

"Why don't you haul your chair up like Tobe?"

"Why don't I not?"

"Don't you want to see?"

"Do I got to?"

"No, sir, you don't got to. Thought you might want to. Be part of our little history."

"Then, I won't." Melvin shook his head and the bangs of his hair fell forward, obscuring his eyes. "History is stupid and I hates fish."

"Hates fish?" Strained laughter. "My sonny boy, you wouldn't be here but for a fish. You wouldn't even exist."

Smack of wood, four legs on the floor. "Like I even cares."

Plug pulled, joy draining, cold wet sink. Lewis found this transformed Melvin impossible to take. Months of moody silence after Wilda left, and Lewis finally sat him down, asked him what was he was thinking, knocked him gently on the skull. Melvin tried to squirm away, but Lewis put both hands on his shoulders, held him in place, "You tell me what's going on in there, my son, or you'll won't be getting out of this chair." To which Melvin replied, "Eventually, I'll grow. I'll get big enough. And then I'll go find her myself." Lewis released his grip, then. Couldn't think of anything to say. Until Melvin was walking away, and Lewis yelled at his back, "Don't ever mention that woman again. For your own good, Melvin. Trust me on that one, my sonny boy. Quicker you forget about her, better off you'll be."

"What was that?" Lewis said. "What did you just say?"

"Nuthin."

"Well, you can just sit right there without budging an inch, do your nuthin, and keep your gob shut."

Toby touched Lewis's fingers, pinched white around the secured hook. "Blue charmer, Dad. Right?"

"Oh, yes, yes. You starts with, um," deep breath, sigh. Lewis leaned over, tightened the clamp securing the vice. "You starts with this here thread and a bit of silver stuff." On the pinewood table, Lewis showed Toby step by step how to create a perfect salmon fly from tinsel, floss, feather, and hair. Twirling thread, adding the items neatly organized on the table, clipping the finished product. Then, with minimal instruction, eight-year-old Toby took his father's seat, two hard cushions propping him up, and constructed his own. "Good, good, yes that's right, what a memory, well done, exactly. You're a natural, my son. By jumpins. A natural." Though loose and bushy, Lewis was telling the truth. Toby had a knack with his hands, the ability to put things together in meaningful ways.

"Can I keep it?" Toby said, fluff of blue and yellow and bristles of brown, hidden hook, resting on his open palm. "Can I keep it for keeps, Dad?"

"Of course, hold onto it 'til we gives it a try," Lewis announced. "See what we catches."

"But what if I loses it?"

"That's the chance you got to take. The chance you always takes. As a fisherman. As a man."

Wisdom fluttering over Toby's head. "I don't want to lose it. I wants to keep it."

"But that's the whole purpose, my son. You got to use them. If it sinks to the bottom of the river or gets swallowed by a fish never to be seen again, then that's what's got to happen" Eyebrows lowered. "You don't get attached to a bloody fly, my son."

Toby crinkled his lips, narrowed his eyes. "Buh, buh, I wants it." And he started to cry, not loudly, but with a pronounced sniffle. "'Tis my fly."

"Oh, for Christ's sakes. Give me that fly."

Toby closed his hand around it.

Metal fly box open, Lewis's own invention already stabbed into the foam. "C'mon, I said. You can stick it in there yourself. Like a big boy."

Second hand enveloping the first, the double fist jammed into Toby's chest, chin bent down over it.

"Fine," Lewis said, snapping the box closed. "Poke your finger. See how pleasant that feels. But you got to grow up, Toby. 'Tis time to grow up." Gentle slap to the side of Toby's head, knocking the boy further than Lewis intended.

Melvin leapt up from his roost in the corner, growled, "Don't you tell him to grow up."

Lewis swung around. "Is you talking to me with that lip?"

"Leave my brother alone."

"You better watch your tone, young man. You're not too big to get yourself in a heap load of trouble."

Step closer. "They calls you a pig, you know."

"What? Who do?"

"Oinks when we goes by. Me and Toad."

"Who, I said."

"Calls us little piggies. Wee, wee, wee."

Lewis yanked open a drawer, tossed his fly box in there, slammed it shut. "Sure they do. Got no respect for yourself.

Hair on you like a goddamned mongrel. Making a mockery of me. You'll be shaving that off right this minute, my son. Shaving it all."

"Like I gives a crap. Wee, wee, wee." Hand twisted up behind his head, fingers pulling back his nose, two stretched nostrils.

"What did you say, my son?"

"Nuthin'."

"What. Did. You. Say?" Ding, ding. Doors closing. Voice ascending. Heartbeat along for the ride.

"I said nuthin'." Quiet snort.

Up from his chair, he had a grip on Melvin. "You said nothing? Nothing? How stupid do you think I is?"

Child mouth in a sneer, singing, mocking. "Do you think I is? I is, I is. Stoo-pid."

Calm veneer disintegrated, and Lewis watched helplessly as his own hands clutched Melvin's skinny arms, muscles firing, dragged the boy to the bathroom. Fistful of hair in one hand, he forced his son's head down into the sink, snapped the switch on the set of clippers he'd used that morning, and they came to life. Making his palm numb with the vibration. He pressed the steel blades against the side Melvin's skull, nicking his ear, trail of blood falling forward, dripping off his nose onto the olive-colored enamel. Verbal shots, "You gonna get that attitude in check, boy. If 'tis the last thing I does. You think you're in for a free ride? You thinks you're something special? No, my laddie. You can think again. Bloody well think again." Melvin did not fight back, lay limp and accepting, arms dangling, and soon the anger left Lewis's hands, and he threw the clippers into the soap-ringed tub, where they cracked into metal and plastic and tangle of cord.

"Dad! Daa-aaah-duh!" Toby was hollering from the front of the house. "Someone's at the door."

Lewis took two deep breaths, rubbed his sweaty hands on his shirt, and strode out into the kitchen. There he found Mrs. Verge standing behind the screen door, big smile, fingernails tapping against the glass. On her hip she balanced a burgundy pot.

Lewis pushed open the door, and short, jolly Mrs. Verge with her tight curls, shiny face, and oversized glasses brushed past him, lighting up the room.

"Thank goodness," she said. "My side was about to drop off." Toby was next to her now, mouth slightly open, and she touched his face. "Wouldn't be too good having an old hip out on your front step, now, would it darling? A bit gross, as they says. Supposing your father wanted you to clean it up?"

Toby giggled, lay his head against her freckled upper arm. This woman who was always warm, and always smelled like comfort. If comfort had a smell.

"Mrs. Verge," Lewis said, rubbing his eyes to gather himself together. He no longer tried to discourage her generosity, had given up that useless line of dialogue a couple of years ago. Now, he just accepted, with sincere gratitude, her turkey soups and moose pies, cherry squares and slabs of fruitcake. Homemade bread, already sliced, bottles of squashberry jelly, or even bakeapple jam if lightning didn't kill the berries. She had brought that first meal the day after Terry was released from the hospital. "He got himself a renewed spirit," she'd told Lewis. "I don't know how you got through to him. What you done and said. But, he's a changed boy. And I'll be forever in your debt for that, Constable Trench."

At that point, Lewis had been unable to look her in the face, as he'd really said nothing, had more negative thoughts during the recovery of Terry than he'd care to admit. So he replied, "Oh, I don't know, Mrs. Verge. Sometimes, you know. Well. Yes. Sometimes. Of course." And in the months to follow, Lewis's recollection of that afternoon adapted, his participation swelled, until he believed he truly had transformed the boy into a solid man.

Perhaps she only intended to do it the one time, but once word about Wilda's wanderlust piggybacked through the town Mrs. Verge arrived regularly. Lewis watched her waddle over to the counter, slide the pot off her side. Plug it in. "All you got to do is twist the dial to there," she said to Toby. "And your belly'll

146

be bursting right after you hears the buzzer." Then, to Lewis, apologetically, "A bit hot for a stew, I knows. But I was going through my freezer. Waste not want not, I always says."

"You won't hear a breath of complaint out of us, Mrs. Verge."

Mrs. Verge's jaw fell open then, not to speak, but in response to something just behind Lewis. She was staring at Melvin, then without hesitation went to him, took his hand, walked him over to a window. Wet the corner of a cup towel, and daubed blood from his nose, the curved line across his face, carefully traced the leak to a tiny laceration near his ear. "Not much to that," she said, pressing a cloth to his head. "Looked worse than it is. You're a bit of a bleeder." Holding his face gently in her soft hands, she joked, "Now, about that style you got. You shouldn't be playing with those things, those clippers, young man. You could've done a real number on your ear. Could've taken 'er right off. One Van Gogh was enough for this world." Chuckling at her own banter. "Terry's working over to Barber Barber's, and he'll give you a clean cut. Unless that's the style you're after." She smiled, hugged his rigid body until he was nearly lost among her folds. Glancing over at Lewis. "Young folks these days. Sometimes they likes to hide behind it, sometimes they don't. Half and half. Newfangled, what have you. I never once made an issue about hair."

"Is that right, Mrs. Verge." As Lewis was watching the smugness spread over the exposed side of Melvin's face, the phone rang. Lewis pressed the receiver to his ear, listened, then rubbed the sunburnt skin on the back of his neck. Hanging it up, he said, "I got to go now."

"Yes, yes," Mrs. Verge said. She plucked an embroidered apron from a hook, leaned forward, tree trunk arms reaching to tie it around her waist. "You go on. Boys'll make themselves scarce, right? I'll just straighten up a few things here and there. Idle hands are the home for the devil."

THEY COULD SMELL the hole before they reached it. Hot muck, drowning plants, still water with occasional clumps of algae bumping against the side. When Melvin and Toby emerged through the bushes, they saw six or seven boys, a couple of girls splashing in the pond. Toby made a rapid scan of the faces, hoping, hoping that Clayton Gibbon would be nowhere in sight. He sighed, but his immediate relief was replaced with trepidation as soon as that particular shark disrupted the surface, popping up for air.

"He's here," Toby whispered to Melvin.

Melvin stopped in a patch of dry grass, a lounge area where swimmers lay down to dry off. Toby stopped too, leaned against Melvin, ball of towel cradled in his arms. "I idn't going in."

"That you is, then," Melvin said. "I didn't bring you all the way down here to get a tan, my son."

"But—"

"No one'll touch you."

Toby scratched his neck. "But Clayton—"

"He's a fucking nosebleed, man. Now get your arse in the water."

Toby kicked off his sneakers, stepped gingerly onto the path, tiptoed down towards the pond, carefully avoiding the scattered pieces of broken glass jutting up like crystals in the mud. He wished he had just gone to the stream in the woods. He wouldn't be able to swim, but at least he would be able to cool down without fear.

Toes touching the edge of the water and Toby felt the charge move up through his legs, weaken them. It was there, he was certain of it. A dirtiness. As though the activities taking place in and around the swimming hole had transferred their wayward energy into the water itself. Necking on the towels, bikini bows untied, fabric slipping, dunking heads, play-humping the diving rock, trunks yanked down to display soggy double loaves. Just coming in contact with the water made Toby feel queasy, nervous. Made his skinny chicken bones want to run back to Melvin.

As soon as he decided to leave, his fears were realized. Some-one grabbed his wrist and he was airborne, stomach smacking the water's surface, hungry gravity pulling him below. Eyes open, through the murkiness he saw white legs and feet, flashes of swimsuit, gunk on the bottom billowing up in great brownish clouds. He came to the surface, sputtering, twisting, found his footing on the slippery bottom. But a ball of wet fur struck his abdomen, someone's big head bending him in half, and he felt hands on his swim trunks, off his feet again, legs kicking, and cool water rushed in around places that were suddenly exposed.

Toby crouched, hands cupping his business end, and his eyes widened as a few feet ahead of him Clayton Gibbon emerged with barely a ripple, Toby's navy blue trunks whirling around the tip of Clayton's finger at high speed, then lifting off, a continual arc, snagged, a dead twig on an old spruce.

"Get me my shorts, you nosebleed." Words big, strength behind them like putty.

"Who you calling nosebleed?" Heel of palm kissing the water, spraying Toby's face. Laughter came from all corners from a hoard of water witches, brazen brutes. Other kids pretending that nothing was happening. No one dared challenge the pecking order. Not if they valued air, liked their shorts on their bodies.

"I wants them now." A squeak.

"Well, go and get 'em yourself, loser." And Clayton dove backwards, did a handstand, emerged, hair a mess of misplaced fins.

As quickly as he attacked, Clayton moved on, joke over, and Toby took mini-steps backwards, trying to find an edge, a corner, a muddy wall, somewhere to disappear until everyone went home. Once there, he held himself, front and back, stomped the bottom of the pond to create a continual blanket of disturbed gunk. Beneath the surface, his chest hiccuped over and over. There was a cry trapped inside there, and Toby would not let it escape through his face. Passed nervous gas instead, and it bubbled up behind his back. Though he wouldn't look directly, he saw one of the Fagan sisters, Angie, staring at him from the side.

He wasn't sure whether she was peering through the water or not, trying to catch a glimpse. But, after a moment or two, he noticed her feet. She was stomping the muck in time with his stomping of the bottom. And as his stomping got angrier, more frantic, so did hers.

Just up the pathway, Melvin sat on the end of a rusty over-turned barrel, lit a cigarette. His chest was bare, and he wore a coonskin hat on top of his head. Shook the tail so that it tickled the skin between his shoulders.

"You looks nuts," Roddie Wall said, and he jumped towards Melvin, tapped the hat from his head, caught it in the air.

Melvin's shag of hair revealed, and his hand went up, clapped over the stubbly section.

Furry hair balanced atop his own sun-crisped scalp, Roddie leaned in, said, "Man, you looks really nuts. You in a fight with a chainsaw, or something?"

Hand coming down, proud, now. "Nope. Lawnmower."

"No shit. You done that yourself?"

"Yeah. That part was bugging me. Took it right off. Did two runs over it with the mower, and said fucking A-one."

"Shit, man. No one said nothing?"

"Nope."

"Wish the old bag'd let me cut my own hair. I could do some-thing cool with it. Shave it right down the middle. Give myself a set of hair ears." Tongue wagging. "Arf!"

"That's why I'm lucky. Got no woman trying to boss me. I don't go in for that shit."

"Yeah, but you still looks nuts."

"That's cause I is nuts."

"Yeah, right on."

Roddie took the hat from his head, jammed it down his trunks, arched his back, strutted with his wings out, display-ing a huge faux mound, furry tail escaping, hanging lifelessly out over the elastic waistband. "Here chicky, chicky. Got some feed for you."

Both boys laughed, and Melvin took a drag on his cigarette, said in a voice an octave up, "You can keep that, now. 'Tis all yours, buddy."

"Right on!"

"Do you think—" Melvin started, but a girly scream shot up from the water, cut the words from his throat. And Melvin was up, knocked Roddie out of the way, dashed down to the black path, mud sucking at his sneakers. Scanning the water, Melvin located Toby, crouched near the edge, sunlight shining through the greenish pond, showing what appeared to be a full body of flesh, arms angled downwards in a tight V.

"What're you doing?"

"Scoochin'."

"What?"

"My trunks, Mellie. Clayton stole my trunks."

"How do someone steal your trunks?"

"I dunno."

Melvin shook his head. "Clayton, you says?"

"Mmm-hmm."

"Fucking drip." Melvin stomped over to the diving rock. "Get his shorts, fag breath."

Clayton stood up. "Who's gonna make me?"

"I'll bloody make you. You fucking quiff. Trying to see my brother's dick."

"Like hell. A fucking wiener's got more draw."

Boys guffawed, and two slapped open palms. Five on five.

Melvin took another step forward, spoke in a monotone. "Get his shorts. Get them now. Or I'll drown you, Clayton Gibbon."

"You will, will you?"

"I'll drown you 'til you're dead." Melvin did not blink the single eye not hidden by hair, and even though he was smaller than Clayton, Clayton backed down.

"Fucking whack-job," Clayton said under his breath, but he turned, dove into the water, swam over to the opposite side of the pond. Cussed loudly as he shimmied up the old tree, scratched his torso on dead sticks. He retrieved the trunks and lobbed them at Toby's head.

"Got 'em! Thanks," Toby called out to Clayton, and Melvin looked up at the sky, smacked his stubble spot with his open palm.

On their way home, Melvin said, "You can't go 'round with a 'shit here' stamp on your head, Toad."

Toby touched his forehead with his fingers, looked for ink on the tips. "What? I don't got no stamp, Mellie. I didn't do nothing."

"Well, sometimes, it's not nothing you got to do. It's something. I won't be around to save you forever."

Toby sped up to close the gap between them. "Yes, you will."

"And one last thing."

"Okay."

"Would you say thank-you to a dog if it pissed on your boot?"

"No, sir. That I wouldn't."

"What if he came back and licked it off. Would you say thank-you then?"

"No sir, Mel. No chance."

"No sir is right. And don't you forget it."

Toby scratched his head, wiggled his toes. Yes, he was wearing sandals, not boots, and a quick scan of the brush revealed no dog in sight. But he said, "Okay, Mel. I won't talk to dogs. Word of honor."

"Good boy."

Before they cut through the trail in the bushes, Toby paused once to look back. Down by the pond, Angie Fagan was still standing there, in the shade, lifting one foot, then the other. Squelching sound lost amongst the screaming and splashing, but Toby could imagine the boggy black mess between her toes, up over her ankles, staining her shins. Claw-shaped streaks of muck on her hand-me-down swimsuit, the loose bands yanked and tied between her shoulder blades. It was her scream that'd brought Melvin to the water, her call of distress. But she was fine, in no danger, and Toby knew she was calling out to help him. He didn't understand why, because he knew the Fagans were rotten through and through. And not just the old farmer, but those sisters, too. No reason given, they just were. He watched her for a moment, until a branch whipped his face and he turned, put his arm up, followed behind his brother.

LEWIS PULLED UP next to the front door, turned off his car. Sat for just a split second before getting out. How many years had it been since he had come through the woods, bursting out into that very backyard? So calm now, a pair of birds hopping, rusting but functional swing set plunked down only yards from the barrel. In the breeze, a plastic swing swayed, and he could see a length of tatty ribbon tied to the iron chain. For a moment he wondered if it had been like that when he and Roy tumbled over the grass, full of drunken joy. He had tried to replay it a million times, but those hazy patches of memory refused to clink together.

One deep breath. Two. Today, more than most days, he kept telling himself to breathe.

Lewis turned to the left, identified the reason for his visit. He saw Eli Fagan's truck parked just a few feet away from a newly constructed cement wall, a retaining wall, perhaps. About four feet high. Someone had stuck a dozen lengths of wooden doweling in front of the wall, coaxed leafy wax beans up the sticks. But it was clear to Lewis that a fine harvest had been spoiled. Leaves and beans were now smears of vegetation over the cement, a number of black contact marks, scrapes of chocolate-colored paint amongst them. As he always did, Lewis surveyed the scene rapidly and meticulously. No immediate danger. He took in everything there was to see, before eyeing the obvious. A tiny smashed car, busted windows, flattened sides.

He opened his car door and took wide strides to reach the destruction. Peered in through the open hole on the driver's side, no sign of anyone injured or hiding amongst the crumpled metal, folded steering wheel, a million sparkling shards of glass. The front of the truck was damaged as well, and it was immediately clear to Lewis that whoever was operating the truck had set about to destroy the little car by slamming it repeatedly into the cement wall. Into the pretty lineup of tender leaves and sweet wax beans.

Lewis went to the side door, rapped. "Constable Trench, here." There was no response, and he eased open the screen door, repeated himself. "Mrs. Fagan. Is you in?" he called. One step into the porch and he could see the hefty figure of Eli Fagan, seated in a rocker. Silence, except for the quiet squeaking of the chair's runner massaging the wood floor. Standing in a patch of sunlight, Lewis began to sweat instantly. He was slightly blinded, resisted putting a hand to his forehead.

Cleared his throat, said, "Mrs. Fagan about?"

"Nope. No, she idn't about. No more."

"I got a call," Lewis said.

"You did, did you?"

"From Mrs. Fagan."

"Well, now."

Eyes adjusted, and Lewis could see Eli Fagan's long face, thick jowls, gray skin. Lewis closed his eyes, breathed through his nose. This was the first time he'd been this close to Eli since, since that day in court. He didn't look quite as Lewis had conjured. There was no sneer, no show of small teeth. No slit eyes, and satisfaction sitting on the crinkled bridge of his nose. Lewis couldn't look at him for more than a few seconds, couldn't see someone who was deflated. Last thing Lewis could imagine was that Eli Fagan was a weak man.

"I need to speak with her direct, sir." Assessing the porch, instead. Piles of shoes and coats. Peeling wallpaper. A damp pink swimsuit balled in the corner. A mess, but nothing unusual.

"That'd be a trick."

"Why might that be?"

154

"She's done here."

"Done?"

"Yeah, she's done."

"Done how?"

"Gone off."

"When might your wife return?"

"She's gone off for good." '

"Has your wife been injured, Mr. Fagan? I did notice the damage to the car before I came in."

"Not that one would see, sir."

"Would you like to tell me what happened? I got a call."

"She was leaving. And she left. Car or no car."

"Yes."

Eli Fagan was quiet for several minutes.

"Yes, Mr. Fagan. Where is she gone to?" A little louder.

"I do believe I killed her."

Lewis's heart began to beat double-time, and he stepped out of the sunshine, deeper into the stale air of Eli Fagan's kitchen. Overturned radio, children's clothes in an unfolded pile, frying pan sitting in the sink with a peeling ring of yellow egg. A stained pair of rubber gloves bunched on the linoleum.

An unopened bottle of whiskey sat on the cluttered table beside Eli, and he held a dry glass in his oversized hand. He began to turn the bottom of the glass around and around the flat arm of the rocker, making a tinkling sound that pecked Lewis's ears.

"Is Garrett here? Your daughters?"

"Nope. Not a soul."

"How much have you had to drink, Mr. Fagan."

"Not a single drop."

Lewis reached to touch a chair pulled out from the table. Glue on the joints loosened, and the chair wobbled when he leaned on it. He spoke slowly, clearly. "I need you to tell me what happened, sir."

"I don't need to tell you nothing. Not one word."

"I believe you do, Mr. Fagan. You gone and told me your wife is dead."

"Did I now?" Soft chuckle.

"Yes, sir. You did."

"Well, then, you needs to be working on your listening, my son. I said nothing of the sort."

"Did you kill your wife, Mr. Fagan?"

"Killing someone don't got nothing to do with they being dead."

Lewis felt his hands turning into fists. Second time today. "You playing games with me, sir? There's no humor in it, let me tell you."

"Go on," Eli Fagan growled. "Leave me be. Leave me down where I is. Down like an old dog on the floor."

"Your wife, Mr. Fagan. Tell me where she is, or we'll take our conversation to someplace else."

"Well, I don't rightly know, now, Constable Trench, her exact location. If I got no car, and I'm right set on leaving, where might I be?" He leaned forward, boots planted squarely on the floor. One workhorse hand gripping a thick knee. His words an auger drilling through black ice. "How did your wife do it, Constable Trench? Just how did your wife do it when she left you?"

Slaps to his cheeks. Lewis stepped back, back through the kitchen, back through the shaft of sunlight, back through the porch and into the backyard, passed the squished little car and the beat-up truck, back into his still-warm seat, down the driveway, unswallowed and suddenly, back out onto the dirt road. He pressed down on the gas, a cloud of rolling dirt behind him. Took a sharp left when he reached pavement, headed straight towards the bus station.

LEWIS FOUND MRS. FAGAN, hunched and scrawny, wearing a long beige coat and a navy scarf tied over her head. Seated on a forest green bench, she was waiting for the four-thirty bus to take her to the ferry. From there, she told Lewis, she was going to head across to Sydney where she would meet her sister. She had thought to drive, but well, that was that. Still, it'd been years since she saw her sister, and it was well within her rights to make a little trip. "You better believe it." Eli and the rest of them be damned. "Going for as long as I wants." Sample a perfect life. Feel a store-bought rug beneath her feet. Did she want to talk about what happened to her car? No, she said. She hadn't meant to call, but she couldn't stop her fingers. Hoped Eli would leave it right where it was, think about what he done. "Eli does on a Monday. Don't think until Friday." If then. "What're you saying, Mrs. Fagan?" "Nothing," she'd snapped. "I idn't saying nothing more than I already said. And I already said too much."

His hands were tied. He returned to his car, sat in the sticky space, windows only cracked. He waited, for a good while, watching her, and she glared back at him. Eyes hard and small. Distrustful, like a bird's. She kept reaching up, sticking her fingers underneath her scarf, tugging it down lower on her forehead. He wondered if she might be bleeding, if he should get out of his car, move closer. But he didn't like the way she looked at him, as though he had done something wrong. As though he had somehow damaged her. When it was her family who had stolen from him. Destroyed something irreplaceable. Here he was trying to help, and Lewis could tell from her tight mouth, narrow eyes, that she begrudged him. Hated him. But he would not leave, would not let her win. He watched her, until the bus pulled up to the bench and stopped. People coming off, going on, and it sputtered black exhaust, chugged away. Lewis looked at the bench, and Mrs. Fagan was still there, right hand holding the edge of her headscarf.

He smirked inside. Feeble woman. Couldn't even muster the strength to climb the three steps to freedom. He drove off, churning up dust behind him. Because he could.

ELBOWS ON THE table, Melvin kept his fork locked in his fist, chewed slowly with his mouth open. Even though he thought his father was waiting to catch his eye, Melvin would not look at him. Partly because he was angry at his father, and partly because Melvin felt guilty.

For months on end, he had dreamt of his mother. Dreamt of her moving around the house, a maze of rooms riddled with shadows and empty spaces, her eyes drained of color. His father was there, too, hidden in different places, behind doors, pressed against the corner of a bookshelf. She jumped every time Lewis revealed his face, no longer handsome, now foreign, frightening, having transformed into a bull, red-eyed, curls of steam shooting from flared nostrils. Melvin was between them, but they would still fight, her matador movements never enough to save her from the being speared by the animal man, dragging her about the bloodied rooms, then tossing her outside, barefoot into drifting snow spattered in red. She lay down, pleading, Melvin pleading, but an eroding wind skimmed away at her crumpled form, until nothing was left.

He saw these scenes so often in his head, with such clarity, night after night, and he had difficulty erasing them when he awoke. Even though he knew nothing of the sort had ever happened.

A second type of dream. Tucked into the intermission of the first. Starless night, and it was him now creeping through the house in pitch blackness, feeling his way along with outstretched hands, moving fingers. Melvin reached the porch, saw her blue coat, glowing ever so slightly in the closet. The flap on her pocket lifted, hovered, an invitation. And in his own bathrobe pocket, he felt the crumbs, and reached in. He was Hansel. She was Gretel. And he would fill her pockets with small morsels of cake. He had promised her that. But as he was making the transfer, his stomach growled—it *was* in the middle of the night—and he relented. Ate every sweet crumb. Licked his fingers. Cake gone, she tottered past him, tugged on her coat, wandered out into a grayish nowhere land, a distant place with undefined edges, an empty television channel. She turned, her shape fading in and out, voice carrying. Telling him she wanted nothing more than to return home, but she was unable to find her way. My darling dear, her reedy voice quivered, my pockets are empty.

She finally left him. Left his nighttime thoughts. And his dreams drifted over into other adventures, riding an invisible bicycle up into blue skies, swimming through a tangle of seaweed and nipping crabs, kissing Barbie Maloney full on her open mouth. But even now, underneath his skin, an awareness lingered. And Melvin looked down into his chipped bowl, slid a lumpy vegetable over another lumpy vegetable. Chewed and chewed without swallowing. He wouldn't look up at his father, as Melvin understood that his father was not alone in his responsibility for the loss of Wilda Trench. Clearly, he was also to blame.

LEWIS COULD SEE Melvin in his peripheral vision, refused to peer at him straight on. And he knew Melvin was doing the same. Melvin did not go to see Terry at Barber Barber's. Left his hair as it was. Two jagged streaks of baldness rising up on the right side of his scalp. Pink bandage covering his ear, pressed neatly into the grooves by Mrs. Verge earlier that afternoon. Melvin had stolen the fly Lewis had made from the metal box, poked the hook through the bottom edge of the bandage. Making it appear as though he was wearing an insect earring. At the dinner table, Toby roared, "I wants one too. I wants one too." Lewis said nothing. Offered Melvin no reaction whatsoever, simply stared down into his bowl, repositioned hot chunks of potato, turnip.

For the first time in years, Lewis did not feel well. He wondered if he had caught a summer flu, and if the first symptoms were a waning appetite and a powerful ache behind his eyes. As though there was a storm inside his head, pressure mounting, and the only possible relief valves were his locked tear ducts. He laid down his fork, rubbed his hands over his face, and then opened his eyes. Once again he was introduced to the empty chair, and resented the fact that there was no one to talk to. No one with whom to share the turmoil of the day. No one to make him a cup of tea, and say, *Things are going to turn out just fine, Lewis. Just fine.* No one to assure him that he had nothing in common with Eli Fagan. Nothing at all. And that the faintest hint of pity he had for the old farmer, that faintest hint trembling on those skeletal legs inside his head, would soon fold in on itself. Fade away. But Lewis knew he had married a ghost of a woman, and that even if she were here, she would still be gone.

Melvin. Ah, Melvin. What was he going to do with Melvin? So gentle as a child, and now he was like an apple dropped one too many times. Skin still shiny, bright, but Lewis knew there were soft spots, bruises, some hint of sweet rot if he were to smell close to the core.

"Melvin?"

Mouth full, he mumbled, "Huh?"

Lewis put down his fork. "Been a long old day, hey?"

"Yeh."

"You alright?"

He didn't look up, grunted.

"Yeah, we went down to the hole, Dad," Toby said, jumping in. "You know, the swimming hole, and me and Mellie had a real good time. No one bugged us. Not even Clayton. No one even tried to steal my trunks, and Mellie didn't need to even save me—."

"Shut it, Toad!"

Lewis cleared his throat. "That's good, Toby. You had a good time too, Melvin?"

"Look. I just wants to eat. Alright?"

"Eat, then," Lewis said, picking up his fork. "Eat, for God's sakes."

Lewis didn't speak again, decided against rehashing the events of the afternoon. It was stupid trying to talk to Melvin when he would barely respond. Besides, he had probably

already forgotten about their fight. Kids were like that. For-
getting things in a blink. So Lewis bent his head, watched his
hands doing what was normal, healthy. What was right. Holding a fork, tines grappling with a mushy potato, lifting it to his
silent mouth.

AS THEY ATE together as a family, Toby never so much as
glanced at the fourth empty chair. He never noticed his brother's elbows on the table, or the mound of stringy meat lingering
in his cheek. He was not aware his father's vision contained no
color, was strictly black and white. Everything was normal to
Toby. His father was his teacher. His brother, Toby's fierce pro-
tector. His little world was exactly as it should be. Toby smiled
wide, and with his tongue pressed a soft carrot out through the
spaces between his teeth. Heart beating with the excitement of
making Melvin laugh.

LIGHTS OFF, DOOR clicked shut, Toby climbed onto a chair and
leapt onto the bed. Scampered over the quilt, and dove underneath the sheets to safety. Complete darkness in the room,
and Toby reached his foot down between the cool sheets, felt
another foot trespassing onto his side of the bed. He ran his sole
over it, felt the hard toes, sharp nails, bones of the ankle.
"Get your foot over, Mellie."
"What foot?"
"Your foot." Toby knocked it with his heel. "Keep it over on
your side."
"My feet is over here."
Toes reaching out again, prodding the icy limb. Pinched it
with his big toe. No ouch.
"Stop that." Toby nudged it again.
"Shut up, Toad. I'm sleeping."
Then a notion spread through Toby's mind, that there
was another foot in the bed. A dead foot. Belonging to no one.
Attaching to nothing. Exploring toes stroking the extra foot

once more. Sharp nails. Rough sole. He could picture it perfectly. An animal foot, claws and coarse hairs and patches of gray-green skin.

"That's not your foot? I idn't touching you right now?" Poke, poke.

Irritated. "Will you shut up? I'm not nowhere near you."

Toby screamed, tore off the covers, ripped open the curtains. Moonlight illuminating the contents behind the sheets. Two feet. Tracing them up the legs. Clearly belonging to his brother. He scowled when he saw the pure joy pulling the muscles of Melvin's face, heard the laughter bursting forth. Melvin's arms and legs assaulting the air, body bouncing, like a roach flipped on its back.

"Gotcha!" Melvin cried when he settled down. "Gotcha good."

"YOU GOT ME," Eli whispered into the darkness. "Got me good." He was lying in bed, staring at his wife who was breathing softly beside him. He could smell her breath, sour and empty, and he knew she hadn't eaten. He reached out and touched the scarf still covering her head, expected her to flinch even in her sleep.

She hadn't wanted much. A few weeks with her sister. But when he came home and found the strange car in the driveway, discovered his wife had purchased the rusty heap with her own few dollars, and intended to drive there, take the ferry, something snapped inside Eli. All he could imagine was her leaving, full of joy, riding in her own car. A sense of permanence stuck him in the throat, and he recalled his wife and her sister dancing at the Legion. Holding hands, swaying their hips, tossing back their heads and laughing. Then, when he saw her that afternoon, head like a plaster of black mud, ring of ink across her forehead, dirty rubber gloves over her hands, he realized she was dying her hair. And his suspicions were confirmed. She wasn't running off to Cape Breton for a simple visit. She was going there to remember who she was.

162

He destroyed it. Got into his truck and rammed the teacup of a car into the cement wall. Smash. Slam the gears. Reverse. Slam the gears. Drive. Slam the gears. Over and over until all that remained was concave doors, folded hood, smashed glass. Destroyed her chance to ride off in style. When he stepped back into the porch, heart filled with a curious calm, she was gone. Stained rubber gloves crumbled on the kitchen floor.

Eli would be the first to admit he didn't know much about women. How to keep them. Eli's father rarely spoke, used nods and grunts and smacks and shaking fists to get his points across. The advice he gave Eli was concise. "My son, you're either a farmer or a pussy—you can't be both. You can run your farm, or you can trot around letting the farm run you. That goes for your woman, too. If you ever gets one. And with an ugly mug like that, I got my doubts. But, if something dumb enough ever crawls into your bed, you remember this. Women is no better than those animals on your farm. Only they wears clothes. When you wants 'em too, that is." Thin grin.

His wife took a deep breath and rolled away from him. Maybe she wasn't even asleep, Eli couldn't guess, found it difficult to think. He couldn't recall the last time he'd been sober in this bed. Tonight, his backside and legs were shaking, but he knew what they were trying to do. Trying to get him to sit up. Stand. Walk downstairs and crack open the bottle he had left on the table. His hands shook too. Fiercely. He could hear his rough fingertips scratching the cotton sheets.

He thought of Lewis Trench, then, swaying inside his kitchen. Eli wondered what that felt like, for Lewis to be so close to someone he hated. Eli couldn't fathom what Lewis Trench had said to his wife. What he had said to make the woman turn around and come home.

But then again, maybe it wasn't Lewis at all.

More likely, she came home for the boy.

20

IN THE BACKYARD of the farmhouse, Garrett Glass squeezed into one of the old swings, leaned his cheek against the chains. He could taste rust from the warm metal, like blood on his tongue. Pressing his bare foot against the hardened clay, he swung gently, and examined the curving woods bordering the yard. Years had passed since he'd ventured down that path. His path. And now, with all the leafy growth and unkempt grass, he doubted if he could even find it.

Closing his eyes, he listened to the creaking of the swing frame as he pushed himself back and forth. So easy to remember those carefree days when he was young. When he was in possession of something perfect and beautiful. Something he had actually created. It had all started with a gift, meant for his mother, but stolen by Garrett. He had just turned eleven years old.

He could recall the very day he had sat on a stool near the kitchen counter, puppy eyes moving between his mother, as she pounded the life out of a mound of sticky dough, and the wrapped gift pushed back into a corner. This gift was not a birthday present, but the one shred of proof that Christmas had come and gone in the world. Other than an evening church service, they did nothing to celebrate—no tree, no shaped sugar cookies, no tasteless orange hidden inside the thin toe of his sock. "'Tis only a godforsaken reason to drink," his mother had said. "And he don't need more of those."

Last day of school for the year, and the gift appeared on the counter. Garrett was hopeful that perhaps it just might be for him. But on Christmas morning, when he placed a cold palm on the top of the box, his mother snapped, "Do that got your name scrawled across it?"

Of course it didn't. "I was just wondering is all," he said now as his mother lifted and slammed the bread on the countertop. Head cocked, eyes wide. "Jesus would want to know, Mom." He blinked sweetly. "He'd want to know what present Aunt Sally sent for his birthday."

She softened, he could see it in her eyebrows. The slightest lift. He could do that, soften her, especially when he played the Jesus card. And he was careful not to use that trick too often. "I suppose it won't do no harm," she replied. "Been cluttering up the room long enough." Cleaning her hands on her apron, she hauled the box out from its corner, blew dust and flour off the top, found the scissors in a drawer, severed the ribbon.

"What is it?" he breathed as she carefully removed the paper.

"Pfft." She frowned. "A camera. Packets of film. Bloody waste-of-a-dollar gadget, if you asks me." She shoved it back into the box, coiled the ribbon, the folded wrap, and poked that in too. "Like I needs a camera. All kinds of family snapshots to be taking. Wants a hole in my head more than I wants that."

"Maybe she was trying to be friends."

"I allows. Slapping me in the face is more like it. That's just her way, it is. Giving herself something to say. 'Oh, I sent my sister a camera for Christmas. Lovely little contraption. And do you know what she sent me? Not even a card. Poor thing. Hard times.'" Mocking tone. "Well, 'tis always hard times, Garrett. Always. Day in and day out. Some people won't never have it easy no matter what they does."

"Are you going to heave it out?"

"Just as well."

Garrett chewed his bottom lip. "That's waste, Mom."

"Waste, you says? Waste was sending it to me in the first place." But she clipped in her slippers out into the hallway, creaked open the closet door, tossed it up into a dark mass of forgotten junk. "Rot up there, for all I cares," she said to the box. Turning back to Garrett, "And that's the final word on that."

Garrett went to his bedroom and closed the door. The air inside the tiny space was frosty, and he crouched near the single narrow window, picked away the ice that grew up over the glass. He had to have that camera. It was his birthday soon, and he had not pissed in his bed in four months. Did he not deserve some sort of present?

He crept to the top of the stairs, spied on his mother through the painted spindles. She gathered the dough in a tight ball, plopped it into a bowl. Slapped it hard, then drew her hand back, and slapped it again. Every time he saw her make bread, she did the same thing, and he wondered if there was some purpose to it. A sound like skin striking skin, and if the dough had been living, it surely would sting. She bundled the bowl in a towel, then a blanket, and she balanced the works on the edge of his stepfather's chair near the stove. Then she left the kitchen, down the hallway, past that closet, into another room, and quietly closed the door.

Garrett did not breathe as he descended the stairs, placing his feet on boards that did not creak. Into the kitchen now, he drew a deep lungful of the yeasty air, and then lifted a chair over the wooden floor, tiptoed out into the hallway. Inch by inch he edged the closet door open, and then slid the chair in amongst the worn shoes. Standing on the chair, he reached, stretched, leaned forward, until he could just touch the box. Scratched at it with his nails. It shifted, and he managed to grip it with the fleshy pads on his fingertips, haul it down from its intended grave.

Door quietly closed, chair returned, and he slunk up to his bedroom, placed the gray shoe-box-sized package on his floor. White writing inside an orange rectangle. Polaroid Land Camera. With a flash. "Sixty seconds from snap to print," he whispered. Lifted the lid on the box, removed the body, black and silver, weighty. Studied the pamphlet, finger with a ragged nail moving underneath every single word. His first photo was an attempt at a self portrait, and he laid the black square of film on the floor, turned around, peeked, turned around, peeked. Nothing but a black hole, spray of light. Second attempt. Something emerging. Nostrils, oversized teeth, smear of hair the color of yolk. Next effort, a picture. Clear and recognizable. He plucked it up off his floor, ran his fingers over his own image, then placed his fingers on his chest, felt the vibration of his pumping heart.

He would only waste one packet of film on himself, he decided. Photographed his hand, his foot, the side of his knee with his leg bent. When he squinted at that last one, it very much resembled a flattened corduroy backside, and before he could contain it, an unholy idea spewed out of a dark corner, flooded his mind. Jack-in-the-box. He tried to shake the thought away, but it would not be contained no matter how hard he stuffed it down, the clasp on this mental lid was broken. He pressed his ear against his door, held his breath, and listened. No sound, only the barely audible clink of hard snow tapping his window. *What would his stepfather say? He'll never find out. But what if he do? He won't never know. Promise me that. I promise, me, now stop bugging, and just do it.* He unbuttoned his trousers, let them fall to the floor. Placed the camera on the family Bible, stepped as far away as possible. Reached, one snap of the back. Waited until the film slid out. Zzzz. Turning. One snap of the front. Quickly dressed, and there they were. Blurry, but he knew what was captured. Those parts of himself that were meant to be covered, only to be handled with a washcloth coated in lye soap. Touching led to blindness and betraying hair sprouting from obvious places. Worse than that, the whole works was apt to fall off in his hand.

Garrett moved closer to the window, to study his handiwork in the natural light, and noticed a flash of deep red moving across the snow. Swiping vapor from the glass, he could see his stepfather with an armload of wood, edging ever closer to the house. Even though he was still a good distance away, panic squeezed Garrett's airways, and he hauled on his trousers, tore all the photos to tiny shreds, poked the evidence down into the cracks between his floorboards. Willed the mice to make off with them. Camera stuffed into the box, torn packaging, remaining film, slid to the farthest corner underneath his bed. Hurried down to the front door, hauled on coat, woolen hat and mitts, ran to meet his stepfather before the old man came to meet him.

FOR WHAT SEEMED like eons, he managed to ignore the temptation that slept in a shoebox underneath his bed. But when he awoke to the sound of dripping, snow rotting and trickling away, and he saw a bird clinging to a still-dormant twig, he knew spring had come. He also knew spring sometimes carried fever as warm fought with cold, and he could already identify the flush rising up in certain parts of his body. Fever worked its way into his muscles, and he did not choose to remove the camera from its hiding spot. He was simply unable to resist as his knees bent, his arms reached, and his fingers clasped. After tucking the camera inside a cloth satchel, he stuffed his coat pocket with stolen pieces of molasses taffy, all wrapped in waxy paper. On his walk, he organized the words of an enticing invitation, left the phrase waiting patiently inside his voice box. Up on the old road, the new sun shone down upon him, and he turned towards the wooded area where youngsters played on Saturdays. Hoping to find the one.

Within a short time, Garrett met an eight-year-old named Cecil Taylor. He was a pudgy and placid boy, whose mouth always hung open just a crack. And even though the days were getting warmer, he still wore a steel gray coat with a ring of matted fur around the hood. Cecil had no mother or father, and would soon be moving to the city, to a home for unwanted boys. A place where someone would love him properly, they said, help him grow into a man. But Cecil didn't care about love, he told

Garrett. Love didn't fill a youngster up. Food was what he was after, and plenty of it.

The boys met on Saturday afternoons in an abandoned ice-fishing hut that someone had hauled up onto the side of Stark Pond. Garrett brought whatever he could find, leftover heels of bread, slices of cold pork, a half-eaten cherry square. Sometimes he'd even manage a thermos of hot tea. One day, Garrett told Cecil his secret. That he liked taking pictures, and he opened his satchel, showed off the stolen camera. Let Cecil touch it. Click the red button several times. "Whoa, whoa. Careful, buddy." In hushed tones, Garrett confided to Cecil that he was working on a project. Something significant. "Huh?" Something momentous. "Huh?" Some big thing. "Oh." A map of the entire body. "Oh, yeah. Maps is good."

School finished, and Cecil was leaving Knife's Point the next morning. When they met in the fishing shack, Garrett asked, "You got any money?"

"Nope."

"Young man can't be going on a trip without a few cents in his pocket."

"What?"

"Should always have a dollar in your wallet."

Cecil shook his head as plowed through a two-inch slab of still-warm oatmeal bread. "I don got no wallet."

"You can earn a bit. I got ninety-five cents, and you can have that."

"For free?"

"No."

"For what?"

"Helping me with my project. With the mapping." Garrett did his best to sound mature, use the three-year age gap to his advantage.

"Huh?"

Garrett gave Cecil a handful of sweaty coins, and even though he was near the point of fainting with curiosity, he kept his voice calm when he asked the boy to undress. Cecil was hesitant, and Garrett said sternly, "This is science. This is art. And you already got paid for almost nothing. That's like giving your word. And if you don't do it," growling, now, "I can tell those men who's taking you tomorrow that you lied. Ripped me off. That you belongs in jail, and not some cushy house for stupid boys." "Uh. Oh." Cecil unzipped his grimy coat with the matted fur hood, and let it fall to the floor.

"I didn't mean that," Garrett whispered. "I didn't. I just wants help with my job. And we're pals, right?"

"Yeah."

"You likes me, right?"

"Yeah, sure."

"You wants me to make a map?"

Cecil nodded. "You won't show no one?"

Fingers ticking his chest, Garrett said firmly. "Cross my heart. I swears to God on my very own life. Sure, you can't swear on nothing bigger, right?"

At first he was shy, but Garrett coaxed him. "How else do you think research is done, Cec?" "Huh?" "This is serious business." "Yeah." And soon Cecil relaxed, at some points even laughed hysterically as though Garrett was tickling him. Moving his limbs this way and that, taking flash photo after flash photo of all of his parts. "Show me, show me," Cecil cried, nearly choked on the molasses candies filling his cheeks. "Hey, take one now," Cecil hollered, as he bent his knees slightly, gripped himself, pissed into the dark hole where trout once emerged. Garrett hunched down, camera pressed to his face, and took the photo.

Garrett carefully documented the curve of the boy's knee, the place where chin became neck, the ear lobe, open mouth, the dip of the last rib above a goose-pimpled stomach. Two bare feet and ten, no, eleven toes standing on the weathered wood. White lower back, dimples above a clenched but chubby backside, turning, bending, lifting. Garrett captured everything. Every single fold of flesh and ripple of blubber. Every inch of

170

skin that covered Cecil Taylor's body. Piece after piece, a human puzzle. Many photos were blurry, of course, but Garrett knew what they were. Besides, the most important ones were crystal. Crystal clear.

"You're beautiful," Garrett whispered when he ran out of supplies.

"Huh?" said Cecil.

"Nothing," Garrett replied. "Nothing."

HE FOUND AN old pickle jar in the barn filled with nails. He tossed the nails near the foundation of the barn, covered them with rocks. In the kitchen, he rinsed the jar with sudsy water, and when it was clean, he carried it to the stream. After he dried the inside of the jar with his T-shirt, he gently placed his photos inside. He put a weighty rock in with the photos to keep the jar from floating away, sealed the lid, and then lowered it into the water, among a tangle of roots and pale mud. Presence disguised by a healthy current, gurgling unwittingly over shimmering blue stones.

Garrett went to the creek every day, extracted the jar, wiped it with a scrap of towel before opening it. For as long as he could spare, he stayed there, handling those images of purity and love with the utmost of care. He would never see Cecil Taylor again, he knew that, but he had him here. Every single piece of him.

THE CROSSBAR OF the swing set groaned, and Garrett opened his eyes. He sighed, looked down at gangly legs, his dirty feet, and the tufts of hair growing just behind his thickened toenails. Even now, sometimes the sight of his adult body surprised him. And disappointed him. When he was a child, his skin was so much cleaner, neater.

Though years had passed since his collection had been destroyed, Garrett still missed it. He was certain those images would soothe him. Satisfy him. If he still possessed his human map, he wouldn't need anything else. But he had made a mistake. He was just a boy, after all. A whiff of laziness. A few lost hours. Everything was gone.

Garrett left the swing, walked across the grass, then along the gravel driveway, ignoring the pricks of sharp stones on his soles. Reaching the end of the drive, he looked up and down at the ditches and the potholes and the emptiness. He raised his arms, twisted and stretched until the bones between his shoulder blades cracked. But none of the tension receded.

21

EARLY IN THE day, a sharp wind awoke Toby from his slumber. Melvin stood near the end of the bed, a fistful of sheets in one hand, pair of black binoculars in the other. Wet wide smirk on his mouth.

"C'mon," Toby whined, reaching for the covers. He had been swimming inside his head, without need of oxygen, and he was about to glide around a bend of coral, swaying plants, sensed he might find something female. "You trying to torture me on my birthday?"

"Shut up, Toad." Melvin balled the sheet, tossed it in the corner. "Wake father and it'll be done."

"What *it?*" Sticking his head back into his pillow, guinea pig hair, his words were muffled. "I don't want to watch no birds."

"Do you think I'd be up at this hour for bloody birds?" Right into Toby's ear, hot breath.

Melvin's voice, with its controlled anticipation, sent a shot of adrenaline through Toby's body, and he rolled out of bed, hauled on crumpled shorts and T-shirt. In the kitchen he jammed dry cereal into his pockets, then followed his brother out into the uncertain darkness of a warm summer morning. They headed north through the woods, and over an orderly field filled with still-headless cabbages and stunted turnip tops, across a dirt road and down into another forest. Moving through the sweet air, Toby held out his palms, clutched the soft fir branches and let them slide slowly through his hands.

"Get the lead out of your arse, Toad."

But Toby wanted to linger, wanted to enjoy this moment alone with his brother, just the two of them, wrapped up inside a place filled with bright new growth, world beyond peeled away. As each year passed, these instants were fewer and further between. Their trout poles hadn't left the porch since spring, and they had not pilfered a single worm from Mrs. Verge's vegetable garden. They hadn't either played a single game of softball in Edgar's field, Toby always a shirt, his brother a skin. And even at eleven years old, Toby would not venture down to the mud hole for a swim. Not without Melvin. He knew no matter how tightly he tied the string on his trunks, someone would manage to tug them down.

Toby crouched, stuck two wiggling fingers inside a perfectly formed cavity in a tree, considered what kind of creature might reside there. Then he stood, yawned, flicked sleep from his eyes, wondered if Melvin and their father would give him eleven bumps for his birthday. Feet and wrists clutched, backside hitting the floor one moment, belly grazing dust from the stucco ceiling the next. Maybe the swings. Side to side. That was a bit easier.

"Geez, Toad!" A hiss. "Should have brought the frigging baby buggy."

"Alright, alright," and he picked up the pace. Trotted through the dense undergrowth, kept his elbow cocked against the spruce branches whipping back towards his face. Even though he wanted to, he never slowed to bounce on the wonky wire fence with the rotting posts.

They came to a fat tree on the edge of someone's property, and under the instruction of Melvin, Toby shimmied upwards, sneakers slipping on the knobby outgrowths, tearing wet bark, turpentine pockets bursting. He reached a thick branch, slung one leg over, hoisted his body into the groin of two major branches, his backside pinched. Melvin followed suit, perched on the opposite side of the trunk, legs straddling the spruce. Before them was a backyard of patchy grass, a rusting barrel beside a great mound of wood junks. Glistening silver, a junk car lay silent, door hanging off, wheels sunk into muck. Other than a faint glow of light from a window on the main floor, the house was bathed in shadows.

THREE NIGHTS OF unusual warmth, and a sticky heat had settled in the crook of Knife's Point, refused to lift. His leg tangled in the sheets, body damp, Garrett tossed and turned, mind sleeping, dreaming, but flesh awake. Inside his bedroom, the air was stale and still, and he leaned his head back, tried to fill his lungs. No relief, oxygen depleted, and his body was exhausted, thinning out. A haze, hovering on the horizon. He spread his arms out, opened his mouth, felt his tongue playing with the scar on his upper lip. Garrett followed his whims, didn't resist as his dream unfolded, as he slid through this sweaty trance.

Floating up, now, he swung his legs over the side of the bed, skin pale in the waning moonlight. He curled his toes, but barely registered the cheap navy carpet he'd purchased from Mr. Clarey. Carpet that was supposed to remind him every morning that he was now a working man. But he didn't want to introduce Mr. Clarey into his dream. Not now. Not ever.

His legs jerked up and down, and he scratched his thighs, twisted the hairs and tugged. Squeezing his eyes closed, he drifted to thoughts of a young boy who had come into the store. Ahh. Skimming his truck along the aisles, one foot tucked underneath his bottom, sliding his backside over the floor. Metal on the truck shimmering as the boy cruised through a shaft of dusty light. If only he could own the child for just a moment. If only he were allowed to love him.

TOBY SHOVED A handful of cereal in his mouth, felt the hard bits pull in his saliva. Spitting flecks of sticky corn, he murmured, "Idn't this the Dawe's?" He glanced at the pick-up trunk near the back stoop, its blackened lights facing them, watching them.

"No, it idn't the Dawes'."

"The Newmans'?"

No response.

"Not the Fagans', Mel," Toby shot out. "Tell me that's not whose house that is."

"Shut it." Melvin tugged up the sleeve of his shirt, looked at his watch. "Any second, now."

"But, Mr. Fagan. Bread us and fry us if we gets caught on his land. Let alone up in his frigging tree."

"Shut your trap."

"And Garrett. That shotgun." Toby could picture Garrett Glass with his gun. He often sat at the end of their driveway, just inside their property line, perched on a rusted metal chair, ripped vinyl seat. He sat there, watching the kids walk home from school, while slowly rubbing the burnished metal barrel with a scrap of towel. Up and down. Up and down.

"Shotgun. Not much good that'll do him. He got to haul it out of his ass first."

Toby shifted on his perch, scraped his front teeth over the top of his thumbnail. "But—"

"Geez, Toad. Do you want to go home?" Irritated. "Go on, then. Get."

Toby stared across the backyard, scanning the walls, the steep roof, the chimney with its broken lip. "I don't want—," he started, and then a light popped on, upper floor, middle window. A bright light, fully illuminating the inside of a room. And then there was a girl, a woman, maybe, stretching, arms up, shirt lifting, skin all over. "Oh," he said. "Oh." Toby stole a glimpse at his brother, saw Melvin, binoculars pressed to his face, mouth open.

"Here," Melvin said through his smirk. He handed the binoculars around the trunk. "You go."

They slipped, and Toby caught the leather strap, gripped now with all fingers, eased the strap over his head in case his hands failed him once again. Slowly he lifted them to his face,

176

squinted, adjusted the slippery wheel for focus. There she was, standing in the brightness, scratching her head with colored nails, moving about the room, her underwear a triangle of mint green covering her backside. Toby held his breath. He had never seen a girl arise from bed before. Surely, he had seen his mother wandering about wrapped in a bathrobe, slightly dingy and thick like a winter pelt, but it was not the same as this. Not nearly the same. Toby peered through the lenses again. He caught her, just as she was closing the bedroom door.

"She's gone," Toby breathed, and he recognized that part of him was thankful, relieved it was over. That she had retreated into her private world, and Toby could now return to his.

"Just wait," Melvin said, shaking his hand. "It gets better. Waaay better."

"Was that Angie's sister?"

"Yeah."

"DeeDee?"

"Fucking A."

"How'd you get here?"

"Through the woods. Like you saw."

"I means, how did you find out about this?"

"Wandering 'round."

"At six in the morning?"

"I was a bit fucked up, if you wants to know."

"I'd say."

"She got to be up on the highway every morning. Selling vegetables and shit from the back of her father's truck. Crap time to get out of bed, but I idn't complaining. Now give the fucking things back."

But Toby didn't relinquish the binoculars, peered through again. Then another light, another room bursting into existence. A bathroom, beige toilet, tub, and the girl appeared there, yanking down her underwear, plunking herself down on the toilet. Toby's stomach tilted as she leaned to one side, wiped, and he swallowed hard as she stood, crossed her arms, pinched her shirt near the waist, peeled it upwards. Pushing the binoculars so hard into his face, he soon saw double, four arms, four mounds of backside, turning, turning, yes, four swollen cups, like white bowls hanging from her chest. Bases painted dirty brown.

He watched her test the water for her shower, and lift one hefty limb over, then the other, behind a plastic curtain now, distorted pink flesh, moving, bending. Toby thought he could hear low humming from behind him, and he started, only to realize the sound was coming from deep within his own throat. Within a few moments, she yanked back the thin sheet that separated them, and she stood there, wet and naked before the mirror, hair in a towel turban. He could see the varying colors of her flesh, arms, knees, and calves fawn brown, belly and backside like shortening with a mild flush.

At once, he was acutely aware of his hands, damp, wrapped snuggly around the textured body of the binoculars. He imagined his palms skipping over her dips and grooves, hitching her skin with sweaty nervousness, hugging her, laying his head on those two white balloons that would surely feel like enormous marshmallows. He wondered if there was milk there. Perfect human temperature. If only he squeezed. Uh.

He gripped the binoculars tightly, felt light-headed as he followed her movements as she dressed, fiddling with fabric, twisting a pink bra, tugging on underwear and shorts, an oversized T-shirt. Then, just as Toby realized he needed to breathe, she stepped towards the wide open window, and stared out though the screen, smiling. She was scanning the woods, and her eyes seemed to settle directly on Toby. He was certain she could see his white sneakers in the rising light, and he twisted both feet, tucked them behind the trunk as far as possible. Teetered on the branch.

"Awww, maaan!" Melvin groaned, shifting his weight numerous times, legs wrapped firmly around the lumpy trunk of the massive spruce tree. "Can't barely see her, and I'm right gone. Feels like I ate a frigging pound of cheese for breakfast. I'm that riled up." He placed the base of his palm near the zipper of his jean shorts, pressed. "Happy birthday, bro. Happy fucking birthday."

"I think she sees me." Words like goose down.

"No, she don't."

"What if she do?"

"Just be quiet. Don't budge."

Toby sat there, heart thumping in his throat, squeezing his air passage, and he leaned his cheek against the cool bark. Watched silently as streaks of sunlight moved across the horizon, rose up over the old, blue clapboard house, above the front door, first story, gliding upwards, protectively, curtaining DeeDee Fagan's bathroom window with natural reflection. Game over. There was nothing left to see, and Toby felt a sigh glide out of his chest.

Just as they began to wiggle from the crooks in the tree, the back door of the house banged open, and Mrs. Fagan emerged, threw two pairs of boots out onto the stoop. Then Mr. Fagan, in trousers and stretched shirt, suspenders dangling by his knees, brushed past her, jammed his feet into one of those pairs, and stomped off the stoop. He surveyed his grounds, then took several purposeful steps in their direction. Unzipped his pants, reached in, released, held himself loosely as he watered his lawn with a never-ending stream of morning urine.

"Shit, man," Melvin yelped. "Shit. The dog's out of his house."

Even from his distant perch, Toby could hear piss turning dirt into spattering muck. "That's gross."

"Who cares. Let's get the hell."

They slid down the trunk, burning thighs and hands, tore through the woods, leaping over roots and shrubs, flying, muddy sneakers barely touching the ground. The binoculars struck Toby's chest each time he landed, bruising the bottom of his rib cage. But he felt nothing, other than the hot need to escape. Panting, inner alarm ringing in their ears, they darted this way and that, burst into the unknown as branches smacked their faces, blinded them. Only when they reached the safety of the other side did they stop in a ditch beside the road. Bending hard at the waist, trying to catch their breath, they laughed between jagged gasps.

GARRETT PUT HIS hand on his crotch, pressed what was rising up. He stood, hauled on a pair of cut-off gym pants and a T-shirt. Crept down the stairs to the front door and jammed his bare feet into a pair of work boots. He could hear water over his head, trickling through the pipes. He could hear his stepfather's mouth, somewhere in the darkness, slurping coffee. Garrett said nothing, opened the door, walked through wet grass, slipped into his car. Slowly, he eased around the back of the property, and up onto the old road. In the queer light coming out of the gloom, nothing was real. He rolled his window down, stuck his head out, like a drunken dog, swallowed the air drifting across his mouth. Beneath his tires, stones crushed and popped a sultry music. He smelled dewdrops dangling from bent blades of grass. Heard a grasshopper rubbing his young legs together. Yes. He was rubbing his young legs together. Garrett nodded, moved forward, stumbling through his delicious delusion, not caring where he was going or what his hands might do.

"FFFF-UCK, THAT WAS close."

"You. Yeah. Ye– yeah."

"If fa– father finds..."

"Hee, hee, he'll skin us."

"Swear," Melvin breathed, hands gripping his knees. "Swear, Toad, you won't tell. On our mother's grave."

Toby stood up, took two deep breathes, squinted in the early light. "But she idn't dead."

"I reckons she is."

"You do?"

180

Melvin stretched, rubbed his backside roughly, as though trying to encourage circulation. "Else she would've come back."

"Yeah."

"Who could resist two young fellers like ourselves?"

"Yeah," Toby snorted now.

"Especially me. I'm that handsome. Got to beat the girls off with a frigging baseball bat."

"Charm the whiskers right off the catfish."

"That's not whiskers, dumbass, they're called barbels."

"Sure, Melvin. They goes around lifting weights in their free time. With their mustaches."

"You're so stupid, Toad," he said, but there was no meanness in his voice, and he wrapped his elbow around Toby's skull, ruffled his hair.

"Stupid? Look where we is. We'll be dead meat if we gets caught."

"No one's going to catch us. I doubts he saw us. Couldn't hold his piss is all. Daughter unstripping in the toilet."

More snorting.

"Besides, she does that on purpose."

"Does what?"

"Leaves her curtains open."

"How do you know?"

"Jimmy told me. Darce told him, and Andrew told him, and she told Jason."

"What she go do that for?"

"She likes it. That's why. Likes being watched." Melvin chewed his thumbnail, spit a peeling off his tongue. "Sometimes there's two or three of us there. Watching."

"Up in the tree?"

"Yeah."

"Holy."

Nodding.

"So you didn't just happen across it. Like you said."

"C'mon. Who do you think I is, frigging Ponce de León?"

"What?"

"Forget it, Toad. Not much harm in it. Gets us up and out, don't it? Bit of fresh air."

"Yeah," Toby replied. "Up and out." He felt a bit shaky, as though he'd been sick, fever just releasing him. He didn't know much about DeeDee, but her younger sister, Angie, was in Toby's grade, and he knew a few things about her. Toby had seen the mother once, remembered her standing outside the school at the start of a snowstorm. The bus had already slid out of the parking lot, and those who lived within a mile had to wait for someone to meet them. Walk them home, in case the storm disoriented them, lured them out in front of a car to meet their demise.

He remembered how Angie had flung herself into that oversized navy snowsuit, hugged it, and her mother's arms remained limp, not even gloves moving. Her face gray and thin and resigned. No tug of a smile on that mouth, while other moms bent on one knee, body braced for impact of a flying child, older brothers guffawing, jamming snow down the skinny necks of their siblings.

Another storm, and no one arrived for Angie Fagan. Perched on the very edge of the concrete step, she waited, swiping each snowflake from the brown paper lunch bag on her lap. A young teacher asked Toby's father to drive her home, and when Angie slid into the backseat, he joked, "Should I read you your rights?" Angie's face was blank. Toby's father cleared his throat as he turned the key, said, "I'll get you right home, maid. Won't be but a minute."

Peering around the edge of his hood, Toby had eyed her with curiosity. He hadn't forgotten how she had saved him that past summer. Saved him with her squeal when Clayton Gibbon had ripped off his trunks. When she peeked back at him, he turned sharply to face the dashboard. Counted the scratches in the plastic until they reached her driveway, long and winding, lined with dead trees that no one had bothered to clear or burn.

She jumped out of the backseat, book bag in one mitt, lunch bag in the other, and skipped past a number of white mounds towards her back door. Toby imagined what was beneath the snow, curled up dead bodies, hungry animals, dozing, pink tongues just behind sharp teeth. His eyes widened when the door slapped open, and Angie's older brother stood there, elbow on the door frame, screen door held in place with his boot. As she began to dart past him, he grabbed her arm, yanked, her tiny head sinking halfway into the neck of her coat.

Driver's side window rolled down, snowflakes tumbling in, and Toby's father said firmly, "Garrett."

And Garrett Glass simply responded, "Constable," before he let the screen door slap shut.

Once the car was turned around, Toby said, "How come no one come get her?"

"Don't concern you," his father replied, shutting off the heat. "You steer clear of that whole crowd. Like I told you a thousand times, nothing good ever growed in or around that house."

But Toby couldn't help but be a little interested in the rumors. Kids would yammer on about Angie Fagan and her sister, say their father made them pee behind a drape, but when they were bad, he burned the drape, and they had to pee in front of him. They said that Angie got her cowlick from her father's fat tongue, and when she walked by they let their tongues hang out, called her "calf brain." "When you gonna grow your udders, calf brain?" Someone told Toby that Angie's father diddled her, and Toby didn't quite know what diddled meant, so he had just said "Cool."

Melvin snapped a stick over his thigh, tossed the two halves into the ditch. "Don't take it so serious. They're all fucked up, anyway."

"Yeah, maybe," Toby said with a faint smile, but inside he felt a dampness, a musty cloth squeezed over his guts. He thought of his metal soldiers, the intricate setups, troops advancing, the battles. That miniature world on the nicked surface of his desk seemed so distant, and he didn't want to let it go. Panic boiled up in his intestines, as he sensed something was happening, and he wouldn't have a choice. His head was full, dizzy, overflowing with a soup of images that made him queasy and giddy at the same time.

"Shit, Toad. You looks like someone just died."

Toby wiped his nose, bit his cheek, wasn't sure whether a laugh or a cry was tucked in his throat.

"I figured you was eleven. Old enough to be a man. See some things."

"Yeah."

Melvin plucked up a shard of shale. "Hand me your finger."

"What?"

"Hand me your finger, I said."

"What? Do you want me to crack it off?"

Melvin grabbed Toby's fist, forced a finger out, pressed the sharp edge of rock into the fleshy tip.

Toby hauled back, shook his hand, "Shit, man," sucked his finger. Mumbled, "What'd you do that for?"

"Get it out of your mouth," Melvin shouted through clenched teeth. "Do you think I wants your spit in me?" He slit his own finger, then pressed his finger to Toby's, let the blood mix and smear.

"Blood brothers," Toby said, and he looked up at Melvin and smiled. "We's blood brothers, now." Sins of the morning losing color as he considered this new and deeper connection.

"Yep. 'Bout time." Melvin licked his finger, smeared the remainder on his jeans, then hugged his brother's shoulder. "We'll do some big things together, Toad. Some day. Wilbur and Orville. That's us two."

Squinting in the sun, Toby cocked his head to one side, looked up at his brother, "I knows who Wilbur is. That pig. With the spider. But who's Orville?"

Melvin stepped aside, made his eyes go googly. "Haven't you never opened a history book? Never in your life?" He shook his head. "You knows, the Wright brothers? Airplane? Human flight? Ding, ding. Any bells?"

184

Toby smirked sheepishly, said, "Oh, yeah, yeah. I knows. Right. Yeah, yeah."

"No you don't. But it idn't your fault. You don't learn shit in school. Moms is supposed to teach that stuff."

"I just forgot is all."

"I'll kick it up, Toad. Get you going on some books."

"Alright."

"Get you some good art books too." Wink.

"I can't draw for nothing."

Base of his hand knocking his head. "Not those kind, numb-nuts. I meant nice art. Pictures of paintings and stuff."

"Yeah. Okay, I guess."

"Man, those books is filled with tits. Asses, too. And you can leave it right out on the counter, and the Verge'll pat you on the back, tell you how good you're doing."

Toby laughed when Melvin grabbed him, one hand to his armpit, the other to the back of his trousers. Hoisted him in the air. "I'll show you human flight. Fly you to the moon, Alice. To the moon." Melvin grunted as he tried to swing Toby, managing a quarter-circle turn before Toby flumped back to earth.

"Could've told you, Mellie. Reptiles don't belong in space."

"Amphibians, Toad. Toads is amphibians."

Grinning. "Yeah, yeah. I knew that. Just testing you."

They were up on the road now, banging about, Melvin smoking cigarettes while Toby kicked stones and stomped in puddles. Toby found a thin stick, dragged it along the soft ground, writing his name, ringlets of mud falling away from the edges of his letters.

"Do you really think Mom's dead?"

"Nah. She's probably off somewhere in some big city."

"Like where?"

"Like Paris."

"Doing what?"

"Eating."

"Oh."

"She's probably three hundred pounds and she got her fat arse stuck in one of those chairs in front of a coffee shop, and all they can do is feed her and splash a bucket of soapy water over her once a week, and she's growing and growing."

"Really?"

"Yeah, really. What did you think?"

"I don't know. I figured she found better kids. Kids she liked."

Melvin shot his cigarette to the dirt, squashed it. "That's dumb, Toad."

"Yeah, I knows."

"Stop saying you knows everything. 'Cause you don't. She was my mother for eight years, and let me tell you, I don't miss her. Not one bloody bit."

"Yeah, me neither."

"She wasn't much of one to begin with. Selfish bitch, if you asks me."

"Yeah."

"And I knowed, as sure as there's shit in a frigging cat, she was just waiting to get out. Get on with it. I knowed that my whole fucking life. Since the fucking second I was born." Authority in his voice. "When she trotted off to frigging la-la-land, I said to myself, fuck that, now I can fucking relax."

"Yeah, I didn't mean—"

"And I tell you this, too," he said, scraping a sharp line with his sneaker, "if someone don't want you, if someone don't think you got at least a few squirts of sunshine poked up your ass, you're better off without them. You and me, Toad. That's all we needs."

"Yeah. You're right."

"And the occasional glimpse of DeeDee Fagan in her baby suit!" Snickering.

Muscles pulling at the side of his cheek, Toby couldn't resist a half smile. As long as he could remember, Melvin had had the capacity to shock him, delight him, empty him out, or fill him up. When it mattered, when Toby wavered on the edge of some gloomy revelation, Melvin was there, shoring up the walls, forcing the sadness out. Toby looked at his brother, lanky body, long limbs, shaggy brown hair, boundless energy, infinite knowledge about the world, even though he'd never left Knife's Point. And Toby knew that whatever well-being existed within him came from having Melvin as a brother.

They heard the slow and steady grind of car wheels creeping along the gravel. They both looked at each other, surprised, as this was a road that rarely saw a vehicle. Toby had the notion to dart into the woods again, but instead he fell in step with Melvin who stood tall, whistled a jaunty tune as though they were out for a morning stroll instead of spying on a naked girl.

They never turned or looked, but kept walking at their even pace, one, two, one, two, as the car approached from behind. Edging into their peripheral vision now, they saw that it was a brown Chevette, rusting holes along the corner of the door, front side nose dented inwards. Wheels slowed their turning, helpless crackles as shale split beneath their weight.

Melvin stopped, turned to look. "Fuck, man," he whispered. "That's her brother."

"Whose?"

"Who do you think, dickwad?"

Toby emitted a low hum, mind awash with the thought of angry hands gripping his testicles, yanking until that thin strip of skin tore. Ow. Ow. Bloop. Gone. Fear squirted from somewhere inside his mouth, tasted like old sweat on his cheeks and gums.

Heads touching, Melvin said, "Jesus, Toad. Wake up a pack of wolves with that sound. Act cool. Act normal."

"Yeah," Toby managed.

"Someone must've seen us. Just say nothing."

"Uh– could be just a run. Sunday drive, sort of thing."

"Yeah. Sure. On Wednesday. Makes good sense, Toad."

They heard coughing. "Hey, bud. How's it going?" Jovial tone.

Garrett Glass's voice plucked a tight thread inside Toby's chest, and he reached out to touch his brother, but Melvin shook him off.

"Going good, Garrett. Out checking a few snares is all."

"Is you, now?"

"Yes, we is," Toby announced, louder than necessary.

"Snares," he repeated, eyelids drooping slightly, head bobbing in heartbeat time. Then he ran his tongue along his top lip, paused in the middle.

Toby imagined he looked somewhat hungry, said, "You can have one if you likes, Garrett. For yourself. One of our rabbits."

Elbow to the ribs, "But we didn't get none. Did we, Toad?"

Garrett cocked his head, smiled at Toby. "You want a job, bud? Earn ten bucks?" His left hand, dangling out the window, lightly stroked the side of the car.

Toby exhaled. All was well. They hadn't been caught.

"What do you got in mind?" Melvin.

"Come here. I shows you. You got to have a look is all."

"What?"

"Come 'ere." Lazy wave. He didn't blink, breathing slowly. "Just you. The little one. See what you thinks of my prize."

They both sidled up to the car, window rolled completely down, and they looked in, newspaper across his lap.

"So, we wants the ten bucks."

Garrett locked eyes with Toby, then shifted the newspaper. One hand was moving beneath, and it took them several moments to realize what he was doing, gripping a purplish shaft, pumping, pumping. He stared at them, eyes glassy and excited, pumped faster.

Melvin knocked Toby sideways when he thrust his hands through the window, pinched his fingers around Garrett's chicken neck. "Dirty fucker," he screamed, and Garrett gagged, banged his head from side to side, gripping Melvin's fingers. Newspaper had fallen to the side, jeans and blue briefs pulled down, bare ass slapping the vinyl seat, Garrett bucking, the prize suddenly limp, knees pressed against the steering wheel.

"Sick fuck," Melvin spat. "Gonna kill ye, ye sick fuck."

Hands on the wheel now, foot stamping on the gas, and the butt of the car shivered, sprung forward, but Melvin didn't release his grip. Didn't let go, even when his feet were running sideways as Garrett drove, feet tripping over themselves, then feet gone out from underneath Melvin, car gaining speed, sneakers bouncing, Melvin yelling but still holding on. Dust cloud choking the fresh air, rocks flying. One second of eternity. Two. Until his elbows buckled, body slid down the side of the car, and he dropped. Head striking a rounded rock near the side of the road. Like fruit splattering. The sound of it coming at Toby in waves.

AT THE HOSPITAL, doctors were hasty when they looked him over. "You gave yourself a good knock, young man." Then to Toby and their father: "A concussion." "What does that mean?" "Essentially, bruised brain tissue." "What does that mean?" "Can't say for sure. There's a lot of uncertainty with concussions." A nurse, flat feet, flat face, shuffled in, snapped on gloves, rinsed bright blood from the oozing gash underneath his hair, bound his head with strips of white gauze. "Vomiting. Headache," she said without emotion. "You might expect some shift in personality. Most likely temporary. Time will tell." She sent them home with instructions on how to properly keep the road rash on his back clean and dry.

Toby placed a red bucket beside Melvin's bed, rinsed it each time the bottom was carpeted with strings of spit, greenish bile. There were hours of fidgety dozing, and Toby gripped Melvin's hand, waited it out. "You should eat to the table, Tobe," their father said. "Else you'll be drawing in the mice." Toby shrugged, chewed more carefully on his peanut butter and squashberry jelly. Even though his father said Melvin was tough, would be just fine, Toby didn't want to leave his brother, didn't want to stop watching his eyes, flickering constantly beneath lids stuck tight, dreaming, rerouting pathways. Body working to bring him back good as new.

When Melvin awoke in the early evening, pale skin, dark circles under his eyes, he looked at Toby's smiling face, growled, "What the fuck is you gawking at?" He kicked off the blankets, jolted upright, then clutched his head, two raking hands, "Sweee-eet fuck. Uh—" Sputtering, vomit shot from his mouth, nostrils, and he fell back onto his pillow, back into the faint halo of dried blood and sweat. "I got to get the fuck out of here," he squealed, still gripping his head. "Get the fuck."

Toby stood, backing away, just as their father rushed into the room. "What the hell's happening?" he said, looking from Melvin to Toby. "Don't give me that goofing around garbage. How the hell did you strike your head?"

"How the fuck do I know?" Melvin growled. He remembered nothing of the accident. Aggravated by the question. Toby blinked, opened his mouth. Closed it. Wished he could extinguish his own memory. Furtive hands sliding up the thick shaft of a candle, clapping the flame. Words tangled inside his head. "Do you wanna see something?" Brother. "Do you wanna see something?" Garrett in the car. DeeDee, too. Naked and aware. Happy birthday. The snarled thoughts all binding his chest, arousing a sick sense of pressure inside his trousers.

"What is it, Tobe?" Adamant, now. "I need to know. This could be serious."

But as Melvin curled into a ball on the bed making tiger noises, Toby shook his head and pressed the tiny slit in the flesh of his thumb. Thought of the matching slit on Melvin's thumb. He looked at his feet, neat hole in his tube sock, talon of a toenail poking through. *Don't try to make me, Dad. I can't. I just can't tell.*

MELVIN GRADUALLY IMPROVED, sat upright in bed, and vomited less often. He was able to watch the small black and white television perched on the dresser for about an hour before the wavering images made him nauseous. His sense of taste and smell had vanished, and the doctor explained it might return at any time. "And what about the aggression?" Father. "Be patient. He'll be back to himself in no time. Be like it never happened."

Six days later, while his fingers padded gingerly over his scalp, Melvin found a lump. "Toad! What the fuck?" Toby,

190

rooting around, discovered a rock still lodged in Melvin's skull. Skin grown up around it.

"Fucking doctor. Should slit his throat."

"Do you want me to get it?"

"Just leave it. Fuck. Just leave it."

"We can wait for Mrs. Verge."

"Fuck." He paced, weaving left and right. Fists like hammers. Ready. "Go on, then. Dig the shit out, man. Dig the shit out."

As Melvin lay on his side, Toby angled the neck of a light towards the injury, found the scab and scraped it away with his fingernails. Pressed until a pea-sized pus-covered stone burst out. He dribbled peroxide into the hole, a raw little mouth, waited until the bubbling stopped, then held a patch of gauze over the cut.

While Toby picked and prodded, Melvin was silent, stared at the wall without blinking. Toby wanted to say something, something that might fix it all, but he couldn't manage a word, and just knelt on the mattress, brown bottle of peroxide pinched between his thighs. He thought of the Mercurochrome designs Mrs. Verge would draw on their bloodied knees when they were younger. Bright red spiders. Snakes. Tree of Life. How easy it was to distract them, urge a smile out from underneath damp salty cheeks.

But there were no smiles, now. Toby was afraid to move, held the patch of cloth in place, his brother's greasy hair sticking out through his fingers. Lifting it for a moment, he peeped underneath, saw the hole where the shard of rock had been lodged. Even though the cut appeared clean, the edges were swollen, skin hot and shiny, Toby couldn't stop dread from making a nest inside his heart. Something was still there. No doubt about it. Something dark and sad and destructive. And no matter how hard Toby cleaned, Melvin's flesh would heal around it, sealing it, pulling it inwards. Not wanting to let it go.

22

OVER THE MONTHS, Melvin's brain still did not connect the dots, and the details around his head injury remained stashed away in an unreachable corner. Their father didn't ask again, and Toby held the secret inside, kept his tongue still. The only other person who knew what had happened was Garrett Glass. And for some time, Toby jumped every time the phone rang, every time the hinges on the door squeaked. Was nervous trekking along the roads whenever a car crept up behind him. He imagined Garrett spewing half-truths to everyone. How the brothers had spied on his little sister as she readied for an honest day's work selling vegetables from the back of a dusty pickup truck. How Melvin went berserk when Garrett confronted the boys shortly afterwards. But Garrett never came, and gradually Toby relearned how to breathe without air hitching in his throat.

He decided it was better that way, to forget about it. Anyway, maybe it had simply been one mistake after the other. He and Melvin just happened to be in the woods, wandering. Hadn't someone mentioned checking snares? Just happened to be climbing that tree. No sinful intentions whatsoever. They hadn't realized they were so close to the Fagan household. Swear to God. And maybe Garrett was not doing what they thought. Maybe his zipper had snagged his parts and he was really only asking for help. Or maybe his hand was gripping something altogether different. Maybe Toby had misunderstood because his body was still confused and aching over the sight of Garrett's naked sister. Maybe.

Garrett was strange and scary, sure, and his lowered gaze made Toby's cheeks burn just a little. But Toby couldn't think of any real evidence that Garrett liked boys. When a man was queer like that, it was pretty obvious, and everyone knew about it. Like Eldon Fleck who ran the convenience store opposite the school. He always wore clean white canvas sneakers, and no one's white canvas sneakers ever stayed clean. And no one kept their jean shorts unbuttoned, shirt spread just so that every kid could see a nest of black hair spiraling a cavernous belly button. Buy your chips or bottles of pop, they knew, but don't touch the loose penny candy. Gum balls. He liked to rub himself and then run his fingers through them, until the candy got so sticky he'd just toss it out for the dogs. Someone saw him do it. They really did. One time some girl found a coarse black hair in her bag of jujubes, and it wasn't from Mr. Fleck's scalp. She stuck her fingers straight down her throat while hanging upside down on the monkey bars.

Those sorts of things were solid clues that a kid could hold on to. Trust in. There were no solid clues with Garrett. Only Toby's shaky memory, and the truth was shifting in a gentler direction each time Toby conjured it up. Softening, melting away, a piece of cold gelatin on his tongue. Toby and Melvin's part morphing into an unfortunate misadventure, and Garrett's part nothing more than a man in a slowed car asking for directions.

MUSIC BLARED, and the beat slid up through the rubber soles of Toby's shoes, made his legs unsteady. He leaned against the curved wall of the stadium, searched the bobbing crowd, finding faces in the shadows and pumping fists. Only a month ago, the cement had been covered with ice, and now it was cleared, dark and smoky and full of an energy that made Toby's muscles twitch. This was his first stadium dance, and he was nervous, wondered if she might finally notice him with his stiff new jean jacket, banana yellow T-shirt. For good luck, he was wearing the braided leather necklace with the silver eagle pendant that Melvin had given him. Melvin gave him a lot of things these days.

Toby hadn't intended for that hard kernel of awareness to burst inside him, a crush to swell and bloom. At the start of the school year they'd shared the same classroom, and he began to stare at her and wonder what her life was like, living in that particular home. Did she sit in front of a television, like any normal family, and spoon up macaroni and cheese from her bowl? Did she brush her teeth while someone else was banging at the door? Soon he began to think about her after school too, and then he began to dream about her. Sitting by a stream, laughing, blue water running over her bare feet. Over a few months, he went from passive observer to an eager boy who couldn't wait to catch a single glimpse of her in the hallway or at the lunch tables, or climbing onto the bus after school. Toby never conjured an image of the girl's sister, or contemplated the reality of the brother. He only thought of her in terms of herself, quiet and strong. Something pretty stuck in a dirty place. Like a perfect purple lupine, growing out of a ditch filled with rusty cans and soggy cardboard and dozens of squashed cigarette butts.

"I don't think she's here," Toby said to his best friend, Ween. Ween scored his nickname due to his tubular body and limbs so short they were on the verge of deformity. To make matters worse, he nearly always wore a knapsack, and instead of just removing it, he'd attempt to access his medical books with the pack still strapped to his back. More than once he was witnessed struggling to reach the zipper with his double jointed arms, as he ran around in a tight circle as though chasing an imaginary tail.

"Do you got a tapetum lucidum?" Ween yelled. He was crouched down, heavy encyclopedia open on his lap, penlight poised in his hand.

"What?" Toby sat on his heels, watched the blur of legs and sneakers, counted the number of times someone stepped on a discarded wad of pink bubblegum.

"You needs those for night vision. And if you don't got them, which I suspect you don't, you won't see her unless she's right in front of your face."

"Oh, yeah."

"Want to walk around?"

"What if she's walking too? And we walks at the same speed?"

"Two bodies traveling at equivalent velocities on a closed circuit."

"Yeah. That."

"You'll never meet. We can wait."

"What if she's waiting?"

"Two bodies at rest." Ween scratched his head. "Shit, Tobe. I don't know everything."

"Yeah, right. That's the first lie out of your mouth tonight." Toby scraped the dirt out from underneath his fingernail, swallowed. He'd told Ween everything about the girl, some days talking nonstop, and Ween never snorted or scowled, only replied, "That's perfectly reasonable at this stage in your development." And Toby didn't mind that assessment either, because Ween wanted to be a special doctor when he grew up, and spent most of the time with his thin nose poked into a book.

"Tobe?"

"Yeah?"

"If you wants to kiss her, make sure you gets a good look at her tongue first."

"Her tongue?"

"Yeah. That's contagious." Ween held up his book, shone his penlight over an image. "Black hairy tongue."

Toby squinted, read. "That's gross, Ween. No one grows hair out of their tongue."

"Well, some poor person did. How else did they get the photo?"

"I idn't going to kiss her anyways."

"Well, you might."

"Nope."

"Someday?"

"Well, if I does, I'll be sure to make sure she idn't got a frigging carpet coming up out of her throat."

"Good," Ween said, and he gently closed the book. "That's good to be careful. Like my nan always says, ounce of prevention, Tobe."

Toby laughed, nudged Ween in the upper arm. He stood up, shook out his legs, numbed from the tightness of his jeans. Then he saw her, circling around with a gaggle of arm-locked girls. She was wearing a short plaid jumper and her dirty blond hair was no longer in a ponytail, but combed out straight, parted sharply in the middle. Perhaps the combination of darkness, the thumping music, and the half bottle of beer he had shared with Ween up in the woods spurred him on, and when she moved past him, he stared without blinking.

Tempo slowed, and Robert Plant's voice wove a slender stream through the air, droning, "There's a laaady who kno-oh-ohs…"

Ween reached behind himself, somehow eased his massive book back into his pack, and was zipping it up. "She looking at you, Tobe."

"Shit," he said, and his fingers crept up his chest, sought out the eagle. "Should I ask her?"

"Why not?"

"What if she laughs."

"Laugh back."

"What if she says yes?"

"You're stuck, then."

"What do I do when the song speeds up? Fast dance? Keep slow? God, it goes on forever."

Ween pushed up his glasses, stared up at taller Toby. "You really asking me this stuff? Man, I don't do dances. You just dragged me here."

"Oh God."

But she was beside Toby now, and she leaned in, her candy breath on his ear. Smell of strawberries and sugar. "You want to, you know?"

Shock stopped Toby's natural functions, and he froze. Ween struck him in the head, and finally, Toby squeaked, "Um, yeah. Yeah, sure. Cool."

Jamming his hands in his pockets, Toby walked beside her

196

into the clump of swaying bodies, and before he knew it they were standing before one another, rapidly assessing where hands went and feet went and if a cheek might brush against a cheek. Toby felt her flared hips just below the belt on her jumper, and her bent arms touched him, palms burning into his shoulder blades. Beat ignored, he moved his feet side to side to side, shuffle, shuffle, like an arthritic man, turning her in contained rounds. He did not shift his hands or face even though he noticed all the boys surrounding him were freely groping backsides and making fox bites on their partners' necks.

The song marched forward, word by word, painfully slowly, and Toby at once wished it would carry on into eternity and that it would be instantly over. He knew he would enjoy the dance much more not in creating the memory, but reflecting on it. All during the dance, he spoke to her nonstop inside his head, told her he thought she was really good-looking and that he didn't care if the other boys were always calling her a carpenter's dream and that he would love to know her middle name. And if she wanted to be something important when she grew up, like Ween did, or if she was more like him, and had no idea and didn't really care. And he mentioned, in silence, that he hoped she didn't like vinegar on her chips.

As soon as the last note faded, Toby dropped his arms, wouldn't look her in the eye. She mumbled something he didn't hear, and Toby said, "Yeah, cool," then turned on his heel and searched the sideboard for Ween. Ween was up in the bleachers, book once again open in his lap, bluish penlight glowing in the crowd.

"I wants to leave," Toby said. "I feels funny."

Ween snapped the book closed, held it in his arms. "I idn't surprised. I bet 'tis the hormones is making you sick," he said. "Page two hundred and sixteen. Really doesn't mean anything, you know. Chemicals from your hypothalamus driving you crazy."

"I think 'tis more than that."

"That's what your brain wants you to think," Ween said, nodding. "You can't trust your brain no more. Or your other parts, for that matter."

"What can you trust?" Toby thought about Melvin, then. Thought about how his brother seemed to be running so fast and hard from invisible ghosts, he barely even noticed Toby anymore.

"Me, Tobe. I can be your voice of reason. So far nothing or no one got a hold of me."

"Thanks, man."

As Toby and Ween came down off the bleachers, Clayton Gibbon struck Toby's shoulder, knocked him into the barrier surrounding the rink.

"Hey, dickwad."

"Watch it," Toby said. "Watch where you're going."

Clayton gripped Toby's arm. "Who you telling to watch it, quiff?" Swung Toby around. "And where the fuck did you get that." Two fingers hooked around Toby's eagle necklace, pulling.

Toby gulped, felt his heart beating, just as rapidly as when he'd been dancing, but with fear now controlling the pump. "Get what?"

"Don't be a spaz, dickhead."

Something in Toby's gut told him to lie about the necklace. "Found it."

"Yeah, like shit. How the fuck did you find it in my fucking room?"

"On the side of the road is where."

Clayton yanked, and the leather stretched, burned a line in Toby's neck, and burst.

"You can't do that," Ween piped up. "That's his. I seen his bro—"

Toby stomped on Ween's foot, said, "That's okay. Just a piece of shit anyways." And though he felt instant guilt for insulting the gift Melvin had offered up, Toby sensed it was smarter to let it go. "Let's blow this place, Ween." Besides, he just wanted to get home, slip into the dark and the quiet of his bedroom, think about every tiny detail of his first slow dance with a girl. And he tried to choke out any image of his father's eyebrows, tangled and low over those eyes, forbidding Toby from ever touching Angie Fagan again.

"NO. NO, HE's in bed. Do you want me to rouse him?"

"Do you think he seen Melvin?"

"I don't expect. Young feller's been in all night." Throat cleared. "And, to be honest, Lew, I don't see your boy around much these days. Not like he used to be."

"Ah." Lewis wrapped the phone cord around his wrist, pulled. "Awful sorry to wake you like this."

"Don't even mention it. I'm sure he'll turn up any minute. Nothing we didn't do to our folks, hey what? Torturing 'em."

"Sure, sure," Lewis replied with an empty laugh, and placed the phone in its cradle. As he left the kitchen, he gently clicked the back door closed. He slid into the driver's seat of his car, still warm, and twisted the key, engine cutting through the silence of a still spring night. Lewis checked the house, waited for a snap of light. Toby had been asleep since he'd come home from the dance, and the last thing Lewis needed right now was the boy waking up. Insisting on coming along. Perched on the edge of the car seat, hands pressed together between his knees. Dread making him stiff.

Lewis drove slowly around Knife's Point. Back roads and main roads. Watching the forest, checking ditches for any sort of unusual hillock. The curled body of his son. Nothing. He made his way towards the water. Parked on a cliff, and got out. Scanned the length of the beach, bright and vast and empty in the moonlight. How many nights had he made this trek? Searching, searching for Melvin. A thick knot of fear clogged his throat, and he rubbed his neck.

Deep inside, Lewis knew Melvin would turn up by morning, his body unscathed, teenaged attitude oozing from his sneering mouth. Though these days, even when Lewis saw his son, face to face, his heart wouldn't stop saying *Your boy is missing. Your boy is lost.* His noisy heart tormenting Lewis until aggravation took over, and he clenched that beating muscle, muzzled it.

MAYBE SOMEONE stole them.
   Maybe somebody did.
   Maybe.
   In the brightness of a full moon, Melvin could make out every blade of young grass covering the backyard. He could see the bumps of new buds on the row of trees between the properties and the glimmer of dampness on the fence posts. But that night, he had no interest in simply seeing the youthful signs of springtime. He only wanted to smell them.
   Two o'clock in the morning, and Melvin was outside the home of his math teacher. Out there, without an invitation. He crept around the corner, scraped his body behind the naked branches of a dogwood, and passed a blackened hibachi perched on the back stoop. Bending close to the grease-caked grills, he sniffed, drew a deep breath in through his nostrils. Nothing. No rank stench of old burnt meat. No whiff of squirted lighter fluid. The part of his brain that announced odors remained silent. Told him he'd just inhaled dead air.
   As he edged along, he kept close to the clapboard bungalow, and finally stopped underneath what he guessed was a bathroom window that was slightly ajar. He never would have considered entering this way previously. Never would have needed to. In the past couple of months, his father had been called to three or four homes, and once word spread around Knife's Point of the break-ins, people stopped leaving their doors unlocked. People weren't afraid, really, but they weren't as open anymore to late night visitors. And so, Melvin had to seek out open windows on the main floor or basement windows that he could wedge open with the screwdriver he kept in his back pocket.
   Other than the odd trinket or book for Toad, an apple or an opened pack of cigarettes, Melvin wasn't intent on burglarizing.

Instead, he was seeking the answer to a question that vibrated constantly within him. Made his teeth chatter with irritation, and skewed his vision. Someone had stolen from him, plain and simple, and he wanted to discover who it was. His objective would confuse the average person, Melvin knew this, but it was straightforward for him. Someone had taken two of his senses. Even the doctor had said so. And Melvin was going to discover who, if he had to rummage through every house in Knife's Point.

He crouched underneath the window, thought about how he missed his smell, his taste. Several months had passed, and his senses showed no indication of returning. During a follow-up appointment with the doctor, Melvin explained how these parts of him had gone missing, and how he couldn't understand where they might be. How, if only he knew where to look, he might find them again. He told the doctor about the soggy sense of worry whenever he chewed a meal, and knew he might as well be eating cardboard. Or, even worse. And how he panicked outside during a wintry night, knowing that no matter how deep he breathed, he couldn't track the sour strand of smoke on the wind or the stench of car exhaust pushed down to the ground by the cold.

"I knows what it's like to be an animal."

"An animal?"

"Taken out of my world. Waiting to be caught."

The doctor shook his head. "You've always been precocious, Melvin. But don't you worry. They'll come back in time."

"No. I got to find them."

Laughing, "You talk like you lost them in a field somewhere."

"Nope. I didn't lose them. They're just gone."

The doctor scribbled a note in his file, said offhandedly, "Maybe someone stole them, then."

"I never thought of that." Seed planted, earth tamped down.

The doctor laughed again, closed the file. "You got a good sense of humor, son." Didn't understand that Melvin wasn't joking.

Melvin climbed on top of a painted bench, balanced on an armrest, sneakers sticking to the thick coat of yellowish paint. Reaching underneath the glass, he unhinged the window and tugged it open as wide as it would go. One foot hoisted over, he hunched hard, then squeezed and quietly inched his skinny body in over the sill. Slid down the wall directly into a bathtub.

Without breathing, he waited in the tub. Wondering if anyone had awoken. Counted backwards from fourteen, Mississippi. No shadow appeared in the faint orange glow from the hallway, and Melvin got to work. He smelled the bar of soap, the sopping facecloth jammed into the corner, stepped out of the bathtub, lifted the lid on the plastic laundry hamper, stuck his nose down into the rank clothes, damp towels. Nothing. Smelled around the sink, opened the bottle of Aqua Velva, poured an ounce down the drain. Smelled the cleaners underneath the sink, smelled the tarnished doorknob and his own fingers.

Shuffling slippers moving across the carpeting, and Melvin stepped back into the tub, turned himself into a shadow behind the shower curtain. Mr. Simms, his math teacher, trundled into the bathroom, stood wavering in front of the toilet. Sat down, sighed, toilet water splashing. Even though he could have reached out and tapped Mr. Simms on the shoulder, Melvin wasn't nervous. He believed he would never be caught. Parts of him were missing now, and as he moved through this night world, he was no longer who he once was. So even if Mr. Simms noticed him standing there, behind the mildewed curtain that released no odor, it would not really be him. Just a portion of him. More like a memory of a past time. He would be a partial projection of himself, and nothing more.

Mr. Simms didn't flush, and eyes closed he wandered back to bed. Melvin once again stepped out of the tub, got down on all fours, smelled around the toilet. Smelled inside the bowl, but was unable to decipher any hint of heavy yellow nighttime pee. Heel to toe, heel to toe, he moved into Mr. Simms's bedroom, where the teacher slept alone. Moonlight streaming through the window, the man appeared gray and calm, hands folded across his chest. Cuticles growing up his nails even as Melvin watched. What if he opened an eye and Melvin chose to reveal himself? Would they talk about differential equations, the business of relating a function to its derivatives? Or would Mr. Simms bolt upright and bust past Melvin, dash to the phone on the wall near the oven? Call Melvin's father? What would Melvin do then?

Melvin stepped closer to Mr. Simms, leaned in to smell the breath. Though he could identify nothing on the warm air pulsing out from Mr. Simms's parted lips, Melvin guessed it would smell like loneliness. Wet wool and boiled onions. The slightest hint of rot. Outside, someone drove by, engine sounding very much like his father's car, and the headlights moved across the wall of Mr. Simms's bedroom. Melvin stepped back into the hallway, out into the cramped living room, framed pictures of long-dead relatives decorating the wall space. The largest, a framed picture of a cat. Melvin smelled the top of Mr. Simms's chair, which should have smelled like years of a resting scalp, but smelled like nothing.

Mr. Simms disliked Melvin because he never had to work at math. Melvin often ditched school for days, showed up stoned, and still aced Mr. Simms's lame exams. But even though Mr. Simms called Melvin a loser for wasting his potential, Melvin recognized that the man hadn't stolen from him. There were no smells hiding there, underneath tongues or bathroom sinks, or inside fabrics or the fridge. So Melvin walked quietly to the front door, unlocked it, and strode out into early morning. The first bird had just begun a tune. Some eager buds burst open. Tips of Virginia creepers starting to snake underneath unraked leaves. But, no smells. Melvin sighed, bowed his head, started the long walk home.

"TELL YOUR BROTHER if he does that again, he may as well stay out."

"Stay out?" Toby said, rubbing sleep from his eyes.

"Yes, stay out. By Jesus, if he lives in this house, he got to live by my rules."

"So, don't come home at all?"

"That's what I said, Toby." To Melvin, "You idn't going to torture me, my son." Then, back to Toby. "Tell your brother he idn't going to torture me. Staying out all bloody night."

Toby sighed, tucked his hands into the pockets of his bathrobe. Navy terrycloth, now a riddle of hitches. He looked at his brother, sunken cheeks and eyes, skin the color of ocean sediment.

"Did you hear, Mellie?" he said gently. "Did you hear what Dad said?"

Melvin, who was not more than six feet from the pacing Lewis, said, "Nope. Didn't hear fuck all."

Toby took another step. "He said he don't want you staying out all night."

"What do it matter?"

"He said he got real worried, Mel."

Lewis threw his hands up in the air. "That's not what I said, Toby. I said, if he does it again, he'll be out on his bloody ass. Can find some other idiot to put up with his nonsense." He ripped his keys off the hook, leaving the wooden hanger at a sharp angle. Kicked open the screen door, yelled over his shoulder, "Tell him, I wants that load of wood piled up in the basement by the time I gets home. He can toss it in through the window, then stack it up. And Toby, you go back to bed." Muttering as the door closed. "Up all night waiting for your good-for-nothing brother."

INSIDE LEWIS'S HEAD, two halves of a single idea were buzzing loudly, yet not connecting. He could sense the near misses right behind his eyes, and the useless buzz was giving him a headache. There was no relief inside his car, so he pulled off on the gravel shoulder, got out. Without thinking, he slammed the door, walked towards the ditch, and with one giant childlike

204

leap he entered the forest. Years had passed since he'd strolled among these trees, and a patchy darkness came down around him as soon as he was a few yards in. It didn't take long to locate one of the winding paths, and even though they were softer, the criss-crossing roots thicker, Lewis's body knew which way to turn, where to lift his foot. He was confident in his choices, and these days, something that simple, that undemanding, gave him comfort.

Drizzle had stopped an hour earlier, but the naked twigs were still dripping. Lewis could hear the drops striking the soggy floor. He reached the narrowest part of the stream and looked up at the sky. The moon had dipped and the sun had not yet crested the horizon. There was no glimmer of a sunrise, and Lewis could already tell the day would promise nothing but dense clouds, faint stunted shadows.

The water reasonably low, he stepped onto the skipping stones, and when he was halfway across he nearly slipped, flapped his arms to balance himself, and there was his brother Roy. The memory rising up before him. How often as children had they stopped on those greasy stones, each holding the other's hands, not for support, but to see who could upset the other. Roy was always the winner, as he was shorter and faster and stronger. Lewis was gangly, and until adulthood he'd never quite got used to the length of his arms and legs. But standing there now, the stream gurgling past him, Lewis realized there was some other reason why Roy always won. Roy was some- one who lunged first, contemplated later, while Lewis studied probabilities and angles. What if. So instead of figuring on how to dislodge Roy, Lewis focused on how to fall without hurting himself.

Lewis crossed the shallow water, walked up the slope on the other side, headed west towards the road that led to his grand- father's abandoned house. He tried to limit those moments when he thought about Roy, as the years had done nothing to sew up the hole inside of him. Still big enough to put a hand in there. Big enough to truly hurt. On that afternoon when Roy was killed, Lewis's good sense was absent. His ability to see what might happen was soused. And Lewis knew if he prodded too long, the truth of his culpability would come out into the light. Why had they trespassed onto Fagan's farm—why hadn't they wandered into town? Though his recollection was rotted, Lewis had the sneaky suspicion he directed Roy there. Through the woods and into Fagan's backyard. Lewis wouldn't have wanted to expose himself, staggering down the main streets, a new constable. Drunk on some bootlegger's potato whiskey. It was Eli's hand who drew the blood, no question there, but Lewis knew he was as much to blame as anyone. On those stepping stones back at the stream, Lewis had only thought about the safety of his own head. Never considered Roy's.

At the end of a dirt road, close to a cliff that lined the ocean, Lewis came to the old house. Some windows broken, others boarded up, long yellowed grass standing in front of the door. Lewis walked up the driveway, saw an abandoned saw beside a few lengths of gray clapboard. Blade on the saw dark orange with rust. Roy had had plans to clean the house up, make it new again. Once he found a woman foolish enough to marry him. He wanted to sit up in bed each morning, he'd often said, know what kind of day lay ahead by peering out at the sea. Tips of the waves iced or bare. None of that would happen now, and Lewis stepped on the saw, felt the decayed metal snap beneath his boot.

Off in the distance behind the house, Lewis saw the outhouse. A weathered box of splintering wood. He went over to it, overgrown grass wetting his pants, and placed his hands on the damp wood. He remembered the afternoon he and Roy trapped their grandfather inside. Roy's idea, of course, but as always Lewis was carried along for the ride. A gusty summer day, clouds running across a blue sky, and the boys saw their pop making his way through the field towards the outhouse, catalogue flapping under his arm. Once enough time was allowed for him to settle, Roy and Lewis crept up, and one, two, three, heave. They slammed the poorly anchored outhouse with their four open hands, and the back lifted, wobbled, tipped. Hit the ground. Flash of white, a dark crevice, and they bolted over the field, guts in knots of laughter, feet not touching the ground. Crouching underneath an outdoor table, they watched the slender man shimmy out through the hole in the wooden seat, narrowly missing the larger hole in the earth. Stunned, he stood, adjusted his clothes, put a hand to his brow, and stared out to the sea. Hobbled back to the house, scratching his head. He and Roy stood whistling, the image of angels, asked what happened. "Gust of wind," he'd replied. "Caught hold to the roof. Good t'ing yer nanny weren't perched in there. She'd never get out!" Guilt soon bloomed, and confession not being an option Roy and Lewis spent three days sawing and stacking a half cord of spruce. Palms weeping, necks and shoulders blistered from the burning sun.

Lewis thought then about Melvin and Toby. And he wondered if they had a single story like that one. He started back down the road. His legs were tired, but the ache felt good, and his headache retreated. Mrs. Verge's house was only a quarter or so of a mile, and he decided to stop by there. It was late enough now, and Lewis knew she would have hot coffee percolating. A chair at her table. A pair of ears that were capable of listening. A word of two of womanly advice.

When he arrived, the kitchen was bright and warm. Mrs. Verge was tucked into a rocking chair, her slippered foot moving her back and forth. Not much more than a fold of fabric balanced in the crook of her arm. A woman, Terry's young wife, was seated at the table, her face tight and pale, like dough made with dead yeast. When she saw Lewis, she stood, but not upright, and starting shuffling out of the kitchen, gripping her zippered bathrobe with her fist. Lewis was not insulted by her turned-down expression, he had seen it often. People who didn't want to be near him, a man who enforced the rules. People didn't trust their own mouths.

"Do you mind?" she said to Mrs. Verge.

"No, honey. You go on. Rest all you can. While you can."

Lewis sat down in her spot, wood still warm.

"Where's Terry?"

"Gone long ago."

"Working?"

"Yes, oh yes. Helping Skipper Neary fix his nets. Terry got a way with knots."

"Right." Lewis looked up at the ceiling. Wondered where the joists would meet behind the drywall.

"The boys?"

Lewis sighed. "You got me, Mrs. Verge."

"Pay it no mind, now. They'll find their way." Voice lowered. "Who would've guessed only a few years ago that my Terry'd be up before dawn earning a dollar, married now, and with this wee one?"

"I guess so." He smiled.

"No guessing about it. Take heart, my son. Take heart."

"Thank-you, Mrs. Verge."

"And look at this, now." She angled her arm so a tiny scrunched face was revealed. "If this don't warm you from the inside out, I don't know what will. Right fresh. Angels still got a hold to him. He's still being born."

"Is that what you thinks?"

"Not what I thinks, Lewis. What I knows. That's why you got to hold them for six weeks or more. Make sure they feels safe enough to stay put in this world."

"That's a nice way to consider it, Mrs. Verge."

"Do you want to hold the little man?"

First instinct was to shake his head, but he could see Wilda clearly in his mind, how rarely she cuddled their sons, how she stared at them with anxiety instead of wonder. And how he was busy, working all hours, keeping the house in good repair whenever he had a free afternoon. He was certain he had unlimited time to connect. Unlimited time to be the best dad. And now, time had slipped away, personalities had set, and he had no idea how to reach his son. All the shouting and shaking and slamming down his fist didn't make a damn bit of difference. Melvin would not stop flailing in the darkness.

"You can't make someone open their eyes," Lewis said. Out loud.

"No, no, he's sleeping. The little lover."

Lewis looked at Mrs. Verge, a lady who wanted nothing more out of life than a happy family, a few good meals, and a reliable fire in the woodstove. "Yes, I'd love to. To hold him. I would, Mrs. Verge."

"Will you stop calling me that?" she whispered. "I have a name, you know. And I'm not old, yet."

"Oh. Oh. I'll try to remember."

Lewis took the child in his arms, stared into the face, slightly yellow with a flattened nose. He sighed again, and couldn't help but relax. Couldn't resist the calm that settled over him. The simple joy he felt being in the company of Mrs. Verge. Peggy. Then, snap, the two halves of that idea collided, stuck. The break-ins. Every targeted household familiar to Lewis and the boys. Melvin out during the nights. Most men would be able to dismiss it. Defend their sons. But Lewis had doubts. And did not believe in coincidences.

SILENCE IN THE kitchen, and Toby went to the cupboard, removed a bowl, found a box of cereal. "You want some?"

"Nope."

"You want toast? I makes good toast. I can burn it just a bit like you likes it."

"No, Toad. I don't want no toast." Melvin pressed his fingertips into his eyes, then massaged his scalp as though he were washing his hair without shampoo.

"Mellie?"

"Yeah."

"You go on. Dad'll be gone 'til supper, and I'll do the wood. I likes doing wood. If you leaves it, it'll be like doing me a favor."

"Yeah, right."

"He was just worried, is all. Didn't mean it."

"Yeah. Sure. He don't get it."

"No."

"No one gets it."

"I do, Mel. I get it."

"No, you don't. And I don't want you to."

As Melvin started across the kitchen, his body went sideways, and he struck his hip on the countertop. He didn't react, righted himself, and made it to the door that led to the hallway.

"Mellie?"

Stopped, held on. "What now, Toad?"

Quietly, "I danced with a girl last night."

"You did?"

"Yeah."

"Cool."

"Yeah. It was."

"How'd she smell?"

"Good, Mel."

"Yeah?"

"Yeah. She smelled real good."

"Right on," he croaked. "Right on." And if Melvin's eyes hadn't decided to clean themselves at that moment, he would have turned to his little brother, said something nice.

23

"GO ON," MR. CLAREY said. "Go on and get a bit of fresh air. You can't be cooped up every day with nothing but carpet and glue. Not good for a young feller."

Garrett watched as Mr. Clarey bent to inspect the underside of a roll of linoleum, the one with the beige octagonal pattern. He didn't like Mr. Clarey, the way he always gazed at Garrett's throat whenever they spoke, instead of his face. And the way he walked around with a thin nail sticking out of his mouth. In an instant, Mr. Clarey could inhale that nail, have it stuck in his throat, and then Garrett would be responsible for getting it out. Or leaving it there.

"Uh, alright."

"Yes, you go on. Where do young fellers go these days to meet a girl?" Wide grin, nail dancing on his white lips.

Garrett blushed, and to calm himself he imagined the sound his boss might make if the nail pierced his skin. "I'll be here by eight tomorrow, Mr. Clarey."

"By Jesus, you will too. You're that kind of worker, Gary."

"Garrett. My name's Garrett." He pictured a longer, thinner nail. Point sharpened.

"Right. Don't get into no trouble now. Watch your bobber, my son." Sharp nod.

Then Garrett pictured how Mr. Clarey would look with his mouth hole trussed. "Yes, sir."

Squeezing inside his rusting Chevette, Garrett gripped the steering wheel. Free time. He wasn't hungry, didn't want to go home. Where to go? Which way to turn? This simple unknown made his palms sweat, and he stuck the key in the ignition, twisted, sighed when he heard the hitching purr. He pulled out onto the street, decided to see where the road might take him if he always turned left. Randomness. He might end up anywhere, see or do anything. Five or six minutes later, Garrett found himself on a back road just behind an elementary school.

He needed to pee, decided to stop, eased the car onto the thin gravel shoulder. Just outside his passenger side window, he saw a dense patch of spruce trees. One branch bent against the glass, leaving a jagged smear of sap. That will be difficult to clean, he thought, sticky and persistent. He got out, stepped around the car and into a weak shadow near the edge of the woods. As he unzipped, legs spread, he faced the school, wondered if someone might see him there. Was watching him now. Peeing. His urine forcing a cavity into the forest floor, spattering up onto his good trousers. Garrett would apologize, act embarrassed. "I never realized," he'd sputter to the teacher. The principal. But no one came across the dirt lot, and he walked out of the woods, got back into his car. Mildly disappointed.

He shifted in his seat, now, eyed the squat brown building with rows of narrow windows. He counted them from left to right. Twenty-three. He pretended that twenty-three was a new number. That the school was a new school. That he had never set foot in that particular patch of woods before. That taking the first three lefts after leaving the carpet shop was a random choice.

Not much separated him from the playground, a few feet of damaged pavement, a chain-link fence, large hole slit in one section. Garrett checked his watch, and breathed with his mouth. Recess soon arrived, and a handful of boys were the first to burst through the double doors. Hello. Checkered sweaters and skinny legs in a blur of brown corduroy. Two wearing knitted hats to ward off the autumn chill. As the gang of them marched across the parking lot, Garrett's lungs stopped functioning, and he pulled oxygen in through his pulsing skin. One dropped a soccer ball onto a hardened patch of earth. And

Garrett's eyes widened, recording every move as they darted about, hopping and jumping, the lucky ball bounding between them and drawing the lines of a jagged star.

Garrett's hand left his upper thigh, crawled over to the other seat. There, his fingers located a puncture in the vinyl of the seat, about two inches wide. As he watched the boys playing, he jammed two fingers into the hole, moved them through the matted layer of stuffing, pushed. There, near the edge of the seat, he located a broken spring, and he rubbed the spring, feeling some type of smooth synthetic batting between his skin and the metal. He closed his eyes for a moment, rubbed some more. And often, that was enough.

"LOOKS LIKE IT might rain." Ween leaned against the classroom window, stared up at the low clouds. "You going out?"

"Nah, I don't feel like it," Toby replied.

"Can I use your rubbers?"

"Don't you got your own rubbers?"

"Yeah, mine got a blow out in the toe. If it rains, my feet'll get wet. I don't need to tell you about wet feet, do I?"

"Go on and take 'em."

Ween slipped his feet out of his indoor shoes and into Toby's rubber boots, a remarkably good fit given their different heights. He was about to haul on his knapsack, medical book inside, but decided to leave it, asked Toby to keep an eye on it. Then he darted out the door, across the paved divider between the junior high and the elementary school. That morning, Ween's mother had asked him to spend recess with his little brother. Yesterday, the boy had come home with a purple ring around his eye, and he told them he had run into a rock. "Did the rock happen to be flying through the air in your direction when you ran into it?" He wouldn't say. Ween's mother feared the boy, who was small and soft-hearted like Ween, was being bullied. "'Tis your job to watch out for him. That's what big brothers do."

They were just tumbling out of the building as Ween approached, and he joined in as they kicked the ball back and forth. At first he eyed every other child, waiting to identify the bully, but there was no sense of menace within their small circle. Soon, Ween forget his task, enjoyed the game, considered how all the running and jumping was good for his cardiac muscle. The ball was hard, overinflated, and when Ween did a running skip kick, kissed the underside of the ball with his boot, Toby's boot, the ball jetted up into space, dove down onto the hood of a car.

"Shit," Ween yelled. He saw the outline of a driver sitting behind the wheel. A man.

"Shit," the other boys repeated.

Ween frowned at them, said "double shit" inside his head. "I'll get it," and he bounded through the hole in the fence. Ran across the dirt road towards the stranger's car.

GARRETT LUNGED FORWARD, fingers freed, banged his chest on the steering wheel. He opened his eyes just in time to see the soccer ball rolling off the hood of his car, into the ditch. Then he saw a squat boy with thick black glasses clamoring through the wound in the fence, running towards him, waving, looking guilty. Garrett pressed his damp back into the seat, felt around his thighs to find his dropped keys. Maybe he could leave before the boy reached him. Maybe he could disappear. The gap was closing, closing, and the boy was smiling, and Garrett felt the ball striking the windshield over and over again, and then the ball striking him, his head and his back, and he had to think of something to make him strong, to bring him back to where he was.

Garrett breathed once, twice, rolled down his window.

"Hey, Mister," the boy said. "Sorry about that."

"Is you?"

"I don't think we done no damage."

"Maybe you should check."

The boy leaned across the hood, stared at the glass, and at the same time Garrett leaned forward, so that he and the boy were only inches apart. He could see that the boy's forehead was not perfectly smooth, but had a bump in the middle, and that his oversized glasses were streaked with grime. Fingers reaching, Garrett touched the windshield. The child's face was not as young as he might have liked, but his body was compact. Garrett could clean his glasses for him. Stroke the lenses so softly on his shirttail.

The boy bounced back, ran around the front of the car to grab the ball. "I don't see nothing."

"Oh. Do you wanna ride?"

"What?"

"Do you need a ride somewhere? I got time."

"No, Mister. I don't need no ride. I got school." He hugged the ball, started to back away, heels on his large rubber boots dragging a line through the dirt.

"Is you sure? We could go somewheres. I can get you some chips."

"Yeah, I'm sure," he replied, then turned and ran, slipped through the fence.

As playfully as he had run towards Garrett, the boy receded, getting smaller and smaller, swept away in a tide of children. And Garrett never blinked until they had all been sucked back into the school, tucked inside cement and peeling boards, and windows that were dark and unwelcoming.

Rain came, huge drops striking the roof of his car. Garrett reached down around his ankles, found his keys behind the heel of his right foot. His muffler backfired when he turned the key, and a bird burst out of the spruce tree, passed just in front of his car. Wings wet, weighted, rain pressed the bird downwards, skewing its path. Garrett waited for it to stop, settle into other branches. Then, reluctantly, he rolled his car around, drove away.

"EVERYTHING GOOD?"

"Yeah."

"No one picking on him?"

"Not for me to see. Guess he really did run into a rock."

215

Toby laughed, closed the encyclopedia.

"Tobe?"

"Yeah?"

"There was this—"

"This what?"

Ween lifted the book off of Toby's desk, slid it into his knapsack and zipped it closed. Ran his hands over the fabric, then lifted it off the ground a little, making sure his treasure was still inside.

"What?" Toby said. "What was you going to say?"

"Nothing," Ween replied, and he slid his knapsack underneath his desk, sat down, locked his feet on either side. "Nothing. Boring over there with those kids. Glad we don't got to go there no more. Glad we're already half growed up."

GARRETT PULLED OUT onto a main road, and saw the police car behind him, Constable Trench gesturing for him to pull off.

Hands clenched around the steering wheel, Garrett stopped his car. Waited for the end.

"You got yourself a flat tire there, my son."

"I do?" Garrett leaned his head out of the window.

"'Tis that road, Garrett. What were you doing in there?"

"Uh, driving. Wandering around, I guess."

"Well, that's no place to wander. Youngsters in there always up to no good. Tons of broken bottles around."

"I'll remember that."

Hand ready to roll up the window, but Constable Trench was still there. Staring at him. Garrett's heart began to knock against his chest, and he had to force himself to not look down.

"Garrett?"

"Yes, sir."

"You still working over to Clarey's?"

"Yes, sir. I is."

"Good. Good for you."

"Okay."

"And Garrett?"

"Yes, Constable Trench?"

Cleared his throat. "You don't have to- have to be—"

"Yes, Constable Trench?"

Hand waving, clearing the air between them. "Ah, go on. Best get that tire looked after. And keep off the old roads."

24

IN A CIRCLE of dry earth, Toby leaned against the trunk of a maple tree near the bank of the stream. All the red leaves still clung to the tree, and while he waited, they protected him from a light rain falling straight down. He watched the woods, wondering if she might show, or if her parents might discover her sneaking away from her house, up to no good.

He didn't have to wait long before he saw her walking through the woods. Hair like string, red pants and jean jacket darkened from the drizzle. Sides of her sneakers were coated in mud, and before she crawled underneath the tree she twisted each ankle, scraped the muck away.

"Hey," she said.

"Hey."

Even though they'd been talking during lunchtime at school, they'd never really spent much time alone together. Toby coughed, shook his shaggy head so his hair covered his eyes. He couldn't look at her face, still pretty even though she was wearing enormous round glasses, navy rims.

"Do your father or mother know where you is?"

"Nope, never told them. Too wet to do anything, so they don't care. You?"

"Dad's working."

"Oh."

"And I told Mrs. Verge I was going to the library with Ween."

"Well, she'll know you're lying for sure. Half lying anyway."

"Ah, she don't care."

Toby glanced at her, saw her hair sticking to her face. Her jacket was open and hanging off, and he could see part of her bra strap riding over her shoulder. He guessed it should be bright white but it wasn't, and that made him think of laundry and clothes on a line, and he wondered if she'd be embarrassed if her mother hung all of her underwear and other stuff out where her brother might see.

Angie lit a cigarette, held it in her left hand, and dabbed at the messy makeup behind her glasses. "So," she said.

"Yeah."

He thought to tell her about what he'd read today. In Ween's book. About Melvin and his head, and how his brain chemistry could be gone off. Explain it to her, and get her opinion. Maybe if he talked to Melvin in a different way, things might change. But he didn't want to betray Melvin, and if he shared those troubles with Angie, that was what he'd be doing.

"Umm. Do you want to play truth or dare?"

Unwanted redness jumped into Toby's cheeks, and he wasn't sure why. "Not really."

"C'mon." She nudged him. "I won't ask nothing hard."

"Alright, I guess." And he shook his hair again, tried to cover his face.

"Okay." She stubbed her cigarette out near the base of the tree. "Okay. Truth or dare?"

"Well, seeing as I don't feel like getting drenched and I knows you'll say something like jump in the stream, I'll go for truth."

"Okay." She paused. "Who was your first crush?"

"That's easy. I don't got no first crush."

"Not fair, Toby. You got to have one."

Toby thought, chewed his bottom lip, smiled a little. "Okay. I got one, but I won't say the name."

"Your mother?"

"No." Toby saw Melvin's young face in his mind now, eyes wide and forever hopeful as he stared at their mother. Toby remembered how rarely she stared back.

"Who?"

"An older woman. You got that right."

"How old was you?"

"Four, I think."

"Mrs. Verge?"

Shook his head. "Not even close."

"Who, then?"

"Miss Penny."

"Who? I don't know her."

"I thinks she's Mrs. Timothy now."

Toby heard a choking sound.

"Mrs. Timothy? That teacher that smells like booze half the time?"

"Ween said she got something wrong with her insides. So sometimes she's fermenting, I guess. That's why she smells."

"Yeah?" She leaned back against the tree. "Can't blame her horse teeth on that. Do she talk or do she whinny?"

"Oh, she whinnies. When I was little, I used to dream about going for a ride on her back."

Snorts, now. "God. You're funny, Toby Trench." A deep breath, composed again. "Your turn."

"Alright. Okay. Ummm. Okay." He tried to resist chewing his knuckles. "Ah. What's the most specialist thing about you?"

She leaned forward, clapped her hands together. "I know. I know. I can touch my tongue off the end of my nose."

"Show me." He glanced sideways, through his hair, saw her thin pink tongue jutting out, and sure enough she could kiss the sharp tip of her nose. "Shit," he said. "Is that normal?"

"I don't see why not."

"Does it go any further?"

"What?"

"I means, can you push your glasses up?"

She punched him, laughed. "Yeah, right, and I'm the only person ever who gave themselves their own cowlick."

Toby shook his head. His body was filled with helium,

and he thought he might float away. "You're funny, too, Angie Fagan."

"So, what can you do? What's the most specialist thing about you?"

"Nothing."

"There's got to be something."

"I'm not much good at nothing."

"Nothing?"

Toby stuck his too-long thumbnail into the fleshy part on his other hand, wished he had something better to say. He struggled with every subject at school, couldn't make anything with his hands, couldn't talk his way out of a Tupperware container, and had the skinny body of a sailor adrift on a raft. "Nope." And then he thought of something small, offered it up. "I likes to saw wood. And my dad says I makes a neater stack than any other soul he knows."

"Oh."

"I knows it don't matter. But I likes to saw wood. You starts with a pile of something, something you can't really use. And then you ends up with something else. Something you can use. And it's quiet, and you can be alone, and you know, you can think about stuff." Thumbnail jabbed in even harder, and the sudden pain stopped his rambling.

"That's cool. Me too."

"Really?"

"Yeah." She lit another cigarette, coughed. "Your go."

"Um. What's it like living with your old man?"

"My dad?"

"Yeah."

"Good, I suppose. He's alright. He don't say much to me. He don't say much to anyone." She shrugged. "He looks at me, though."

Toby leaned forward. "Like what?" Controlled tone.

"Like it hurts him. Hurts him to see me exist in the world, you know?"

Back against the tree again. "I know."

"Deep down he's really a good person. But it's hard for people to see through all that build-up."

"Yeah. Build-up. Crust."

She laughed. "What about you? What's it like living with the fuzz? Does he go all cop on you all the time?"

Toby laughed lightly. "Nah. He's alright. He's a bit tough, yeah. Especially on Mellie. Don't know why." Scratching his chin. "I think he don't like Mellie cause he's soft."

"Soft? You're trying to tell me Melvin Trench is soft? On what planet? Pluto?"

"He is, Angie. I know he don't act it. He's kind of, um, wolf on the outside, but just sheep underneath."

"Well, I'll take your word for that." She pushed up her glasses with the back of her hand, glanced at Toby. "You go."

He didn't have another question ready, tired of the game, but was surprised when one burst from his mouth. "Did you get a good mother?" And as soon as it was out, dangling in the air between them, he wondered if she might think the question was more about his own heart rather than hers.

"What?"

"Nothing. Dumb question."

"No, it's not. No question is ever dumb, Toby. She's decent, I guess. I don't know that I'd call her motherly. We gets what we needs. Food and clothes and stuff for school. But my brother is her favorite. She's thinks he's something special."

"Garrett?" Clearing his throat.

"Yeah. She don't say it, but you can tell. You'd think he'd be gone by now. Out living on his own. But no, he's still up in his little room. Like a freak."

"Really?" Toby resisted the urge to snort.

"Yeah, she makes his bed and irons his clothes. Picks up his socks. Kisses his cheek, and checks his teeth before he leaves for work. It's pathetic. I tell you, if she weren't old enough to be his mom, you'd guess they were husband and wife."

"You two don't get along?"

"Get along? He's been nothing but an ass to me since I can remember. So, no, we don't play checkers or nothing."

Toby shook his head, felt a small checkmark of relief.

She took a deep drag, waved away the smoke. "Do you miss your mother?"

"My mother?"

"Uh, yeah."

"Nope."

"Not at all?"

"I don't remember even having one."

"Do you think she'll ever come back?"

"What?"

"Come back. See what you growed into."

"How could she come back?" Toby folded his arms across his chest. "She's dead."

"You think?"

"Well, she just as well be dead. And Mellie'll say the same, I can tell you that."

"I heard she's living in a store somewhere."

"What? What did you say?"

"Yeah. Selling all sorts of, well, crap."

Toby jumped to his feet, cracked his head on a low branch. "Who told you that?"

"No one. I don't know."

"Who told you?"

"I can't remember. I just listens, that's all. I hears stuff."

"Well, it idn't true."

She pulled her knees up to her chest, stuck her cigarette into the damp earth.

"Okay."

"It idn't true. You hear me?"

The rain had stopped, the world had opened up again, and they were no longer the only ones in existence. Toby looked at Angie then through sober eyes, saw how she really was. Tough mouth, glasses too big for her face, hair that needed washing, raccoon rings of eyeliner around her eyes. He stepped out from underneath the tree, felt exposed, and quickly checked to make sure the zipper of his jeans was fully up.

Who were they kidding? The two of them, meeting there in secret, pretending there was something sturdy beneath both their feet, as though they could walk across air, find each other in the middle.

"I just remembered," Toby said. "My dad wanted me to do something."

"Yeah?"

"Yeah."

"I didn't mean nothing. By what I said. I really didn't."

"That's alright. I don't care where's she at. Don't need her. Don't give a shit."

She cocked her head, took off her glasses. And even though she didn't squint, he knew she saw him, too. Lanky, and shy, and ears that no amount of hair could hide. He had told her he liked to saw wood. And what seemed sincere and decent then now brought a flush to his cheeks. He liked to saw wood. So stupid. So nothing. So him.

25

TOBY USED A pen to write the note, even though he had to cross out several mistakes, and ink globbed as he paused over certain words. He wondered if she might notice that, how his writing slowed when he had to write the important parts. The parts about being together for a whole year. The parts about fighting and making up. The parts about falling in love.

Someone rummaging in the hallway, and he folded the paper rapidly, jammed his hand into the closet. Found what he thought was his jean jacket, slid his fingers down until he located a pocket, and he hid his feelings there.

DEEP IN THE woods behind his house, Melvin knelt on the forest floor, leaned forward, blew on the glowing twig positioned just under the shredded newspaper. The paper smoked, then caught fire. Without smothering the flame, he constructed a tiny teepee with the dried splits he had stolen from the shed. Fire gaining momentum, he layered on a couple of logs, patiently poking the base, balling the rest of the paper, tossing that in. When it crackled with strength, Melvin stood up, went down the slope to the stream where he and Toby played as a child, and filled his cut off apple juice can with water. Reaching into his pocket, he retrieved a handful of small mushrooms someone from school had offered him, beige with nipple tips, dropped them in with the water, stirred with a stick. He hooked a length of wire through holes in either side of the can, twisted, and hung the can over the crook of a hefty branch. Bringing it up to the fire, he suspended it, then sat down, branch balanced over his knee, waited for his special tea to boil.

"Fuckin' wild trip, man," a boy named Jarrod had said about the mushrooms he'd plucked in a field riddled with cow manure. "Be whatever you wants to be."

"Do it work?"

"Yeah, it works. Works good. Fuck, man, I was sure I'd turned into an orange. Fat and juicy like. And I was freaking right out when I thought Russ the faggot was trying to peel me."

Melvin snickered. "Yeah, right. You sure there idn't shit on these?"

"Shit? You won't give a fuck about eating shit when it hits you right here." Hollow knocks to the skull.

"How do I know these idn't poisonous? That you're not trying to poison me?"

"Look," he said, grabbing one from Melvin's hand. He pinched the edge gently. "See, it turns bluish. Like a bruise. That's the real deal."

"Man," Melvin replied. "You should be a frigging scientist."

"That's your department, buddy. Not mine."

"Not no more. I idn't got no fuckin' department, man. I am department-less."

Although he'd heard about the high before, Melvin was doubtful, figured he'd end up vomiting. Or give himself the runs. But he was willing to try. After twenty minutes or so, he removed the can, stuck his nose into the steam. Nothing. Not even a hint of a smell. When it was cool enough not to burn, he gulped the tasteless tea down, felt it coat his empty stomach. Then he tossed away the heads and stems, even though Jarrod told him he could eat them. Make his journey last a little longer.

"Yes, I is the mushroom man, the mushroom man, the mushroom man," he sang quietly while he waited for something to happen. "Yes, I is the mushroom man who loves to, to, to... I don't know what I love." Head bent, murmuring. "I don't know what loves me."

As he sat cross-legged, smoking a cigarette, Melvin's stomach gurgled, and he burped. Tasteless, though his eyes still reacted, and they stung. The back of his throat tickled, and he knew that if he didn't get up his digestion would course in the wrong direction. So he stood, put his hand against the cool trunk of a silver birch, and didn't bend at the waist. If he gave gravity a chance, he would throw it all up. Melvin decided he had wasted his time. This was right up there with Jarrod's other ideas, to smoke banana peels or black tea, inhale bathroom freshener sprayed into a garbage bag, or swallow a tablespoon or two of ground nutmeg. *Try it,* he'd say. *It's wicked.*

Melvin was about to turn and walk home when he heard the stream, such a pretty tinkling sound, and when he looked he noticed the surface of the water sparkling in the moonlight. Just a quick look, he thought, and as he made his way down the slope, the trees began to lean in towards him. Wrinkled bark, almost faces. Could they be smiling, nodding? Hey, cool. Hello. And for a short moment he was aware that his trip had suddenly commenced, and that he was stepping through a forest door. Lifting one foot over the threshold. Then the other. In this new place, branches lifted and fell, and Melvin could see that they were caressing each other, rubbing knobs, pine-covered mittens slipping into holes in the bark, rooted toes curling. Holy shit, he thought. So much for propagation with cones. Trees actually fucked. Then Melvin laughed, and the trees laughed back, their afterglow eyes weeping turpentine.

When he reached the water he stared down at his reflection, watched for a while how the water skeeters stretched his skin, turning his head into a prickly burr. He thought to sit down, as the edge of the crystal stream was breaking apart, and Melvin had the vague notion that a liquid he had swallowed was creeping upwards, drowning his brain. He watched the rippling water, flickering patterns of light and sound, and using his mind power he slowed down the sparkles to a near standstill, could identify individual shapes. And he grew excited, trying to take it all in, every math principle, sine and cosine in full bloom, waves and bell curves, infinity repeated infinitely. All the secrets of the physical world were right there, floating on the surface of the water, theorems and truth about time and space. In plain view. What a clever hiding spot.

He had to see where he was, how he fit into this heavenly reveal, and he looked down, fingers in the water, touching his reflection. At the same time his hands were moving through the stream, he could sense his hands gliding over his face. Opened his mouth, fuck-off finger poking into the watery hole, no tongue, no teeth, and Melvin snapped his limb back. A moment or a lifetime of panic, compressed. Wanting the lights again, he waded out into the stream, fabric sucking up the water, but all the light collapsed into a pinprick, everything now contained in a point so small, so bright, his knees buckled. Here he was, Melvin Trench, witnessing the origin of the universe, the primeval atom, and the Big Bang about to happen.

He carried himself backwards, allowing room for the explosion, but he was cold, took deep breaths through the open wound in his face, knew that if the sun didn't shine soon, his ears would freeze, fall off. Tumble away like leaves caught in a blustery day. In the sky, an enormous crescent sun obeyed, and Melvin stood, walked straight across the black water, a solid shiny table, reflecting the blinding light. But he moved too close, and soon his skin was peeling, onion layers, and Melvin began moving backwards through his own flesh. He could see the cells and the nuclei, and feel the bags of cytoplasm cushioning whatever form he had adopted. Continuing his journey towards the light, towards full understanding of this new nonphysical realm, he realized that there was nothing to leave behind. That his very genes had unraveled, and he had now become light.

He willed his mother to appear, and she hovered before him, a knotted star. But he was unable to touch her, to feel her, to untangle the cluster and comprehend her betrayal. Suddenly, he was back inside a body, a mass of night and shadows, metal skin inches thick, his entire being suspended in a layer of gelatin. "Go." Inside his consciousness, her voice arrived. "Go see what's in the barn." Easy enough for you to say, he would have shouted. If he had a tongue. He wanted to pull mounds of darkness down around her. But when he reached, the drapes skirted sideways. He could not do it. Could not harm her. Up until the moment she had vanished, so many years ago, she had been a perfect, perfect mother.

THE COFFEE WAS cold and tasted like mud, but Lewis drank it anyway. He had made the decision to take a little run, and needed to stay awake.

"I'm going."

Toby twisted his head around, but Lewis noticed his eyes did not leave the television screen. "Alright."

"I'll be gone for a while."

"Uh-huh."

Then Lewis felt a twinge of shame, said, "I'll be out by myself."

"Okay, Dad. See you later."

Lewis grabbed the keys from the hook and quietly closed the door to the house. He stood on the bottom step of the back stoop and glanced at the woods. For a moment, he almost walked over, found the old path, thinking he'd find Melvin at the end of it. Lost and in trouble. But he chastised himself for more foolishness. So many nights he had tried and failed to find his son. Like trying to pinpoint a shadow in the darkness. Not a single trace until, early morning, the boy's body reassembled in the kitchen, limbs and trunk moving sluggishly, his eyes low and tired and hiding something. Lewis tried not to focus on the flurry of break-ins. Nothing ever stolen, just items shifted, touched. There had been a lull in the reports lately, but it still gnawed at him. He had never been able to catch the culprit. Catch, he was certain, Melvin. Lewis gripped the flaking handrail, stared at the woods again. Listened for some sound of fear, but there was only a gentle whistling. Just the wind riding out through the trees. He went to his car, hauled the door closed. There was only so much he could do, he told himself. As a father. As a constable. Only so much.

No questions were asked when Lewis stopped in and borrowed Terry Verge's prize Mustang. As he drove up onto the highway, he told himself he would just wander for a few miles, enjoy the rumble of an eager engine. His weight against the leather seat when he pressed hard on the gas. The stars in a clear fall sky. But Lewis knew where he was going. As he always did.

THE LIGHT OF his mother faded out, but Melvin still heard her words. Go. You'll find your truth in the barn. He turned around, located the heavy wooden doors of a barn, one set opening onto another set, opening onto another set. After a single forever had passed, he stepped into the damp structure, pigs in a circle, heads bowed with reverence, and in the center was a manger. A bed of straw. Melvin squinted, saw that his brother was sleeping. Toby, fully formed, naked, fetal position, in a pouch of clear fluid, and waiting patiently to be born. Tiny fingers reaching out, testing the membrane. Beholding Toby, Melvin felt clean and good inside, and he knew that his brother was like the trees. Full of rings. Timeless and chubby with purpose and purity. Melvin wanted to touch him, protect him, but there was someone else standing above them. In the loft. Curtain separating the two.

"Open," Melvin thought, and the curtain spread. Folding sheets of newspaper. Crinkling. A hooded man stood on the platform, arms out like Jesus trapped in the stained glass at the back of the church, sweat marks underneath his armpits moving outwards, coating him. A layering of deep-fried grease. Wind blowing back his hood, and the man was revealed. Skinny, in navy overalls, faded knees. Smirking, smacking a rubber chicken against his thigh. Smacking, smacking. In a rhythm that made Melvin's body jerk. And smells suddenly flapped though the air, car exhaust and unwashed bodies, sour breath and cheap pine tree freshener. He had it, Melvin knew. So obvious. This man had Melvin's sense of smell.

230

As Melvin's blood began to rush about through highway tunnels, flattened disks tumbling over each other, bending, squeezing, trying to flee, he witnessed the chicken turning into a peachy colored gun, and the man aimed the flaccid barrel directly at the manger. At Toby's neonatal head. Melvin could see Toby's eyes open wide, Toby's hair like a million arms, soft and waving in the fluid. Melvin rushed forward, elephant legs, rolls of loose gray leather weighing him down. Hands now blocks of sand, ready to crush the man's narrow skull, but the tide pushed Melvin backwards, backwards, washed him towards shore. Hands dissolving, settling to the bottom of the stream, watery fingers working to knit him back inside himself. Rolling out of the water, Melvin knew he was on the side of the stream, hidden underneath a heavy book. Godly hand tearing away sheet after sheet. Weight becoming lighter. Gradually, he became aware of reinhabiting his stiff body, felt his face resting in the cold muck that oozed up between the trampled blades of sharp grass.

For a while he lay there silently, had no desire to move while the rest of him arrived from beyond. Then, just before sunrise, he felt a spirit move over him, touch down. Announcing that someone was watching him. Would take care of him, if he held onto the truths that he learned. If he believed everything that was revealed to him. A baby still lived inside Toby. Threatened. Melvin could stop searching, stop sneaking in through opened windows and unlocked doors. The thief had been revealed. And someday soon, Melvin was certain, he would kill Garrett Glass. Kill him dead.

NEAR THE TOP of a spruce tree, an owl gripped a branch with its white claws, then locked her rolling eyes on the child. Since the boy had stumbled down the short path to the stream, he had not moved, had not blinked. He lay there, head twisted to the side, body curled, one bent wing dipping into the steam. Every time he opened his mouth, the owl twitched her ear tufts, waited for a gentle hoo. But no sound emerged. And she loosened one foot, tightened, then leaned, loosened the other, tightened. The sight of this fledgling made her uneasy. Somewhere deep inside the hollow of her flight feathers she understood he was motherless, pushed too soon from his nest. Broken and lost.

A mouse quivered in the shadow of a shrub, then darted across the deadly gap of open space. Reaching the boy, it pressed its body to his hardened jeans, skittered up towards the pocket of his jacket. Nose under the flap, the mouse began to tear away strips of a hand-written note, working, working with its long yellowed teeth. Bunching the damp shreds inside inflated cheeks.

With inbred patience, the owl watched, waited, and when the moment was exactly right, she dropped from her perch, cut soundlessly through the air, diving downwards, wings extended, beak wide open. Swooped over the hapless child, and in one snap removed the tiny violator. Swallowed it whole.

THE FIRST FEW times he'd come, Lewis had been filled with anger. Tempted to take a brick and at three in the morning smash out the front windows. Destroy the one possession she somehow managed to love. Love so much more than him and his boys. But now, the anger had faded, and only a dry sadness remained. Making him suck spit from the crevices of his mouth and swallow over and over again.

Lewis arrived in the city and parked across the street. As he always did, he watched Wilda in the faint glow, dusting and rearranging. Padding among the items. Pausing to lean her head against a worn bookshelf. That night, as Lewis spied, she came to the entrance, stood there, hands touching the glass. Lewis hunched down, worried she might spot him. The humiliation of such an encounter would gut him. But soon, she turned and touched the wall. The store went black, and she dissolved into the shadows. He waited several hours more, until all the drunkards had passed without disruption, then cringed as the car growled into life, and he made the journey home.

232

Over the years, he had watched her hair grow and her style change from skirts to trousers, and the displays in her front window shift only slightly from what was there to more of the same. Not once was she out, and not once did she have company. And as much as Lewis's insides wanted him to step right up to her and ask why, his hand not once touched the handle, opened the door. His foot never met the ground of that thieving city.

IN THE EARLY morning, Toby couldn't find his note anywhere. He checked every pocket of his jacket, ran his hands down the sleeves. Had he stuffed it into Melvin's jacket pocket instead? Same style, color, only three sizes larger. Toby dropped to his knees, checked the floor of the closet, a jumble of shoes and gravel and dust balls. Nothing. His first love note had vanished, and his face went instantly red, even though he knew Melvin wouldn't rib him. Wouldn't joke. Still, when he glanced at the pen and paper, he didn't have the stomach to compose another.

He went outside, followed the rising sun until he came across a stretch of dandelions, growing in a protected area near the side of a large rock. The flowers curled outwards, just waking up, and he plucked them one at a time, wiped the sticky milk from the stems on his jeans.

He walked towards their meeting place, and smelled the intense odor of spruce, as though the warmth of morning was releasing what the night cold had consumed. By the time they met at the boulder, the flowers were closed once again and limp in his fist. He hid them behind his back, but his fist wouldn't open. Wouldn't let them drop into a shadow. And he cringed as he watched his hand move out around his side, and hold them up to her.

She stuck her nose in the handful of flaccid weeds, leaned her head onto his shoulder. He thought to tell her about the note, but decided against it. When she looked up at him and smiled, a dusting of yellow powder on her nose, he realized he didn't need to write anything. She already knew.

26

Bubble at the bottom of a thick dark drink. Knocked free, floating upwards.

"Toad! Wake up."

"Ah-huh."

Breeching the surface.

"Something happened."

"What?"

"I need to tell you something."

One eye open, Toby turned towards his brother, rigid and shaking in the bed.

"What? You had a dream?"

"No, no. I knows something."

"You knows what?"

"Someone is coming for you. Coming to get you. And I knows there's no way out from it, and these ones trying to help you can't do nothing for you. They couldn't stop no one. And I was just there and I was waiting in the dark for someone wanting to hurt you, and I couldn't look everywhere at once, and I had to turn my head, and even though I got us into a corner, I still couldn't see everywhere I needed to see, and I couldn't even breathe, like someone was stomping on my chest, and I knew it was only a matter of time before someone showed up to kill you. Take your life away. Leave you in the black. And I decided then and there I'd rather put a gun in my mouth before I sees someone do that to you."

Silence.

234

"You fucking fall asleep on me?"

Eyes wide open at the sound of Melvin's queer trembling voice. "No."

"Someone's coming for you."

"No, they idn't. Was just a dream, Mellie."

"'Twas fucking real, man. Scared the shit right out of me." Flapped the covers.

"It was just a dream, I said. I wouldn't lie to you."

"Yeah. Not like everyone else."

"No one lies."

"They do, Toad. They all do. Someone's coming to get you. Maybe me, too. But I don't care about me. You got to be safe, Toad. Safe."

"I got no one coming for me, Mellie. I swears."

"You do. You do." Starting to whimper. "I knows, Toad."

"Did you take something?"

"What do that mean?"

"I means did you swallow something that might, you know, give you funny dreams or something?"

"It idn't dinner, Toad. You don't get it. Don't you hear the rumbling?"

"What rumbling?"

"Like a piece of junk car. Idling."

"There's no car, Mellie."

"Listen!"

"Okay, okay." He didn't understand, and the sound of his brother's mewing frightened Toby beyond anything he'd ever known. He would fight to the death for his brother, but how could he fight something he couldn't see? Couldn't hear?

"Someone's coming. Things is gonna change soon. Soon. And I can't see everywhere. I got blind spots."

"Is your head hurting? Should I get Dad?"

"No, fuck, no."

Melvin lay ramrod straight, and his skinny body shook in the bed.

"You sleep, Mellie."

"Can't."

"Yes, you can. You don't be scared, Mellie. Sleep and I'll watch for a while. I'm a good watcher. I won't barely blink."

After a while, Melvin turned on his side, brought his knees up towards his chest, and Toby lay next to him, curled his body around his brother's, trying to hold what was left together. He felt the sharp points of Melvin's spine through the damp T-shirt, wished he knew how to pad them. Lids pressed back, Toby kept his promise as best he could. Stayed awake. His owl eyes trying to find some light in the darkness.

A ROLL OF pure white shag. Garrett's final payment. He'd lost his job at Clarey's Paints and Carpets after working reliably for six years. Most people would guess he was fired, or maybe he simply didn't perform well enough as a salesperson. But nothing could be further from the truth. Garrett quit. Plain and simple. He told Mr. Clarey that he would never set foot in his store again.

What started innocently enough turned into something vile. Eventually, Garrett understood, it was bound to. During those years of work, Garrett and Mr. Clarey rarely conversed, and when they did, Mr. Clarey never met Garrett's eyes. Instead, the man gazed at Garrett's throat, at his Adam's apple. And Garrett was aware of this look of appetite in his eyes, as though the three cans of wieners hadn't quite filled him up. Garrett didn't trust Mr. Clarey. Not in the least. A man who often pressed his nose into a roll of underpad, inhaling deeply.

Mr. Clarey had called Garrett into his office at closing that day, and when Garrett slipped in through the door, Mr. Clarey asked him to close it.

"Close it?"

"Yes, my son. This is a business meeting, idn't it? These things got to happen behind closed doors." And, eyes fixed on Garrett's swallowing throat, Mr. Clarey winked. Winked.

"Oh. Oh, okay." Garrett was nervous that he'd been found out. Perhaps Mr. Clarey had discovered the box containing his supply of carpet cutters was nearly empty. Garrett had stolen over a dozen of them, hated to not have one in his pocket, in his hand. The clicking blade had become a source of comfort.

"Come 'round here," he said, and patted the chair next to his. "Come have a look, my son."

Garrett stepped around the wooden desk, and sat down on the chair. Seats nearly touching.

"You want a drink?" Mr. Clarey hauled open the lowest drawer to his right, plucked out a bottle.

"No. No sir."

"Suit yourself, my son."

And Garrett watched as he opened the bottle, splashed an ounce or two into the glass. Mr. Clarey had clean, shiny fingernails, and hairy fingers that made Garrett nervous. Garrett imagined Mr. Clarey could touch anything with those stubby, pale digits, and no one would ever feel upset. Think there was something wrong. Innocent doctor's fingers. "Really, Mr. Clarey. I got to be on my way."

"Hold your horse, boy. I wants to talk to you."

"You do?" Garrett's blood began to flow faster.

Mr. Clarey sat back in his chair, screwed joints creaking when pushed off onto the two back legs. He rubbed his bulbous belly. One leg bent and up, trousers climbing, and Garrett stared straight ahead, would not allow the bare skin on Mr. Clarey's leg to come into view. "Glass, you knows I got a boy, right?"

"A boy?"

"Yes. My boy, Wayne."

"Oh, yes. Wayne."

"My son. And I knows, after these years, you heard me complaining about his lifestyle. Having babies with any woman he could poke it into," a nudge here, "working just enough to pay for his booze. He don't want nothing respectable."

"Okay, Mr. Clarey. Okay."

Mr. Clarey snapped back to four legs, put his arm around Garrett, and drew him closer. "Have a look at this paper," he said.

Garrett saw a jumble of numbers and rows, and smelled Mr. Clarey's breath and some spicy cologne. He was close enough to count the deep pores on his gullet, to fear what lived behind those whiskers crawling out of his nose.

"We've had a stellar year," Mr. Clarey announced, and he leaned over, gently slapped Garrett's thigh. "Best ever. And I got some wonderful news. I wants you, Gary. I wants you."

Shallow breaths, dizziness, and the numbers blurred. Garrett looked down, trembled as he saw Mr. Clarey's hand, five, ten, fifteen fat white fingers. Touching him. *I wants you.* He could feel the dirty adoration through the thin wool of his dress pants, and as he watched those fingers lay there until they aged a year or more, teasing, teasing, then slid down the side of his thigh, returned to their rightful space. *I wants you.*

"We're moving up. Bigger space. More selection. People is loving their floor coverings, and putting out good dollars to make their homes nice. We's on a roll, my son." Chuckle. "No pun intended. And you're the best there is. You know that? You could sell ice to the Eskimos, as they says. I wants you to be my right-hand man. Do you hear me, Gary? Do you hear me, my boy?"

But Garrett didn't hear a word of it. He stood, knocked over his chair.

"No," he breathed. "No, Mr. Clarey. I won't do nothing no more."

"What?"

"You got to find someone else. 'Cause I won't be your boy."

Mr. Clarey shook his head. "I'm real surprised you feels that way. I thought we had a good thing going."

"We never had nothing going. Nothing at all." Garrett reached into his pocket, felt the carpet cutter. Gripped it, slid his fingers up to release the blade. He'd do it if he had to.

"So, you're done?"

"I'm done."

"Done, done?"

"Yes, Mr. Clarey."

"Well, well, well." Still shaking his head, arms folded across his chest. "I owes you. Eight days. You can come back for that."

"I won't then."

"Well, we got to settle something. I don't want to be owing someone. That's not the way I does business."

Garrett looked around. Saw a leftover roll in the corner. "I'll take that. White shag." And I'll keep the carpet cutter in my pocket. Click out, click in.

"Go on, then. If that's what you wants. But I tell you, you got me run right over. I thought we was a team, Glass. You and me. Putting down carpet in every house in Knife's Point."

Garrett plucked up the roll and ran out the back door. He darted down the alleyway and into the street. A group moved past him, dipping in and out of stores, nodding and smiling. Acting strangely normal. Garrett didn't understand the world. Didn't understand the people living in it. But he knew enough not to strip naked, even though, more than anything, he wanted the bright sunlight to clean his skin.

"DAD?"

"Yes, my son."

Toby leaned against the doorway of his father's room. A square space filled with papers and books and hooks and feathers and rods and reels. As the years went on, Toby found his father spent more and more time tucked away inside that room, hunched over a tying vice, fashioning miniscule flies that were never used.

Toby's palms were sweaty, tongue dry. He was about to open his mouth, and betray his brother.

"I needs to talk to you."

His father didn't turn to face Toby. Instead, he reached up and angled the neck on the silver lamp.

"Now?"

"Um, I guess so."

"Shoot. I'm all ears."

"Well. I. Well."

Toby heard a gentle chuckle, saw his father's shoulders lifting and falling. "Is this girl problems, Toby? You'd be barking up the wrong tree if it is. Maybe Mrs. Verge can give you some advice. She's a wonderful lady, really wonderful. You know that?"

"No, no. Not girls."

His father swiveled around, looked at him over the top of his glasses. "What is it, then? You in trouble?"

Toby reached behind him, pinched his own back, and spat it out. "Mellie. It's Mellie. I needs to talk to you 'bout Mellie."

Instant redness in his father's pale cheeks, accelerator pushed, words rushing out. "I got nothing to say about your brother. He got to pull himself together, 'cause believe you me, believe you me, Toby, as soon as that boy hits eighteen, he's gone. Earlier, if I can't take it no more."

"I don't think he's right, Dad."

"Damn right he's not right. Hasn't got a word in his head to say to me. Gawking at me all the time like I done him over. When I haven't done nothing but work to put food on his plate and clothes on his back."

"He talks to me. Talks to me a lot."

"I don't want to hear none of it."

Toby bit his lip, stood up straight. "I think he's fooled up, Dad. In the head. Fooled up. He keeps saying awful queer stuff. Sometimes in the middle of the night."

"Waking you up?"

"Um. Yeah."

"You keep your door locked, my son. He got his own room for years now, and he got no business bugging you when you needs your sleep."

"I don't mind."

"Well, you should. You needs to focus on finishing school. Getting a decent job. Making yourself into something."

Toby felt the air in his lungs grow heavier. "I'll be alright, Dad."

240

"I'll tell you something, Tobe. Just to let you know what we're dealing with here. You remember when all those homes got broken into?"

"Yeah."

"Well, that was your brother. Your very own brother."

"What?"

"Yes. Your brother. No doubt in my mind, though I didn't catch the bugger. He's lucky he gave it up."

"I don't think—"

"Well, I don't got to think. I knowed. Got no idea what was going through his mind, what he was after. Boggles the brain, it do. And I would've hauled him in, too. Treated him no different than any other beggar. There's no honor there, my son. Not one ounce."

"Mellie wouldn't—"

"And let me tell you something else, Toby. I've been around a lot, and I seen what's coming into this place as fast as some crowds can carry it. And that old crap'll mess with your mind. Confuse the shit right out of you. Christ, two nights back, I had one rabble-rouser out doing a jig on Widow Murray's lawn, going on about leprechauns and clovers, and then not four hours later I had another young feller up crowing on his roof. Thinking he was a bloody rooster. Could've at least waited until the sun was coming up, don't you think?"

Toby smirked slightly, nodded.

"I can promise you this, Toad. If your brother ever cleans himself up, settles back down, he'll be as good as new. As long as he's got his nose in the gutter, he's going to talk garbage. There idn't a single thing wrong with him that he hasn't brought on himself. And there idn't a single thing we can do to fix him."

"You sure?"

"I seen enough to know."

Toby sighed, allowed the faintest breeze of relief to touch him. "Don't tell Mellie I was on about him, alright?"

"Don't you worry none. You go on, now. Find your friend, what's-his-name, and tell him to get his face out of that book."

"Ween?"

"See if he wants a job."

"Alright."

"Beds got more weeds, now, than vegetables. Mrs. Verge, Peggy, went to all kinds of trouble to plant it, and we needs to look after it. Show her we cares. You and your friend work a few hours, and I'll pay you both."

"Really? How much?"

"Oh, enough to make you both happy, I reckon." He swiveled around, picked up a few strands of hair from a scrap of buck tail, started twisting black thread, attaching it to his fly. "Now get on," he said over his shoulder, "before the day is already over."

LEWIS TOOK A deep breath, leaned his rib bones against the table. Pressed for a moment until it hurt. Then he slumped back in his chair, looked down at the fly he was making. Too much head cement, and the eyelet was coated. Useless, now. He could never attach a line unless he scraped it out, and he couldn't be bothered with that. Loosening the vice, he plucked the fly from the jaws, threw it into the plastic garbage pail near his feet.

Lewis made a fist, stood up from his chair. He hated this feeling lodged in his craw for so many years. Now thriving there. He could cough and cough, and not dislodge it. So many times he had talked up one side of Melvin and down the other, and not a word moved through the boy. And though Lewis could barely admit it, it was true. Some part of him had given up trying to find Melvin. No longer sought him out. His son, filling the air around Lewis, but rarely present. Lewis had taken his place on the edge of the woods. Always waiting, blind and wobbly, not understanding a shred.

MRS. FAGAN HEARD a rumble, pulled the curtain aside in time to see Garrett's brown Chevette easing down the gravel drive. The car stopped, and she watched him climb out, reach into the backseat, struggle with something. Bending over, yanking, his

242

grip slipped, and her son fell backwards on the crushed stone. Not a curse from his lips, he was up again, brushing away the dust from his trousers, grabbing, finally hauling out a roll of carpet he must have crammed into the small space.

She went to the door, called through the screen. "You need a hand, my son?"

"No, I got it."

"You buy that?"

He carried it in the crook of bent elbows. "Nope. He give it to me."

Mrs. Fagan extended her arm, opened the door and allowed him to pass. "Why, that was nice of Mr. Clarey. You must be a hard worker."

"I is."

"I knows, my son. I knows."

She watched Garrett balance the carpet, making his way through the kitchen, into the hallway, up the stairs. He paused, halfway, called down to her. "You want this in your room? I can keep the blue one."

"Oh, my Lord, no," she replied. "You deserves it. Put it down on your own floor."

"You sure? It don't get no nicer."

"I'm sure."

He clamored up the rest of the stairs, closed his bedroom door.

Mrs. Fagan sighed. Somehow, this house, rickety and full of whispers, had become a home for herself and her son. Even though he was fully grown, he lived with her still. In the room he had occupied since he was a boy. When her older daughter was grown, Mrs. Fagan had rooted her out, and she would do the same with the younger girl, as soon as possible. But Garrett would stay. Garrett was a good boy, strange, yes, different, yes, but he was a decent son. Maybe she hadn't loved him enough, or protected him from Eli. Maybe he had been damaged somehow, when lost under the ice pans for those long minutes. But what sort of son offers up a reward he has earned to his useless old mother?

She went to her son's room, opened the door, and there he was, on his knees, spreading out a scrap of beautiful carpet. "Looks nice," she said. "Might be hard to keep clean."

"I'll be careful, he said. "I won't make a stain."

"No, you won't," she replied. "I'm sure you won't." Garrett Wesley Glass was a good boy. A good man. No one could tell her any differently.

27

FOUR TIMES THE phone had rung that afternoon. Four times he had answered it. No one there, only a faint guttural sound on the other end. He screamed into the receiver, screamed that he would come through the wires and beat the living shit out of whatever was on the other end. "Do you hear me, you fucker? Do you hear me?" But there was no response, and the strained croaking gradually petered out, replaced by trickling water. Receiver clenched in his fist, he busted holes in the wallpaper, and then, with one swift yank, Melvin tore the entire phone from the kitchen wall, slammed it onto the floor.

He popped down the back steps, ran to the swelling stream. Something was coming, he had known it. And he was right. Someone or something was trying to send him a message, trying to tell him what to do. Messages everywhere. Letters in the crooks of the branches, I's, L's, K's. Though he pulled them out, lined them up inside his mind, he couldn't decipher them. Ilk. Lik. Ikl. The letters wouldn't make words, wouldn't reveal their meaning. He tried to light a joint, but the twist of paper slipped from his trembling hands, lost among the trampled grass, icy muck. He wished for a bottle of beer, a mouthful of rum, anything to numb this hyperawareness. Spaces were opening up inside his head, pockets full of shadows, seams ripping. What will it take to fill me up?

As he paced up and down the edge of the stream, wind whistled in his ears, turned his face in different directions. Look here. No there. Try up here. Look there. Like a frightened bird, his head flicked left and right, scanning and assessing, trying to ride out the drums beating in his blood, as they hailed forthcoming understanding. Marching towards him. Marching towards him. It's coming. Then, at the very tip of the stream, where the river wound its way around a gentle turn, Melvin saw something. Drifting down the center, lazily, riding the tiny ripples, dipping beneath the black surface, rising up again. He crouched down, fingers in the mud to balance himself, and he was silent as his eyes grew the vision of an eagle. He focused in on the remains. Boom. A body, splayed like a newborn's, pale underside, arms and legs outstretched and bowed at the joints. He saw a white rounded jaw, belly spread out on either side. A drowned toad. A dead toad. Toad. Toad. Gliding closer to him like nothing at all. Boom, boom.

And it all made sense. Wooden puzzle pieces snapping together inside that open space. The sounds on the phone. The croaking. The trickling water. The letters in the trees. Kill. Kill. Kill. Boom. No time for questions, no time for weakness. Melvin understood what he had to do. This was his final warning. The time was now. He closed his eyes, saw the colored picture plastered on his eyelids. Of a man. A man who would die.

He turned on his heel, raced back towards home. Was unable to see that the item floating down the river was nothing more than a scrap of birch bark.

GARRETT CAME UPON the young boy while he was strolling on the beach. The child, maybe seven or eight, was seated on damp stones, chewing a hole through the cuff of his wool sweater. First glance in the dimming light, and Garrett thought he looked familiar. Something in the bulge of his cheeks, eyes too close together, smooshed nose. Maybe the old gray coat on his back, matted fur encircling the hood. Though he couldn't quite place him, parts of Garrett's body sensed he had known the child before.

Within a few feet of the boy, Garrett tripped slightly, palm coming down on a dead sea urchin, brittle spineless dome crushing under his weight. "Shit."

246

Mouth open, damp sweater falling from his mouth, the boy stared, wide-eyed.

Even though it never hurt a bit, Garrett crouched, inspected his hand, flinched and shook it. He squeezed his thumb, licked, as though it were bleeding. "That sure do smart." He directed his voice out over the sea, careful not to speak to the boy. It was best, Garrett had learned, to let them speak first.

Only a second or two, and the boy piped up. "Sure, I sliced my foot up on some rusty tin can when I was six. Doctor gave me a needle this big."

Garrett glanced over casually, saw the boy's hands two feet apart. "That make you cry, kid?"

"Not one bit. I don't cry over nothing."

Light laughter. "Well, now. I hates needles. I'd squeal like an animal if 'twas me." Garrett leaned his head back, let out a high-pitched piggy yelp, ended with a few snuffles.

The boy giggled, and Garrett saw the rotted front teeth, adult teeth, and knew that the boy liked sugar. And when the smile lingered, Garrett could tell that the boy would also like a friend.

"You chewed a good hole through your sweater, there, guy."

"Yeah."

"When I was little, I did that too. When I was nervous. You nervous?"

"Nah. Just hungry," he said, and laughed again. "My nan got dyed beets or something, and she don't eat no cookies or nothing. Won't have it in the house. And all she cooks is fish and brewis for supper. I told her I'd rather eat glue than that junk."

"Whoa."

"She said sometimes hot dogs rolls up on the beach. So, I'm waiting."

Garrett nodded. Thoughtful voice, "You might be waiting a long old time."

The boy sighed, and his mouth hung open just a crack, full bottom lip. Garrett cocked his head, couldn't resist staring at the boy, at his mouth. That familiar feeling washed through him again, and then he remembered. So many years ago. The boy in the fishing shack. That boy. Garrett had brought him scraps of food. Sometimes salvaged from the dog's dish. What was his name? Garrett had no idea. But he could blink, and see the photographs. The shape of the boy's calf. The flabby lobe of his perfect ear. The small of his back, right where his body split in two. Blood rushed through Garrett's veins, and the beach tilted slightly beneath his feet. Sweaty palms, and he licked his thumb again, tasted salt.

Garrett had this overwhelming desire to grab the boy, cup a hand firmly over his mouth, steal back to Eli's house. No one was home, and no one would catch him. But the boy might fight, might kick or bite. Garrett touched the fabric of his pocket, traced the outline of the carpet cutter. Somebody just might get hurt. Better to talk him there. Try that first.

"Do you know what a map is, kid?"

"Yeah, sure. Who don't?"

"You ever meet anyone who makes maps?"

He shook his head.

"I made one once. When I was younger. Had to hire someone about your age."

"What?"

Garrett smiled. "That's right. The last feller I hired needed a few dollars. I reckons you could use that, too. Buy yourself some chips and gravy. Half dozen hot dogs."

"Really?"

"Yes, sir. You're half growed, half a man, my son. You should be able to make some decisions on your own, right?"

Garrett was resolved, he would do whatever it took. He wanted to keep this one.

IN THE EVENING light, Toby stood in a pile of fine damp saw-dust, one hand gripping the wet spruce, the other pushing the blade down through the wood. Almost through, and he cracked the junk away from the log, watched it fall into the small mound to the left of the wood horse. He wiped his running nose on his

248

glove, took a clear deep breath. The sweet scent of wood and the newly arriving cold air, tinged with chimney smoke, filled his lungs, and for a moment made him happy.

Toby hauled the shortened log over the horse, began to saw again, when he noticed a shadow form cutting a straight line across the front grass. Without question, Toby could identify the shape of his brother's thin shoulders, oversized coat, legs like whittled sticks. He watched Melvin stomping over crushed stone, every muscle flexed. "Hey, Melvin!" Toby shouted, but Melvin did not turn or look, just leaned forward, propelled into the house, taking the stairs two at a time.

Waiting there in the yellowish light of the porch, Toby's blood began to move in the way it often did when something was about to happen. He let the saw hang by his side, and could feel the weight of it tugging at his wrist. Moments passed before his fingers opened, and the saw dropped. Teeth biting into the tender bark of a log. Toby walked slowly towards the back steps. Took them one at a time. The clanging sounds coming from inside the house stopped suddenly, and Toby paused. Breathed rapidly. Waited for a burst of nerve to arrive inside his stomach. Ah, there it was, and he jumped the last two steps, clamored into the house.

Inside the kitchen, cupboards and drawers hung open, rifled though. Knives and forks spilled onto the linoleum. Phone wires sticking out of the wall, three perfect circular holes, receiver still stuck in one. But no sign of Melvin. He was gone. The house was empty.

GARRETT HAULED AN old box out from underneath his bed, let the boy pick through it. Sepia-toned hockey cards, a bag of cat's eye marbles, a handful of dinkies with chipped paint.

"You can have something if you wants."

"Really?"

"Yeah."

"Gee, thanks."

The boy scratched his chin, choosing carefully among six or more comic books.

"Do you want a bar?"

"Sure. I likes bars."

Garrett reached up behind him, grabbed a Turkish Delight, handed it over. "You can trust me, you know."

"Yeah?" he said, peeling the wrapper off, jamming two curves into his mouth. Mouth full, mumbling, "My nanny tole me neba trust no one who say dat. Means you canned. Daz why dey's sayin' it."

Garrett laughed, ran his fingers through his piece of white shag.

"I think she was mad at my pop. Doing stuff that idn't no good."

"Sometimes pops is like that. Doing no good."

"Yeah."

"I just want to be your chum is all."

"Don't you got no chums your own age?"

"Well, it's hard."

"Why?"

"Just is, is all. I don't know why."

"'Cause you looks funny?"

Garrett laughed again, touched his hair, the tiny scar on his upper lip. He felt more charming than he had in ages. "Do I, now?"

The boy shifted, crossed his legs, and Garrett could see a hole in the bottom of the child's dirty sock. A flash of pink skin beneath.

"Hey, what's that?" the boy said, nodding towards the arm of a threadbare chair.

Garrett plucked it up. "A carpet knife. I got lots of them. I used to be a carpet man."

"I thought you made maps."

"One map." Garrett coughed. "That stuff is hard work, you know. Can't be doing it all the time."

"Oh."

"Never mind. Want to see?"

"Yeah."

Click, click, click, Garrett gripped the orange plastic, pushed his thumb up the side, blade extending. "Want to try?"

"Yeah." The boy played with it for a moment, ribbon of metal clicking in and out. Turning it in the light so that it glistened. Click, click.

"Careful. 'Tis like a razor. Could take part of you right off." Licking his lips.

The boy retracted the blade, lay it back on the armrest. "You got more bars, Mister? One don't never fill me up."

"Yeah, I got lots more."

"I wants one."

Garrett crossed his legs, too, leaned his chin on his hand. "Well, chum, you got to take that shirt off."

"My shirt?"

"Yeah."

"Why for?"

"I needs to see your muscles. Make sure you're in good shape. Can't be stuffing your face with bars if you're already covered in fat, right?"

The boy jumped up, tossed aside his dirty coat, hauled his jersey top over his head. He punched his naked stomach lightly with one fist, then the other. "I got muscles," he said, faux growl in his throat. "I got good muscles. Do you want me to lift you up? I can, you know. You don't think, but I can. Lift you right off the ground, Mister. Roaaarr."

Garrett covered his mouth with his hand, shook his head. "No, no," he breathed. "You'd hurt yourself." Sweat trickled down between his shoulder blades, and he knew, beneath his overalls, his skin was flushed. He got up off the floor, went to his night table. The drawer scraped open, dry wood against dry wood, and that sound obscured a second noise on the floor below. A pair of rusty hinges, the back door grinding open.

GARRETT GLASS. Melvin knew the way to his house. He'd been there many times before. Not so long ago, he'd spent many mornings hanging from the tree out back, watching Garrett's sleaze of a sister flash her pasty skin.

Damp hand on a cold metal handle, Melvin opened the door slowly, and walked inside. He stuck his nose in the air and sniffed. Like a feral dog, he sought some thread on the air, and was not surprised when he found it. An odor, droning low. When he glanced about in the dim light, he saw the source, a pot on its side, blackened bottom. Another sniff, and other smells threaded their way through the dim light. His nose, useful once again, detected the stale fat from a deep fryer, a cluster of bananas turning black on the windowsill. This was the right place. Garrett Glass was the thief. Melvin had no doubts, now.

He slipped out of his shoes, and in his yellowish socks crept across the kitchen floor, into a hallway, up the narrow staircase. He kept low, back bent, hands touching each step, two up from his feet. His blood pooled in his chest, pulsing, pulsing, and Melvin knew that if he didn't listen, didn't act right now, nothing would ever be the same again. In some world, some other space, his feet had made this walk a million times, and they knew where to tread. Not a single creak from the wide floorboards. In his hand he gripped the wooden handle of a serving fork. Two sharp shiny prongs. When Melvin had pulled open the drawers in his own kitchen, this was the only utensil that glinted.

In the upstairs hallway, Melvin found the room. An amber glow eked out from the cracks where door met frame, the inch of space that had been shaved from the bottom. Melvin stood there, holding the fork behind his back, staring at the rectangle of blackness, the circumference of light. No place to think. No choice to make. He was the only one. To open the door and bring out the brightness. Kill that man, hiding in the closet. That man, hiding under the bed. A thief. A threat.

Behind him, the phone screamed. Once, twice. And Melvin turned to stare at the black contraption, receiver jumping off

252

the hook. Three rings. The shrillness moved through Melvin's body, and he knew who was calling. To check. To see. Go on. Hurry. Yes, he would. He paused for only a moment, wiped his stomach with his left hand. He knew there was a glass tunnel of churning water living in there. Filled with tadpoles and debris, a bunch of loose snapshots no eye should ever see. It often made him feel like vomiting. But if he finished his task, did what was required of him, the water, his insides, would be clean, pure. Not so much as a ripple moving through.

Someone held Melvin. He felt parts moving over parts, cradling his arms, taking his hands, so gently, a puppet on a taut string. This is the right thing. The only thing. He nodded, was thankful for the guidance, did not resist. Watched his hand open the door, and on a tongue of wind he was carried inside. Face to face with Garrett Glass. The devil in navy overalls.

Garrett sprung up from the ground, hovered, his bare feet just inches above a flat white cloud. He opened his mouth, and Melvin could hear a sudden stutter, Garrett spitting foreign words. "What the hell? You better get yourself gone, 'fore I gets the shotgun!" Melvin sniffed the air, could smell the lie of sugar, and the truth of grown-up sweat. He brought the fork around, and Garrett's skinny white wings fluttered up, palms outwards, "Hey, hey, hey, now, now, now. Just wait. I got money. Whatever you wants, b'y. Just wait. You can have my carpet. Just wait, now. Now, now, now, now." One wing, dipping down, and Melvin saw the man clutch something, heard a click, click, click.

Melvin didn't hesitate, lunged forward. Stabbed with sudden force. Buried the two shiny prongs of the serving fork deep into Garrett's gut. They came together, for a moment, hugging, almost like old friends, and Melvin felt the full weight of the man against his chest.

Warmth seeped through Melvin's clothes, and then, as he opened his arms to release, something pierced his side. Garrett fell backwards, struck the wall, and Melvin looked down at his own belly, lifted his shirt. He'd been cut, too. In the shape of a pink smile. Red beading formed at the corners. He knew his tunnel had been sliced, bright water was beginning to leak out. Streaming. He took three steps backwards, sensed two segments of flesh, top and bottom, once knitted together, now slipping against each other. A pair of greasy lips. He slumped back against the bed, breathed deeply.

Liquid coursed down his shirt, over his faded jeans, but Melvin was not alarmed. The fear that had held him by his throat for months and months had evaporated. And he lifted his face to the ceiling. To the sky. The temperature in the room dropped, and he began to shiver. It was then he noticed a boy, hunched, a few feet to his left. Melvin leaned, tumbled onto his side, his elbow sinking into the soggy shag. He looked down at his hand, now a snowflake, and he watched the ice crystals crawl out towards the little boy. Crawl backwards through his body. Shivering harder now. Color draining from his lips. "We can go home now, Toad." He moved his crystal fingers further. To touch his brother. A second snowflake. Touch him, and bridge the space in between.

STANDING INSIDE THE kitchen, Toby was shaking. Even though the spoons and forks were quiet on the floor, the aggression was still cutting through the air. He stared at the holes in the wall, the broken phone, and suddenly he wanted to talk to Angie. Wanted to talk to her badly. Even though they'd been going together for a full year, Toby had never called her. They had worked to keep everything between them a secret, but at that moment he had to talk to her. He needed to hear her say that everything would turn out okay. No matter how bad it got, a time would come when life would be normal. Life would be kind. "Another storm," he'd say, using their private code. "Occurring or imminent," she might reply. "Squall already moved through. Damages moderate."

He unplugged the phone in the kitchen, ran to the hallway. Dialed her number, let it ring. Once, twice, three times. Then a pang in his stomach made him hang up. Her voice would not be enough for him right now. He would have to see her smiling face, her solid body. Smell her hair, the faint smell of her scalp, and have proof that she exists. Tonight he would march up to her door, stare her mother and father straight in their squinting eyes, and tell them "She may sleep under your roof, but the one part that keeps her alive belongs to me. And there idn't nothing you can do about it." If Mr. Fagan held up his battered fists, challenged him? After a whole year of secrecy, Toby had had enough. Tonight, if gloves were raised, he would strike the old man down. Beat him into a mushy speechless pulp. Anything for a sliver of her love.

Tugging a wool hat down over his ears, he stomped through the kitchen, out into the night. In a flutter of a wing, he reached her door. Courage tempered by the brisk walk, he tapped lightly, rephrased the words that sat on his tongue. "Might I see your daughter? Might I talk to Angie for a minute?" No one answered his tapping, and Toby pressed his face hard against the metal screening, stared into the kitchen. Someone had left a light on over the stove, and it threw a faint glow on the mound of shoes and jackets in the porch. Then, as he was about to turn and walk home, he spotted something. Just beside a plastic bucket of metal pieces, Toby spied another pair of shoes. Separate from the others, neatly laid side by side. Sneakers, white with blue stripes, heels worn where the owner scuffed. Toby knew they were Melvin's.

Courage moved out of his heart and into his muscles. He opened the screen door, and stepped in. Took three more steps into the kitchen. Directly above his head he heard scrambling sounds, and his stomach flip-flopped, contents squelching. Without thinking, he moved through the kitchen and into the hallway, slowly moved up the staircase, step by step. Found a door ajar, and he knocked it with his toe, closed his eyes as it creaked open.

Blood everywhere. On the walls, the carpet. Toby sucked in his breath, saw Garrett Glass, slumped, holding his stomach.

Sheer curtains billowed with the salty wind, and when they parted, Toby saw a pair of young fingers, gripping the sill, slipping, slipping, then a loud thunk as the owner fell to the earth below. Toby rushed to the window, stared out across over the moonlit backyard, saw a child, pale arms and back, limping over the frozen lawn. He turned, discovered a layer of his brother's clothes on the opposite side of the room, strangely full as though they were stuffed with bloody hay. Surely, it's just his clothes. Just his clothes. Just his clothes. Toby tilted his head, tilted, and his knees nearly folded when he saw Melvin's hands, his head, somehow tucked under the metal bedframe, hidden.

He ran to Melvin, hauled him out, wrapped his arms around his torso, squeezed. Melvin's bloody clothes were slippery against Toby's skin, and Toby tried to sit him up, then thought to lay him flat. "Shush, shush," he whispered into Melvin's cold ear. "Someone's coming for you. Someone's coming. Going to be alright."

"Help!" he cried. "Help him!" But no one answered.

His brother lay dying. Toby began to whimper. No one was coming, and he was too afraid to get up and find their phone. He needed to hold his brother, hold Melvin, and be present. He couldn't allow himself to steal away inside his own head. Melvin would not die alone.

ELI FAGAN TRIPPED over the shoes in the front porch. "Christ Almighty." A pair of white and blue sneakers right in the middle of the mat. For several moments, he stared at those sneakers, wondering where they belonged. Whose feet had just been in them.

Something propelled him forward. Made him aware. In the kitchen, he looked up, saw a bright bug near the fluorescent light. Closer inspection, the bug was growing, spreading outwards, not a bug at all. He stood directly underneath it, and watched as a black drop formed, fell, struck him on the forehead. Reaching up, he wiped it, looked at the blood on his dirty fingers.

256

Upstairs, he could hear someone grousing, and he gripped the banister, ascended the stairs as fast as his prickly bones would carry him.

Once inside his stepson's bedroom, Eli's farmer mind calculated things at an extraordinary rate. He saw Garrett lift a hand towards him, heard him moan, "Me, father. Meee." And he recognized the Trench boys, one clinging to the limp body of the other. He clenched his jaw, rubbed a hand over a wrinkled forehead, spoke, "Get away from him."

Toby was defiant, didn't budge. "No, sir. I won't."

"Get on, I said."

"I won't let go."

But Eli Fagan gripped his arm, yanked, broke Toby's grasp. Then he stepped behind Melvin, eased the boy back, put a pillow under his head. Felt his clothes, fabric already sticking to the wound. He didn't lift the clothes away, removed his own shirt instead, balled it and applied pressure.

"Go," he said to Toby. "Call."

"Call?"

Eli shook his head. "Call the operator, my son. Call your father. In the hallway."

Toby stood there, mouth gaping, lungs constricting.

"Go," Eli growled this time. "Don't got much time."

"You got to save him, Mr. Fagan. You got to. He's my brother."

Toby found a phone in the hallway, perched on a tiny table, chair attached. He scooped up the receiver, stuck his finger in the right hole, twisted all the way, waited ages for the plastic dial to reorient itself, number to connect.

"Operator."

"Missus Bussey? Missus Bussey?"

"Yes, darling."

"We needs help. I'm at the Fagan farm. My brother is hurt."

"Who's this?"

"It's Toby."

"Okay, lovey. Hurt bad?"

"Yes, yes. Bleedin'. Bad. Cut."

"Oh, my lovey, lovey. Oh my. Just one sec, and I'll get some-one out there." He heard her making another call, after a moment, she returned. "Want me to call your dad?"

"Yeah." He sat down. Closed his eyes.

"I got him here for you," Mrs. Bussey said after a moment. "I'll connect."

Toby took a deep breath, felt his father on the other end before he even spoke.

"You there, Toad?"

Toby couldn't speak. Words hitched in his throat. Incompre-hensible. How could he form the sentences, tell his father that Melvin's goodness was drifting away? Drifting out through that open window, and Toby was unable to close it.

PART FIVE

28

MOST AFTERNOONS THAT fall, Mrs. Verge prepared warm meals in
the Trench kitchen, rabbit covered in pastry or stew and dump-
lings. Tonight, she served up mounds of steaming pasta with
spicy sauce of ground meat and tomatoes. "You won't believe
that's moose," she said as she laid two plates on the table. But
most of it went uneaten, Toby being absent, and Lewis's stomach unable to accept more than a spoonful. He picked at the rest,
rearranged it on his plate, and finally scraped back his chair
and left the table.

"I'm sorry," he said. "Was delicious, though. What I tried of it."

"Yes, I allows."

"No, no really. It was good." He put his fist to his stomach,
pushed. "Toby'll eat for sure when he gets home."

"You can try again later," she said as she placed a second plate
upside-down on the first, slid the works into the fridge. "You
got to be gentle on yourself. You got to remind yourself you
done the best you could."

Lewis shook his head, put his hand up to stop her. He
couldn't hear those kind lies. "I'm going out," he said.

"Working?"

"No. Remember they sent in that young feller? Wish they
didn't. Gives me too much time on my hands."

"Oh, yes. Blessing in disguise if you asks me. Working yourself into the ground all these years. Nothing wrong with a bit of
help."

"No, nothing wrong," he said as he took his coat, shut the
door quietly behind him. He closed his eyes, leaned the back of

his head against the door, felt the moist air on his cheeks for a moment, and then walked down the steps.

He wandered over the dirt road, picked his way through an overgrown path in the woods. The brisk movement calmed the sadness that had settled into his legs. He hadn't intended to go anywhere in particular, but that night he found himself standing on the edge of Eli Fagan's backyard. Face against a wet tree, he stared out over an expanse of slick black grass. The house and barn were dark, empty, nothing more than uncertain silhouettes in the night. Maybe there, maybe not. He reached up, touched a low branch, fingers running over the knobby bark. Instantly, he could imagine Roy. Bounding through the woods, his strong shoulders and back oiled with sweat, perhaps even gripping that very branch, swinging, and then tumbling out into the backyard. Towards his own death. Lewis moved out from his shelter, spray transformed into icy drizzle. He walked a dozen steps straight ahead. Squinting, he managed to see the remains of the old barrel, a circle of rusting teeth sticking up out of the tired lawn.

When he reached it, Lewis stomped the edges, and some of it crumpled, a shard of it stuck into his boot. He sat down in a sodden patch, thought about how his brother's blood was still here, on this very spot, still feeding the grass and the earthworms, and the dandelions. Still breaking down every winter as life decayed. Picked up again when spring fought its way back through the snow. If. If, on that day, I had kept my head stuck underneath that sink. I had opened a can of beans and wieners to feed his crying stomach. I had grabbed his wrist before he tore off through the woods. I had held him tighter on this very spot. I had said good-bye.

Cold winds slid across Lewis's open mouth, and he found it difficult to breathe. These days all he thought about was Roy. He could do that, stick a poker into those old embers, let them sputter and smoke. Choke him, blind him. But he couldn't think about his boy. Not yet. About everything that a good father might have done to prevent things or fix things, or make things better. Lewis couldn't manage to think about any of it, though the weight of regret stunned him, made him feel as though a jokester had found a hole in his back, filled his entire soul with sand.

ELI RESTED ON a bench in the barn. He'd been puttering about for most of the afternoon, cleaning tools, sharpening blades, organizing bolts and screws and straightened nails into butter tubs. Things would be tidy for Angie, he'd decided. All ready. She would have enough on her young shoulders when the time came. She didn't need a mess.

The afternoon passed away and night drifted in. Eli was lost in shadows. Beside his thigh was a lantern, and he placed his hand on the cold glass chimney. When he lifted it, he caught the bitter odor of kerosene, knew the cotton wick was ready. But he didn't strike a match. He hated the dark, the way his hands disappeared, lost at the end of his arms. But, more and more often, he sought out these quiet places filled only with absolute blackness. Reasoning that, given time, he might get used to the sensation of night pressing in on his skin.

He leaned forward, removed the tweed hat from his head. Pinching it in his fists, his fingers worried the fabric. Only a few weeks earlier, Eli had been to visit Doc Rideout. Overnight, his body had morphed from tight leathery pelt and good stores of fat to a heap of saggy paper skin, protruding bone. He'd been vomiting bile and blood daily, felt a painful fullness in his guts, and there were visible sores on his tongue. After a battery of tests, Doc pronounced cancer. "Started in your stomach, I reckons," he said, "but now it has progressed to your tubing, your throat and into your mouth."

But Eli knew the doctor was wrong. Not about the cancer, but the point of origin. Without doubt, it had started on his tongue. All those words, all those things he needed to say, laying dormant inside that muscle for years. Festering. Finally emerging the only way possible. Craters that formed from the inside out. And still, he continued to swallow it all down. Instead of speaking, he pushed those words further into his body. "Do you want to know how long?" Doc had asked. Eli shook his head. "We'll do everything we can," he continued. "We have the means to make you comfortable."

And there it was. Just like that. One moment moving through a day like any other, taking care of business, hauling limp stalks from the earth, gathering muddy potatoes. The next moment, open face pressed up against the great abyss, straining to see, hands flailing through cold blackness, feeling nothing. That was where he was headed. Eli was certain. Pulsed through that tight ridged channel, no pink light this time. Born again into a wide open space. Pitch dark. Eternal emptiness. He sensed the icy breath already moving to encapsulate him, brushing against the tip of his nose. Not much longer.

He would be alone, he'd make sure of that. He wouldn't allow Angie to witness him fading away. And what with the woman he married? Up and gone. Once the boy was in the ground, she plucked her clothes from the drawers, handful of dollars from a slit in the mattress, and left with her sister. Papers arrived within the week, and at first Eli didn't understand. Copies of an application to dissolve ties between Mr. Fagan and Mrs. Glass. Then it struck him. In a final squirt of spite, she had stripped herself of his name.

Eli leaned his head back against the splintery wall. Any filament of brightness in the barn had withered, and night filled the entire space. Even though he had been a terrible husband, he had done what he could to protect her that afternoon. Keeping the truth to himself all these years. She never knew her son. The boy that he was, the man he became. And Eli had long ago realized her love for that boy was the only thing that held her together.

So, that's one good thing I done, he thought. He looked upwards, blinked. Wasn't it? One good thing?

Eli dropped his hat, put his head in his hands. So difficult now to keep reflection at bay. Hard work had kept his conscience clear all these years, but with muscles now like shriveled fibers, he could no longer settle his mind. He looked upwards again, into the endless darkness.

"I am a…" he spoke. Nothing more than a whisper, but the echo inside the box of his barn jolted him, made his spine straighten. "I am a farmer." His tongue contorted to shape the sounds, and the words burned as they made their passage.

No, you is a puss. A bloody puss.

Gone soft, my son, gone soft.

Eli folded his fingers together, ignored the extra voices, did not resist when his mind stuck in a claw, dragged out long dormant memories.

So many afternoons during those summer months, the boy would disappear for hours at a time. Leaving Eli with irritable cows, or weed-riddled fields, or a leak in the roof of the barn, rain on the way. Eli went looking for him that one day, and the bend in the long grass was as good as any arrow showing him the boy's direction. Eli tramped through the woods, and found him perched by the stream. Stopping in the shadows, he watched the boy haul up a glass jar, hidden in the river. Waited as he opened it, and dumped all his filthy secrets out onto the grass.

He saw the boy rocking on his haunches before a stack of photos, putting Eli in mind of some sort of queer animal. Sucking on the skin of his bare knee. Before Eli stepped forward, he felt the very air change. Heavy now. As though weighted with something forbidden. Something ugly. He believed Lucifer was lingering around the boy, drawing circles through the air, and his heart knocked hard against his ribs as he rushed out from the brush.

Eli overtook the boy. Added ten years to his age when he saw the photographs. A child, a child, naked, sprawled on a wooden floor in some, leaning against a wooden wall in others. White under-grown flesh. Pillows of baby fat. Big wide smile. Teeth locked together with what Eli could only guess to be a mouthful of old brown candy. He even thought he knew the child's face. His face. For that was all he could stare at. The face. And as he stood there, stunned, the boy danced. Hopping from one foot to the other. Eyes glazed and shiny, like someone gone mad. His hands flapping. A flightless, frightened bird. He began rambling stupid stories. Nothing believable, as Eli knew, the devil had hold of his tongue.

His first instinct was to drown the boy. Without a second thought. Drown him in the stream. Be done with it. Hold his head under. Until he went limp. He reasoned it was no worse than scooping kittens into an old sheet, and tying them to the muffler of his truck. And for a long moment, he did. The boy gaped up at him from beneath the rippling surface, but the water wouldn't take him, wouldn't do its work. And while Eli hated that child, he feared him, too. He let him go. Let him breathe. Then, as the boy crumbled and sputtered on the grass, Eli jammed every photo into the jar, twisted the lid thinking one might escape. He never spoke a word, stomped out through those woods, jar locked in both hands. Sleeves of his shirt were wet from the stream, rest of it wet from his sweat.

In a rusting barrel, he burned every last one. Struck them with a fork that was handy. Eli was senseless with disgust and anger and some sort of queer deep unease. And he couldn't help but remember his long dead uncle. His father's brother who lived in the room below Eli's. Every evening, creeping upstairs, suffocating Eli with his weight. Drunk and fumbling. Sour reek from down there. Stench like rot in a barrel. *Say hello to my pet, Elias.* Every night. *Say hello to my pet.* Here. Those smooth handfuls and handfuls. Turning him over. There was joy in being someone's favorite. Small, simple joy in that. Sweets under his damp pillow when he awoke. But that was a window long painted shut. Long painted shut. And Eli would not take a knife to it now. No. But it could have been him trapped in that jar. Could have been him.

Hands between his bony knees, Eli leaned forward into the darkness of his barn, and listened. For something. He could sense his thoughts were in the air above him, like a texture or a layer. Rough against his crown. And he wondered how such a disturbance could hover there so silently.

Eli slumped his back, snapped the sole of one boot with the sole of the other. Another claw, tugging, tugging, more memories of that summer afternoon. Roy Trench coming out of nowhere, grabbing his shoulders. Constable Trench right behind him. And then everything just clashed together. A thousand voices calling "timber" in Eli's head. He couldn't hear or see or think. And all he could really recall was the dimmest notion to cover it up. As much as he threw at his wife, hard as he was on her, something in him said she didn't deserve that. To see that. To know she birthed something spoiled. She was a mother, first, who loved her son.

Well, he could save her from the truth about that boy. Her own flesh. Flesh she wouldn't let go. And he hadn't meant to move his arm in the way he did. Hadn't meant to have such force behind it. Strength in his clenched jaw, riding right down through his hand. A strike. A push. A twist. Eli's hand covered with blood, and even after he'd washed, it hid in the cracks on his knuckles, grooves around his fingernails. Like stubborn dirt.

So many years, he had worked to confuse himself. Erase the sins of the boy. Must the actions of a youngster mark out the grown-up he becomes? And so, Eli allowed the boy to stay. Living under his roof. And, in his head, he changed Roy Trench into a scheming trespasser, who was bound to do his property harm. Though he never could quite trick his mind fully, and he'd never been able to forgive myself for stealing someone's life.

Of course, that wasn't the end of it. Eli understood things like that don't end. They settle deep in the dirt, instead, just waiting to be kicked up. And now, a lifetime later, when the circle closed, when the dog finally caught hold to his tail, what choice did he have? Those two boys in the room that night. Life pooling on the floor. What could he do? Should he let the runt who had infected everything pass away? Should he let the runt be and tend to the healthy stock?

Pain spiked through his drug-numbed flesh, but Eli spoke again. Slowly. "I am a farmer. And, may God punish me. May He punish me for all eternity. But there was never any question."

He unclasped his hands, took several quick breaths through his nose. Waited. Hard rain tapped the window behind his left shoulder, and hand gripping the rough windowsill he hoisted himself up a few inches. He shifted the old curtain, glanced out across the backyard towards the empty house. And there, in the middle of the lawn, was a murky shape, as though a foreign stone had risen from the depths, settled there.

Eyes adjusted to the night, and when he looked up at the rafters of his barn he could just make out the cross of wood. He shook his head slightly. Eli knew who it was. He turned to look again. After watching for several minutes, he reached for the lantern, lifted the glass chimney, and, with a match, lit the blackened tip of the wick.

THE HEAVENS OPENED up and icy rain pelted down, striking Lewis's scalp, the last few strands of hair slithering back and forth. He didn't seek shelter, stayed next to the disintegrating barrel until he was soaked through and through, and his skin began to swell on his body. He never noticed the light bobbing across the backyard, until a glove and a glowing lantern appeared right in front of his face. Someone gripped him firmly underneath his arm, guided him to his feet.

"You got to go on," Eli Fagan said to Lewis. No trace of anger in his voice, but no softness either.

"Yes."

"Idn't doing no good to no one."

"No."

Eli lifted his lantern, and for just a moment, in the pitch blackness of that backyard, there was a radiance between the two of them. Reddened eye meeting reddened eye. And in that instant, Lewis felt nothing. The hatred he had cradled for so long was gone. In its place, a curious whisker of something else.

"Eli."

"Don't."

"But—"

"I wants to see your suffering no more than you wants to see mine."

"You done something and I needs to—"

Wet blackness once again, Eli had blown out the light. Voice from somewhere beyond. "Get on. Take what you got. I only—" A pause, sound of boots squishing wet grass. "Oh, I only—"

Lewis took several steps, reached into the night, wanting to touch Eli's shoulder, wanting to grip the farmer's waxy coat. But Eli was gone, swallowed in darkness, and for a moment Lewis was disoriented, wondered if the old man had been there at all.

SHOULDERS HUNCHED, ELI shuffled across the backyard, didn't slow when the wind stole his hat, lifted his strings of hair. When he reached the back of the house, he turned to look, but the yard was empty. The stone gone.

He rested against the door frame. The handle of the lantern was cutting into his finger joints, and Eli leaned, dropped it onto the stoop. His teeth clacked against each other, but Eli didn't feel cold at all. Sweaters and trousers wet and heavy, but inside the dragging fabric his skin-draped skeleton felt lighter than it had in years. And he lifted his face in the dark rain. Opened his mouth, let the clean drops rinse across his tongue.

AS HE MADE his way home, the rain lightened, and the moon peeked out through a crack in the clouds, making the naked world shine. He walked up his driveway, towards the warmth of his trim house, past the logs Toby had been cutting a month ago. Lewis bent to throw a few errant junks of wood back to the group. He stared at the pile, at the saw, blade rusted, and tried to assure himself that tomorrow, he and Toby would work on that together. Finish cutting, stacking a neat row against the shed. He could hear Mrs. Verge, Peggy, in his head, her kind words. Tiny steps. That's all anyone can ask.

29

DECEMBER PASSED INTO January, without as much as the toot of
a metallic horn. Toby didn't mind the quiet, and he spent many
weekend afternoons in the woods, cutting down birch, hacking
bare branches with his tomahawk. Sweating inside his coat, his
sweater, often working in nothing more than a T-shirt. Sometimes, at noon, Angie would find him, bring him a thermos
of something warm, and they'd sit in the tamped-down snow,
talk for a while about nothing in particular. He couldn't look
her in the eye, had asked her to stop coming, but she refused.
Said, "I don't know who you think you'd be helping, but it's
neither of us." He wanted her to stop caring about him, but she
told Toby she couldn't manage it. "Fine, then," he said. "Give it
some time, and you will."

One afternoon, when he finished his work, he walked about,
thumped heavy boughs with his fists, let thick layers of snow
tumble down onto his head and the hood of his coat. He didn't
turn towards home until the wet cold invaded every square
inch of his young body. Pushing his legs through the foot of
sticky snow, he wondered what it might be like to lie down and
sleep. Would he dream of Angie? No, he knew he wouldn't. He
wouldn't allow himself the comfort. If he dreamt at all, he'd
dream of Melvin.

He walked into the kitchen, and there was Mrs. Verge, balancing on a chair, pinching runners from a spider plant. Fresh
snowfall outside shot white light into the room, and Toby could
see a yellow glow coming off her wide sides. He stood there, in

271

dripping boots, jacket hanging open, damp scarf letting go, a bright blue puddle on the floor.

Mrs. Verge turned, jumped slightly, frame jiggling. "Oh my gosh, Tobias. You startled me. Near stopped my heart."

Toby's mouth fell open just a shade, and he said, "What?"

"I said you near stopped my heart."

Toby shook his head, "I never meant to, Mrs. Verge."

"You never said nothing when you come in."

"I never said nothing. No."

With deliberate steps, she held the table, eased herself off the chair. Came over to Toby, and placed her strong hands on his shoulders. "My gosh, darling. You looks like death warmed over. You're working too hard. There's enough wood in the basement and shed for half of Knife's Point."

"I likes to cut wood."

"But—"

"I'm good, Mrs. Verge."

Hands on her hips, she tutted. "All this talk of being good. Being fine. You men people. I tell you, 'tis run its course, buddy boy." She plucked up his scarf, yanked his coat from his arms, hung them both over a chair.

Toby turned to leave the kitchen, but she clutched his wrist. "Not so quick, my son." Spun him around, caught him in an embrace. "Now," she said. "Now, I got you."

"Mrs. Verge?"

"You let it out. Right out."

He squirmed, bleated, "Let what out?"

"You knows, Tobias Trench. You knows exactly what got to be let out."

Toby tried to catch some air, and he smelled something floral and soft on her clothes. While his own mother had been nothing more than a draft, skulking around his ankles, here was Mrs. Verge, fully present, a hot oven, door wide open. He was lost in her fleshy folds, face plastered to her chest. "Nothing to let out, Mrs. Verge," he mumbled. "Nothing."

272

"You don't get off that easy," and she squeezed, tighter and tighter until he coughed. "I idn't letting you go no time soon."

He waited, encased in her fat arms, soft breasts. Finally, he mumbled, "You're hurting me, Mrs. Verge."

"I'll be damned," she said as she released her grip. "You men. The whole load of you. All alike."

"I'm good, Mrs. Verge. Honest, I is."

"Well, you won't escape my tongue that easy." Hands on his shoulders again. "I got something I needs to say, and you best remember it."

"Yes, Mrs. Verge."

"You is you, Tobias Trench, and you is not your father or your mother, and not your brother, God love him. You is young and you is able, my son, and there's a lot of lovely things in this world, lots of good, and the snow looks so clean right now, but that will go too, and you'll have plenty of mud before you finds another spring. But spring will come, it always do, with green grass, and enough birds singing in the mornings to drive you right batty. Do you get what I'm saying, Tobias?"

"I does, Mrs. Verge."

"You is a special one, Tobias."

"I idn't, Mrs. Verge."

"Yes, you is. I knowed it since you was young."

"No, Mrs. Verge. Melvin was special. He really was." Toby looked out the window, tried to study the blankness of the winter sky.

"You can make this all good," she said, hugging him again. "Just grow yourself up and live a happy life. Simple as that."

30

TOBY WALKED TWO steps behind his father. He kept his head down as he passed a man wearing only faded pajamas. Bottoms shrunk, riding up over the ankles. Feet without slippers. The walls were painted a sickly green, the color of a plant long denied sunlight, and Toby could not see a single picture, not a single image mounted to break the long stretches of nothing. On either side of the corridor, some doors creaked open, unfocused eyes peering out, others closed, moans and stutters slithering around the door frames, sounds that burrowed into Toby's head. With every breath, the smell of cleaning chemicals and sour cotton edged further up his nose, and he knew it would take some time to dislodge it.

There was nothing worthy of a giggle in the hallway, but Toby could barely keep it in. He looked up at the ceilings, so much higher than they needed to be. And Toby wondered if the building was built that way for the crowd it housed. Not enough room in your head? Well, there's plenty of extra space up here. The very thought made Toby pause, fingers touching a door frame, bent at the waist to accommodate a silent full-body laugh.

A few feet ahead of him, his father slipped to the left, disappeared inside a room. Toby stopped just outside the door, leaned against the wall. He couldn't go in, he couldn't do it. Not with this type of laughter rollicking through his body. He closed his eyes, swallowed hard, and chomped the inside of his cheek.

"Hey, son." Toby heard his father's voice, and he leaned in closer to the door to listen.

"Hey."

"How you getting on?"

"Good. I'm good." Voice flat, and Toby thought, unfamiliar.

"You need anything?"

"Nah."

"You sure? 'Tis no trouble, Mel."

"Well. I could do with something to . . . to read."

"Magazines? Word search, or something?"

"No, I means books. Some good books on places. Different places in the world. I likes to think about where I might go someday."

A pause, then, "You got it, my son. We'll hunt you down some of that."

"Thanks, Dad."

Toby heard the whine of bedsprings, and then his father saying, "You know. I been thinking these days a whole lot about fishing. Something I used to love when I was a young feller. And it come to me, in all these years we never fished the Grayley together."

His father paused again, and Toby waited.

"There's a cabin upriver a good ways. Used to go with my father. Fly fishing first thing in the morning. Cooking up whatever you caught."

"Sounds nice."

"When you gets all better, when the doc says you're a hundred and ten, that's the first place we're going. You and me and Tobe."

Toby held his breath at the mention of his name. Then, the bedsprings groaning relief, his father up and barking gently, "Tobe, Tobe. Where you got to?"

Don't be a puss, Toby told himself, and before he could think any further he rolled himself around the corner, into this new home. A small room, practically empty, a bed, a pressboard closet, a stretch of curtainless windows near the ceiling. And a boy.

He hadn't seen Melvin in months, and some days Toby wondered if Melvin were even alive. But there he was, sitting up and seated on the side of the bed, dressed in pale blue drawstring pants and a white T-shirt. Skinnier, and his once long hair now shaved close to his round skull. A winding scar, reminding Toby of the accident, visible in the black fuzz on the back of his head. Melvin's tongue kept daubing his bottom lip, and every few seconds he winked. Hard. With both eyes.

Toby stared at the marks on Melvin's skull. Then he glanced at his father, wide smiling mouth but wet eyes. Inside Toby's gut, the desire to laugh suddenly tumbled across the floor, now replaced with something else. Flat fish flopping over, pale soft belly exposed.

Toby couldn't look his brother in the eye, mumbled. "You good?"

"I'm alright, Toad."

Toad.

Toby choked out, "I miss you, Mellie."

"Yeah." Big sigh. Melvin rubbed his crown with his knuckles, and then he stood, moved towards Toby. "You been missing me a long time."

The tips of warm fingers moved across his back, Melvin's hand touching him, and Toby hiccuped. He leaned forward, cheek against his brother's ribs, and at once the hiccuping broke through, and sobs tumbled out. Toby wrapped his arms around Melvin and cried. Long and hard. Cried for not being good enough to keep a mother, and cried for the ghosts that moved through the walls of their home. Cried for Melvin, and the voices that spoke to him, whomever they might be. Cried for the anger that filled up their father, and the words that were trapped in the man's throat. Cried for Mrs. Verge, a spoonful of human sugar. Cried for how beautiful the world could be whenever Angie smiled. Toby held on, and Melvin curled his tall frame over him.

"Gonna be okay, Toad. Things is gonna get better. They is. You'll see."

After some time, Toby sat on the bed, pressed his runny nose into his sleeve. He stole sideways glances at Melvin until he was

276

shy no longer. Then, as they chatted about nothing and everything, he reached over and took Melvin's hand. His brother's
fingers were cool and slightly swollen, didn't feel quite normal.
But they didn't feel bad either.

"HE DON'T REMEMBER none of it."

"He don't?"

"Nope. I'm sure it's all in there somewhere, though."

"Yeah."

"Not like you. I knows you'll remember it. And I don't know
what's worse. Either way, Toby, it don't never really leave you."
Lewis placed a hand on the back of Toby's neck as his son bent
his head, shoveled fries from the shiny plate. He could feel
Toby's spine on his fingers, several points and dips, and Lewis
had to swallow when he realized how rarely he touched Toby.
He expected the boy to draw back, but he didn't. Instead, he
continued to eat, managed a quiet, "Mmm."

"But that's a better place for him there, Tobe. Than behind
bars. He got a chance there. To figure out what's going on with
his head and make himself better."

More fries.

Lewis stared at his reflection in the window, watched his
mouth open and a few brave words emerge. "You know, we was
always together. Me and him."

"You and who?"

"My brother."

"Uncle Roy?"

At the mention of the name, Lewis bristled, waited for the
inevitable jolt of grief to clamp his jaw. But instead, he was surprised to discover some sense of pleasure residing in his chest.
Uncle Roy. And the curious desire to share with Toby.

"Oh, and what an uncle he would've been. Always finding
some way to have a bit of fun, he was. Sometimes good ways,
sometimes not so good ways. If Roy didn't find trouble, trouble
was bound to find Roy."

Toby smiled.

"Every year when we was little, we'd get a barrel of clothes and magazines and stuff sent down from Montreal. Well, one year there was a mix-up, and we ended up with a barrel of mannequin legs. Mother couldn't figure out what use we could make of those legs, but she wouldn't dare toss them out. Told Roy and me that we could have the load of them if we wanted, as long as we didn't waste."

"Did you?"

"Sure did, Tobe. Balanced them up on a sleigh, dragged them over to Stark Pond beyond Dilly Green's house. Cleared away the ice, and had ourselves a hockey game using the legs, now, as sticks. Bit awkward, and you're apt to get struck with a scrap of plaster in your eye, but they worked alright nonetheless."

"You're joking."

"That I idn't, my son. We played a good bit, the fellers took good care of their legs. Dilly and his brother stole their mother's black stockings, pair of shoes, dressed up the legs we gave them. Leaned them against a tree, pair of her pink drawers stuffed with rags balanced up on top, and her garter belt clipped around and on to the hose. God, we all had a good laugh at that, as you can imagine, until she showed up at the ice, calling the boys for supper. Saw her lower half naked in the woods, and I swears she looked down at herself first, like she was checking, and then turned like the beet, snatched those legs, tore off up to the house. So mad now, the snow melted around her. Dilly and the other one never saw their legs again. Said she took a hammer to them. Crushed every bit of plaster 'til all was left was a metal rod."

Toby laughed, shook his head.

"Dilly was some upset. He had plans to get his leg signed by The Rocket."

"You're kidding."

"No, sir. Best laid plans, they say. Funny how it seems like just yesterday." A sigh.

Toby munched, said through his cheeks, "That's a good story, Dad."

278

"Yeah. You can't make that stuff up."

"You should tell that one to Mellie, too. Next time."

"You think?"

"Yeah."

"I just might." Lewis shook his head slightly, smiled to himself. Then, to Toby, "You full?"

"Yeah."

"You sure? Could get another plate if you wants. We're not in no rush."

"Nope. Stuffed." Belly clap.

Lewis placed four one dollar bills on the table, wedged the corners underneath Toby's empty glass. Toby looked at him, expectantly, but Lewis did not stand up.

"We ready?" Toby said.

Lewis swiped his hand over his face. "Tobe?"

"Yeah?"

"There's ... there's something else I wants to mention." Lewis noticed Toby's body stiffen, his mouth close, and he quickly added, "Don't worry, my son. Nothing serious. Nothing serious. It's about Wilda."

"Who?"

"Your mother."

"My. Mother."

"Yes."

"You talk to her?" Aggression in the boy's tone.

"Yes, Toby. I have."

When Lewis called the day after, he expected her to answer in a singsong voice. But, she didn't. Her hello was timid, questioning.

He never introduced himself, used his constable tone to announce the news, "It's about Melvin." Then, just in case, "Your son."

Shallow breathing on the other end of the line.

"There was trouble. An argument or something. He, ah, he ... nearly died. I thought you should know. What's happened and all. Where he is. And ..."

A strangled, "And?"

He bit his bottom lip, closed his eyes. Pushed out the words. "He killed a man, Wilda. Killed someone."

Sucking sound, then. Like water lapping over the opening of a dark hole.

"But it weren't his fault. No. It weren't. He didn't know what he was doing."

Lewis waited a long minute for her to say something. But there were no words. Silence on the other end of the line, and he wondered if the connection were broken. Wondered if she had the gall to hang up on him. But then, he caught it. A grunt, followed by some snuffling. Ever so quiet. A riddle of sounds, making him think of a newborn pig.

"And what do she want?"

"She's been to see him a number of times, you know. I don't know what to make of it. She wants to see you, too, Tobe. Wants to talk to you. When you're ready."

AS HIS FATHER spoke about Wilda, the fries tucked inside Toby's stomach felt hard and sore, and he hunched forward. Toby stared down at the greasy plate, wished he hadn't finished everything.

He couldn't help but think about the afternoon she left them. Abandoned them. Though he had trouble picturing her face, he could easily recollect her back, the shape of her shoulders in that long coat. Blue or gray. He remembered hauling Melvin home through the snowstorm. How Melvin wouldn't move, and Toby thought he might be dead. And how he tried to get him to drink something sweet to make him feel better. A pitcher of purple liquid sitting in the fridge, and Toby knew Melvin loved purple. And being so young, he was certain something purple would fix things. But the two glasses were stuck together, stuck right together, and as much as he pulled at them, they would not come apart. Wedged tight, one squarish glass nestled nicely inside a round one. He was hurrying, didn't think, poured the ice cold drink into the first glass. Picked it up to bring it to Melvin, held it carefully, and the bottom glass, the one that was holding on, exploded. Shards of glass went everywhere. Fragments sticking in Toby's hands and wrists, into the mittens dangling from their strings, a spray of crystals across the countertop, windowsill, inside splashes of purple on the floor. Toby was afraid to move, afraid to breathe, gazed for a long while at the second sticky glass that somehow was cupped inside his hands. Gazed at it until forever had passed, and then he dropped that too.

"Is that smart, Dad? Is that a smart thing to do?"

"I don't know."

"Letting that woman slink back into his life like that?"

"I don't know, Tobe. I don't know."

"Look at all the damage she done. You know he's just barely holding it together."

"I don't know."

"What if she screws him over, again? Did you think of that? Screws him over."

"Christ," Lewis yelped, slammed his fist on the table, plate jumping. "I. Don't. Know." He pushed his chair back, put his face in his hands. "I really don't, Tobe. I been to see her a couple of times. She don't seem like she was. She don't. She looks like she had a hard go of it, these years. Like she's gone through some real misery."

"Misery? Give me a break. Don't tell me you pities her. Don't tell me."

Calmer, now. "No, Toby, I don't pity her. But I can't keep my sights on what's passed. I can't live like that no more. I don't know why bad stuff locks one person to a spot, while it drives another one off. I don't know why she done what she done. Maybe she regrets her choices. We all regret something, don't we? What I knows is that she's there for Melvin today. And she's doing him some good. I asked her to be careful with him. And that's all I can do. Is ask."

Toby sighed.

"I should've just left you out of it," Lewis said. "Never mentioned it at all."

"I'd rather know."

"Well, what do I tell her? She's waiting for me to call."

Toby spotted a nickel, then, perched on the table. Lewis started flipping it over and over with his fingers.

"Well?"

"Where is she?"

"Not far."

"Fine."

"Fine what?"

"I'll go. And I'm going to tell her straight out she better watch it with Mellie."

"That's fair." Lewis plucked up the nickel.

"Fair?" Toby shook his head. "What do fair got to do with it?"

THEY WALKED ALONG a winding street, up a hill, past an open window. Someone inside was playing an accordion, leather wheezing, pitiful sound assaulting the air. A row of shops now, one stuck to the other, and Toby wasn't watching where he placed his feet. He stumbled on a crack in the cement, fell sideways into an alcove. He stood, brushed white dust from the sides of his navy pants, noticed a mermaid carved into a wooden placard hanging on the door. Tail curved, hair in a tumble of curls hiding the mermaid's face, chest bare, miniature breasts exposed. He stared for a moment, then glanced at his father.

"This is it," Lewis said.

Toby was surprised, peered in through the shiny glass, saw a lot of dark wood, shelves, piles and piles of stuff. Junk.

"This?" A sign to his left read "The Curious Mermaid."

"Yeah. Open the door."

Pressing the metal tab with his thumb, Toby pushed the door open, stepped up into the dimly lit store. Rows of dolls and doll heads, some without eyes, a brown jug with a chipped lip, used

282

jewelry inside a glass case, mismatched cups and saucers and plates and bowls, an old fashioned washbasin hanging from the ceiling, a tub filled with hundreds of buttons. Folded quilts draped over a rack, yellowed doilies spilling out of open drawers, a dartboard, a pair of leather shorts for a child. The only sign of life was the row of African violets lined up on a windowsill that never saw light. And an orange cat, sucking on a blanket in a worn wingback chair.

"What is this place, Dad?" Toby whispered.

"It's where she lives."

Quieter, "Oh."

Then he heard someone call, "Just one minute."

Toby leaned to the side, saw her back, arms raised as she placed a candy dish, milky green glass, on a top shelf. Short brown hair, and he saw her neck and her ears, and his heart began its tattoo even before he saw her face.

His mother. Toby blinked. Standing there. Turning now. Facing him. Eyes, just like his own, staring for a moment, then looking down, rising to meet his yet again. A head, in the waves, bobbing, drowning. Toby wanted to take a step backwards, but didn't trust that his feet would find a solid floor.

She walked towards them. "Hi Lewis."

"Wilda," he replied, then he strolled away, behind a row of shelves.

She kept her hands behind her back. "Hello, Toby."

Toby didn't say anything.

"How are you?" she said, and Toby saw her draw in a long, controlled breath.

How are you? Such a loaded first question. How was he? On the walk over, a sick heat had mounted inside him, and he had planned how he would handle it. How he would yell, tear a hole right through her. But now, face to face, he felt dizzy. Confused. She wasn't what he'd expected. Not at all.

He looked above her, beside her, around her. Then something caught his eye. A small framed picture on a table behind the till. Taking two steps forward, he was able to make it out.

The image nothing more than a square of snow, and in the middle two boyish faces, ruddy cheek fused to ruddy cheek, happy and smiling wide at the camera. Oh, God. It was that very afternoon. Toby stared at the photo, at Melvin's shiny eyes. His brother. Completely oblivious to the dejection that was about to settle in his heart.

Toby's voice cracked when he blurted, "Why?"

A squeaky "Oh."

"Why do you got that out there? On bloody display."

He heard her breathing through her mouth, and she whispered, "I look at it every day."

"You look at it? You look at it?" He kept his back to her. "That's the dumbest thing I ever heard."

No response.

"Gawk at some Polaroid, when you could've had the real thing. You could've had him. That's all he ever wanted, you know. A bloody mother."

Toby turned to her then, saw her face was contorted, chin pulled back, thin skin on her neck shaking. And he wanted to stop his words, but they barreled out. "Weren't all bad, you know, Missus. It weren't. You missed plenty of good. Plenty of good."

He noticed her shake slightly and the air seemed heavy and stuck in his lungs. Too much going on inside of him, too many cracks and crevices filled with emotion, and he couldn't smooth it out. Part of him wanted to watch that woman cry, and at the same time another part wanted to make everything better.

"I made tea," she said weakly.

"Tea."

She took a few steps, sat on a wooden stool, stared for a moment at the seat opposite her.

He closed his mouth. Hadn't realized it was hanging open. Wilda. His mother. He really didn't remember much about her, but the image he had held onto all these years was far prettier than the reality. She was thin and shaky and he could count the veins on the sides of her face. If he looked at her for long enough.

284

And when she brought her hand to her face, he saw the tips of her fingers were bluish, as though she were cold. Or maybe nervous.

"Do you drink tea?" She held the pot, filled two mugs on the small table.

"It don't matter."

"You don't have to."

"No."

"Yes?" she said, lifting a tiny jug.

He turned his head towards the bay window. "Yeah. A bit."

She dribbled milk into his tea, slid a spoon next to his cup.

"I've been to see your brother. Melvin. Been to see him quite a bit."

Toby sat down, exhaled. "Yeah. Us too. Well, not quite a bit. We was just there."

"We talk. A lot. He's doing much better. He had a hard time understanding what happened, but he ... he's taking the help they are giving."

"Cool."

"That's a difficult thing, to accept comfort." She stirred her tea in figure eights, nodding slowly. "Yes, he's doing well."

She was wearing a worn cardigan over a flowery blouse, navy slacks, and when she crossed her legs, he saw she had bony ankles.

"Toby?"

"Yeah?"

Silence expanding between them, and her mouth smiled. Her head wavered slightly, lids lowered, and she whispered, "I don't even know how to begin."

Her voice, so soft, connected with some sleepy part of him. He glanced at the framed picture again, and felt that scheming laughter tickling his voice box. Dying to burst free. He wanted to hold his rage, grip it in his fists, but he couldn't manage, and it was slipping, slipping. He leaned, his head just over his tea, felt the steam warm his chin, his cheeks. He thought of Mrs. Verge then, squeezing him, telling him not to judge. Not to be angry.

It don't make anything no better, she'd say. Only blacken your own heart. He held the handle, wrapped his left hand around the cup. And pulled it across the wooden table towards him. What could he say to her? What could he say? He slurped, stared at his hands. Hands that, even after all these years, still remembered touching her. And he opened his mouth, managed, "You make good tea."

31

STANDING BY THE side of the stream, Toby bent over, rolled up
the wide legs of his jeans. Too hot for the heavy fabric, but when
he dressed earlier that morning to fish with Terry Verge, the
salty air had made him shiver.

He sat down in a bed of flowering clover, let his legs dangle over the grassy lip, and dipped his feet into the cool water.
A gentle current made his legs sway, and tadpoles grazed his
soles each time he flicked his numbed toes. Leaning back on his
elbows, he thought about Melvin. Slowly, things were improv-
ing. While living in that building Melvin had finished high
school, and they encouraged him to teach some of the others
math and physics. Today, for the first time, Melvin was allowed
to leave for a couple of hours. A lunch out with Wilda. Both
Toby and his father laughed when Wilda called, said Melvin
had requested fish and chips, peas, dressing and gravy. A meal
so simple. There was talk of an afterwards, of a down the road,
when Melvin would be allowed to come home. But Toby didn't
think about that. Didn't like to think too far into the future.

He heard someone approaching, and twisted, saw Angie
coming through the woods behind him. When she reached the
grass she flicked off her sandals, plunked down beside him, and
slid her feet into the water. She drew in a sudden breath at the
chill, then edged closer to Toby, hooked one white ankle behind
his.

"How did I know I'd find you here?"

"You could smell me?" His jeans were smeared with blood
from the fish he and Terry had cleaned on the stage.

She laughed, nudged him. "You is ripe, I give you that."

He gripped her hand, felt the tiny stab of her ring on his palm. A square green stone, a bright yellow band. Something from Wilda's store. At first he was concerned about giving his girlfriend a used ring, but Wilda insisted that jewelry wasn't the same as people. It didn't hold on to history. Toby gave the ring to Angie at Christmastime last year—they were watching television in her basement apartment, and he had hidden the box at the bottom of the popcorn bowl. With Angie's father and brother gone, her sister lost and wandering in Toronto, and her mother living somewhere in Cape Breton, he wanted her to know that she'd never be alone. He wanted her to have that promise.

"How's it going with Mrs. Verge?"

"I don't know. Alright, I guess."

During the winter, Mrs. Verge had moved into a spare room. Terry came over and painted it bright yellow, brought a mattress, a night table, a lamp, and a few boxes in the back of his truck. Toby's father had claimed he was reluctant to have Mrs. Verge move in, but when he began complaining of curious aches, a dry cough no one actually heard, everyone agreed it would be easier to have her close by. After her first night, the aches disappeared, and his father never again mentioned a cough. Not a week later, Toby had walked in on the two of them, sitting side by side reading, shoulders touching, and unless he was mistaken the air had more charge than what he'd expected.

"Three's getting to be a crowd."

"Yeah?"

"I think Father's trying to oust me."

"I doubt that."

"He said I needs to start thinking about my future. Think about where I's going."

"Going?"

"I idn't going far."

"Far like distance, or far like becoming a big honcho type far?"

288

He reached up, removed her glasses. She had pretty eyes, green with perfect flecks of yellow, and he liked to see them without the distraction of those thick lenses. He slowly cleaned the smudges using the inside of his T-shirt. "I don't know. I idn't good at nothing."

She grabbed her glasses, pressed them onto her face. "Will you stop saying that? It idn't true."

"Yeah. It is."

"No, Toby. It idn't. You're very good at some stuff."

"Tell me one thing, Angie. One thing that counts." He was joking now, prodding her for a moment of adoration.

She paused.

"Told you so."

Pouting. "I was thinking about how to word it."

"I'm only pulling your leg, Ange. I'm happy without being a big brain or running the whole province. I don't want much."

"No, really. I want to say it. You're, you're," she gripped his chin, turned his face to hers, "you're like good dirt."

"I'm what?" Blinking.

"Good dirt. Good soil. Stuff grows right in you, you don't need to go searching for it."

"Stuff."

"Yeah, like, like love." She blushed, but continued. "You're good at that, Toby Trench. You're good at being kind. Not many can say that."

Toby lifted his feet out of the water, watched them drip, the water spatter. He laughed, but it sounded hollow. "Oh, c'mon. Good try though, darlin'."

"But it counts. It really do. And if you don't believe me, you deserves a good crack on the ear."

He lay back on the grass, put his arm over his eyes. "Not too hard, I hopes."

"You'll find out." Angie got to her feet, then leaned out over the stream, let her hand strike the surface of the water, a cold spray shooting up over his body.

"Hey!"

"Hey, yourself," she said, and slipped into her rubber sandals. "I got to go."

"Where to?"

"The Verge boy. They wants me to watch him for a bit."

"Oh, yeah."

She bent, kissed him upside-down on the forehead. "You coming?"

"No, I'm just going to think a while."

"Think or dwell?"

"I don't dwell, Ange."

"See you later?"

"Ween's home for the weekend, so we're going to knock around for a bit."

"Alright."

"But after that I'll see you. Whether you likes it or not."

"I likes it," she replied, her voice soft and girly.

He felt a quick pinch on his ear, a little shake, and then he heard her walking back along the path, wet feet squeaking against rubber, the crunch of dried leaves, a few snapping twigs. He didn't understand why she walked all that way just to spend a few moments with him. He didn't understand, but he didn't question it either. Even though he was only nineteen, and he never claimed to know much, he had already learned that love was a peculiar thing. Something you couldn't bottle or drown. He'd seen it mount a bus, stretch down long highways, weather years without snapping. He'd hauled it over a snowy road, wrapped its feet in nubby blankets, and coaxed it back to life. For as long as he could remember, he'd felt the steady weight of it on his young shoulders, and the undeniable warmth of it in his stomach. He'd watched as it spied, moaned, lashed out, choked, and destroyed. And when hope was lost, he had discovered it again, healthy and blooming in that space between him and Angie. An empty sort of space where love did not belong.

Somewhere above him, he heard crying, and he opened his eyes, squinted. High in the air, a large black bird with its

290

wings outstretched drifted across the blue sky. It made a neat loop, turned, and coasted back in the opposite direction. Toby cupped one hand to his forehead, and with his other he reached upwards, fingers stretched, tracing the bird's graceful path. Side to side, higher and higher, it soared. Toby followed the bird, so sure and steady on its path, gliding, looping, until it disappeared into the brightness of the sun.

ACKNOWLEDGEMENTS

I WOULD LIKE to thank the Ontario Arts Council for funding this project. Thank-you to both my agent, Hilary McMahon, and Chris Labonté at Douglas & McIntyre for believing in me and my simple story. Thank-you to Barbara Berson, my editor, for her wisdom, her patience, and her caring. I am grateful to my early readers: Nancy Lundrigan, Ann Diakiw, Aniko Biber, and Randy Drover. Also, thank-you to my twin nephews, Robert and Colin Morgan, for sharing parts of their lives. I am indebted to my dear friend Nathalie Kavianpour for helping me at every turn. And finally, a thank-you to my husband and children for their encouragement and their sweetness.

NICOLE LUNDRIGAN is the author of three critically acclaimed novels: *Unraveling Arva, Thaw,* and *The Seary Line.* She grew up in Newfoundland and now lives in Ontario with her family.